The Herb Knot

Jane Loftus studied 16th Century European History before taking a postgraduate degree in Modern Political History. As a lone parent, she worked in Winchester Waterstones before taking a job in IT. This novel was written in the evenings while she was raising her son. Hugely passionate about the Middle Ages, she drew inspiration for this novel from the medieval layout of Winchester which has been painstakingly documented.

The Herb Knot

JANE LOFTUS

ONE PLACE. MANY STORIES

HQ
An imprint of HarperCollins*Publishers* Ltd
1 London Bridge Street
London SE1 9GF

www.harpercollins.co.uk

HarperCollins*Publishers*
Macken House, 39/40 Mayor Street Upper,
Dublin 1, D01 C9W8, Ireland
This edition 2025

2
First published in Great Britain by HQ,
an imprint of HarperCollins*Publishers* Ltd 2025

ISBN: 9780008755270

Set in Minion by Palimpsest Book Production Limited, Falkirk, Stirlingshire

Printed and bound in the UK using 100% Renewable
Electricity by CPI Group (UK) Ltd

This book contains FSC™ certified paper and other controlled sources
to ensure responsible forest management.

For more information visit: www.harpercollins.co.uk/green

JC and BW
"Buster!"

Glossary

Batiste	very fine linen
Bliaut	a style of dress
Bodkin	a needle threader
Braiel	a belt to secure braies
Chalon	type of cloth, often used for blankets
Chaperon	a hood which covered the shoulders
Cheveril	soft leather
Costrel	a drinking vessel, often made of leather
Dickedinnen	luxury woollen broadcloth from Ghent
Ells	unit of measurement for cloth
Gambeson	padded armour
Gongfermour	cleaner of cesspits
Groot	a silver coin, used across Europe
Jeetje	exclamation in Dutch
Jettons	tokens for counting
Liripipe	a long tail on the end of a hood
Mazer	large drinking bowl
Melomel	a fruit/berry mead
Misericorde	very slender dagger (can be viewed in Winchester Museum)
Palfrey	a riding horse
Pancheon	a type of mixing bowl

Perse	a blue/grey fabric
Pipkin	a pot with a spout
Rouncey	a sturdier riding horse
Scaerlaken	Flemish scarlets; fabric made from high-end English wool and coloured using expensive dyeing techniques, fetching a high price
Scrivener	a copyist/notary, usually writing legal documentation
Siskin	green cloth, originating in Flanders
Talbot	medieval hunting dog
Tippet	adornment for the sleeve of a dress, resembling a long streamer

Prologue

August 1346, Crécy

The branches folded over them, crackling like a dog biting on chicken bones. Raphael and his mother wriggled beneath low shrubs and coils of fern. Even in moonlight they would be difficult to see, but it was not the place of safety his mother would have chosen. It was his mistake that had forced them to stop here.

His first mistake.

'When did you last see Christophe?' His mother pulled him close.

'By the big oak.'

'Tch!'

'I'm sorry, Maman.'

The big oak was where they'd entered the forest. It was where enemy soldiers roamed, blood-soaked after a day of battle. There would be looting too, and worse. It was why a woman and two children had left a cottage that was no longer safe. And now one of the children was missing.

'He told me not to wait. He said he'd catch up.' Raphael's tears could be heard in his voice. He'd ruined everything. He should never have let go of Christophe's hand. Now, they had been forced to stop where Christophe might still find them. They should be further towards the heart of the forest, not here.

It was all his fault.

'Don't cry, *mon petit*. He'll know where we are.' Raphael's mother, Marianne, reached for his hand. 'I should have paid more heed.'

She'd been calling gently as they walked, to make sure the children were still following. Raphael had answered. But he'd spoken only for himself. Christophe had fallen behind long before she'd become aware of it. They were supposed to hold hands, but Christophe had kept stumbling, dragging Raphael down with him. In the end he'd told Raphael to go ahead, that he'd catch up.

I should have waited.

Christophe would surely find his way here. He had Raphael's precious St Joseph scapular with him. Raphael wore it always, but Christophe had been afraid so Raphael had given it to him. It would guide him here; it had to.

Raphael and his mother lay for a while on their stomachs, the leaves above them gently shedding raindrops from the earlier storm. The damp earth smelled rich and strong and caught the back of Raphael's throat. His ribs began to hurt and he tried to move, but there were footsteps now. Marianne pressed her fingers to his lips.

The footsteps came faster and louder. A man entered the clearing, his outline bulky as if he were wearing armour. There was a shadow of something in his hand, something that glinted for a brief moment as a dull beam of moonlight caught the edge of it. Raphael felt his mother's hand tighten on his again.

Who was this man? A mercenary? Genoese? There was more moonlight now but it still wasn't enough to see for sure.

'*Anglais*,' Marianne whispered.

When Christophe crashed into the clearing like a hunted deer, the mercenary had already begun to walk away. Had Christophe arrived but one minute later, his and Raphael's lives would have taken different paths. But at the sight of the child, soiled and trembling, the mercenary turned on his heel. He had his arm wrapped around Christophe's neck in an instant, pulling tight until his feet barely reached the ground. Christophe's hands pulled at the mercenary's arm but to no avail. Raphael wanted to cry. He could feel his mother tense beside him and he was afraid. She was ready to move; he felt a shudder under her skin.

Don't go out there. Don't go.

It was over before she had a chance. The flash of a blade, the sound like a sigh as it cut across Christophe's neck, his cousin's body flung across the clearing as if it were of no more consequence than a slaughtered calf.

'No.'

The voice did not belong to Raphael, or his mother. They had been so fixated on Christophe that they hadn't noticed the arrival of another soldier. He wore no heavy armour, just a gambeson and sword. The weapon sat snug and familiar at his waist.

The soldier's tone was flat but his face was angry. He stood between the mercenary and Christophe's body where it lay, half in and half out of the clearing, partially shrouded by the darkness of the trees. Raphael didn't speak English, but it was clear that the soldier was remonstrating with the mercenary. He shook his head, his face tight. The mercenary responded with anger. He prowled around the soldier, shouting at him.

And then the soldier touched the mercenary's arm, and moved in for an embrace that did not seem unwelcome.

They must know each other. They must be friends.

But there was to be no truce and no contrition. The mercenary pushed the soldier backwards at the last moment. There was a loud crack, and the weight of a man landed on top of the bushes that protected Raphael and his mother.

A sharp branch cut into Raphael's ribs and he cried out. He pushed his fist into his mouth but it was too late.

He had made his second mistake.

He felt his mother's lips against his ear. 'Stay still. Stay still.'

His cry had betrayed them both and there was a lightness beside him where she'd been. When he dared look out he saw that the mercenary had her now, his arm around her waist.

The weight that had pinned Raphael down shifted and now the soldier moved towards the mercenary. He glanced at Christophe's body, pausing to cross himself, and then reached for his sword. The mercenary threw Marianne to one side, and raised his own weapon.

Run, Maman. Run!

But she didn't run. She lay on the ground where she'd been cast aside like a rag doll, and almost imperceptibly shook her head. The soldier was their only hope. He had to win.

The mercenary struck first, but his aim was poor and he moved slowly, his armour hampering him. The soldier swung to one side, his movement lithe and sure. He edged towards the trees, away from Marianne and away from where Raphael was hiding, towards the place where Christophe had entered the clearing. He was drawing the mercenary to him.

The mercenary advanced, sword pulled back. Rage drove his weapon and again, the soldier jumped to the side, graceful as a cat. The mercenary's breath came heavy, the armour clanking like a rusted bell.

When the mercenary drew for a third blow, he fell, toppling over Christophe's body, which still lay where it had fallen.

'Whoreson!'

Now the soldier could take him, a sword through the joint of the ill-fitting armour, at the neck, the thigh, where the blood would flow.

Raphael ran through this moment so many times in the years that followed. Why did the soldier hesitate? Why did he give his enemy enough time to react; to get to his knees and thrust his sword upwards?

The soldier looked down. His gambeson had been slashed

open. And then he fell, sideways, his face turned towards where Raphael lay hidden.

The mercenary hoisted Marianne over his shoulder like a sack. She made no effort to struggle as her dark hair tumbled loose and exposed the white skin at the back of her neck. Her captor stepped over Christophe's body and out of the clearing. The gap in the trees closed behind them. Where once she had been, there was only a flicker of movement as the leaves settled gently back into place. And then nothing.

Raphael began to cry. How could he stay here and not run to her? But he had to stay; she had forbidden him to move. So he waited, his heart thumping in his ears, salt tears sliding into his mouth. What if the soldier wasn't dead? There was blood on his gambeson, a lot of blood, but . . . he was breathing.

Anglais. Anglais were the enemy.

But . . . Raphael bit his lip.

He tried to save Maman.

What should he do? He was still crying, and his breeches were stuck to him. He cried even more, out of shame. Maman would have to clean him, as if he were a baby.

Suddenly, the silence was broken.

'I know you're there.'

Raphael gasped. The soldier was speaking French.

'Can you pray with me?'

The blood pooled around the man, soaking into the red-stained earth, so heavy and fresh from the rain. The first weak rays of dawn now hit the clearing, making the air shimmer around where the soldier lay. Raphael could see that he was young – not much older than his mother.

'I'm sorry. I tried . . .' The soldier coughed, frothy red bubbles erupting from the corner of his mouth. 'What is your name?'

'Raphael.' He edged forward towards the dying man.

'Raphael. *Angele Dei.* I die in good company, then.' The man reached inside his gambeson. The effort caused him great

5

discomfort, and he winced, his eyes rolling backwards, but he eventually pulled out a flat, broken disc. A seal matrix, likely made of silver, of the kind used to make a mark in wax. Whole, it would just about have fitted into Raphael's palm, but it was incomplete and jagged at the edges, and no bigger than a sheep's eye.

'Where . . . where is the other half!' The soldier's hands fluttered at his gambeson as he searched for the missing piece, causing more blood to spill from his mouth and down his neck. 'You must take this to my father . . .'

The soldier held out the broken seal.

Without thinking, Raphael reached forward and grasped the man's fingers, but they were cold; death was coming for him.

'He will make amends and . . . let me rest.' The soldier was finding it harder to speak now. 'My father . . . to Winchester. Winchester. Please. Bring him this. Bring it to him.'

The soldier's voice, beseeching, offered no choice. And so, Raphael nodded, making the promise that would bind him to this man, the man who had tried to save his mother, until the promise was fulfilled.

The soldier closed his eyes and didn't open them again. His breathing grew harsher and gradually diminished. Raphael prayed for him, reciting the *Angele Dei* gently into the still, morning air until the fingers he held slowly unfurled and the spirit departed.

Raphael gripped the seal matrix and, keeping near to the ground, pushed himself back with his elbows, the dirt clinging to his body as he retreated once more into the safety of the ferns. And there he waited.

There were footsteps. The danger was still around him. He laid his head low on the ground. He didn't look at Christophe's body or that of the soldier. He couldn't bear to.

Raphael couldn't see who entered the clearing. He was so far back that all he could make out were feet, pacing around the bodies. He heard more English being spoken, then a howl of grief and the sound of crying. A hand came down to rest gently on the forehead of the dead man, and then moved inside the open gambeson, probing gently. The missing part of the matrix seal was taken from the body. Cut off by the force of the blade, the piece had been there after all, and now it was found.

The feet stopped by Christophe's body, the hand coming down again to close his lifeless eyes.

'*Requiem aeternam dona eis, Domine.*'

But then, to Raphael's horror, the hand took the scapular from around Christophe's neck. The stranger stayed only a few moments more before disappearing in the direction he'd come from.

Was this man a scavenger looking for trinkets? But that didn't make sense. The scapular was just a crumpled square of cloth. And the man had been crying. Scavengers didn't cry.

The morning was cold; the rain had doused the heat of the previous day. Raphael would stay here until he heard voices he trusted, or his mother came back for him. And then they would go home, together.

But his thoughts were suddenly shattered. From somewhere deep in the heart of the forest came his mother's scream, so loud that the air shivered and trembled around him. Her cry drove a nail into his heart. Then it stopped, and her echo died away, leaving him in silence.

Raphael's head sank into the earth. Dirt was in his hair and his nose and his mouth, but he no longer cared. Like the matrix seal, he was sundered.

His mother would never come to take him home.

Chapter 1

Spring 1361, Ghent

Three dozen linen shirts; twenty pairs of slippers; fifteen ells of woollen cloth, azure; fifteen more in deep brown; two dozen bedspreads; four dozen surcoats, caps, hoods, liripipes, belts, pins, tippets, stockings, gloves.

Rafi marked the final column in the ledger, followed by a flourish of his initials: *R.D.* He sat back in his chair, rubbing the soft stubble on his chin as he waited for the ink to dry. Page after page listing the finest cloth and merchandise Flanders had to offer. The warehouse was full of items piled on tables, neatly organised so they could be packed efficiently and dispatched to the draper in Winchester.

The raw wool for these items had arrived from England many months ago. Rafi had never seen so many woolsacks. The cog had been almost keeling over when it had sailed up the Leie. The duty on the wool alone must have cost a fortune. But they had made such beautiful things with it. There were none so fine as Flemish weavers and no wool as fine as English wool.

The draper's cog would arrive within the hour, and when it docked there would be work aplenty in the loading. But until then, all was quiet even with the warehouse shutters open. The only sound was a light breeze gently rattling the wooden slats.

Rafi enjoyed the silence. Ten years in a monastery under the kind care of Brother Johannes had acclimatised him to it, and he hadn't known how much he would miss it until it had gone. He patted his chest, feeling the familiar bump of the locket that encased the half seal he wore around his neck.

It had been fifteen years since that night in the forest. He'd neither fulfilled his promise to the soldier, nor avenged his mother, and he knew he would never fully heal unless this burden was lifted. He was ashamed of his cowardice. How much longer would he stay here, festering – a year, ten years, so many years that he would be bleached bone in the earth?

The boat with these goods would leave for Southampton tomorrow. Perhaps he should go with it, add some adventure to his life. But he had neither the courage to stow away, nor the money to buy passage. He barely had two groots to rub together, and even if he had enough to secure a berth, he'd have to buy his way out of his contract with his master. He would never save that much, not until he was old and grey.

Footsteps on the quay: the cog must be here. Rafi ran his finger lightly across the lettering on the ledger. Dry, no smudges. His hand shook as he laid it on the fine goatskin. Bleached bone in the earth.

Rafi slammed the book shut.

The warehouse opened onto the quayside where the boats unloaded. The bulky oak hull of the cog reared out of the water as it dipped and bobbed along the river. It was barely sea-worthy – the dark wooden strakes were in need of repair, and the sail was ragged but the merchant who had sent it must have known from experience that it was trustworthy. No one with any sense would load such valuable cargo onto a ship liable to sink – and the merchant who owned this particular vessel, and this particular cargo, was no fool.

Outside, Rafi shielded his eyes against the sun-sparkled water. He smiled. Adam, an English apprentice who would be returning home with the ship, was striding towards the warehouse, late as usual.

Rafi shook his head as Adam tripped and nearly fell headfirst onto the cobbles. 'You would not need to rush if you were on time.'

Adam grinned. 'I know.'

'Everything is in order.' Rafi tucked his hands into his sleeves and shivered.

'You need some meat on you; that is all!' Adam thumped Rafi on the back. 'I expect you have finished everything already, have you not?'

'Some of us are reliable.' Rafi pursed his lips, but could not prevent the smile that came instead.

'Dull is what you mean. Dull.' Adam stood on tiptoe. 'Where is everybody? Are we expected to load this thing on our own?'

The other apprentices should have been emerging from the workshop, which was at the far end of the grey-cobbled quayside. There was no one to be seen, not even their master, Gamelin van Loo.

'I suppose we might as well start filling the crates.'

Adam rolled his eyes. 'Oh, must we?'

'Now, or later – it will still need to be done before the morning. I have organised everything; you only have to lift and carry.'

Adam patted Rafi on the head as if he were a small child. 'You are a marvel, so clean and neat. Those years in the monastery were not wasted.'

'Indeed! Not so. It was always my fate to be the nonpareil of apprentices.'

'Ha! You cannot have been born so perfect. It must have been all that praying.'

Rafi laughed. 'It is called taking your responsibilities seriously.'

'You are too particular.' Adam yawned.

'And you are not particular enough.' Rafi smiled. 'Come. It

will be faster with two.'

'You will miss me when I leave with the ship tomorrow. Your heart will break. Very well, very well. Don't look at me with those peevish eyes.' Adam rolled up his sleeves. 'I'll soon have this done. You are too puny to keep up.'

It was no lie; even if he wasn't 'puny' Rafi would find it hard to match Adam, who was built more like a plough horse than a man.

The cog began manoeuvring towards its berth. It would take a while for the sailors to unload the newest batch of woolsacks from England, but in the meantime, he and Adam could at least get the crates and barrels packed. By the time Rafi had gathered his first armful of finespun breeches, Adam had already filled two containers and was well on his way to filling a third.

'Boys, boys!' A red-faced man appeared at the door. His long cloak dragged on the ground, the hem muddied, leaving a brown trail behind him. His belt was tied far too tight for his girth, making his belly stick out beneath it like a wine barrel. He clapped his hands and shooed Adam away from the boxes.

'Now now, we can finish all this later. Heaven forbid that I send you back to your master without a proper meal and a mug of wine.' Van Loo leaned forward and lowered his voice. 'I wouldn't like Hugh Le Cran of all people to think me a cheapskate!' He laughed uproariously, his chins wobbling.

Rafi raised his eyebrows. Cheapskate? That would be an unlikely conclusion. Van Loo had laid out his best merchandise for the English draper. If Hugh Le Cran of Winchester wasn't impressed, Rafi could only imagine the man was wealthier than a king.

'We shall miss you, Adam.' Van Loo clapped Adam on the back. 'So come, I have a feast laid out for all my dear boys in your honour. And with sustenance, you will work faster. Ha!'

'We're not boys,' whispered Adam, 'we're both over twenty years!'

'Ssh!' Rafi nodded towards Van Loo, shuffling ahead of them to the workshop.

The shabby table, normally piled high with bolts of finished cloth, had been cleared. Seated around it were a few of the other apprentices – Willem, Vincent, Jacob and Mathys. All of them slept and worked in this building, save Mathys who toiled in Van Loo's weaving factory, in the centre of the city.

'Now, I expect all of you' – Van Loo nodded at the gathering – 'to attend to the loading of these crates after we have eaten. And we want to make sure that we get rid of Adam on the morrow, of course.' He chuckled.

'Well in that case I shall work harder than ever,' said Mathys, nodding and smiling from the end of the table.

Adam pulled a face. 'You are so helpful.' His Flemish accent was heavy, but the sarcasm needed no translation.

Mathys glared back but quickly adjusted his expression when he realised Van Loo was staring at him.

'Now' – Van Loo opened his arms wide like a benevolent king – 'we eat.'

The food was no different to what they usually ate at this time of the day, save that there was a little more of it, and Van Loo had provided an extra treat in the form of an egg custard pudding. It did not look particularly fresh.

Adam tentatively dropped a slice of salted herring on his plate. Rafi tried hard not to laugh out loud.

'If you had but stayed a little longer,' Rafi whispered, 'you would have grown fond of it.'

'No thank you. I thought Le Cran's salted pork was bad enough.' Adam pushed the fish around with his fork before finally thrusting it into his mouth. He looked as if he'd been force-fed rat entrails.

'Ah!' Van Loo had overheard them. 'Salted pork and bad English ale. What else does Le Cran have on his table?'

'The ale suits me, unlike this fish.' Adam shuddered. 'He has a fancy for French cheese, and Spanish wine, although we get to taste little of either.'

'You only ever talk of meat and ale and women and never of

your master's workshop,' said Mathys, helping himself to a second slice of herring. 'That must mean it is very poor compared to ours. I do not expect he has a weaving factory.' He grinned smugly.

'It's cleaner. And tidier.'

Everyone laughed. Van Loo was notoriously haphazard in his habits. Rafi had taken on the responsibility of organising his master's affairs several years ago, making sure his desk did not collapse under an avalanche of correspondence, but as fast as he could clear one jumble of papers, another would appear.

'I am sure he can afford the time to spare,' said Van Loo. 'Some of us, like me, have agents and customers to attend to.'

'He certainly can afford it, but he works as hard as any merchant in Ghent,' said Adam.

'But he is only so rich because his father was rich, not through any talent of his own,' said Rafi. 'Or so I thought.'

Adam shook his head. 'If I gave you that impression, then abandon it. The family nearly lost all their money when the father died. Hugh is not the eldest son—'

'Ah! That would be William,' interrupted Van Loo. 'Came back from the French wars, nearly destroyed them all, then vanished, pfft!' Van Loo waggled his chubby fingers over the dishes. 'The French have caused enough trouble for us merchants, too. Malcontents and fools, the lot of them.' He pounced on a fat piece of chicken.

Adam patted Rafi on the back. 'Sorry.'

'Ah, Rafi,' said Van Loo as the juice from the chicken smeared his chins. 'You have been here for so long and speak our language so well, I almost forget you're from Picardy.' He wiped his face with the back of his hand. 'Delicious!'

'I cannot imagine Le Cran's workshops being better than this.' Mathys nodded towards Van Loo.

'My apprentices are the pride of Ghent! I am sure there are a dozen Adams in Winchester, or in any city.' Van Loo leaned forward. 'No offence to you, Adam, of course. But how many are there like Rafi? His learning, his languages, and so artistic!'

'A few, I expect,' replied Adam, inspecting a watery bowl of pottage, 'but I would think they all get paid a lot more than you pay Rafi, so they wouldn't mix with the likes of me.'

Van Loo wagged his finger. 'Come now. You leave tomorrow, and so you grow bold. I shall miss you, nonetheless.'

'I won't,' muttered Mathys.

'My heart is breaking.' Adam speared a large wedge of cheese and crammed it into his mouth, washing it down with a hearty swig of ale. 'Finally. Something edible.'

'Le Cran has his hands full, I can see. Well, good luck to him. So long as he keeps sending the fleeces to me, then I'm a happy, happy man!' Van Loo heaved himself to his feet. 'Finish what is here.' He pointed to the remains of the meal, the pudding still untouched. 'And then to the warehouse with you. There is a lot to do.'

Van Loo shuffled towards the door that led to his quarters, filling a mug as he went. 'If you are all done by dusk, then perhaps I will allow you to visit the Blue Swan but . . .' he turned to look at Vincent who had whooped loudly at the promise of a trip to the inn '. . . only if you have that cargo fully packed and presented in neat rows and tidy lines. Get to it.'

Vincent shot out of the door almost immediately. Jacob and Willem were not far behind. Mathys mopped the remains on his plate with some bread and then pushed the dish of leftover herring towards Adam. 'My parting gift to you.'

Adam poured himself another mug of ale. 'Let them get a head start, eh? Mathys will work hard enough for two if it gets him to the inn faster, I'm sure. I'll do him a favour and drink this so he can get on with it.'

'Oh no you don't. You can bring that with you if you like, but you'll do your fair share.'

'You are very dull, Rafi.'

'And you are very lazy.'

'I know. I know something else, too.' Adam drank deeply from his mug.

'Do I guess, or do you tell me?'

Adam leaned forward. 'Do you think old Van Loose-Lips will make you a journeyman?' Adam paused. 'He's keeping hold of you because you can eavesdrop for him in the market. You're like a walking Tower of Babel. He won't pay you for it, you know.'

'As if I don't know that.' Rafi hadn't meant to say it out loud.

'Get on that bloody boat then. What's he going to do, swim after you? Ha!'

Jeetje! That would be a sight to see. A land whale, sinking like a stone in the water.

'You know why I can't.'

'Come. Come with me to the Blue Swan tonight and explain. I will bet you one mug of ale you'll agree to get on that boat tomorrow.'

Rafi took Adam's outstretched hand. 'Very well. You know you're going to lose, don't you?'

'I never make a bet I can't win.'

'Then you are about to experience something new.'

Rafi was almost out of breath by the time he reached the Blue Swan. The tavern was full, and the press of bodies combined with the heat from the fire felt like a furnace-blast after the chill of the evening quayside. This was a popular inn frequented by apprentices, sailors, fishermen, and couriers who went from merchant house to merchant house. Why go into the centre of Ghent when you could drink here? The ale was cheaper, the food passable and the clientele less particular.

Rafi stood on tiptoe until he caught sight of Adam, waving to him from a table near the kitchens.

He made his way over and took the mug of ale Adam offered to him, raising it aloft. 'To friendship!'

'To friendship.' Adam clinked his mug against Rafi's. 'Drink up!'

God's teeth, but the ale was frothy and strong. Adam would have drunk two, or even three, before Rafi was halfway through this one.

Adam smiled. 'That's the spirit! Just think, I will be gone this time tomorrow. *We* will be gone this time tomorrow.'

'Not this again.' Rafi's shoulders sagged.

Adam finished his mug and waved towards the bar for another one. 'Yes, this again. We have a bet, remember. You can tell me your excuses, but the only thing stopping you is yourself. I've said this a dozen times.'

Rafi loosened the neck of his shirt. Instinctively his hand went to the chain around his neck.

'And the sooner you sort that out' – Adam poked at Rafi's chest – 'the better it will be for you.'

Rafi jerked back. The hard metal of the hollow locket pressed against him as Adam pushed at it then pursed his lips. 'You will never be free until you find the other half. And what of the man who gave it to you? Does it never bother you that you're breaking a promise to a dead man?'

Rafi sighed. Of course it bothered him. It had bothered him from the day he first held the thing in his hands as a terrified child. Apart from the clothes he'd stood up in, it was the only possession he'd taken with him when he left France. That and the bundle of dried marjoram he kept in a book by his bed.

'The damned thing won't shatter inside that locket,' said Adam, frowning at Rafi who had clutched his hand over his shirt where it covered the locket. 'I sometimes think it would be best for you if it did.'

'It would be best for me if that whole night had never happened, but it did and I have to live with it.'

'I'm sorry. I know how much it matters to you, and we are here tonight to solve your problems. So, come, let me look at it. I promise I'll be careful.'

Slowly, Rafi pulled the chain over his head, the locket emerging from his jerkin. He held it in his palm and opened the clasp. The broken seal was thin and flimsy, more of a token than anything of practical use. It would have been much the worse for wear after all these years if Brother Johannes hadn't had the idea of making a protective case for it, enlisting the help of one of the local craftsmen who prayed at the abbey of St Michael in Antwerp. The material was cheap, but no matter. It had done the job.

Adam shook his head. 'It makes no sense to me. I can see a bit of a tree, and is that a duck, standing on a stone? It looks like a child's hand-made it. And these letters are nonsense to me.'

'*ulligiS . . .*'

'What devilry is that?' Adam pulled a face.

'*Sigillu*. It means seal. It is made in reverse, see. But it helps little. If we had the other half, we would know whose seal it was.' Rafi closed the locket again and tucked it safely back inside his clothing.

'Who has a duck on his badge?'

'A man who makes feather beds? A farmer? It could be a goose – their feathers make good pens.'

Rafi had used goose quills many times in the monastery. A bishop, then, or a lawyer who wrote for a living? How would he ever know where to start?

'And the man who killed your mother has the other half?'

'The man who found the dead soldier has the other half. I saw him take it.'

'And he is in Winchester?'

'I can't be sure, but I assume he is. At the very least he must have known the dead soldier. He . . . he cried over him. But all I know for certain is that the soldier's father lives, or lived, in Winchester because he told me.' Rafi patted his chest. 'But since he was bleeding to death he may well have been delirious. And don't forget I was only five years old at the time. Perhaps my memories are all wrong.'

Adam sighed. 'You have to do something about it. It will eat you up otherwise.'

By way of an answer, Rafi took a small mouthful of his drink and looked around the inn. The other apprentices were sitting with the captain and crew of the ship. They were already drunk. They would be lucky not to crash the cog into the banks of the Scheldt if they carried on like this.

'I know.' Rafi did not want to catch Adam's eye. 'I know. But I am afraid.'

And it was true. He was afraid of the unknown, of leaving his small but comfortable world here in Ghent. The sun rose and set on days that were reassuringly similar to the ones before and the ones to come. He did not have to think too hard about what to do next – he did not have to think too hard about anything.

'And that is your excuse? Fear? Then put it to one side. Do you want to find the man who killed your mother or not? It is that simple.'

Was it really that simple? How would finding the owner of the seal help him find the man who had killed three people in cold blood? Christophe, Marianne, the nameless soldier. It was likely the two were linked, and the dead soldier had known his killer, but this was no guarantee. As for the here and now, he had no money, and he couldn't countenance stowing away on a boat; such deception was beyond him. And even if it were of no consequence to him, there would be repercussions at the abbey where he'd been brought up. The Van Loo family had made donations to St Michael's for several generations. It was why Brother Johannes, a cousin of Van Loo, had brought Rafi here when it became obvious that the monastic life was not his calling.

It was why Van Loo had got him so cheaply.

He was trapped.

'No, no, stop thinking about this and that. Pretend that all of your problems have been solved.' Adam snapped his fingers. 'There. Gone. Now, answer the question, a simple yes or no. Do you want to find the man who killed your mother?'

'Of . . . of course. Yes. Yes.'

'Finally! Then you know what to do.'

'It's not like that.'

'Here come the excuses.'

More ale had been brought to the table. Two gulps and Adam was halfway through his cupful. Someone was going to have to carry him back to their lodgings tonight.

'It's very easy,' said Adam. 'You'll never be able to buy yourself out of your contract with Van Loo, so forget that. There, one problem gone.'

'And you expect me to buy passage with money I don't have?'

Adam swigged from Rafi's mug. 'I will vouch for you as you have always vouched for me. You looked after me when I came here to learn Van Loo's trade all those months ago; you were the only one who tried to make me feel at home. I spoke not a word of this godawful language, but you helped me and I cannot thank you enough. I'm almost fluent now! What? Why the peevish looks again?'

Rafi smiled. Adam's accent was so thick it was often impossible to understand what he was saying, although it did improve the more drink he had in him.

'If not for you I wouldn't have been able to talk to all those pretty women in the market. I owe you many nights of . . .'

'I don't want to know.'

'Haha! So proper. But I mean it – I know the others mocked me behind my back. But not you. If I vouch for you, you won't be turned off the boat.'

Rafi was taken aback by Adam's words of gratitude. It was true that the others had laughed and ridiculed Adam's lumpen Flemish, especially Mathys. Rafi had taught Adam in the evenings, and Adam had grasped the rudiments quickly enough, and it had helped Rafi with his own English. In return, Rafi had been dragged away from his evening routine of perpetual reading and drawing. He'd seen the inside of more taverns in the past few months than in the whole of his life. And he'd enjoyed the companionship more than he'd expected. It was an odd alliance, but they had both gained from it.

'And when I get to Winchester, then what? How do I live? What do I eat?'

'Get a job with Le Cran,' said Adam as if it were the easiest thing in the world. 'You can write. How many languages have you taught yourself? Jesu, I can scarce keep up with my own. He likes clever people—'

'So, I go to Le Cran and say, "Please, can you give me a position. I have no job because I ran away from my last master by stowing away on *your* ship without your permission." He will think me a very solid fellow, will he not?'

'Don't tell him.'

'You're drunker than I thought,' said Rafi. 'You think Van Loo won't work out where I've gone? He will send to Le Cran and ask if he's seen a puny boy about the place and demand that I am sent back.'

'He might not. Besides, there are other merchants.'

'Oh come. Surely even you can see the obstacles. Please. Let us speak of something else.'

There was silence. Adam shrugged.

'Come on, let's not argue.' Adam raised his goblet in the direction of a fair-haired woman who had just entered the tavern. The sailors and apprentices began to whoop and holler. 'This will be fun.'

Rafi blushed.

'You are better suited to a monastery. You need to liven yourself up.'

'I disagree, but thank you for the advice.' Rafi rubbed at his smoke-filled eyes.

'You did not like the colour of the robes?' Adam grinned.

Rafi hesitated. In many ways, the colour of the religious life had been the perfect match. There had been much to love and give him succour – the silence, the order, the routine he had clung to as a child. There was the garden inside the cloister, the roses, the droplets of dew on the comfrey, the crunch of the snow as he walked in prayer in the winter, the thyme and rosemary that reminded him of his mother. Brother Johannes had rescued him and the monastery had sheltered him. But it had not been enough.

'I lacked the required spiritual certainty,' said Rafi.

'It has never stopped anybody before!'

Rafi smiled. 'That may be true. But it stopped me.'

'Well,' Adam said, rubbing his chin. 'I may as well enjoy this while I can. Le Cran does not approve of his apprentices staying out late. He would come in and drag us all back to our rooms if we behaved like this.'

'And you will be married soon.'

Adam waved his hand. 'That's no obstacle.'

'It might be for Ailith.'

'She will do as she is told.'

Rafi sipped some of his ale. The roof of his mouth was dry. The smoke was bitter and made him cough. 'She might not be so forgiving if your eye keeps wandering. And you have not written once.'

'I cannot write well.'

'I would hold the pen for you.'

Adam thumped Rafi on the back. 'I will keep her busy enough with babies.'

'She holds a position in a house, you told me?'

Adam licked his lips. 'Yes. A very – very – rich and charming widow called Joan Cuppyng. Exactly the sort of woman who, were I as wealthy as my master, I would attend to immediately.'

Rafi put his head in his hands.

'You're too innocent.'

Rafi said sternly, 'You risk your soul with the sin of lust.'

'I shall make sure I'm shriven before I leave this life. You know the words – you can say them for me in my hour of need. When

I'm rich, I shall appoint you as my religious adviser.'

'No, thank you. I hereby decline your offer.' Rafi blinked. 'I need some air. My eyes are burning. You join the others. I will take a walk, maybe go back.'

Rafi left the inn, tripping over a foot that he suspected had been stuck out deliberately.

'Watch out, *kleine jongen!*'

Jesu, even strangers felt they had the right to comment on his appearance. As if he didn't get teased enough every day.

There was nobody on the quay now. All were abed after their suppers, or drinking in the Blue Swan. But there was a woman and her young child, hurrying from the furthest end of the quay where the water lapped against the side of the last building on the waterfront.

Van Loo's workshop and office.

The swaying lamps from the ships docked on the river guided her steps, flickering over her as the breeze lifted them to and fro. She was well dressed, a merchant's wife, perhaps. She wore a deep green gown over a russet kirtle, and a black cloak held by a silver brooch. The tallow light made it glint and shine. The boy at her side was about three years old. He was holding his arms up to his mother, wanting to be carried. Perhaps her husband was one of Van Loo's customers, and she was on her way home after purchasing some cloth. By the look of her, she could certainly afford it. She could also afford a manservant, so why was she out here on her own at this time of night?

As the woman bent to pick up her child, Rafi saw a shadow move behind her. He straightened, alert now. Perhaps it was a trick of the light, but then the woman's head turned, only slightly, as if she were conscious of danger but too fearful to acknowledge it. She hurried on again, towards where Rafi was standing. Her head remained slightly turned to the side, aware of something, or someone, following her.

She was almost running now. She would see Rafi soon, surely.

He remained still. The stretch of quayside behind her was full of shadows but there – yes, there was something there. The shape of a man, moving swiftly to match her speed, keeping away from the edge of the quay, away from the light of the boats. She stayed in the middle of the walkway, as if the shifting lights could protect her.

The shadow revealed a man who caught her and drew an arm around her neck. She jerked back with a gasp.

The man held a blade to the woman's neck, then cut along the section of her cloak that was secured by the brooch, not caring that he took a lock of the child's soft hair with it. He ripped the silver clasp from the piece of cut cloth, leaning in towards her. A thief, a common thief, moving silently between the gaps that separated the warehouses, waiting in the dark. She would have walked past him and not even known he was there.

Rafi was as scared as he had been in the forest and she was as still as his mother had been. Why? So that the child wasn't frightened? But if she called, then someone would come. But – dear God – that someone was him. He was the only person here. He tasted the sourness of the ale he had drunk earlier.

Rafi fumbled at his belt. All he had was a small knife that was used for cutting the crate bindings. It was too blunt to cause much damage; it could barely cut cheese, but it was all he had.

The thief began to trace his blade along the line of the woman's cheek and she whimpered. At the sound, Rafi came to his senses. If he didn't act soon the woman would lose more than a brooch.

'Leave her alone!'

The thief instantly loosened his grip on the woman who immediately took her chance and ran towards Rafi. He held out the crate knife. Even in this light the thief would see how much the knife wavered. Rafi gripped so hard his nails began to dig into his palm.

'Run! The inn. Ask for Adam B . . . B . . . Bixham.'

It took no second bidding, not that Rafi had the breath left to repeat himself. Her footsteps faded as she retraced his path back to the Blue Swan. She was not the sort of woman who would frequent such a place. Perhaps she would keep running, and leave him here, and Adam would come too late. Perhaps he should run too: he could outrun the other apprentices, so he could surely outrun this thief. But he didn't think his legs would hold him. His bones were water. At least if the woman and her child were spared, his life wouldn't have been a complete failure. What did it matter if he died here?

The only sound now was the fluttering of canvas flags from docked ships; that, and the voice of a thief.

'That was a costly interruption.' The thief looked towards the inn. 'Your lady friend will alert the rabble. I should kill you quickly, then, and take the few groots you have.'

The thief took the crate knife by the blade and pulled it from Rafi's hand. By the time he'd thrown it on the cobbles the sound of voices further down the quayside had cut through the darkness.

'Damn her.'

Rafi found himself bent double as the thief punched him in the groin. He squeezed his hands between his thighs as the thief pulled the purse from his waist.

'You're not worth hanging for,' the thief whispered, then he slipped away, vanishing down one of the many alleyways, a maze that led to the centre of the city.

The sour ale rose in Rafi's throat again and he stumbled to the edge of the quay on his hands and knees, vomiting into the Leie. He lowered his head and pressed it against the cobbles. He was no longer cold – his shirt stuck to him, his hair lay slick against his forehead.

Where was Adam? He'd thought he'd heard voices and so had the thief, but no one had come. Had the woman abandoned him after all?

He had no idea how he would make it back to the workshop. He could barely get up, let alone walk the full length of the quay.

'Bloody hell, Rafi, I leave you for two minutes and you start a fight!' Adam pulled Rafi to his feet with one arm. 'You look terrible, man.'

Rafi pushed his damp hair back from his face. The woman and her child were standing behind Adam.

'Where is the blackguard, then? Did you see him off? You must have bored him to death, Raf.'

'I had my trusty crate knife.' Rafi tried to smile.

'Oh well, no wonder you saw him off, with such a mighty weapon. This is Mevrouw Schellekens, by the way.'

The woman stepped forward. The child was still in her arms, his eyes beginning to close.

'You saved my life. I cannot thank you enough.' She was still shaken; that much was obvious. They would have to get her home quickly. With Adam here as a shield it was unlikely the thief would risk making another appearance.

'Where do you live, Mevrouw?' asked Rafi, who was just about able to stand up now that the tide of nausea had begun to subside. 'We can walk with you.'

The woman gathered herself. 'It's behind the inn.'

Behind the inn, where the streets grew narrow and drew close into shadow.

'We will see you home. Adam?'

'Oh yes, yes, of course.'

Rafi stepped beside her as they walked along the cobbles, past the Blue Swan. There was plenty of light shining through the door of the inn. Light and voices. Safe, warm and far removed from the menace of the dark, flickering quayside.

Mevrouw Schellekens guided them along a narrow alley, the inn on one side, a warehouse on the other. There were chains coiling from the walls, held in place with loops of cold metal. Smooth and worn and slippery, as Rafi almost found to his cost. As they passed between the two buildings the light was sucked away, only for a few steps, but Rafi felt the hairs on the back of his neck prickle. How could this woman have felt safe walking home through here? Why was she abroad so late without a chaperone?

'There.'

They had gone from a dark place to an open square. Mevrouw Schellekens gestured to a large, three-storey house, tallow candles in lamps on either side of the doorway. No, these were not tallow, but beeswax. So this woman was very rich, or very wasteful, or perhaps both because she could afford to be.

She turned to Rafi as they reached the door, the light from the candles bright on her face. She was young and pale, still in shock. She would need a strong glass of mead and a posset to calm her. 'What is your name?'

'Raphael. Raphael Dubois.'

'Well, Raphael,' she said, kissing the top of her son's head as he shifted his weight in her arms, the missing lock of hair a jagged reminder of how close they had come to harm. 'You have done me a service I shall not forget. You are a guardian indeed.' She smiled. 'I'll take a manservant with me in future, although I did not expect to be out so late.'

Rafi nodded. 'All that matters is that you are safe. The man who attacked you is at fault; you are not to blame.'

She looked at him, questioningly. 'You are one of Van Loo's apprentices, are you not? I have seen you with him entering the guild when my husband has been there.'

'Yes, I work for Van Loo.'

'He has a fine young man in his service, then. Take care, Master Dubois. And thank you, Adam Bixham.'

Rafi and Adam were silent until they reached the quayside. Adam stank of ale, Rafi of something worse.

'That was fine workmanship. Looked like one of Van Loo's pieces and she wore it well. Would look better without, eh?' Adam thumped Rafi between the shoulders.

'Now is not the time.'

'Never is with you!'

Rafi chose not to remonstrate further. He still felt sick. What if

Adam had not been on hand to help him? Tomorrow, his friend would be gone, heading back home on the cog. Rafi would be on his own. There would be no Adam, no solid rock of a man to stand beside him if another thief stepped out of the shadows. Now it had happened once, Rafi would forever fear the dark of the quayside. The next time, a viper with a knife could bite at will.

The next time could be Rafi's end.

Chapter 2

Winchester

Edith and her two companions were bent together over the herb bed in the small garden near the abbey infirmary. They worked industriously, digging with their large wooden spoons and dibbers, and even their fingers. Into each hole they made in the soil, they would drop a seed or a cutting.

'Ailith, you look exhausted.' Edith glanced at her with concern.

'I cannot stay in this position any longer!' exclaimed Ailith, her fair hair sticking to her forehead.

'Here, let me help you up.'

'You are a saint!' Ailith took Edith's outstretched arm gratefully, wiping her muddy hands on one of the few clean spots left on her apron.

'I think I'm finished here too,' said Edith, appraising the herb patch. 'The dark comes too early still. Agnes, I think we should stop for the day.'

'As you wish.' Agnes nodded, smiling. She clapped her hands to rid them of soil and dirt and stood with Edith to consider their day's work.

'The tail of this winter has been mild,' said Edith, 'but it may not stay that way and we may be lashed by it yet. Let us hope these little sprigs will last the spring. There may be frost to come.'

'And the parsley too,' Agnes said, pointing towards the back of the soil bed. 'I will need them for the ague, to mix with goat fat and rue.'

Edith smiled. 'And the parsley too. You are learning fast, Agnes. Domneva will make a herbalist of you yet.' Edith put her arm around the young girl's shoulder. 'Shall we see what Sister Domneva is doing inside?'

Domneva was laying out the herbs she had collected last summer, some of them kept in oil, others simply tied in bunches and hung from low wooden beams on the ceiling of the infirmary. She crumbled some of the leaves of rosemary, and pulled at the spiky lavender heads, the dusty pungency filling the air. Edith breathed in deeply. 'I have missed these smells over the winter.'

The nun smiled and nodded, offering Edith a pestle and mortar.

'May I help?' Agnes ran her finger along the row of bunched herbs hanging from the ceiling. They swung gently to and fro, releasing even more scent into the room. Ailith coughed pointedly, but Agnes paid no heed.

Domneva thought for a moment. 'A test,' she said. She pointed to the end of the table, which was clear of pots and jars and glass containers. 'A cure for a surfeit of food, to ease the passage of wind through the gut.'

Agnes clapped her hands and began to search for the ingredients. Edith smiled. The girl had gone straight for the jar of liquorice on the shelf above the table, which was precisely what Edith would have done.

'I shall be glad when this cold weather is all done for good,' complained Ailith.

'I am sure you will.' Edith had started to pound oil and mallow leaf together.

'Although . . .' Ailith pouted '. . . spring and summer bring problems of their own.'

Edith paused. 'Aye, well. Matters need to be cleared up. Sooner rather than later.'

'There would have been nothing to clear up if a certain person had not vanished overnight.'

Edith hesitated. She had heard talk only this morning from Nell, the senior maid in the Le Cran household. Adam was on his way home, perhaps this very day, and it seemed that Ailith was blissfully ignorant. Well, what good would come of telling the girl now, when she would find out soon enough?

Edith held her tongue and started to mix some of the concoction she was making with her finger, to check the consistency. Domneva looked over her shoulder.

'I don't think I have ever cried so much in my life.' Ailith ignored the lack of response and continued to complain.

'You did cry a lot, as I recall,' replied Edith, 'for a whole week at least. Well, three days, mayhap.'

Ailith's shoulders sagged, and Edith immediately felt remorse.

'I am sorry,' said Ailith softly. 'You have had your own tragedy. You put me to shame.'

Edith blinked and focused on the mortar. Her auburn hair had escaped from her wimple, but her hands were too wet with oil to push it back in without getting grease everywhere. She let it flop in front of her eyes.

Domneva saved her by taking the spoon and retreating to the far end of the table, where Agnes now had a selection of herbs and powders lined up on dishes.

Edith sighed. 'I am content. My children are healthy – what more could a mother wish for?'

Before Ailith had time to answer, Agnes had started clapping again.

'I am done. I have my selection. Here are liquorice and chamomile and wheat flour. I would cook them into a porridge and recommend the patient eat it every day for one week. Is that right, Mother Domneva? Have I passed your test?' Agnes skipped up and down, her face beaming.

Domneva smiled and then stroked the girl's cheek. Edith watched, wondering at how Agnes always had such a mellowing effect on everyone around her, even someone as taciturn as the abbey nurse.

'You have passed,' said Domneva.

Agnes threw her arms around the older woman's waist and then, realising what she had done, took a step back. 'Oh, I am sorry, Mother,' she said, noting Domneva's startled face. 'I am just so . . . pleased!' She skipped out of the door and around the herb garden several times.

'She is talented,' remarked Edith.

'She is.' Domneva glanced out the door at Agnes, still running around like a hoyden. 'And so young.'

'Well,' said Ailith, 'not *so* young. She is fourteen this year. May, is it not?'

Domneva nodded.

'I had met Will when I was fourteen,' said Edith, quietly.

She felt Ailith's hand squeeze hers. 'I hope I am as good a mother as you when my turn comes. And I pray you find happiness again, for you deserve it.'

Edith held on to Ailith's hand for a few moments, then busied herself putting her mixture into a glass jar and straightening her wayward hair. She was calm now and was able to bid farewell to Domneva, Ailith and Agnes without them seeing the tears she had held back.

The evening smelled of woodsmoke as Edith passed out of the abbey gate. Instead of heading back to her cottage, she strolled towards the cathedral, moving beyond the precincts to walk along her favourite path, by the waters that ran through the meadow on the south side of the city. The air was fresher here, and she needed to clear her head. Ailith's words had agitated her, but it was not the girl's fault. Ailith was young and meant well, but she had gone to the crux of the matter. Edith longed to be happy too, but she feared her chance was gone.

Edith could see the outline of St Catherine's Hill as she looked along the line of the water meadow. Underneath the hill the body of Ailith's father lay, buried in the plague pit. Edith's three brothers were also there, and her parents, too. The only person she had left from that time was her sister, Hilda. Edith sighed. Best hurry home. Hilda would be looking after the children, and it was getting late.

She turned back, to the streets where the tanners lived and worked, and where she too lived, her apprehension growing stronger with every step that took her along the streams that ran fast through the centre of the city. What mood would he be in tonight? Would he even be at home? With luck, he would be spending their money in an alehouse. Letting him drink away their hard-earned coin – her hard-earned coin – was almost better than having him in the cottage. If Le Cran had not been so lenient with the collection of rent, they would be out in Beggar's Lane with the rest of the poor.

She knew why he did it; she knew why he sometimes let his servant Roger pass by and not ask for the pennies she owed. But it could not last. He could not grant her charity forever. She feared that day, which would surely come, when she would find the wooden spike hammered into the earth outside the door. The spike that told the bailiffs they could enter. Were it not for her children she might choose poverty anyway, anything other than what might be waiting for her now.

The fumes from the pits where the tanners worked filled her nostrils; the putrid scent of animal skins left covered in ordure and urine so they could be scraped more easily. In some cases, citizens used the pits for waste, hoping not to be fined by the authorities. Whatever the cause, the end result was the same. The stench was like a blow to the stomach; she had never got used to it. She pushed open the door to their tiny cottage. The fire flickered weakly. Her crock pot kept warm nonetheless. Weak fare, barley pottage, but it would fill their bellies.

She sensed him before she saw him. She didn't want to be alone with him, so turned to go. 'The children,' she said weakly. 'Hilda will be waiting.'

His face was as sour as his breath. 'Not so fast, little bird.' He gripped her waist, tight. His fingers dug into her. Even drunk, he was able to hold her fast.

'Thom, I need to bring them home. It is time for them to be asleep.'

'Where have you been? Opening your legs, no doubt? How much have you earned?' He laughed in her face, his hands locked around her.

'What does it matter? You would have it spent before tomorrow was out.' She regretted her words as soon as she said them.

He pushed her backwards and she fell against the table. She didn't bother to right herself. He would only push her again, and again.

'I should never have bothered with you.' He began to untie the woven cord he wore around his breeches. 'You were already used when I married you, but still you cannot be grateful.'

Should she just turn around and save him the trouble? Once she would have fought, and scratched at him, but she was tired. There was nowhere she could run, not even to Hilda. He would have dragged her out by the hair in front of her children, and she would never let them see that.

She turned, and pulled her kirtle down and over her shoulders, covering her breasts with her hands before bending over the table, face down. Better get it over with quickly.

'There's a good girl,' he said. 'You know what to do.'

She knew what to do and she knew what was to come. But even so, she could not quite stifle the cry as the first blow fell between her shoulders.

Chapter 3

Adam woke with a sore head.

Rafi was faring little better, although in his case it was lack of sleep rather than a hangover. Every time he thought of the thief and the kick to the groin, he winced and had to stop what he was doing. As the others loaded the items into the cog, he ticked them off, missing some of them and double ticking others. His work had never been so untidy.

'*Kijken!*' Mathys nodded towards the workshop. Van Loo was ambling towards the cog, waving genially to the sailors on deck.

'Boys! Boys! Are we ready yet . . . What is it, Mathys?'

'Rafi saved Liesbeth Schellekens from a robber last night. She was nearly sliced in two!'

Van Loo waved him away. 'Do you think I would not already know? Tch!'

'Menheer Schellekens will buy more of our cloth!' Mathys laughed.

Van Loo nodded. A smile lit up his face. 'Well, well, what a stroke of good luck that was. This will reflect well on us all.'

Rafi recalled the woman's face, and the soft lock of the child's hair as it was sliced cleanly away. It had not felt like a stroke of luck at all.

'Mathys, take some wine from the shelf in my office. The best you can find. Bring it back out here with two cups.'

Mathys scuttled away.

The crate sagged as Van Loo shifted himself. 'You deserve more than wine, young man. More responsibility, maybe. Here.' Mathys had returned with a bottle. Van Loo sniffed it. 'When I said the best, I didn't mean a bottle as good as this. And you've opened it already.'

Mathys squirmed as Van Loo glared at him. 'Well. There's nothing for it. Rafi, take this. Consider your work done for today. And you, Adam, you may have a few minutes, since you also contributed to our good fortune.' Van Loo poured Adam a smaller cup of wine.

'There will be none left!' Mathys peered glumly at the bottle.

'Oh, did you save Liesbeth Schellekens from being cut in half? No, you did not. So get on with your work – and you will have to shift twice as hard and twice as fast to make up for wasting my best vintage.'

'But you said . . .'

'Enough! Now, I wish to discuss matters with Rafi. Get on with you.'

Mathys didn't wait to be insulted further. He narrowed his eyes and selected the box that Adam had been about to load. It was far too heavy. He staggered backwards and landed on his backside on the cobbles.

'*Lomperik!* Get out of my sight!' Van Loo launched himself to his feet and nearly went the way of Mathys. 'Come, Rafi. We shall away to the warehouse. There's too much distraction here. They are nearly done anyway.'

The stones on the edge of the quayside were slippery; deep green fronds of seaweed clung to the cobbles, glistening and perilous. The three of them wisely kept away from the edge as they made their way to the warehouse. If Van Loo went over there'd be difficulty enough getting him upright, let alone having to haul him out of the Leie with a fisherman's pole.

'Well, Adam.' Van Loo held the young man by the shoulders as they reached the building where they'd stored their wares the evening before. 'You've been a great help these past months. We'll make a man of you yet!'

'Thank you, I have learned much from you.'

'Have you?' Van Loo's beady eyes narrowed. 'I do hope not. Try not to give too many secrets away, hmm? We do not want you weaving your own dresses. I will be on the next boat out of here if you tell Le Cran how we do it.'

'Have no fear. We could never manage anything as fine as this.'

'Splendid!' Van Loo relinquished his grip and turned to Rafi. 'You have learned much too, I think,' said the merchant. 'And your actions last night should not go unrewarded. Maybe it is time we thought about your future, eh?'

The words were like the sweetest melomel. Finally, the promotion he deserved, more silver in his palm to save and buy his way to freedom.

'I was thinking . . .' Van Loo was swigging wine from the bottle and wiped his mouth with the back of his sleeve, the berry red liquid staining the material. 'Maybe we should raise you to clerk, in charge of the ledgers. How would that sound? No, no, you think about it. We shall talk more when I return.'

'Clerk?' The melomel had proved to be sour. Not even a journeyman. He would be writing pretty lines of profit and loss for the rest of his life if Van Loo had his way.

'Yes indeed! There is no one else I would trust with my paperwork. Not a single person! We will try it, let us say, until Michaelmas.'

'And then?'

'Then we can think about giving you a little extra coin.'

'In six months?'

'Yes. Not long to wait!' Van Loo beamed.

This was not a promotion. And even if Van Loo genuinely thought it was, he still wasn't going to pay Rafi for the privilege. Curse Van Loo. He would forever take advantage.

Without thinking, Rafi downed his cup of wine in two large gulps. He was aware of Adam's surprised expression and was surprised at himself. The wine started to go to his head.

'Well, it's good to see you celebrating, but do not overdo it.' Van Loo covered his vintage bottle with the voluminous folds of his cloak. 'And now, Adam,' he said, turning to the young man who towered above him. 'I am to the guild at noon so must return to my office in preparation. I bid you farewell. May you have good fortune – you will need it, with Le Cran as your master!'

Van Loo chuckled, pulling his cloak tight around his rotund body as he ambled along the quay, which was now empty of crates, barrels and boxes. The ship was fully loaded. Even the apprentices were nowhere to be seen. They would be preparing the workshop for the next batch of woolsacks from England already.

'Well,' said Adam. 'Clerk in charge of the ledgers.'

'Indeed. What a privilege.'

'Come on, do not be downhearted. Let us sit by the river while I finish my wine. You have had yours already.' Adam strode across the quay and sat by the side, legs dangling just above the water.

After a pause, Rafi followed. He was light-headed and stumbled as he came to perch beside Adam.

'Damn and blast Van Loo!'

'You have a fine title now,' said Adam. 'Clerk. Of the ledgers, no less. Did I not warn you?'

Rafi ran his hands through his hair. The cog sat low in the water, belly full of boxes. It would leave soon. Out to the North Sea, then onto the narrow channel to dock at Southampton. His chest tightened.

'Though I must say,' Adam continued, 'how you did not punch his fat face, I will never know. What a bargain you are.

Penmanship such as I have never seen before, drawing, and how many languages now?'

Rafi held up five shaking fingers.

'*Five*? Are there even that many languages in the world?'

'My Castilian is very poor. I am surprised he promoted me as highly as he did.'

'Such sarcasm from such a small fellow.' Adam cursed as his shoe nearly fell into the Leie. 'God's teeth, I only have one pair. And you, my foolish friend, only have one life. Come with me, for pity's sake. You see how the land lies here.'

'I cannot. He has me in chains. He has the monastery in chains. If I leave, he will probably ask Brother Johannes to repay the food and lodging I've been given for the past five years. He will certainly ask for more than he paid for me.'

'Then ask Mevrouw Schellekens for a position. Van Loo would be riled up if you worked for his rival. It would be worth it for that alone. I'll warrant her husband would pay you what you were worth – she may even give the monastery an endowment to reward you. What is there to lose in the asking?' Adam patted Rafi on the back then quickly grabbed him before he fell off the edge of the quay. 'All the merchants here think so highly of you. I have heard them talk.'

'Well, none of them have come calling.'

'Sometimes, you have to call first,' said Adam. 'You just sit and . . . what is this?'

Liesbeth Schellekens, as if summoned by the mention of her name, was marching purposefully along the quay towards them. A tall, neatly dressed servant followed behind her, his eyes scouring the decks of the boats, looking this way and that.

Rafi and Adam stood immediately, wiping their breeches and tunics, Adam clumsily kicking the cup that had held his fancy wine. It fell into the water with a plop.

'By the pox-riddled bowels of . . . Ow!' Adam glared as Rafi kicked him on the ankle.

'I have found you, Raphael.' Her voice was transformed from the night before, sultry and rich now that the fear had left her. 'Pieter, please.' She extended her hand, and the young man dropped a purse into it, bowing smartly.

'Master Raphael,' she began, 'you did me a very great service last night . . .'

Adam giggled, and Rafi nudged him in the ribs. The woman stifled a smile and continued, 'Please accept this as thanks from me and my husband, Menheer Schellekens – and, of course, my son.'

'It was nothing,' Rafi stuttered, 'anyone would have done the same.'

'But they did not. You did.' She smiled at him, her white veil fluttering in the breeze, held in place by a fillet of gold thread. 'Take it.' She held out the purse.

Rafi was unable to do anything other than open and close his mouth like a fish on a hook.

'Take it,' she repeated, grasping his hand and placing the purse in his palm since he seemed incapable of accepting it. 'There are fifty florins here. I trust this will be enough. I hope so.'

Rafi's head spun. Fifty florins. This was an enormous sum. This was . . . he did not know. He could not begin to comprehend the magnitude of it.

'Should you ever need help, ask for me by name. I am still in your debt. Good day, Raphael, and you of course, Adam Bixham. May Saint Bavo keep you both.'

She nodded to Pieter, and the two of them marched back across the cobbles, her scaerlaken gown flowing and shimmering like a pool of ruby as she went. Pieter ran to keep up as they passed through the alleyway that last night had seemed like the entrance to hell but today was shining in the sun. Liesbeth Schellekens. Fifty florins. *Fifty florins.*

Rafi held his breath. As soon as he said it, as soon as the words were out of his mouth, it would make it true. He opened his lips, but his tongue was too dry to let him speak.

Adam was shaking him. 'This is a miracle! God loves you, Raphael Dubois!'

'I . . .'

'Say something, man!'

Rafi wished Adam would stop shaking him, but at the same time realised that his friend was the only thing stopping him from crumpling to the ground.

'I . . . will leave with you.' There, the words were out. 'How . . . how much is passage?'

Adam finally let Rafi go. 'What is wrong with you?! I have told you, no need to pay. Keep your florins; you will need them.'

Sweet mother Mary, this was too much. 'I have to pay. I have the money now. It is dishonest not to. And . . . and Van Loo. Oh Adam, I can spare the abbey!'

'Van Loo deserves nothing.'

'But Brother Johannes does. Do you not see that at least? I will pay for his sake. Do not let that boat sail without me.'

The oars were being readied as Rafi ran to the workshop. They would push against the side of the quay and propel the cog into the middle of the Leie, which would join with the Scheldt. Then, they would be in open water. He did not have much time.

Jacob was in the workshop, parading around in a new hat. 'What do you think?'

'Where is Van Loo? Has he left for the guild yet?'

Jacob nodded sulkily towards the office. The room still reeked of yesterday's herring. How many times had Rafi lain his head on a pillow, rank with the fingertipped scent of eel or cod; or pulled on breeches that reminded him of yesterday's supper? This room held the imprint of their daily lives, layer upon layer. It clung to their clothes and spoiled their sleep. It had suffocated him.

Van Loo was at his desk, hitting the sleeve of his cloak with a book. Rafi had told his master repeatedly not to place the candle so close when he worked. The flame had finally caught on Van Loo's clothes and now the fine russet wool was scorched.

41

'What is it?' said Van Loo, inspecting the damage.

The boat would leave soon. There was no time for prevarication. 'I am come to bid you farewell. It . . . it is my intention to . . . leave with Adam.'

Van Loo narrowed his eyes. 'What's got into you, Dubois? I have just raised you and you repay me with this foolish joke?'

'It is no joke.'

Van Loo threw the book at Rafi's head. 'Clerk not good enough for you, eh? You ungrateful boy.'

Good enough? After five years of service, spying on foreign merchants in the marketplace – which none but him could do – acting as a ledger clerk *already*? No, it was not good enough. It was nowhere near good enough.

'I am better than a ledger clerk. And you know it!'

Van Loo hauled himself to his feet, a small spiral of smoke rising from his sleeve. 'I own you, boy, don't you forget that. You'll clean the privy for the rest of this week, and the next.'

'You don't own me anymore.' Rafi placed three florins on the table in front of his master.

Van Loo stared at the coins on the table, then his eyes darted to Rafi's belt. 'And you expect that to recompense St Michael's for your loss? And me?'

Rafi hadn't expected it at all. He'd deliberately pitched his offer low. Van Loo would always want more.

'Here.' Rafi tossed two more florins onto the pile. 'St Michael's debt, in full. No doubt you can replace me easily enough. I am cheap at the price after all.'

Van Loo swung his fist towards Rafi's braiel, hoping to clutch the purse, but he wasn't quick enough. Rafi was already heading towards the workshop exit.

'You could have left and I would never have known!' Van Loo stood in the doorway to his office, furious. 'St Michael's would not have suffered. I pay them to say prayers for my eternal soul. I have invested too much to stop now. You have lost your money for nothing, Dubois. Maybe you are not as clever as I thought you were.'

'Then you are well rid of me.'

Rafi pushed past Jacob, grabbed his cap and cloak, and then reached for the book he kept beside his cot and which he could not leave behind. He had shared this room with the others for five years, a dormitory by night, workshop by day. He would miss the other apprentices, but he had burned his bridges. He had to leave, now. Van Loo would block his escape. The man was already shuffling towards the door, indignation writ large.

'Goodbye, Jacob. It is a fine hat. It makes you look most distinguished.'

Adam was beckoning from the deck of the ship, waving urgently. The chains had already been pulled from their moorings and if Rafi didn't hurry the gangway would be too far to reach.

Rafi ran. He was fast and light and made it to the ship before the gap was more than a dainty leap from the quay. The wind caught his breath as he slid down the side of the boat in relief, the cog edging away from the silver-grey cobbled landing and leaving no time for regret.

His precious book was in his tunic, his locket was around his neck and his purse was safely tied to the braiel that kept his breeches secure.

He had left nothing behind.

Chapter 4

The cog felt smooth as silk as it was coaxed along the Leie, like sliding across a glassy lake in winter. The speed with which his old life dropped away had taken Rafi by surprise. The wharf, the warehouse, Ghent itself – had shrunk to a pinprick by the time he had dared look back. Everything had gone. The only certainty was that the *Lady Cecily* was bound for Southampton whether he changed his mind or not. She was gentle and kind and they had been surely blessed by Saint Bavo.

Until they reached the Channel.

Navigating their way past Vlissingen had given him the first sign of things to come. The silver-frothed water snarled at the side of the cog and the smooth lake of glass had shattered. How would they find England when the sea and sky had merged into a fearsome wall of metal grey?

'You look pale. I think we should sit with the cargo, but it might be full of bilge water. Here, let's throw this old sailcloth over ourselves and hope for the best.'

Rafi slid across the deck behind Adam and down the ladder into the hold. The *Lady Cecily* was hardier than she looked. There were droplets of rain spattered on the surfaces of the crates, and a few dirty pools of water here and there, but the cargo looked to be sound.

'If you need a slop bucket there will be one lying around somewhere,' said Adam cheerily.

'My stomach is unscathed. It is my balance I fear for.'

'Not long now. A few hours at most.'

Rafi was glad the apprentices had been so diligent in their packing. Except . . . there was more of it than he recalled. He edged his way towards a barrel and kicked it. 'I do not remember signing for this.'

Adam laughed nervously. 'Just a bit of extra cargo.'

'Just a bit?' Rafi had now counted five extra crates.

Adam pulled the sailcloth over his shoulders and curled up beside some sacking. 'Get some sleep.'

'What is going on? Adam? Adam, answer me!'

Adam drew the sailcloth over his head.

The boat lurched, throwing Rafi back against the ladder. He sat where he'd fallen, staring at the lump under the sailcloth.

'There might be a few extra barrels of ale on board.' Adam's voice was muffled.

'Ale? That is no ale, unless it can disguise itself as bolts of cloth!'

Adam shuffled out of his shelter, his dark tunic open at the neck, the muscles in his chest and torso pulling the kersey tight to bursting. He smiled sheepishly. 'We sent a consignment of wool to Van Loo last year, as you remember well. Indeed, you were there to receive it and receive it you did.'

Rafi nodded.

'Well, the ship wasn't quite as heavy when it set out as when it arrived. Some conveniently placed rowing boats along the coast might have had some extra woolsacks, which might have found their way on board. I expect Van Loo was happy enough to receive them.' Adam grinned, no longer sheepish now he had decided to tell the tale.

'But . . . one pays dues on woolsacks leaving the harbour, so what of these? What of wool that is on boats hidden in coves and inlets? Woolsacks which, as you say, might have found their way on board. Where are the dues paid on those?'

Adam shrugged. 'That's not my business.'

'How did I not see them when the ship was unloaded?'

'The *Lady Cecily* has many talents. And, like all ladies, she has secret places and only opens them up to a lucky few.'

Rafi could not believe what he was hearing. What the devil had he walked into? He was on a ship carrying goods made from untaxed wool.

'And Van Loo knows about this, you say?'

'Don't be naïve, Rafi, of course he does. Le Cran saves money on duties, so he charges Van Loo less when the goods cross the Channel. Which means Van Loo can buy more and make lots and lots of pretty dresses for your new friend Mevrouw Schellekens. And very nice she looks in those pretty dresses too, although I expect she'd look better without—'

Rafi held up his hands. 'Stop.'

'They're all doing it, you know.'

'That does not make it right!'

It was far from right; it was illegal. Duties had to be paid on all wool passing through the ports to help pay for the king's army to rampage all over France. The cost of exporting wool to Flanders was becoming prohibitively expensive as the war dragged on, but smuggling?

'Oh, don't be an old ditherlug. The more money Le Cran makes, the more he pays me. He will be selling *scaerlaken* and *dickedinnen* on Drapers' Row come Friday morn. The finest cloth that money can buy.'

'Who else knows about this?'

Adam shrugged. 'Everyone on board, at least.'

Rafi sank down on the seat next to Adam. If the customs men caught them in Southampton, they would be thrown in jail.

Adam would not be able to vouch for him then, and Le Cran? Why would Le Cran care about an anonymous passenger, fleeing his former master? No, he would be left to shift for himself. If only he had paid for passage on a pilgrim caravel to Canterbury instead of a clinker full of contraband.

He had best keep his wits about him. He would need them.

Three hours later, dangling from the side of the cog over the vast blackness of the Channel, Rafi wondered if being caught by the customs men was actually all that bad a prospect. The sea was in a better temper, and they were closer to the shore. But it was night-time, the port was a few miles along the coast, and he was clinging to a rope, the other end of which was being held taut by Adam and two men he'd never seen before. They waited below in a rowing boat, torchlight flickering as Rafi twisted in the wind.

Adam, several sacks and a payment for Le Cran were going to disembark where no customs men would find them. Rafi had begged to stay on board but the captain had refused and had as good as thrown him over the side with the rest.

Rafi slid further and further towards the water, the muscles of his arms burning as they held his weight. The rowing boat was getting closer. One of the men with Adam had hands the size of bear paws. Surely he would catch him if he fell?

'We can see you. Martin can swim like a fish. If you land in the water he'll have you out before you know it.'

'That is not as reassuring as you think it is.'

There were hands grabbing his calves, and then an arm around his waist. 'You can let go.'

Rafi could not let go. Adam had to prise the rope out of his shaking hands.

'Don't suppose he'll be up to rowing then, d'you think?'

A bottle was pushed between Rafi's teeth, and a sweet warmth flowed through him.

'Mead,' said Adam. He was grinning. 'Should do the trick.'

Hands pushed him onto a seat. Adam and two other young men were looking at him, bemused.

'Our new friend is warming up. That mead must be good stuff.'

'This is Martin,' said Adam. 'He works on Southampton Docks.'

'The fish?' said Rafi, weakly.

'And this is John.'

John, the bear, nodded and grabbed a pair of oars.

'They will take us to an inn just outside Southampton. Le Cran owns it, so no one will ask questions. We stay there tonight, make for Winchester tomorrow.' Adam took an oar. 'I do not think you are up to rowing. Just sit still and keep warm.'

On John's count of four, the men began to row, firmly and strongly.

The coast, lit up by the moon, dipped and rose as the boat rocked its way across the Channel. All was calm. The oars hit the water with a thwack and then swished gently through the waves. One-two; one-two. Rafi sat rigid, hands tucked inside his woollen tunic, cap pulled down as far over his head as he could manage. It would have served him better to row. Martin, John and Adam had the sheen of their labour on their foreheads, and it would have given him something to do to stop the crash and clatter of his thoughts. More things – too many things – than he could imagine in a lifetime had happened over just two days. He thought about how his life had been: so ordered, so easy. But always, in the back of his mind, and around his neck like a millstone, was that unfinished business. That task to complete at some undefined point in the future.

Rafi bowed his head and prayed: for his mother, for Christophe, for the dead soldier and for himself. His own *Angele Dei*, whispered in his heart, the same words he had spoken so quietly in a forest many years ago.

The point in the future was upon him. It was now.

Chapter 5

Rafi and Adam left the outskirts of Southampton at dawn. Bed and provision had only been made for one, so they had shared their food and a cramped room.

The innkeeper was sending several kegs to a sister tavern in Salisbury and offered to let them ride in the cart, driven by an unenthusiastic carter. Passing along the great forest once so beloved of King William the Norman, they reached the pretty village of Romsey in good time. The closer they got to Winchester, the more Rafi began to relax.

'I cannot believe I'm nearly here.' Rafi almost asked Adam to pinch him but hastily thought better of it.

'Aye, well, make the most of it. You have money and time on your side. There is entertainment aplenty if you know where to look.'

'I'm not here for entertainment. Oh . . .' Sticky droplets spattered Rafi's tunic as the cart dipped into a muddy rut.

'Don't be so foolish. When else will you get a chance?' Adam lay back against one of the kegs. 'Get a cheap inn and you are set fair for a year at least, the amount of money you have.'

'I don't want this to take a year. I have risked my neck getting this far; why would I sit back now?'

'Nonsense. You were never going to fall into the sea and Van Tight-Purse was never going to pay you enough.'

'Easy for you to say.'

'Well,' Adam said, closing his eyes. 'You have a merry seafaring adventure to tell the ladies. Although don't tell them too much. We don't want people finding out about our trade arrangements.'

'*Your* trade, not mine.'

'You were on that boat too, and you knew what was going on, so you cannot deny it now.'

'But . . . I got on that boat in good faith! I had no idea!'

Adam raised his hands. 'But by the time you got off, you had every idea. Did you report it to the customs men? No, you did not.'

Surely Adam was joking? As far as anyone was concerned, Rafi's name wasn't even on the passenger list. So that was an end to it. Adam would surely not give him away?

'But—'

'Haha! You should see your face!' Adam walloped Rafi so hard his ribs nearly burst through his jerkin.

The cart stopped, jolting them both forward. 'You can walk from here. Somborne be near as good as.' The carter's charity had come to an abrupt end.

'Two or three more miles wouldn't hurt!' Adam protested.

'I be already gone out of my way. Begone!'

'Misery guts.' Adam leaped off the cart and shrugged his tunic back on.

'Is he a Frenchie?' the carter snarled at Adam.

'He is from London.'

The carter pointed his whip at Rafi. 'That be worse. I would not have had him set foot on this cart had I known.'

'You would not have much choice if it came to it. My master owns this cart and you with it.'

The carter jumped down and stood close to the horse, guiding the animal slowly in an about-turn. He glared all the while at Adam and Rafi until his neck nearly twisted back on itself. The horse clopped obediently until they were facing opposite to where they had started, towards Salisbury and away from Winchester.

'Quite a performance!' hooted Adam.

'May your children shit on you,' came the cheery response as the carter plodded on his way, not bothering to look back.

'I don't suppose,' said Rafi, tucking his book under his arm, 'that I am going to be very popular.'

'My advice is to say you are from Flanders, which is more or less true.' Adam began striding along the same road as the cart, but eastward. 'Most people care little, but some might try to stab you if they think you are French.'

'Stab me?'

'I am not being completely serious. Come on.'

The path was rutted with cart tracks, churned up during the rain, frost and snow of the winter months, but it wasn't impassable, and they didn't need to clamber to the side too often to find a foothold on the grassier edges.

'I shall be glad to see Ailith again,' called back Adam. 'She will warm me up soon enough. Although 'tis not too chilly once you get moving.'

'And what about your brother?'

Adam's pace slowed. 'I'll be glad to see him too. You'll like Ned, I expect. He is sensible, never puts a foot wrong. Like you, he would pay for passage on a boat even if there was no need.'

Rafi smiled. 'You are lucky to have a family.'

'Not all families are worth having, but yes, Ned is a good brother. He has looked out for me all of my life.'

Rafi's shoes were getting soggy, and some of the cold mud was seeping through the soles. They were leather shoes, but ancient. An apprentice did not earn enough money to replace them as often as needed. Maybe he would treat himself to a new pair. After all he had been through, he surely deserved it.

A family member who looked out for him: that would be a fine thing. Christophe had taken that role once. A kind and gentle playmate, whose broken body lay in a deep, green clearing.

I let go of his hand.

Rafi was not just here for his mother and the soldier who had died trying to save her. He was here for Christophe, too. He bit back his tears and walked on.

'I wonder how different things would have been if Christophe and . . . my mother were still alive?'

Adam stopped and turned, the sun behind him. A golden giant. Youth, strength, family. Rafi would have swapped two of those just for the third. Adam had them all and it made him brave.

'You can't dwell on that. Think of what you have. I wish I could read like you. I wish I could pray like you.'

'I can teach you to pray,' said Rafi, quietly.

'There are devils on the cathedral, and devils in some of the books, like the ones you have painted I expect.' Adam paused. 'When my parents died of the pestilence, no priest would come in. I sometimes fear for their souls. It was a cruel way to die.'

Rafi sighed. 'I do not think God needs a priest to tell him who is and who is not worth saving.'

Adam's eyes widened. 'You make a terrible monk – that is blasphemy!' He crossed himself.

Rafi shrugged. 'Now you know why Brother Johannes decided my future did not lie within the walls of a monastery.'

They were nearing the top of the hill now. The woodland began to thin out, the road curving and sinking down onto the other side of the incline.

'So, these people who wish me harm because I'm French,' puffed Rafi as he made the final few strides up the hill, the backs of his calves screaming for mercy. 'What about Le Cran? Is he to be one of them?'

Adam laughed. 'Highly unlikely. Especially if you are useful. If you are, he would care little if you were the devil himself.'

52

Adam quickly made the sign of the cross again. 'He would get his steward Roger to do away with you anyway.'

'Well, I do not need to meet either of them and nor do I want to. Besides, I am Flemish, as you said.' Rafi squelched to a halt as Adam stopped suddenly.

'It is impossible *not* to meet either of them. Le Cran owns half the city and he makes it his business to be seen. Roger goes before him, smoothing the way, getting rid of problems. If he thinks you're a problem you will need to make yourself small. Mind you, I will enjoy seeing you pit yourself against him. You lose all of your meekness when you get a chance to sharpen that tongue of yours.'

'I am small. Who would be interested in me? I'm covered in shit and my shoes hardly look like shoes anymore, just clods.'

'Oh, sweet Raphael, you have no idea. You could be a gong-fermour for all anyone cares, but Roger will take an interest regardless. Any newcomer and he will hear about it.'

'I have nothing to hide. Save my accent.'

'Pah! Most people in Winchester can barely tell you where Salisbury is, let alone France; don't fret too much. But I warn you . . .' Adam was serious '. . . there was a middle son, Richard. He was killed in France. Roger was his servant. Roger has been with the family probably all of his life, but he was very close to Richard. If you need to worry about anyone, it is Roger, not Le Cran.' Adam strode forward again. 'But then, Roger is a foul-tempered barnacle and likes thinking ill of everyone.'

By all the saints, it seemed he had enemies already and he had not even set foot in the city yet. It had crossed Rafi's mind several times on the journey, the fact that he might face hostility. England and France were at war after all. But he had pushed the thought to one side to make space for other, much more pressing matters.

'You'd have to watch out for Roger anyway,' Adam called behind him. 'He's as salty as a fish barrel and just as rancid. But you may fare worse than others, so be on your guard.'

They were almost at the top of the hill. If the going were not so sticky, Rafi would enjoy himself more. It might not be particularly warm, but it was bright and Hampshire was so . . . so green. If he could capture that colour in paint, imagine the illuminations he could have made. Alas, he had to watch his step rather than the scenery. Blast this mud! He feared for his toes.

'Flanders, then,' he said. 'If they can believe I am from London, then surely they can . . . oh my!'

They had begun the gentle descent almost without noticing, and as they rounded the last of the trees, Rafi lifted his head and gasped. Below them, sitting in a peaceful valley in the loop of a river, was the city he had dreamed of for fifteen years. The sun bounced off the honeyed walls of the cathedral, and the spires of the churches were so many he could not begin to count them. The light sprinkled gold on the walls of the castle, sitting snug at the western entrance, the gate open to Aetheling Street, the road that entered from Somborne and Wilton, with its travellers, merchants, friars, priests and apprentices.

Adam turned, his eyes shining. 'Home!' He began to canter down the hill.

Rafi devoured the view. It was quite magnificent. The cathedral was a wonder. How could this city be in decline, as he had heard it said? And if it was in decline, what must it have looked like in its pomp?

I am here. Maman, Christophe. I am here. I will find who did this to you.

Winchester. England. Three days ago, he had been on a quayside in Ghent with nothing more than dreams. He had imagined the path he would take, the places he would go for information – the same as in any other great city in Europe. Guildhall, castle, churches, abbeys. They were all there in front of him, but this was not his city and he did not know where to start.

What a great multitude of spires. So many of them. Enough to make his hopes plunge like a stone down a well. Big religious houses received endowments and offered spiritual services and masses in perpetuity for the rich and powerful, but it was not just the cathedral. Smaller churches also held secrets. They would have seen plenty of marks and seals.

Which one should he ask at first? What were they all called? Would the priests be helpful or hostile? Would they offer information willingly or would he have to pay? It would take days – weeks, maybe even months. And then there were the merchants, and lawyers. Where would he stay? Would his money last? What if he was robbed? What if . . .

Stop making it worse. None of these things have happened, and none of these things may ever happen.

'Halloooo!' Adam was beckoning to him from halfway down the hill.

Adam . . .

Adam was his only friend in this strange place. Rafi ran, then slid down the hill on his backside, eyes on Adam, the purse of pretty golden florins bumping against his hip. The castle drew closer as he hurtled onward to join his friend.

They entered through the Westgate, their eagerness speeding them downward until they joined the bigger, main thoroughfare that ran from Salisbury and through to Stockbridge and then into the city. There was more traffic on the road now, carts, horses, servants pushing barrows filled with goods. His feet were sucked into the chaos of the mud, breeches soaked by the spray kicked up from a heavy cart. Well, that was that. No point trying to save his clothes now. The drapers had better be as good as he had been told they were, for he sorely needed them.

'Come, this way!'

They were well inside the gates now, standing in front of the castle, looking down the main road, which ran west to east through the city. Shops, with shutters drawn up and wares displayed, lined the route. Saddlers, skinners and goldsmiths to the left, cutlers and shoemakers to the right. There was so much choice and here, just what he needed: a shoemaker. Soft shoes of calfskin, sturdy boots, for riding maybe. Fancy shoes with scalloped rims and decorated strips of leather for contrast. All very nice but too extravagant for his tastes. Perhaps there were plainer styles inside. He was about to poke his nose through the open shutter of the next shop along when Adam grabbed him by the arm and pulled him away.

Now they passed along Spicers' Row. What was this smell? A perfume so strong it made the nose prickle. Spikenard, that was it! And galangal, warm and sharp too. There was something else, something he couldn't catch. His nostrils had the memory of it but . . . ah. Sweat and drying goatskin. That would be from the skinners and the parchment makers. But these spices, the quality was exquisite. And the colour here, the brightness of the saffron in particular – how many times had he used paint like that in the scriptorium?

He would expect to see no better fare even if he travelled to Spain or the Levant. One day, maybe he would, once his search here was over. He would eat rich, dark olives, shiny like beetles in glistening oil, and there would be no Van Loo to call him to work. He longed to tarry, but Adam pushed him on further down the high street towards a row of bright canopies and open windows that jutted further into the road than the rest.

'This is the drapery. See that?'

It was hard to miss. The largest shop on the row. The shutters were pulled back so that passersby could see right inside, to where the dresses and shirts and leggings were placed neatly on shelves. Projecting from the window was a counter, a piece of wood that folded outward, held in place by rope looping upward to two hooks above the opening. It kept the counter steady and firm so that the shopkeeper could display his wares. Rafi rubbed his eyes – these were just like the goods he'd helped load onto the *Lady Cecily*. Hoods, gloves, liripipes, linen shirts, tapets, caps, ells of cloth piled one on top of the other. This must be it: Le Cran's shopfront. Well, this was one drapery he would be swerving past at speed.

'This is the best spot in the city for selling, and this is the best shop in the whole row and belongs to Le Cran. Everyone passes this way. I have slept on that floor many a time. Come on, follow me.'

They turned right past the city pillory and the Helle Tavern where, according to Adam, there was an excellent cellar with much ale and fun to be had. Rafi was less enthused. The doorway reeked of piss, although such considerations had never bothered Adam before.

They were in a narrow alleyway now, tight enough to suck out the daylight, but not so tight a space that it could not contain a church, or at least the doorway to one. Surely this building could not back on to the tavern? Drunks and penitents squeezed together in one place?

Adam was out the other end of the alleyway already. Very few men could match Adam's stride and Rafi was definitely not one of them. Jesu, what had he just stepped on? A dead dog! The ribs of the poor animal were clear through what was left of its flesh; he could feel the imprint of them between his toes. He leaped back, repulsed. By the time he had gathered himself, all he could see of Adam was the top of his head – thank the heavens his friend was so tall.

Rafi stumbled out into the main marketplace, which sprawled outside the cathedral perimeter, held back by the walls. It was chaos. There were spicers, herbalists, potters selling ceramic jugs and bowls, baked goods, vegetables, shoes, woad, dozens and dozens of people milling and weaving their way through the displays, feeling, measuring, appraising. The ground was uneven and littered with barrels, baskets, stray dogs. Rafi's ears rang with strange accents. His English was good, but the local tongue was almost incomprehensible. Some of the words sounded less than kind, especially when they were accompanied by a sharp nudge to the ribs.

The wall enclosing the cathedral had a gate for worshippers to come in during the day, keeping the marketplace firmly at bay. But there was as much chaos within the walls as without. At the west end of the church was scaffolding, buckets and hammers and bodies being lifted on ropes as the masons got to work on the new door. Rafi was astonished at the scale of it. He would have liked to get closer, but now was not the time to get lost. No matter. There would be time to come back to talk to the cathedral clerks and priests about his seal and time to get a closer look at the building.

Adam had drawn a crowd, most of them women. He waved to Rafi. A few heads turned, but not many and only for a few disappointed seconds.

'I must away, ladies. And you, you take care of yourself. If you need anything . . .'

Adam's admirers began to disperse, leaving the path clear enough for Rafi to get through.

'It is as well you're so tall. I'd have lost you before I left that alleyway. Oh . . .'

A woman stood behind a stall, neatly arranged with culinary and medicinal items, mustard, sweeteners, bags of powder douce, crushed yarrow leaves for cuts and bruises. She was slender with sea-green eyes and the hair that stuck out at the front of her headdress was a warm auburn. Her clothes were worn, the material thin and frayed in places. A boy of about three or four was etching marks in the dirt under the table.

Adam nodded at the woman. 'Well, Edith, I expect Ailith has missed me. I had best make haste before she finds out from someone else that I have returned. She will be all the better now I am home, eh?'

'She . . . will be glad you are safely back.' The woman smiled.

Adam had not noticed her hesitation, but Rafi had. She had barely been able to look at Adam as she spoke, and her smile had not reached her eyes. Her lips were drawn tight, and her hands played absently with the items on the table, moving them a fraction this way and that and then back to their original position. He ought to buy something rather than stand here gawping, but then Adam tugged at him again.

'Nice woman, Edith,' Adam said as he ploughed his way towards the far end of the market. 'Not very lusty, but she is not really to my taste anyway.' He dug his elbow into Rafi's side. 'Mind you, 'tis hardly surprising. The poor woman was widowed.'

'Oh,' said Rafi. She seemed so young. And the child too. It could not have been so very long ago.

'Her husband used to work for— Bella!'

Adam rushed forward, his arms wide. A dark-haired young woman ran towards him, and he instantly enveloped her in a bear hug, which turned into a display of bottom-squeezing in very little time.

Rafi's cheeks burned. The English were very tactile; it was not what he had expected. Although that woman had been very quiet and solemn. And her stall – it was hard to make out now, there were too many people in the way. A fragment of a memory, of his mother at market with her dried bundles of herbs and cure-alls.

Now he could see. The boy had crawled out from under the table and she was holding him in her arms. The child nestled into her neck, and she finally smiled, not cautiously like before, but with genuine warmth.

'Enough gawking. You are drawing attention to your foolishness. This way.'

Rafi shook himself, like a goose emerging from a pond and shaking the water from his wings. 'It is you who draws attention to yourself.'

'Nonsense!' roared Adam. 'It is the English way.' He waggled his finger under Rafi's nose. 'You will grow hearty in no time!'

'I am happy as I am.' Rafi smiled, running to catch up with Adam who walked with the long, confident strides of a man who knew where he was going.

They were skirting around the edge of the market now, closer to the cathedral. It was enormous. Where did the building end? The nave was so long. And no spire, no fancy turrets, just a tower. Square and squat, punched into place by Norman fists.

'Here we are,' said Adam, interrupting Rafi's train of thought. 'Minstergate. Just through here and we are at Le Cran's house.'

And there it was. The house of Hugh Le Cran, on the corner of Calpe Street and Minster Street, with its enviable view of the cathedral and all who passed within the walls. A view like that must have cost the owner a small fortune.

It had two large storeys, and what looked like a small extension on part of the roof, like a lookout. The house was enclosed within a wall, with a large wooden gate, currently open to admit visitors on foot or horseback. The path led through from the street, along the side of what looked to Rafi like extensive stables. On the side opposite the stables were the medicinal herb beds, with a row of lavender plants, three deep, lining the path. His mother would have loved to have seen this; she had such an eye for plants and herbs. 'Follow that passage there, see. You will be back on the high street again. You can loop around here all day and look at the shops over and over if you like, but now' – Adam patted his breeches – 'I need to give Le Cran his payment. And explain the mysteries of Van Loo's weaving.'

'You . . . how?' Rafi's mouth dropped open. 'You cannot do that! You promised Van Loo, and you did not even see how it was done!'

'Oh . . . did I not, Master Rafi? You were not with me every hour of the day.'

This was not right. It did not sit well.

Adam folded his arms. 'Van Loo would do the same, and he did not honour his promise to you, did he?'

'He never actually *said* he was going to make me a journeyman, or steward. It is as much my fault for thinking it!'

'Stop making excuses for bad people. It doesn't cure their

devilry and you will still be in the same shit as when you started. Sometimes you have to take things for yourself.'

'No, Adam.'

Adam shook his head. 'And what if, say, the only way you could find out who killed your mother and that soldier was by lying, or taking something, or hurting someone . . . would you be holier than thou still?'

'I . . .'

How could he answer that question? All he had considered so far was finding the path that led to the answer. He was determined to avenge his mother and Christophe but he would worry about the *how* when he had the *who*. As for the family of the soldier, they would surely be glad to receive the missing part of his seal.

But . . . was that really true? Whoever it was might be less than glad to discover how Rafi came to have half of it in his possession. They would know their son or husband or father was dead. But they might not know the manner of his death.

Murdered. Would he lie, to spare them that?

'Adam, I . . . Adam?'

Adam was staring at the entrance to Le Cran's house, hands bunched into fists by his sides. He was breathing rapidly, the muscles of his cheeks clenching and unclenching. The sight that had so unmanned him was that of a woman, visible through the open gate. She was young and wore a haphazardly laced dress, her apron hanging at a jaunty angle around her swollen belly. She was extraordinarily beautiful. She was also very clearly with child.

From Adam's reaction, Rafi guessed that this had to be Ailith. And if it was, then the baby she carried was either very late, or belonged to someone else. Adam had been in Ghent for nearly a year, far too long for this child to be his.

She had not seen them yet. She was engrossed in amiable conversation with a man who, apart from the darkness of his hair, was almost the mirror image of Adam.

Ned and Ailith? Could it be . . .

The couple had their heads bent towards each other and Ned leaned in to kiss her. It was as she turned away, smiling, that she saw them. Her exclamation drew them to Ned's attention and there was silence.

'Go.' Adam's voice was little more than a croak. 'Take the inn near the stocks, beside the Helle. Not the other one. He doesn't like . . . just go. I'll find you there.'

There was nothing Rafi could do. It was not for him to interfere but he had never seen Adam so shaken. It was best he left, found the inn and waited for Adam to return. Not that he knew when that would be – Adam would have duties to attend to and then this . . . family matter.

Rafi found the inn near the stocks, beside the Helle, or was it near the Helle and beside the stocks? There were two inns. Which one was he supposed to avoid? Damn it, he'd take the one near the Helle.

It was a decision he would soon come to regret.

Chapter 6

The innkeeper at the Tabard, John Marsh, received Rafi less than enthusiastically, offering him a bed for two pennies in the cellar with the stable boy. When pressed for a better room, preferably for one, Marsh glared at Rafi's shoes, peeling caked mud on the chipped tile floor.

'A shilling. And a shilling and two pennies for breakfast. Now.'

Rafi saw how Marsh must see him: sweaty, dirty and smelly. Penniless. No surprise that Marsh doubted his ability to pay.

Rafi had a few coins in his purse from when he'd bought a pie in Southampton. One shilling and two pennies were duly handed over.

Marsh shifted and crossed his arms over his grease-smeared tunic. 'Where you from?'

'Flanders.'

'Flanders.' Marsh nodded. 'Good. There are a few of your countrymen in the city – they like to fight but they also like to drink and that suits me very well. Come, come this way.'

The inn had a high ceiling and a firepit in the centre of the room, smoke spiralling upwards towards the tiled roof. Over the firepit hung an iron bar, supporting pots of unappetising pottage and dubious-smelling stews. There was light enough to see, and a wooden box of tallow candles was laid by, and iron rings on the wall, which could take a rushlight for when the day turned to dusk.

It was not worth what he had paid. The rushes were unkempt, and the tables were stained and greasy. Marsh himself was no better; there was filth under his fingernails, and his breath was stale.

'Come on,' said Marsh. 'Lodgings are out there, next to the stable. Hurry up.'

The lodgings comprised a long, low building. It held a common sleeping room with one or two doors leading off to private chambers. Or at least, they masqueraded as private chambers, but they did not seem very secure. The room was only slightly more salubrious than a pigpen. The mattress was lumpy, the air fetid. The covering on the window was little more than a sack with holes in it. Wooden boards were stacked up against the grey plastered wall.

'Is this . . . is this a storeroom?'

'What of it. It's what you've paid for, so either take it or sleep in the stable.'

'I paid for a room, not a cupboard.'

'You paid for what I say you paid for.' Marsh left before Rafi had time to object further, slamming the rickety door behind him.

Rafi sank onto the mattress. He was too tired to argue. The money he'd paid was gone so he may as well make the best of things. He rubbed at his face. It was gritty, salty from the sea journey. At least if he looked like a rakish pirate there would be some consolation. But then he recalled the looks of disappointment he had encountered from Adam's admirers earlier. A cursory glance had told them all they needed to know.

Three days he'd travelled, not knowing where he would next lay his head. He was out of place here – the voices, cadences, smells, everything made him realise how far from Ghent he was. Adam was all he had, but Adam was unlikely to be of any help, not after what he'd witnessed earlier.

There was no point moping. He had best head out and find clean clothes, shoes and a bite of bread and some ale. But not here, not at the Tabard. He had paid for this so-called bed for one night, and it would be one night only. If he hadn't already parted with his coin, he would leave now, but he was damned if he was going to let Marsh have something for free. The man set his teeth itching.

The Chequers, the inn near the stocks, was obviously where Adam had intended him to go. The innkeeper, who answered only to the name of Serlo, was exceedingly amiable and assured Rafi that yes, there would be a bed available from tomorrow night and yes, Adam did drink here from time to time and if Rafi wished to wait he was more than welcome to do so.

'But, pray, kindly remove your shoes and leave them outside as you are making the place smell mightily of cat piss and privies. If you can pay I care little how tidily you dress but I must say, I can do without the smell. People will think it is my cooking and I do pride myself on my potpies and provenance, so if you do not mind?'

A not unreasonable request, delivered with barely a pause. And, damn it, the potpies did look delicious. Rafi paid his penny and was given a tender feast wrapped in pastry. It was as he was wiping rich gravy from his chin that Adam, who appeared to have aged several years since this morning, came through the door.

'Whore.' Adam dragged a stool across the floor and thudded onto it.

Serlo was at the table with a mug of ale before Adam had time to ask for it. 'It is good to see you back.'

'Well, I'm glad someone is happy.' Adam snatched at the mug and tipped the contents into his mouth, liquid snaking down his neck and onto his shirt.

'Ah.' Serlo knotted his brows. 'I see.'

'You do, do you? A belly that big is hard to miss on a woman,

I suppose. It's almost as big as yours. I expect everyone has been laughing behind my back!'

'Not so, Adam, do not . . .'

'Don't tell me what to do. Here, take your money.' Adam threw a handful of coins at Serlo, most of them scattering under the table. Rafi stooped to pick them up.

'Oh, can you stop being so bloody perfect for one moment? If Serlo wants his money he can get it himself.'

'And if you want to remain at this table' – Serlo took the coins from Rafi and retreated towards the cellar stairs – 'you can mind your tongue.'

This was going to require delicate handling. Rafi had not seen Adam in such a mood before. He could be quick to anger, but was usually quick to lighten again. Not this time.

'Before you ask, yes I have spoken to her. And never will again, nor my brother.' Adam slammed his mug hard onto the wooden trestle.

'What has happened?' Rafi asked softly.

'Her broken heart healed very quickly. And who was on hand to heal it for her? My brother. Who, it would appear, had always loved her and no doubt' – Adam jabbed his finger at Rafi – 'was pleased as a cat with a gutted pike to hear that I had left. He didn't wait very long to open her legs, and nor did she think to stop him.'

'Adam. I can understand that this is a shock, but . . .'

'I speak as I find!' Adam raised his voice. Half a mug of ale and he was already drunk. Chances are he had been drinking before he got here. 'And you understand nothing . . . Nothing!'

'She looks close to her time.' The spilt ale on the front of Adam's tunic had begun to darken. 'Things do not always run smoothly. You would regret it if anything went awry.'

Adam scowled. 'Lily words. And if you intend to press me with a fine speech about how I will get over it, save your breath. I have already done so. She's not worth the bother.'

'The child will be your flesh and blood, Adam.'

'It will be *his*, not mine. He is not my brother anymore.'

'You do not mean that.'

'What would you know?'

Rafi chose not to reply. Whatever he said was going to be wrong. It was Adam's pride, not his heart, that hurt. He had never once said he loved Ailith, had never accepted Rafi's offer to write to her. He had looked at other women – and probably more than just looked – plenty of times in Ghent. And Winchester too if his earlier performance with Bella was anything to go by. If he had loved the girl, Rafi did not understand how he could behave the way he had. Adam had not fed their love. It was no wonder hers had withered so fast with no sustenance to keep it secure.

'Say it, go on. You might as well.'

Rafi would prefer silence but Adam would prod and poke until he got an argument. He wanted someone to blame for his own mistakes, and Rafi was the nearest target. Well, so be it. Perhaps some home truths were needed.

'You never wrote . . .'

Adam pushed his mug to one side and leaned forward over the table. His breath was sour.

'Are you blaming me for this? Is this my fault – is that it? Fine friend you are.'

'I kept telling you – only you were too cloth-eared to listen. And don't talk to me about friendship. You have not been honest with me.'

They locked eyes for a moment before Adam sat back. 'What else could I do? My master bids me and I obey. He sent me to spy on Van Loo; 'tis done now.'

'Not quite done. You blabbered like a halfwit. Your master might have thought it was because you were tired from the journey but it seems my suspicions were correct.' A hand picked up Adam's mug. 'Ale, and women. As usual.'

The hand belonged to a man with a tight mouth and a piercing eye. 'Is this the miscreant who stowed away on the boat?' His attention was on Rafi now.

'He paid. I told you.'

'So you say, but judging by the state of him I say you lie.' The dark eyes travelled up and down Rafi's body, coming to rest on the bare feet under the table.

'Not that it's your business, but I did pay.'

'Not my business? Tell him, Master Bixham.'

Adam groaned. 'This is . . . this is the steward I was telling you about.'

Salty as a fish barrel and just as rancid. Roger Writel. Rafi's plans to avoid the man had been dashed already.

Roger pulled up another stool. It seemed they were to have the pleasure of his company. Serlo scuttled across, a helpful little beetle with three mugs on a tray. Rafi had not asked for any ale. Adam grabbed his before the tray had even been set down. Roger cupped his, but did not drink.

Now Rafi could get a better look at him. The steward was wearing a badge on his worsted surcoat, which Rafi presumed marked him as Le Cran's servant. His narrow face was deeply lined, especially around the sides of his mouth, like furrowed soil. A man could grow turnips on that face and still have room for a second crop. Coupled with his closely cropped hair, Roger looked like an angry cadaver.

Roger began to tap his long finger on the splintered, sticky trestle table. 'Your master will want to speak to you tomorrow, so make sure you are sober by then.'

Adam grunted.

Rafi eyed the badge. No ducks, no geese, no trees. Le Cran was not the mystery owner of the seal – at least that much was resolved.

'When you have quite finished, why not tell me what you are doing here. More to the point, explain how someone in such a state of dereliction is able to afford passage on a ship.'

By all the saints the man was rude, just as Adam had warned.

'I have business here. Family business.'

'Do you now. And what family business would that be?'

'My own.'

'You do not understand.' Roger leaned forward. 'You were on the *Lady Cecily* without permission.'

'I paid.'

'So you keep saying. But as soon as you set foot on board, your business became my business. I will ask you again, Frenchman. What are you doing here?'

'I am from . . .' Rafi caught the slight shake of Adam's head.

Roger smirked. 'No, you are not. I can hear it a mile off. I will tell you why you are here. You are—'

Adam snatched at Rafi's mug. 'He's not going to tell anyone what was . . .' Adam slurred more quietly, 'what was on the ship. He didn't know until we had cast off.'

'And you expect me to believe that?'

'It's the truth.' Rafi was growing exasperated. How many times would he have to tell Roger that he had paid honestly for passage and had his own reasons for being here – reasons that had nothing to do with wool smuggling or whatever else Le Cran was up to.

Roger shook his head. 'I do not believe you and I want you gone.'

'Believe me, I do not want to be here. The sooner I can leave, the better.'

Adam had finished Rafi's drink and now looked beseechingly at Roger's. 'C'mon. You are not going to drink it.'

'And neither are you.' Roger poured the drink into the rushes underneath the table.

Adam lurched forward, smashing his knee into the side of the table. 'Jesu!'

'Serves you right.' Roger's face was like granite. 'Be in the workshop tomorrow by dawn, and if you are one second late I will have you cleaning the privies so fast your breeches will be covered in shit before you can count to ten, and as for you' – the piercing, dark eyes bored through Rafi – 'I will make sure you are out of here by the end of the week, if not before.'

'You cannot tell me what to do.'

'Oh yes I can. So you either tell me what you are really about or I have you thrown on the midden. Or, if I am feeling charitable, jail. What is it to be?'

The finger started tapping on the table again.

'Why would you throw me on a maiden?'

Roger narrowed his eyes. 'Are you trying to goad me?'

'Midden, not maiden.' Adam belched and let out a stinking breath. 'The midden is the pile of shit outside the walls.'

'Midden,' repeated Rafi. 'I didn't know this word before.'

'You'll know it soon enough if you carry on with this caper.'

Jesu, this was not going well. There was no way Rafi could afford to be thrown out of Winchester before his search even began. He had no doubt Roger would do it. There was nothing for it, then.

'I'm looking for somebody. They know who killed my mother and I have reason to believe they are here.'

Roger's look of surprise was somewhat gratifying. 'I must concede that I was not expecting a lie as elaborate as this. In Ghent, I take it? In which case, why not look there?'

'No. Not in Ghent. From . . . the war, just outside Crécy.' There was no point in lying about that at least. Roger had already worked out that he was no Fleming.

Roger's face tightened, the lines deepening. He reached for the pouch at his waist and threw some money on the table. 'Tell Serlo that is for the spilled ale. You can pay for your own, and his.' Roger nodded at Adam. 'But take my advice and get out of here.'

'But I was telling you the truth!'

'I doubt it.' Roger scowled at Adam. 'And make sure he spruces himself up or he will get a kick in the cods tomorrow.'

'But . . .'

'Crécy, you say? That was years ago. You weren't even born.'

'I am twenty years old!'

'You look about twelve. You should have chosen Poitiers – at least it would have been more believable. How many men d'you think there are in this city who would have been there?'

'I cannot claim to know that.'

'Dozens and dozens. And dozens more. So how convenient for you that you cannot possibly leave until you have spoken to all of them when in fact, you are snooping around asking questions and spying for whoever it is who sent you here. Van Loo, no doubt.'

This was monstrous. 'How many times do I have to tell you?'

Roger waved his finger. 'I would take care if I were you. There are dozens and dozens of bowmen too. They will be keen to know where you are from. I have a bow in good condition. I doubt I am alone in that.'

'Your . . . you have your . . . you were at Crécy?'

Roger pushed his stool back. Adam had slumped forward, head on the trestle table. Roger kicked him on the ankle. Adam did not wake up.

'Like many others. And if you are not out of here by the end of the week, I will string that bow and put an arrow in your guts myself.'

'He ain't as bad as he seems,' said Serlo after Roger had left.

'He is worse,' Adam groaned. 'How the hell am I supposed to be up by dawn tomorrow? Rafi, get me back to Calpe Street, for the love of God.'

Like old times: carrying Adam back home after an evening of excess. But this wasn't Ghent, this was somewhere Rafi did not belong. Roger had opened his eyes to yet more danger. How could he not have realised that there would be men here who had borne arms in northern France, Picardy, Crécy? How long had it taken him to walk into one such man? Less than a day. He'd probably encountered several already. Marsh, maybe; Serlo, too. How could he ask about his mother, or explain where he had got the seal, without giving away where he was from?

He was stuck now. Stuck like a pig in a ditch. To move forward was to give himself away. But if he didn't move at all he would find no answers. He could guess the answer to one puzzle, though.

Why did Roger not throw him out of Winchester right now? He could march Rafi down the street by the scruff of the neck and kick him through the city gates – none would lift a finger to stop him. But what good would that do? Surely it would be better to keep a troublemaker under observation than risk him slipping into the murk to carry out his foul deeds?

It was as clear as day. Roger was going to spy on him, a cat weaving silkily between the ankles, getting in the way, holding everything up until persistence paid off and it finally got what it wanted.

Well, the cat would be waiting a long time, for there was no mystery here. If Roger wished to waste his time, then let him. Indeed, it would add a certain piquancy to a task that Rafi had already begun to realise would be a lot more difficult than he had imagined.

Chapter 7

Rafi woke. Where was everybody? Jacob, Willem, Vincent . . .

Oh. Now he remembered, now he felt the unfamiliar bumps in the mattress. And outside, voices, a language he understood but did not inhabit. The ceiling, low, with traces of damp in the corners and the smell: musty, cloying. For a few moments his senses struggled to keep up with his mind as they readjusted to these new surroundings.

The Tabard. Jesu, he would have to get out of here today. Serlo would take him, on condition he did something about his shoes before crossing the threshold again. Rafi had not expected personal hygiene to be a particularly English concern, but it was most definitely of concern to Serlo. Very well, the sooner the issue was resolved, the easier he would breathe.

A bucket of cold water sat in the corner. Rafi sniffed it, dipped his finger in a few times, fearful of what it might contain, but other than a slightly stale smell, it seemed safe enough. He plunged his head in; the icy shock brought everything to wakefulness. He shook the water from his hair like a dog in a stream. More alert now, he removed his shirt and splashed water over his chest and shoulders, looking around for something to wipe himself with. Nothing.

Waiting for his skin to dry, he took one of the boards that had been propped up against the door. There was paper and charcoal too. It seemed that Marsh was making some kind of sign for the front of the Tabard. The penmanship was as underwhelming as the quality of the hospitality Marsh had shown him.

Well, there was jest to be had here. Rafi wiped his hand on his breeches and reached for the charcoal. The soft weight of a drawing implement on his palm sent a tremor through him, and he smiled. He forgot the ache in his back and hips. For ten minutes his attention was wholly fixed on the paper, his hand moving deftly across the surface.

'I will show you what I think of your so-called inn.'

The shapes took form. The entrance to the Tabard, with the firepit and hooks, two rats hanging over a pot, chairs overturned, Marsh relieving himself into a bowl of pottage.

'No doubt you would serve this for breakfast if you could.'

Oh, how he had missed this. It had been too long since his hand had lifted a brush from a paint pot, rich colour sliding across parchment. He could not stop now.

A woman – he would make her angry, perhaps he would have her stab Marsh in the guts. She was respectable, her dress prim and rich, like Mevrouw Schellekens' beautiful scarlet gown. Soft hair, smudged slightly to frame her face, the smile reaching her eyes . . .

Rafi's hand stilled suddenly. He put the paper down as if it had bitten him.

After he had dressed, he glanced at the drawing again before leaving the room. No. He had not been mistaken. It was her, the woman from the stall. Edith.

Marsh was raking the ash from the firepit. He had his back to the open door and didn't notice Rafi as he slunk along the side of the building and out on to the high street. No need for goodbyes. He hoped not to see Marsh ever again.

The bells were ringing as Rafi made his way back up towards the Westgate. It was terce, late already, the third hour after dawn. At St Michael's, he would have been hard at work in the scriptorium by now. In Ghent, he would have made several trips to and from the guildhall or the marketplace. Adam, with his sore head and injured pride, would have been dragged from his cot by Roger hours ago.

Emerging at the height of the morning was almost sinful, but who was going to condemn him for it? Brother Johannes? Van Loo? There was only himself and he had no intention of repenting his own sloth.

I can do as I please now.

Rafi well remembered where the shoe shop was, the one with the fancy items. Perhaps there would be less ostentatious styles hidden inside. Or perhaps . . . damn it, why bother with old leather slops anyway? Why not have scalloped shoes, just this once? Had he not earned a little respite?

And now, clothing. Winchester was full of drapers. Any of them would do – bar one. He would be avoiding Le Cran's establishment. How well he knew the items he would find there, for had he not helped design and pack them? The quality was assured, but he would not be buying.

He was instead measured for a set of clothes in a small, tidy shop. There were ready-made items in out-of-date styles but the seams were neat and the cloth well cut. So much for gold thread and smuggled *dickedinnen*. This would do him nicely. He bought two linen shirts, some breeches and a tunic of light wool in a tabby weave. He picked out a piece of perse broadcloth to have cut into a three-quarter-length surcoat, with the rest for a hood, dark blue with a chaperon for his shoulders in case it got cold.

Now that was a fine way to spend the morning, far better than being cursed by a carter and growled at by a belligerent innkeeper. He looked better and no longer smelled of cat piss and privies. Now to settle himself in his new room and get on with his search.

Where to start? The cathedral – no reason to put it off. He had been brought up in the Benedictine order; the monks here followed rules he knew well. He imagined being embraced by friends, welcomed into the waiting chamber while the clerks listened to his tale and assured him of their assistance.

Instead, he was ambushed by Roger, lying in wait for him outside the Chequers.

'Where are you going?'

'That is not your business.'

'We have already had this conversation, Dubois. Are you looking for your paymasters, perhaps?'

This was pointless. Rafi began to edge past Roger, but found his arm caught. 'Let go of me, Writel.'

'Not until you tell me where you're going.'

Rafi shrugged. What was the harm, if it got him on his way? 'The cathedral. Happy now?'

'You think one of the monks murdered your mother? Oh my, this tale weaves tighter and tighter.'

'I am going to ask them if . . .' He was going to *show* them, not ask them. He could take his locket out right now and show Roger as well, a man who, according to Adam, knew everything about everybody. So why was he disinclined to do so? It could save him a lot of trouble, and Roger had been at Crécy after all. But he had seen the man's badge; it was there on his tunic right now – a wine bottle and grapes, the mark of a vintner. It was more than likely that Le Cran was a vintner as well as a wool merchant. Many of his kind traded in more than one commodity. So, that explained the badge, and since there were no trees or feathers, it was a waste of time pursuing Le Cran further.

But there was another, less worthy reason. After only two days in Winchester, Rafi had been treated with derision and contempt, first by Marsh and now by Roger. If there was even a small way in which he could aggravate and mislead, then that seemed perfectly fair.

'They may recognise the man from my description.'

Roger laughed. 'A description? From . . . how old were you?'

'Five. I have a remarkable memory, for I am a remarkable person.'

'Oh dear. This is very poor. Can you not do better? Describe this man to me. Mayhap I know him.'

Rafi thought fast. 'Bright ginger hair, seven foot tall, Saracen helmet and linen pantaloons.'

Roger narrowed his eyes. 'You mock me, Dubois.'

'Think what you like. I'm going to the cathedral anyway. Are you going to follow me?'

'You think you're so clever. But you are not. Where did you get this if you're a lowly apprentice?' Roger flicked at Rafi's new tunic, which parted to reveal the heavy purse tied to his braiel.

Rafi took a step backward. 'I earned this fairly.'

'Oh, come now. Look at these,' Roger stepped on Rafi's toe. 'Finest Cordoban leather. Earned my arse. Unless you stole this, someone is paying you handsomely for services that involve more than just winding ells of cloth.'

Jesu, his foot was being crushed. He pulled it out from under Roger's heavy boot, nearly falling backwards. 'Leave me be. If it saves you time, after I finish at the cathedral, I shall be visiting the abbey, which I can see from here is at the east end of the—'

Roger's hand was around his windpipe. 'You go to the abbey and I swear to God I will kill you.'

Rafi coughed, and the air stuck in his throat as he struggled to free himself. It was hurting; he could not catch his breath. Roger held him for a little longer before sending him sprawling into the dirt.

Rafi's breath came in gasps, drying his mouth. He struggled up. Unsteadily, he began to pat himself down, hands shaking. His purse was still there, thank the saints. But . . . his book. Where was his book?

He sank to the ground again, turning around and about on his knees, looking between barrels, under moss and stone. Pigs had run down the high street this morning, escaped from the butcher's yard, and foraged in the heaps of waste outside Serlo's cellar. No matter – Rafi dug his fingers into pig shit and detritus, desperate to feel the hard edge of his beloved book. But it was not there.

No, no, no, no! He remembered now. The drawing. It had so unnerved him he'd left in a rush this morning. The book was still at the Tabard. He turned towards the cursed building. There was no sign of Marsh. Perhaps he could sneak in the side. The door to the room he had slept in was so rickety, who would know if someone bashed it in?

'Lost something?' Roger followed his gaze and then, before Rafi had a chance to get to his feet, sprinted down the alleyway between the two inns, darting through the side door that led to the kitchens where, seconds later, Marsh could be heard roaring expletives.

Rafi was up as fast as he was able, still coughing, but the sludge and mess was slippery and he fell again before he could properly right himself. He shook as much of the mess off his hands as he could, then slid into the yard.

Marsh was coming out of the room Rafi had slept in last night, the drawing and the book in his hand. Rafi lunged forward but found his arms pinioned by Roger. 'You will see what it means to cross me now, Dubois.'

'No!' He kicked back at Roger's shins but Roger was too strong and was able to hold Rafi far enough away to avoid the flailing heels.

'Writel has told me all about you.'

Rafi stopped dead. Marsh's face was contorted with hatred.

'Bring him inside,' said Marsh. 'I have something to show him.'

Roger forced him forward, into the main body of the inn, towards the blazing fire pit. Marsh held up the drawing. 'I suppose you thought this was funny, did you? After all the kindness I showed you. Not so funny now.' Marsh threw the drawing into the pit.

Rafi began to struggle again. He knew what was coming next and he had to stop it. Roger tightened his grip. 'Oh no. We're not finished here.'

Roger was a sinewy man, maybe twice Rafi's age, but he had Adam's strength. When Rafi struggled, he felt Roger's muscles tighten, hard as rock.

'There goes your fucking book!' Marsh tossed the book after the drawing.

Rafi could barely breathe. The flames danced before him, the corners of the book curling as the orange tongues licked at the pages. His body sagged. It was pointless struggling now.

'Why? Why did you do this? What have I ever done to you?'

'Flanders, you said. Flanders my arse. You lied to me. Killed my boy, they did. You. You and your kind.' He prodded Rafi with his finger as he spoke. 'Get out of here before I put you on the fire as well, you blackguard. Get out of here!'

Rafi stood where he was. He could not leave the flames. He could not tear his eyes away.

'I would kill every last one of you with my bare hands if I could. Get away.'

Rafi could take it no longer. He had lost something precious. All he had left of his mother had been held in that book, a single sprig of marjoram. The heaviness in his heart was intolerable; he had to get away from it. He ran from the inn and through the yard, across the high street, dodging a cart almost too late. That would have solved his problems, to be crushed to death under the wheels. His heart had been wrenched asunder, so what difference did it make if his body was broken too?

He kept running, paying no heed to whom he pushed out of the way, not looking where he was going until he could go no further. He had reached the great door of the cathedral, the stones new-cut and sharp, the scaffolding reaching high, the clang and crash of the masons' hammers ringing in his ears.

Inside, Rafi fell to his knees and rested his head against the cool, smooth tiles. He was shattered. He still had his money, but he would have swapped all of it, even years of his life, for his book and his treasured herb.

He crawled to a corner, not caring what people thought and there he remained, in a dark, quiet place, hugging his knees to his chest. He was vaguely aware of the mumbling of penitents, their feet shuffling along the nave as they made their way to the transept. He looked up at the motes of dust held suspended in the light that filtered through the windows, the beams growing wider and wider as they reached the nave, little pools of light on the floor. He hid from them, pressing his head down towards his chest so that he saw only darkness. And then he remembered.

Five years old, motherless, he had run back to his house near the forest, trying not to look at Christophe's body as he emerged from his hiding place.

There had been no one there. The garden had been trampled, all his mother's vegetables and canes and wild garlic squashed and ruined. And inside, her earthenware pots smashed, dried peas and barley spilling out of their sacking, tables upended, chairs thrown against the wall and splintered. Soldiers. They would have found nothing. That was when he knew his mother had gone for good. She was so tidy and so ordered, everything in its right place, everything just as it should be. Not like this.

He tried to clean up, for her sake. He wanted to put the table upright again, but it was too heavy for him. Her broom was broken, the handle snapped and only a jagged stump for him to hold on to. It cut his hands, left splinters in his soft fingers. He tried to pick up the broken pots, finding all the parts and pushing them together to make them fit, but they could not hold, and nor could he reach the shelves to put back those items that were still intact. There were no chairs left to stand on, and he was too little.

Night fell, and he was still alone. He waited until dawn and then, hungry and bewildered, he decided to walk towards the village of Crécy. He had been there many times with his mother and would surely be able to remember the way.

At his feet, as he left the broken cottage, was a bunch of marjoram and a bunch of thyme. They had fallen from one of the beams on the ceiling. The thyme had almost disintegrated, flattened by careless boots, dusty from the dirt floor with just a few woody stems held with cord. The marjoram was in a better state, but delicate. He breathed it in. Hers had been the last hands to touch it. He pushed it into his jerkin, nearly crying when some of the leaves stuck to the rough wool. It was precious; he could not allow it to break or shatter. It was all he had left of her.

Without his mother to guide him, he had gone in the wrong direction and after several hours had become lost and disorientated. He hid by the side of the boot-trampled path as a tall, black-cloaked figure emerged further along the route. Rafi's mouth was dry, and he had not eaten for two days. He was faint with hunger, and when Brother Johannes found him, scratched and bleeding behind a blackberry hedge, Rafi had offered no resistance. The monk had gently picked him out of the thorny bushes and carried him in his arms, for several miles, to the next village.

It was Brother Johannes who had saved the little sprig of marjoram, rapidly falling to pieces, by placing it gently between the pages of a prayer book, where it had remained until this day. Until, on this day, it had been cast into a fire.

His knees still drawn up to his chest, and his head pressed hard against them, Rafi cried, great gulps shaking his body as he sat in the corner of the enormous Norman church in this alien city, miles from home. He wept until he was exhausted. No one stopped to comfort him; the feet continued to make their way up and down, to and from the altar; the spears of light continued to shine, none troubled by the small, singular figure in the corner. Rafi was unseen and insignificant, and for that he was grateful. His grief felt so deep he could drown in it. It had taken fifteen years for the tide to finally rush in.

What devilry had taken hold of Roger? At the mention of the

abbey, he had become wild and enraged. What was in the abbey that Roger was trying to hide, that had led to this – the burning of his memories? Rafi could see the book now, the pages curling and charring and turning to dust in front of him, the little sprig, what had been left of it, gone forever. He would find out. This was not to be endured. He had lost his mother once, and now he had lost her again.

Chapter 8

Rafi stepped out of the cathedral into the sunshine. He recoiled from the brightness of the day. How could the sky be a canvas of such joyous blue when inside he felt nothing but the darkest misery? He was shaken and heartsore.

He wished he were back on the quayside in Ghent. His hands were empty, his heart ached for his mother and his cousin, and the soldier weighed on his conscience. The enormity of the task felt like the bite of a wolf's teeth around his neck. And yet he had come all this way. It could not be for nothing; it must not be for nothing.

He would not turn back.

He shielded his eyes before stepping into the light again. What had his mother taught him during those late winter days when her seeds and plants defiantly stayed beneath the warm coat of the soil? What was it she had always said?

Persévérance.

It would not be the cathedral he would ask at next; it would be the abbey. He would search for the seal's owner, and maybe that would lead him to the man who had taken his mother. If he found more than Roger had bargained for at the same time then so much the better. Let Roger fret, let him lose sleep, let him waste time trailing a nobody through the streets all day. The man could rot in hell for all Rafi cared now. Remembering how much he had enjoyed drawing the ill-fated picture of the Tabard inn, he now felt an urge to purchase parchment and pen and retire to his room. When he was younger, his thoughts were often sharpened while at the task of illumination. Perhaps something similar would work for him now.

'Lamprey. Best lamprey!'

Rafi had not been paying heed to where he was going. His footsteps had taken him out of the cathedral precinct and back into the tumbling marketplace. The voice belonged to Bella, the woman who had welcomed Adam so warmly yesterday. She was at a stall gutting and descaling fish, her sleeves rolled above her arms, viscous fluid spattering her apron. She placed the chopped and diced fish in the basket of the woman in front of her before moving on to the next customer. Taking an eel from the barrel by her side, Bella deftly clubbed the wriggling creature over the head with a ragstone, which she also used for sharpening her knives.

If he was close to the fish stall that meant he was . . . oh no. She had seen him, the woman he had drawn this morning, the woman brought to life on the page. Edith.

She was standing by her stall, where the edge of the market met the path to the high street. The boy was in his favoured spot under the table, but this time he was joined by an older girl with frizzy hair. They looked like brother and sister and were playing with stones and what seemed to be spindle whorls marked with patterns. So the woman had two children. It would not be easy for her. Adam had said she was a widow and it seemed she had to feed these little ones too.

Most people passed her by. The better spice shops were on Spicers' Row, which he had passed yesterday with Adam.

But Rafi was drawn to her table, strewn with simples and

many workaday herbs that he recognised and knew well, and some more unusual ones. A dish of saffron, some orange peel preserved in brine, such as the Spanish trade ships were wont to trade in Ghent before making their way to London. The import of such items was expensive, yet the woman's clothes were poor and almost threadbare. It did not seem worth the cost to sell such wares when the stalls on the high street took the greater share of trade. How could she afford them?

She was watching him. He had tarried too long, staring at her. Perhaps he could ask her what the church was called, the one in the alleyway near the dead dog. It would be an excuse to speak to her.

Rafi pretended to consider the open bags in front of him, keenly aware of her, watching her out of the corner of his eye.

She was not plain by any means, nor was she a dazzling beauty like Ailith, although this didn't bother Rafi one jot. Her hair escaped in soft tendrils from the grubby white headdress that sat haphazardly on her head, the same colour hair as the girl playing at her feet. She put him in mind of his mother, or maybe it was just the sight of these herbs, which were comfortingly familiar to him. Perhaps it was little more than that, the trappings of his past, the reminder of someone he had loved and lost and missed every single day. But something about her would have made him stop anyway. He didn't understand what it was, why the light blurred around her, why she made him feel more alone than ever.

Rafi picked up a small herbal sweetener tied in a cheap piece of fabric. She had stitched the edges neatly and evenly with black thread, each straight line interspersed with a cross. The sweeteners were stacked in little wooden bowls, which had been carved around the outside with swirling patterns. They were unvarnished and partly faded in places, but very prettily done. Rafi held the posy in the bag and sniffed. The scent took him back to childhood summers.

'Lavender and . . .'

'Yes?'

He hesitated. 'It has the slightest smell but . . . meadowsweet?'

And now she truly smiled, and it transformed her. Her face blossomed, the cleft in her chin smoothing out as her cheeks dimpled. As the smile reached her eyes, he saw a vibrant woman step out of the shadows.

'No one ever guesses!'

Rafi smiled at her delight. 'Then I shall buy one,' he said. 'And remind myself of home. Oh . . .'

Dear God. He had forgotten about his hands – they were covered in pig manure. The lavender had obscured the worst of the smell but now he stared at the caked grime on his fingers, cheeks scalding. What on earth must she think?

He dropped the sweetener back on the counter and began to rub his hands on his breeches, realising that this probably made him look even more ridiculous and yes, his face was now burning like an oven. What with the tears still caked on his cheeks, he must look a pretty sight indeed.

'Where . . . is home?' She avoided looking at him, pushing the sweetener forward on the table.

'Um . . .' Rafi clapped his hands together, letting loose a cloud of dried muck. At least most of it had come off his fingers. 'Flanders.'

'Ah, of course. You were with Adam. How is he?' Her face wore an expression of acute concern.

'He . . .' Adam had been drunk the last time Rafi had seen him. Drunk and angry. 'He was not his best when last I saw him.'

'No. I can imagine. And you? You seem . . . not quite your best either?'

Rafi's felt his cheek. Not quite as warm as it had been. 'I've spent too much time in the sun.'

'I meant . . . you seem a little upset.' Her concern was now directed at him. His face still bore the salty marks of grief. His eyes, he realised, were damp. The rakish pirate look had failed to materialise yet again, just when he needed it most.

'A little homesick.' It was no more than the truth. 'How much for this?'

'A penny.'

Rafi fumbled in his purse. He had a penny among his florins. Two pennies, in fact. 'I will take another.'

There were many to choose from, powdered in pouches, dried in bunches, leaves loose in cloth bags. 'Can you choose? I fear I cannot make up my mind.'

She did not hesitate and he wondered, later, how she could possibly have known.

She held out a pouch.

It was marjoram.

The tears sprang again as he held the pouch to his nose. He dropped the two pennies on the table, thanked her and zigzagged back through the alley that led out to the Helle. She would think him rude, but it couldn't be helped. What a fool he was, to sprinkle pig dust on her table and then cry in front of her.

The breath he drew caught at the top of his lungs, but he held it, leaning against the side of the Helle to steady himself. The smell was no better than it had been yesterday: stale urine and tallow. It looked as if the building doubled up as a shop. It was tall, three storeys high, whitewashed like the Chequers, with thick timber beams, a handsome, gabled roof, and a chandler's shop at the front. Candles, fat and squat, tall and fine; tallow of course, and the more expensive beeswax variety; church candles almost as tall as a man; smaller ones for placing in front of a plaster saint. And down below, when the shop closed, the ale would flow.

Rafi didn't wish to tarry longer. The stench was too much. He wandered towards the apothecary shop, up the hill towards the Westgate. Perhaps there would be paints here, and a little time spent away from his cares would be time well spent. He put the two herbals in his purse and weaved his way through the street.

He paused outside the apothecary shop. The window was lined with green and blue glass urinal bottles. They were so beautiful it seemed a shame to use them for such a mundane purpose.

Rafi edged closer to the window to get a better look. The shop was empty save for an elderly man, sitting behind the counter staring intently at the contents of a copper alembic. There were shelves and boxes and vials and dishes lining the walls. And there, reflected in the glass window, Rafi saw a man, not moving, merely standing and observing.

Rafi straightened and spun around. The man, in cloak and hood, shifted a little, but made no attempt to disguise the fact that he was staring at Rafi. Who was he? Rafi hadn't seen him before. Was he one of Roger's lackeys, keeping an eye on him? He was very well dressed; Rafi's experience in the cloth trade was enough to tell him that. He earned more than an apprentice, that much was clear – too much to be a lackey.

The man put his hand to his hip, nudging his cloak open to reveal a sheathed dagger. Rafi's skin prickled. He could go back along the high street until he got to the Chequers, but he didn't fancy being followed. He chose instead to enter the shop with the intention of asking the apothecary if he could leave by a different door. It would be a strange request and no doubt would be refused, but it was better than any alternatives he could think of.

The smell of the shop took his breath away; the sharp clarity of camphor laurel, the tang of which made his nose tingle. Each bottle on the wall labelled with a beautiful hand, neat and firm. Quicksilver, copper salt, ox gall, salmortis, orpiment, indigo woad. Five years dropped away in an instant; he was back in the scriptorium, sunlight falling through the windows onto parchment, the quill firm in his hand, his knife neat on the desk beside him. He glanced anxiously through the window. The man was edging towards Parchment Street. Perhaps there had been a mistake and he'd been waiting for someone else. That seemed most likely. Rafi couldn't imagine what business such a man would have with him.

'May I help you?' The old apothecary looked up.

'Oh, no. I just . . .' Rafi gestured towards the window. 'The glass is wonderful.'

'Indeed,' the apothecary said, smiling.

Rafi leaned forward. The alembic was opaque so he couldn't see what the apothecary was concocting, but he recognised the vitriol crystals in the shallow pancheon on the counter.

'Ink?'

'Yes, yes indeed!' The apothecary frowned. 'But I have changed the quantity of copperas to see if it weakens the tint.' He held the bowl and rotated it gently, his eyes keen as he peered into the bulb. 'You know something of crystals, I take it?'

'I have made ink before, that is all.'

The apothecary looked up then. 'A scholar?'

'Of sorts. May I look around? I don't wish to disturb you.'

'Of course.' The apothecary went back to staring into the bulb of the alembic.

Rafi looked along the shelves. The bottles, boxes and philtres were like precious jewels to him. Madder root, gum arabica, mandrake, oil of mint, linen bandages. And oil of linseed.

'Ah!'

The apothecary looked up, eyebrows raised.

Rafi was beaming. 'I've used this many times, to bind paint.' His head suddenly filled with memories.

'I have heard walnut oil is more efficacious.'

'It can be a little dense.'

'Oh, that is a shame.' The apothecary was dismayed.

'May I buy parchment here?'

'No, but there is a good parchmenter nearby. Do you know your way to the castle? Simply turn left out of here and head up the hill. He has quills and brushes, and I can provide you with ink.' The apothecary raised his head. 'It looks as if your unsavoury friend has left now.'

So it seemed. There was no one standing opposite the shop any longer, and the entrance to Parchment Street was empty.

'I would have come in anyway.'

The apothecary smiled. 'I expect you would. And please do come back. I'll mix you some ink in anticipation.'

There was no sign of a pursuer when Rafi left the shop. He took a few moments to check up and down the high street to reassure himself before continuing his progress uphill towards the parchmenter.

Winchester was a busy city. Every day dozens of traders and visitors flooded in and out of the Westgate, and then congregated just inside the walls where all the fine shops and inns were clustered. There were obstacles everywhere: kegs, barrels, shop signs of varying quality, which he could not help but inspect. Some were done very well and some were crude and badly made. He could make a living here if he ever needed to, painting shop signs. Perhaps that's what he should do – make a life for himself as an artist once his search was over.

As well as obstacles, there were animals, particularly in the area around the Shambles where the butchers did most of their trade. The animal pens were poorly secured and Rafi had to dodge at least two porcine escapees, squelching his way through animal waste that leaked through the boards over the city water channels. It was here that he fell, and, as he wiped pig sludge off himself for the third time in one day, he noticed the man from outside the apothecary shop, watching from a little way up towards the Westgate, arms folded, eyes keen as a hawk hunting for prey.

Rafi checked for his purse, stamped his feet to clear dirt from his shoes, and took note of a narrow passageway that he assumed went towards the cathedral like the alleyway near the Helle. Wiping his nose on the sleeve of his tunic, he checked to see if the man was still in the same spot.

He was not. He was now walking directly towards Rafi, heading downhill, gait quickening as he went.

Jesu! How was he to disappear quickly? The man had made it clear that he was armed so this was not a friendly approach. The alleyway offered him a possible escape route and might lead him back out to the sprawl of the market. He had nothing with him this time, not even his feeble crate knife. But he was fast. He dipped behind the butchers' stalls, crouching between barrels and stinking pig carcasses as he ran. The man momentarily halted, eyes searching animal pens and under tables.

Slowly, slowly, Rafi edged backwards, down Hammond's Passage, away from the high street.

Into a dead end.

There was no exit here as he had hoped. Or if there was, it was blocked. A gate and a high wall, which he could climb if his fear had not made anchors of his legs. There was no crevice, no tiny gap he could slither through, and the light from the high street was already being sucked away by the shadow of the man who had followed him.

He was trapped.

The knife slid out of the sheath with the briefest glint of metal, heavy footsteps crunching on the loose stone.

The man was tall, clean-shaven, dark hair falling below the collar. He wore a badge on his tunic – three feathers embroidered with silver thread. And the knife, held steady and tight.

Rafi backed away, instinctively. He tripped over himself and fell on his backside.

'Up you get, little one.'

The back of Rafi's shirt was wet and cold and his guts roiled. He could no more get up than he could fly. He turned and retched violently against the wall, acid burning his throat, his ribs screaming as he heaved and heaved again.

'Finished?'

Rafi wiped his face with the back of his sleeve, his arm shaking. He pushed himself hard against the gate, his hair sticking to his head, the foul taste in his mouth making him gag again.

The man squatted in front of him. Rafi kept his eyes on the knife.

'I want information.'

Information? What information could this brute possibly want from him? 'I . . . have . . . no . . .'

'We saw you; you came in with that empty-headed lump. And now Le Cran is selling mighty fine breeches and stockings. You help him sneak those in?'

Mother of God, it must be one of the customs men. As if he was not in a mess of trouble already with Roger, now he was beset by both sides. He shook his head wordlessly.

'Do not lie.'

Rafi's head was slammed backwards as a fist smashed into his face. Warm blood sprayed out of his nose like a fountain.

The customs man cracked his knuckles and blew on his hand. He remained squatting in front of Rafi, completely composed, keen eyes as dark as a rook's feather.

'You were on that leaky boat. We saw you.'

Rafi groaned. The pain was bad enough when he had first been hit, but now a hot agony was spreading through his face and down his neck.

'And we saw you, helping the fair-haired idiot out of the Chequers. And then' – the man was relentless – 'there you were, chatting away to our friend Writel.'

Rafi's cheek was warm and throbbed as if someone were kicking him from inside his face. And outside his face. He dared not speak. Everything the customs man said was true, but if he tried to explain that he was an innocent bystander he feared for his teeth.

'You have been here for just a few days, yet you know all the important people who work for Le Cran. Now, how can that be, if you are not with him?'

'I work . . . worked for . . .' Rafi spat a mouthful of blood onto the dirt. 'Van Loo,' he finished.

'But now you do not, and now you are here.'

'I . . .' Rafi ran his tongue round his teeth. At least one was loose, hanging by a bloodied thread.

'How much extra cloth was on that ship?'

It was as Rafi had predicted. He had warned Adam. He knew no good would come of this.

'I told you . . . I worked for Van Loo. I . . .'

'You were on that bloody boat and I saw you speak to Writel. How could you not know?'

'I had never clapped eyes on Writel until I got here.' Blood was thick in his mouth now. He spat again.

The customs man stood up. 'You lie. You are close to Le Cran and you will bring us proof that he is a cheat.'

'But . . .' Rafi's stomach lurched. 'I cannot.'

'Cannot? Or will not?'

'I have never even met him!'

'Make sure you get the evidence I require.'

'But . . .'

The customs man thundered out of the passageway, each footstep a hammer blow to Rafi's throbbing head.

Rafi stayed where he was, sitting in the corner of an alleyway with his blood-soaked shirt and his loose tooth and his broken face. His injuries needed tending. He would have to go back to the Chequers and call for a surgeon to remove the tooth, call for a compress, call for valerian. And then he would think, for he had to find a way to avoid both Roger and now the customs men. Where in Winchester could he do that? It was not big enough for him to be able to hide for long.

He had been here less than a week and had never hated anywhere so much.

Chapter 9

In the end, no surgeon could be found, so Rafi's back tooth was pulled by the apothecary. The procedure was quick and relatively painless – the tooth was already half out and it took such a tiny tug that Rafi could have done it himself were he not so squeamish.

Serlo proved to be an excellent host and went in person to the market for a restorative.

'You are a sight, young Rafi,' said the innkeeper, bustling about and propping his guest up on pillows.

'You are so kind. You barely know me.'

Serlo paused. 'You are the same age as my son. Were he lost in a wild and dangerous town full of madmen, like Salisbury or Southampton, I would hope someone would look out for him. And besides, I am being nice so that I get a good reputation and steal all of Marsh's customers. Once Marsh is done for, I swear I shall treat you like a dead horse. And methinks you will scrub the cellar for me with a good heart in return for my attention.'

'Scrub the . . . Ow!'

'Hold still. You are worse than a barrel of eels.' Serlo pressed the compress to Rafi's face. It had come from Edith's stall. It warmed his cheek and it comforted him to know that it was her hands that had filled the pouch with the herbs that now soothed him.

He chose not to stay in his room, coming downstairs to get a bite to eat once his gum had stopped bleeding. Ale and pottage was as much as he could endure, and even then he had to mash it with his spoon to soften it. It didn't help that Roger had seated himself at the opposite side of the inn, watching him.

'Been asking about you, hasn't he – you and the brawl in the Shambles earlier. I said I knew nothing – which is no more than the truth.' Serlo cleared his throat. The lack of gossip clearly pained him.

'I cannot say as I know much either. I will say this – I'm being accused of spying from all quarters when all I want to do is . . .' Rafi pretended his tooth was hurting again. Roger had warned him – bowmen everywhere. How could he be sure Serlo would not turn him out? He was nothing like Marsh but Rafi didn't wish to test the water.

'Without wishing to be rude, young Rafi, you're not doing a very good job of spying.' Serlo put his cloth on the table and sat opposite, his stomach pressing against the worn wood of the trestle. 'First, Marsh throws you into the street, then you get beaten up; you have Writel following you around and goodness knows what else. I'm more than happy to let him drink my ale 'til day turns to night but he's not one to sit here on his arse, not without good reason. And you' – Serlo touched the cloth of Rafi's tunic – 'you're no prancing dandy but those clothes are good quality. Not saying you're a wrong 'un but you sure attract them. Bit of a mystery, you are, and no mistake.'

Rafi pressed his hand to the locket that lay on his chest. Should he, could he show Serlo the seal? Would he end up on his backside in the street again, looking for somewhere else to stay?

'My son saw everything.' Serlo tried to lean forward but his stomach got in the way. 'He is a butcher, like me.'

'A butcher?'

'Why so surprised? You've tasted my potpies. It takes a discerning eye to select cuts of meat like that.'

'Well, now you come to mention it.' So that explained why Serlo was so much better with meat than with pastry. He could cut a pork chop as fine as you like, but his griddle cakes were a travesty.

'When you get to my age, chasing pigs down the street loses its appeal. My son can look after that for me, and make sure old Marsh gets naught but gristle from the butchery.' Serlo's laughter nearly tipped the table over. 'He's probably watering the ale as well.'

'I did wonder why it tasted like weasel's piss.'

Serlo chuckled. 'You know, we get our brew from Mistress Ailith. She is a marvel. Finest ale this side of London. Adam lost a good woman there, but it was his own fault. Spends his time with Bella now, fumbling with her undercarriage I shouldn't wonder.'

'Why would he fumble with her carriage? It's got fish barrels all over it. Is he helping her pull it through the market now?'

Serlo hooted so loud Rafi feared his ears would be blown off. 'Not *that* kind of carriage, lad! Undercarriage. You know?' Serlo gestured towards his breeches. 'Under her . . .'

'No need to explain further!' Rafi held his cup of ale to his cheek.

'Oh my! You are greener than I thought.' Serlo picked up his cloth and started cleaning the table. 'But to get back to the nub of things, as I say, my son saw everything. Roger saw everything. Ah! Didn't know that, did you? Well now!'

It was certainly a surprise. But then, Rafi had been so intent on getting back to his room after being attacked he had paid little heed to anything else.

'You know Le Cran owns the Tabard?'

'No, I had no idea.'

Serlo nodded. 'Well, he does. So any mischief you cause for him, can't say as I'll be sorry.'

Rafi sighed. 'But I don't wish to cause any mischief for anyone. I just want to . . .'

Oh, to the devil with it. He would take a chance and hope for the best. Lifting the locket over his neck, he placed it on the table. 'I just want to find out who owns this.'

Serlo peered at the half seal. He picked the locket up and held it as close to the tallow as he could. He shook his head as he handed it back.

'No idea, young Rafi. But to be honest with you, I've little use for seals and letters and the like. A shake of the hand is all the surety I need for an exchange of meat and money.'

Rafi put the locket away. 'It is no matter.'

'It clearly is, lad, since it's why you're here. Where did you come by such a thing?'

This would be the test now. Rafi glanced over his shoulder. The smoke from the tallow and the steam from skillet were not enough to obscure Roger's face. The man was staring intently at Rafi's table like a dog waiting for a bone.

Rafi closed his eyes. 'France. Where I was born.'

'Oh my! No wonder Marsh was so upset. Ha!'

Rafi opened his eyes. Far from throwing him out, Serlo was gurgling like an infant at play.

'You . . . do not mind?'

Serlo shrugged. 'I couldn't care less. You pay your way here and that suits me. And you've curdled Marsh's piss, which I mind not one bit. But look now, the beast has arisen.'

Rafi had no need to look. He felt Roger approach, a chill crawling down his back as if he were walking through a grave-yard at midnight.

'If you don't mind.' Roger loomed over the innkeeper.

Rafi nodded to Serlo, who moved aside to make room. 'If you need me you know where I am.'

'Bring him another ale,' growled Roger.

Serlo winked at Rafi and shambled through to the heat and steam of the kitchen. Roger took his seat, unasked.

Rafi's pottage was cold; he had mashed it so much it had

turned to a green liquid, but eating it gave him somewhere to look other than at Roger. His day had been bad enough already without having Roger make it worse.

Roger drummed the table, the *tap, tap, tap* of the finger that seemed to be his trademark.

What was he playing at? How long would it take him to explain what the hell it was that he wanted?

'Well.' The tapping stopped. 'It seems you may have been telling the truth. Or some of it at least.'

Rafi sucked at his pottage, pushing it to the side of his mouth where his teeth remained unscathed. 'I have no interest in what you think.'

'You should. You gave nothing away. My master wishes to reward you.'

What was this? Insufferable man! 'After what you did to me? I want nothing from you.'

'How could I predict that Marsh would burn your possessions? As far as I was concerned you had already left. I could hardly have known you'd be stupid enough to leave something behind.'

Rafi put his spoon back in his bowl to give his hands something to do other than punch Roger between the eyes. 'But you still wanted him to do me harm, so as I say, I want nothing from you.'

'Very well. At least tell me what he said.'

Such persistence. 'How close were you?'

Roger shrugged. 'I was standing just by the entrance to Hammond's Passage. Close enough to hear a good amount, but not everything. Once he cracked your mouth open you were annoyingly muffled.'

'For the love of Saint Bavo, could you not have stopped him?'

'I wanted to find out who he was and how much you were prepared to tell him.'

Rafi could hardly believe what he was hearing. 'You let that man beat me up?'

'I didn't expect him to punch you in the face.'

'You didn't expect Marsh to set fire to my things either.'

'Perhaps you should pay more heed to your welfare.'

Rafi half stood to leave when something gave him pause. What had Roger just said – he wanted to find out who the man was? Surely he already knew?

Rafi slid back into his seat, his face hurting from the slightest tremor as he sat. 'Are you telling me that you don't know who he was?'

Roger's hands curled around his mug. He had not drunk a single mouthful as far as Rafi could tell. 'Tell me, why should I know?'

More games. 'Because when we spoke yesterday, you as good as accused me of spying. Adam made reference to what was on board and you made no denial. Who else would it be? Tax collectors, duty collectors. You thought I was going to tell them what I had seen, and give away who had put me up to it. Not that there is anyone, as I keep telling you.'

Roger allowed himself a tight smile. 'You have some of it, but not all.' He continued to not drink.

'Are you going to tell me what the "all" is?'

'Well, since you have taken a beating on my master's behalf then so be it. No one is chasing us for duties.' Roger leaned towards Rafi and lowered his voice. 'We know all the customs men and they know us.'

Rafi started forward. 'You mean . . .'

'Hush.' Roger raised his hand. 'It is of no consequence. We all profit in our own way.'

Was anyone honest in this city? Rafi was beginning to wonder if Winchester was populated entirely by thieves and liars.

'I would know if you had spoken to them,' Roger continued. 'They would tell me. It would topple the quinces for all of us, and none of us want that. But you might have spoken to someone else, to someone who wishes to undermine my master – a rival, perhaps. They do exist, you know. Men are ambitious. Perhaps someone in Ghent wanted to take a cut of Van Loo's profits, and, failing to persuade the fat old gizzard, decided to take matters into their own hands, with you as the pawn.'

Rafi slumped in his seat. 'I am not interested in any of this. Will you just leave me be?'

'Sorry, but no. I am convinced you're not working for the man who beat you up. I heard you refuse to reveal anything incriminating, which you could very well have done, which is why my master wishes to reward you.'

'I would surely incriminate myself if I admitted anything. Reason enough for me not to talk. Nothing to do with your blessed master, I can assure you.'

Roger made circles with his mug, staring at the ale as it swirled inside. 'And yet I still wonder. Who is this Raphael Dubois, I ask myself, who appears out of nowhere, with money round his belt, yet who worked only a short while ago as an apprentice?'

'I was rewarded for . . .'

Roger waved Rafi's indignation away with a flick of the hand. 'And who now finds himself beaten up by what looks like a man of means, asking about my master Hugh Le Cran. You can see why I might be left . . . wondering.'

'Is it so difficult to believe that this is a very vexatious series of coincidences?'

'Yes. Extremely difficult. You will come to Minster Street now and explain yourself to my master, and then we shall . . .'

Rafi shook his head. 'No, I am not going anywhere. And even if I wanted to, my head hurts, my jaw aches and I need to sleep this off with a good dose of valerian.' Valerian that Serlo had acquired earlier from Edith, which would make the taking of it even more desirable.

'Tomorrow, then.'

'No.'

Roger slammed his mug on the table, drawing curious eyes and gossip-thirsty glances. 'I don't think you understand. He wishes to offer you a position. Not as an apprentice, something much better.'

'I do not wish to become involved in other people's business and I would appreciate it very much if you didn't try to get involved in mine.'

'You don't say,' Roger growled. 'He will pay you well.'

'I have money.'

'For now.'

Rafi gripped his belt. 'Are you threatening to rob me?'

Roger pushed his chair back, not heeding that it fell over with a clatter. He leaned over Rafi, face surly. 'I give you less than a week. You will be knocking on his door like a supplicant.'

'This is a poor reward, then. It sounds like a punishment.'

Roger looked him up and down. 'Whoever he was, he will come for you again. What are you going to do – throw one of your fancy shoes at him? From the cut of him, I'd say he was a soldier of some sort. You don't stand a chance.'

Rafi had already worked out for himself what his chances were against such a man around the time he'd been spitting blood into a pewter dish after the apothecary had finished with him. The man in Hammond's Passage was expecting information of some kind and had not accepted Rafi's refusal. Roger was right. This wasn't the last of it. But getting involved with Le Cran was not the solution. It would only prove the assailant right, convince him that Rafi was indeed part of Le Cran's chain of dishonesty. Whatever choice Rafi made, he'd likely get another fist in the face if he didn't mind himself. If it was going to happen anyway, he may as well keep his conscience clear.

'I said no. And you hardly came to my rescue earlier. Great bowman you turned out to be.'

'I don't carry the bloody thing around with me, you idiot!' Roger's raised voice drew more interested glances. The tavern had filled since Roger's arrival. The sweat had mingled with smoke and cooking meat. It reminded Rafi of the Blue Swan and all that he had left behind.

Rafi stood. He was on a level with Roger's chin but it was better than having the man hover over him like a foul miasma. 'You want to know what that man wanted and the best way to do that is through me. You couldn't care less if he slices me finer than Serlo slices his pork bellies. I am useful to you, but once you get what you want, you'll have me thrown into the castle moat. I want nothing to do with your miscounted woolsacks and misplaced kegs. I am here for one thing only and as soon as I am done, I shall be gone.'

Roger nodded. 'I see. As soon as you're done. Very well. We'll see how long it takes you to be done. Le Cran can close as many doors as you try to open.'

Roger pushed past Rafi, face surly, then turned briefly. 'One week. I give you one week.'

One week. Rafi knew in his heart it would take longer than that, especially now that Roger was even more determined to block his way.

Worse than that, someone else was pursuing him. A soldier, was it? Sooner or later that soldier would come for him, demanding information. The soldier wasn't an official of the crown; he was not here to collect duties. Roger had said as much. So who was he? Why was he so interested in the provenance of Le Cran's breeches and stockings?

Rafi clenched his hands to stop them shaking. He had no real idea as to the extent of Le Cran's wrongdoing. The excess wool and cloth had been hidden so Rafi had not been able to enter anything in the ledger. He had no idea how much there was or who else might be involved.

He had nothing.

Nothing but half a seal, a broken tooth and a dozen unanswered questions.

Chapter 10

In the short time Rafi had been in this godforsaken place, all he'd found out of any use was that Le Cran was not the owner of the seal. Yet all roads led to this man he had never met. Roger had followed him on behalf of Le Cran; a mystery assailant had followed him in order to find information about Le Cran. But the road Rafi most wanted to travel, the one leading to the seal holder, was the one path that didn't have Le Cran at the end of it. But at least knowing who didn't own the seal was better than knowing nothing at all.

Still, Serlo was trying to help, albeit in an unexpected and potentially hazardous way.

'Good morning, young Rafi. Your mouth looks less swollen and you look less forlorn and I have a plan in mind that may well kill two birds with one stone and I am sure you will be all the better for the hearing of it.'

Rafi rubbed his eyes. He had barely finished his first mouthful of breakfast – a piece of bread soaked in weak ale and mashed to a form that rendered it almost unrecognisable. 'Whatever plan it is, you may need to deliver the details with less speed, for while I understand much of what you say, my English does not always keep up.'

Serlo placed a wooden token on the table. 'Bring that to my son and tell him you are taking delivery of the meat cart today.'

Rafi scratched his head. 'The meat cart?'

'Indeed.' Serlo rubbed his hands together. 'Mal will recognise the token and know it comes from me. You take the cart and deliver meat around the city to the places he tells you.'

'And this helps me . . . how, exactly?'

'I thought you were a bright boy.' Serlo tutted and whipped his cleaning cloth from his belt. 'It will get you into a lot of places. Maybe there will be some clue to your seal lying on a barrel while the maid goes to the steward for payment. Or perhaps you can sneak around.'

'I'm not really the sneaking kind.'

'Needs must, lad! There are at least five churches who take our wares, several fancy merchants like your friend Le Cran—'

'He's not my friend.'

Serlo ignored him. 'At least three of the shops inside the gate use us, old Raymond the saddler for one.'

Rafi was touched by the trouble Serlo had gone to in thinking up this scheme, but felt compelled to turn it down. 'I fear I would ruin your business. I'm no salesman. I would put people off if anything.'

'You have it wrong, lad. I'll be honest, you won't turn many heads among the young lasses, but the older ones will love you and they . . .' Serlo leaned forward. 'They are the ones who run the households. They will see your pretty face and want to mother you. They will ask for extra pork. Haha!'

Rafi blushed. 'Serlo, please.'

'I jest, I jest! But it will start a conversation for you. Much easier than knocking on a door, stranger that you are.' Serlo pushed the token towards him. 'And I am not lying about you being able to sell more to a certain type of woman. You may not be as handsome as Adam but you have a way about you. Not to mention those fancy shoes.'

Rafi remembered Adam's friends in the market. 'You have no idea how wrong you are.'

'I am never wrong about meat!'

Rafi laughed. 'Very well. There is some merit in what you say. I'll admit I was nervous about knocking on doors with no guarantee of a welcome. I suppose a fistful of mutton chops will smooth the way.'

'That's the spirit!'

By the time the meat cart had been loaded, Rafi was beginning to regret his decision. He had received instructions from Mal, which he could barely remember. The list of customers was very long and had to be committed to memory but Rafi at least recalled the names of the churches. Once he was done with those, he would have to return to Mal and ask him to repeat the rest.

To make matters worse the cart was unstable. It had two wheels and Rafi had to pull it along carefully to make sure it didn't tip over. The one saving grace was that if anyone tried to attack him today there would be plenty of witnesses, and the butchers from the Shambles would respond with their fists if there was any risk of their meat coming to harm.

The day yielded little. Two drunk priests who could barely remember the name of their own churches but who were remarkably adept at counting out exactly the right number of pennies for their supper. Father Alfred at St Maurice's was kindly but could not identify any of the marks on Rafi's seal.

Surprisingly, Serlo's prediction that Rafi would delight the more mature women of the city was proved uncomfortably correct. Mistress Alice, a maid at the house of Alun Lattewelle, had Rafi sit at her table, piled high with laundry, while she examined a haunch of mutton – an examination that involved her leaning over Rafi's lap for no obvious reason and which seemed to take an eternity. To her credit she did buy more than had been put aside for her, but the prospect of asking any questions about seals or any other business was secondary to Rafi's desire to get as far away from her as possible.

There was an awkward moment at the house of Roderick Cowper, whose wife Iseult asked Rafi for a measure of chops the same weight as her bosom and could he measure both carefully, please. Not wishing to lose the sale, but reluctant to attempt the kind of measuring Iseult clearly desired, Rafi was saved by the irate appearance of Roderick and his two dogs, the former hurling a handful of pennies on the table for his meat, the latter growling menacingly as they chased Rafi out the door.

Two more houses, involving more acceptable transactions, brought at least some information, albeit of a negative kind. Henry Marchmont had a seal, which was kindly shown to Rafi by an elderly maid who fussed over him, offered him bread and cheese and would have chatted for hours had she not been called away by her mistress. The Marchmont seal, alas, did not match Rafi's in any way, and nor did the badge on the coat of Simon Cappin from the house of Hubert Le Fain.

Rafi had returned to Mal with an empty cart and very little in the way of positive information.

'Well done getting out of Mistress Alice's kitchen in one piece.' Mal placed several slabs of unidentifiable offal in a small wooden container and handed them to him. 'Sorry if she undid your braiel but you seem to have survived. Can't say I was sorry you took my place but I still feel bad for you.'

'My braiel remained intact, fortunately. What is this?' Rafi held up the offal box.

'You must have really taken Mistress Alice's fancy because she bought all of Raymond the saddler's usual order as well as her own. This is the last one you need to deliver. He's just up the hill. He's a little . . . loud but he knows everyone who comes in and out of the city because his shop is right inside the gate. You'll hear him before you see him. Just follow the roar.'

Rafi grimaced. But at least this was the last futile trip he would have to make today. Well, perhaps that wasn't entirely fair. He at least knew that the seal did not belong to Le Fain or Marchmont. Along with Le Cran he could eliminate three Winchester families from a list that, he feared, could keep him in the city for several years at the rate he was going. Assuming his florins didn't run out first.

Raymond the saddler proved to be an amenable fellow, but as loud as Mal had warned he would be. His shop was filled with saddles, of course, but there were also leather gauntlets, gloves made of beautiful soft cheveril, reins, bridles trimmed with squirrel fur. Castilian imports, good quality.

As Rafi had feared, Raymond could offer no clues.

'Not familiar with it, lad,' said Raymond, peering at the broken object inside the locket.

Rafi dropped his shoulders.

'But that's because I've not been looking out for it. I will now, won't I? But in return, you can do me a little favour.'

Everyone wanted favours today. Even people Rafi had only just met. He could do with some favours himself, but it seemed unlikely he'd ever be on the receiving end of any.

Raymond thrust a tattered bridle into Rafi's arms. 'Just outside the gate, to the left near the stone pillar and down a pathway. There's a bit of the moat that's filled in and I've a stable nearby. Bring this to the boy there. I'd go myself but some blackguard would steal something while I had my back turned.'

'Right.'

'Cheer up, lad! You don't even need to go through the gate. There's a gap in the wall someone your size can easily slip through. You'll be thanking me should John Marsh ever come chasing you after the curfew bell has rung – oh, don't think I hadn't heard.'

Rafi winced, waiting for Raymond to reach for a bow and gut him with one shot, but instead the saddler roared with laughter. 'We heard you'd drawn gizzards and rats, and goblins and demons on his sign—'

'There weren't any goblins or demons.'

'There should have been! That he saw fit to tell us how clearly you'd seen him just shows what a fool he is. Everyone knows he runs a foul inn. The new owner will shut him down soon for sure and no one will be sorry.'

Serlo was delighted with this news when Rafi finally trudged back to the Chequers.

'Le Cran most surely will shut him down if he finds him watering the ale and putting gizzards in the soup and now everyone will think he does because of you – put gizzards in the soup, that is. I'm not sure about the ale but I did say it tasted like weasel's piss so I'll warrant he's either selling old ale or pissing in it himself.'

Rafi escaped to his room before Serlo could draw another breath. Trying to be optimistic he supposed he had at least some more acquaintances in the city. Butchers, saddlers and, once he'd delivered the bridle at Raymond's request, he had also found a secret route through the walls, which might be useful should a deranged soldier or French-hating innkeeper think to attack him again.

He would take whatever solace he could wring from the day, but from now on there would be no more meat deliveries. Tomorrow he would make good on his threat to search at the abbey. He would speak to the abbey clerks, not the abbess herself – he doubted he would gain an audience with her. Clerks would have records. Clerks always had records.

If it put Roger's nose out of joint, then so be it.

Chapter 11

Rafi slid across the sticky ooze bubbling up through the uncovered waste channels that ran down the high street. Someone ought to do something about this. Didn't this wretched city have a mayor? Because if it did, he hadn't done a very good job by the looks of it.

There was the Helle backing onto St Lawrence's church and the passage that he had walked several times now. He could reach the abbey this way, past the cathedral wall and out through the postern gate in Colebrook Street. Adam had given him directions to all the important places as they'd travelled from Southampton on the cart. 'Start at the Westgate and follow the smell. Your nose will take you to Shite Lane. That's where you'll find the postern gate.'

The abbey was right down towards the river, which marked the eastern limit of the city. It was through the Eastgate that travellers and visitors came from St Giles Hill or Beggar's Lane, and further out towards the villages of Easton and Alresford.

That end of the city was certainly pungent. The tanners and fullers lived here. Rafi tried to stop breathing in as he passed. The smell of animal hide and urine was strong and sharp, and then there was the stench of human ordure from the latrines at

Maydenchamber.

St Mary's Abbey, once called the Nunnaminster, rose up before him now. The building was dwarfed by the shadow of the cathedral nearby, but it was still impressive. He slipped down the side of the building, down to Colebrook Street, close to the postern gate and midden. He held his breath again.

He could see through the gate into the abbey grounds. West of the main building, there was what looked like an infirmary, and a dormer attached to the inner cloister. To the north was the chantry chapel. The doors to the abbey itself were open, and he could see a long nave flanked by huge columns. It had two towers – one more than the cathedral, and taller too. The stone was silver-grey and the edifice plain and simple. The Itchen bounded it to the east, and a stream ran through it, providing a pretty fishing pond with water for laundry, cooking and brewing. The church had been founded by Queen Ealhswith, wife of King Alfred. He had made this city his capital, and the abbey was much loved.

As Rafi reached the end of the passageway, he froze. Edith, a basket in one hand, her little boy holding the other, appeared from the direction of the cathedral.

She didn't see him at first; she was concentrating on the boy at her side. Her wimple fell forward as she leaned down to talk to him. Placing her basket on the ground, she pushed the wimple back, where it sat, skewed. 'Not again!'

'Not again!' repeated the child, and they both laughed. She kissed her finger and placed it on his nose.

As she straightened, she caught sight of Rafi and smiled. He had been anxious at the thought of seeing her again. The last time they had spoken was after Marsh had burned his things. He had been tear-stained and distressed. Yet here she was smiling and not as horrified to see him as he had feared she might be. When the boy tried to pick up his mother's basket, Rafi walked forward.

'Would you like me to help you with that?' He held the basket out so that it was closer to the boy's little hands.

'Ooooohhhh.' The child reached out to grab it.

'Leof, we say thank you.'

The boy shook his head, the soft brown curls as light as duckling feathers. 'My basket.'

'So why do I have to carry it?'

Leof thought about this for a moment, then shrugged, and ran through the gate into the abbey grounds.

'Sorry, I have no wish to upset the boy.'

She laughed. 'He will have forgotten already.'

'Thank you,' said Rafi. 'For the sweetener, the other day.'

She did not answer for a moment. 'I am Edith, by the way. And I think you might be Rafi?'

'Yes. How did you know?' He was pleased that she did.

'Ailith. She works for Le Cran, and Adam . . . well, she will have heard.'

Had Adam not said that Ailith worked for a rich widow? Well, no matter. 'I have only seen her from a distance. We have never met.'

'Ah, then you'll have noticed . . .' Edith looked at her stomach then up again quickly. 'The baby arrived late last night. A girl, Judith.'

They did not speak for a moment or two. They could hear Leof from inside the abbey grounds, chattering to someone, babbling nonsense.

'You seemed a little upset the last time we met . . .' She looked away.

'I had lost something precious.' Rafi hesitated. 'Something very precious. A sprig of herb, which I had carried for a long time.'

'Ah. Marjoram?'

Rafi nodded, then looked at his feet.

'Are you . . . a herbalist? Or do you just like plants?'

Rafi shook his head. 'No, not particularly. I mean to say, I do like plants, but . . . I am not explaining this very well.'

Edith tilted her head, waiting for him to continue.

111

'I mean, my mother was very skilled indeed, and when I was young I used to help her,' Rafi continued. 'I could never make plants thrive, but I was good at working out what should go where. Or so she told me.' He paused. 'I expect she was just humouring me.'

'And you help her still?'

Rafi's face fell. 'I . . . She died a long time ago. No . . . it is . . .' He was startled by Edith's expression of dismay. 'How could you know? But I wish I could still help her, yes.'

'So . . . are you here to visit the herb garden? The nunnery has an excellent selection, but I'm not sure you can go in there.' She blinked up at him.

'Oh! No, I had no idea.' He hesitated. 'I was here to speak to the clerks. I hoped to, anyway.'

Edith was thinking, her brows knitted together and her hair falling over her eyes. 'Look, maybe you could . . .' She pushed at her unruly fringe. 'Here is an idea. Come with me. I'm here to work in one of the houses here – the abbey owns them. The couple who live here are old and cannot tend to the garden very well, and Sister Domneva asked me to help. She wouldn't wish me to do heavy work, but . . . you could? And maybe you can help me decide what goes where in a new patch?'

This was not what he'd come here for. And he had little time to spare if he was to get out of Winchester before losing any more of his teeth. It had been many years since he'd done any gardening anyway, other than when Brother Bertrand reluctantly gave him planting duties at St Michael's. It hadn't happened often; he killed more things than he sowed. His talents lay in the scriptorium, where he'd spent most of his time with quill and paintbrush. But it wasn't Brother Bertrand asking him now. The request had come from someone far more appealing. Surely he could afford her an hour?

'Why thank you. I would like that.' And now he didn't know what to do next. Should he follow her through the path between the abbey and the cottage garden, or should he go first? They both stepped forward together and then laughed. He gestured to her to lead.

'Maybe Sister Domneva can tell me where you can find the clerks today,' said Edith over her shoulder as they entered the abbey herb garden. 'Or . . . maybe not, but then . . . maybe. Oh, what am I saying, I'm talking nonsense.'

'No, not at all.' Rafi could not imagine this serious, thoughtful woman ever speaking nonsense.

'Well, I can hear her in the infirmary. I'll speak to her. I need to rescue Agnes from Leof anyway; he will chatter her to death!'

Edith crossed the tiny, overgrown passageway that separated it from the abbey, and then disappeared through a wide gate, through which Leof could be seen running in circles around a sweet-faced young woman, presumably Agnes.

The distant clink of a pestle pounding against a mortar could be heard from the near end of a long building, which sat at right angles to the abbey. The gate that opened from the passageway was big enough to give a reasonable view of some of the buildings and grounds, but not all; that would have been too much to hope for. That this gate was open at all was an unexpected gift. Sister Domneva would have been expecting Edith so must have opened it. He was a hidden guest at a forbidden feast, free to view the infirmary and herb garden, set back from the main abbey, so neat and precise, so like the one his mother had kept in the patch outside their cottage.

Rafi waited, praying that Sister Domneva didn't send him away. This was not his domain. If the sister asked him to leave, he would abide by her wishes, but he dearly hoped she would not.

The girl, Agnes, was standing near the stream with a bucket. She waved at him just as Edith reappeared from inside the infirmary.

'She doesn't mind – I suspect because you've come at a convenient time. She is infested, she says. The warmer weather has emboldened the weeds.' Edith smiled. 'But she insists that you stay only in this garden. I hope you understand.'

His heart jumped. He could stay. And he suddenly cared less about gaining admittance to the abbey itself than he had half an hour ago.

'Of course,' he replied. 'I lived in a monastery for ten years. I will be mindful and do as she asks.'

'Oh, I will tell her. It will reassure her.'

Rafi waved back at Agnes as Edith went to the infirmary again to fetch a shovel and a small cutting implement.

'Sister Domneva says she would be pleased if you could remove some of the ground glutton, and the chickweed. I'll mark out a space, and we can plant some little herb seedlings for you.'

'But then I won't be able to buy them from you.'

Her face became serious. The smile had gone. 'No matter. This is a better place.'

They worked quietly for a little while. Rafi began to sweat. He pushed his matted hair back from his face and kept going. His back was beginning to ache and his shoulders were getting stiff. It was the happiest he had been for a long time.

Straightening for a moment, Rafi watched as Leof wandered over to the fishpond. It was just after sext. The sisters had taken their meal and were free to read and work until nones. Agnes picked little Leof up and started to count the ducks in the pond, while he gave each one a name.

Edith joined him as he watched. 'I can always trust Agnes to keep an eye on him.'

'He is a happy boy.'

'Yes, yes he is. My youngest.'

'You have a daughter too. I have seen her with him.'

'Yes, Tilly – and there's Simon, the eldest. He's eight now.'

'You have three? And one of them eight? You cannot be old enough!'

She laughed. 'You are kind. I was sixteen when Simon was born. Not much older than Agnes there.'

Edith went back to her work, bent over the herb patch with a wooden dibber, making neat, even holes in the earth. Rafi tugged at a long, twining arm of groundsel. He dug down carefully, following the line of the root, mindful not to snap it off and leave the smaller root tendrils behind. He scraped away a shallow channel and then pulled gently, removing the entire plant, before moving on to the next one.

'You're doing well there. Domneva will insist you come back!'

'Maybe I will. If . . .'

They looked up. Leof was on his back, with Agnes tickling his tummy. His giggles had become louder and more high-pitched.

Sister Domneva came to the door. She stared at Rafi, stared for a long time. It was unnerving yet he was unable to look away. She held him, even from this distance. There was little of her that he could see, her features all but hidden by her wimple. Eventually, she gestured with her hands towards Agnes to quieten the child, and then silently returned to her work.

'Was that her, Sister Domneva?'

'Yes. She has a kind heart, once you chip away at her.'

Rafi held up his hand to his face. His fingers trembled slightly. The nun's gaze had peeled something from him, stripped him bare.

'What is it?' Edith had stopped what she was doing.

'I . . . am not sure. Perhaps she disapproves of me.'

'Not when she sees how much of that groundsel you've dug up.'

Her smile restored him, and he returned to his labours, Leof's babbling, childish talk floating across from where he and Agnes played. The girl seemed to smile all the time, and Leof clearly adored her.

'Who is Agnes?' he asked.

'An orphan. No one knows who her parents are. She lives with the laywomen here.'

Edith laughed at the sight of Leof chasing the ducks. The sun shone in her eyes, and she put her hand up to shield them from the glare. The dibber in her hand was covered in dirt. The earth had caught beneath her fingernails and smeared her apron where she had tried to wipe it away. Rafi painted her in his mind. She had an aura of calm, of browns and greens, warm russet. She was, too, a beautiful autumn sky, peach gold and soft. But . . . a bitter wind followed behind, pushing the clouds too fast, drawing down the day. He readied the pigments he would need, focused on the flow and ebb of her movements. He shook himself when he realised she was staring at him.

'Agnes,' said Edith, 'is both an open book and a mystery to us all.'

She put her dibber on the grass and sat back on her heels, her hands clasped lightly on her apron. 'She's nearly fourteen now. The abbess adopted her, along with an endowment. No one knows where it came from – the abbess would never reveal such a secret.' She looked directly at Rafi. 'Do you know what they say of her parentage?'

Agnes was still playing with Leof. Her beauty was mesmerising, she dazzled brighter than the sunshine bouncing off the pond. A young woman with an endowment and such grace. There would be suitors queuing for her hand in a year or so, he had no doubt – should she wish to leave the abbey, that was, or if her mystery patron reclaimed her when she came of age.

'I have no idea.'

'There is a chantry chapel here. The priest says masses and there are a few wealthy folk in the city who pay him to do so. Other than the priest and the abbess, one other person holds the key.'

'A steward to a cloth merchant by any chance?'

'Yes! How did you know?'

'A lucky guess.'

'Well, 'tis none other than Hugh Le Cran who pays the most for the surety of his eternal soul. But Roger Writel who holds the key, and collects some of the rents from the houses nearby. So he is here often enough, and is close with the abbess.'

'So, you think Le Cran . . .?'

'Oh no,' Edith shook her head so vigorously her wimple nearly toppled into the flower bed. 'He hardly ever comes here, and when he does he ignores Agnes completely. He's passed her on the street and not given her a second glance.'

'Then you think Roger . . .?'

Edith shrugged. 'He treats her almost like a father but in truth, nobody knows. Save Roger himself, and possibly Domneva and the abbess.'

'Domneva?'

'She is close to Agnes and has taught her everything she knows about medicine. Agnes is skilled beyond her years. She often attends as a midwife in the city; her reputation is such that she's often asked for. She has more freedom than Domneva, not being a novice. Not yet, anyway. It is she who attended Ailith. Roger often walks her to and from deliveries, stands nearby like an obedient puppy waiting for her. She's very young to be a midwife yet she is more than capable. She is . . .' Edith tilted her head, thinking of a word, '. . . extraordinary.'

'Oh?'

Edith nodded towards the infirmary. The pestle and mortar had suddenly stopped clinking.

'Sister Domneva has taught me almost everything I know. I've never met anyone as skilled or as knowledgeable in herb lore as she. She has both an intellectual understanding and a . . .' again, Edith searched for a word '. . . prowess, an instinct. People will turn to her, rather than the surgeon or the apothecary, when they have any illness or ague. But Agnes . . .' Edith picked up her dibber again. 'I would say, and Domneva would no doubt agree, that Agnes will surpass her teacher if not this year, then the next. If anyone knows her secrets, it is Domneva. But I doubt that even Agnes knows the truth.'

'The nurse does not mind that her pupil may outstrip her?'

Edith shook her head. 'Quite the opposite. But, of course . . .' Edith sighed. 'When Agnes turns fourteen, she'll have to choose.

117

Either to bind herself to the abbey or leave. She cannot be an adopted daughter of the abbess forever.'

'When will that be?'

'This month. She has but a fortnight left to decide.'

Rafi sighed. It was likely that Agnes would choose to stay in the abbey and take the oath. Would that be a waste of her talents? If the abbess were wise, she'd put Agnes to work in the infirmary with Domneva, but she would always be bound.

'It is a pity,' said Rafi. 'She should run the apothecary shop.'

Edith pushed her dibber into the soil. 'The apothecary is very ill. I fear he will not last the summer. He has no family and when he goes . . .' She shook her head. 'What a waste. He would be honoured to have someone like Agnes come after him, he's told me so himself. But it is not to be.'

Saddened, Rafi returned to his groundsel, his fingers feeling their way once again down the length of the root.

'You said Agnes delivered Ailith's child? You are friends with Ailith?'

'Yes, and Adam.' Edith tutted. 'He treated her very ill.'

'I . . . well, I have not seen him since. He was very angry. I did not realise Ailith worked for Le Cran. Adam told me she worked for a rich widow – Joan, I think the name was?'

'Joan Cuppyng. Or should I say Joan Le Cran. She married again last Christmas.'

Rafi stopped what he was doing. 'You know, I have been here less than a week and that name comes up over and over again. They should call this place Cranchester. I am never rid of him but have never set eyes on him. I wonder if he exists in legend only.'

Edith laughed. 'You will meet him for sure. He was mayor and will no doubt be mayor again. He is also mayor of the staple – any wool coming through Winchester and he has the measure of it and counts the taxes.'

Oh, this was too much. Mayor of the staple? No wonder he was able to get away with so many nefarious activities.

'He sounds very talented.' It was too sharp. Well, so be it.

Edith covered her mouth with the back of her hand but failed to hide her smile. The fact that she had tried delighted him. If he could but take that hand . . .

'Talented, you say? Aye, it would seem so.'

Damn him.

Edith continued. 'He is certainly very handsome. It was no wonder he captured Joan. He could have had his pick of women even richer than she was – and she had plenty of suitors when her husband died, but she turned them all away. He chose her and she chose him. I do believe it is a love match. And when she married, she brought her servants with her – including Ailith.'

Rafi now detested Le Cran more than ever. Handsome, was he? Handsome and dishonest with it.

'I see.' Rafi ripped a piece of groundsel up without due care and hurled it across the garden.

Edith looked at the groundsel for a few moments, scratching her head. 'Well.'

'What of Adam, then?' Rafi wished to change the subject.

'He didn't tell Ailith he was leaving. It was May Day and she was the May Queen. He'd promised her the world the night before, and . . .' Edith blushed. Rafi could guess the rest. 'She waited all day. She looked so pretty – pretty for him, and all for nothing. She cried so much I thought her heart would break. Ned had to carry her home. Adam never said goodbye, just took what he wanted and left. What if she'd been with child?'

'I . . .' Rafi sighed. 'I had no idea.'

'I'm glad of that. I would not like to think you knew.' Edith blushed again. With her frazzled auburn hair, pink cheeks, filthy nails and apron, Rafi could have gazed on her all day.

Edith picked up her dibber and started poking holes where they shouldn't be. Rafi's job was to point out where things would look best, but now both of them had completely lost grip of geometric precision.

'Ned said he would marry Ailith,' Edith continued, 'but as it turned out, there was no child. But they grew close. They grew close very quickly because Ned had always loved her and . . .' Edith shrugged. 'I always thought he was better for her than Adam. So perhaps Adam did her a favour. She is happier with Ned. If Adam is upset . . .'

'I told him to take more care, so many times. I had no idea how bad it was.'

Edith started pushing seedlings and small sprigs into the holes she'd made while Rafi watched silently. What a fool Adam had been. More than a fool. Carelessly hurting someone and walking away from the consequences. It was callous and selfish. They were not words he wanted to associate with his friend, but it was the truth of it.

'So . . .' Edith's voice was soft. 'Your little sprig of marjoram. So precious – was it from a sweetheart?'

Rafi blushed, sinking his hands into the channel he had just dug to hide his embarrassment. His fingers eased their way around the fibrous mass at the bottom, and he tugged gently, coaxing the root. 'Well . . .'

'Yes?' Her wimple had tilted to one side now, a ship about to keel over.

'I have never had a sweetheart to give me such a token.' The weed came out as sweetly as one of Serlo's pies from the oven.

'Oh! Be careful!' She clamped her hand over her mouth, dusting her face with a sprinkling of chalky earth.

He saw the dimples in her cheeks, but he was not embarrassed by her amusement as he fell on his backside, the groundsel in his hands. There was no mockery in it.

She turned back to her work and tugged viciously at some sweet cicely. 'Hmmph! Wretched plant.'

'It is inoffensive!'

'I do not much like the name.'

She hacked at it, her hair going everywhere. Her wimple had

120

finally come off and her hair was tangled, like a nest.

'You will make it grow more if you cut too much.'

'Aye well, it has its uses.' Edith recovered her headdress, smeared with dirt now. She made a face and Rafi tried not to laugh as she pulled the wimple back on, badly.

The bell rang for nones. He had been here for three hours! He'd come here to talk to an abbey clerk, yet here he still was, in the garden with his sleeves rolled up and dirt on his new linen collar. He didn't care. He hardly believed how much time had passed. He wished he could catch it in his hands and hold it tight, but the bells continued to ring.

'We had better leave.' Edith was suddenly anxious. She curled once more into the ball of tension he'd seen at the market stall, before she'd smiled at Leof; before she had captured him. 'The sisters will need to attend to their prayers. Leof!'

While they waited for the boy to come towards them, Rafi thought to ask: 'I need to find some plants to make colours, for painting, you see. It will give me something to do in the evenings.'

'Oh.' But Edith was distracted. At the sound of the bell her demeanour had tightened, she had become as brittle as glass. He wondered if he'd done or said something wrong.

'Danemarch Mead. There is some good moss there, near Tumbling Bay.' She didn't look at him.

'You go there?'

'When I can. If my sister looks after the children I can go after supper and before the curfew bell. The moss is springy and tough. It makes the best poultices for wounds. Mix that with goose fat and it can heal anything, I am convinced of it.'

Her eyes scoured the abbey grounds for Leof who was taking far too long to come towards them.

'Leof! Please hurry.'

He could hear the panic in her voice. It tore through him.

The sisters began to trudge towards the abbey. Domneva emerged from the infirmary and left something on the doorstep, a bunch of dried herbs, tied with string. She locked the door behind her and did not look back.

Leof ran into his mother's arms. Her basket was full of good things from the herb patch, but her face was troubled.

'I can carry this back to the stall if you cannot manage it,' offered Rafi, knowing already that she would refuse him.

'No. I thank you, but I had best be on my way. The Durngate is that way.' She pointed. 'Follow the wall around, and you will find the marshes.'

Her mood, suddenly brusque after the easy way they had talked together, cut him. She turned, not even bidding him farewell. But she went only a few steps before a man stepped through the postern gate and blocked her way down Colebrook Street.

Rafi was with her in less than two strides. For one of the rare times in his life he was bigger than the person who now confronted him. 'The lady wishes to pass through here. Can you step aside?'

'Lady, is it?'

Rafi recoiled as soon as the man opened his mouth. Ale. A lot of ale. Stale and sour and sickly. 'Please, could you move?'

'Pleeeassse, could you mooooove!' The man danced in a circle, mockingly.

Leof sat quietly on Edith's hip, his head resting against her shoulder. 'Pray, sir, could you leave us be?'

It took Rafi a few horrified seconds to realise that she was talking to him. Sir?

'Popinjay.' The man looked at Rafi's shoes. 'You could afford her, then, for a few pennies.'

Rafi's face was boiling. 'How dare you . . .'

'I dare . . .' the sourness came closer '. . . I dare because she is my wife.'

'Your . . .' He could not look at Edith. He could look only at the ground, the ground that swam and rose up to meet him before receding and rising again.

Wife. How could Edith be married to a man such as this? Was she not a widow?

'Thom, let us go.' Her voice was fragile as she stepped around her husband and carried Leof through the postern gate. She kept her head low, rubbing her cheek against Leof's hair for comfort.

Thom spat at Rafi's feet, aiming the spittle so it landed on the toe of his shoe, a glistening, viscous mess. His grin was virtually toothless. The man was so drunk he could barely stand. Rafi could have pushed him with the lightest touch and had him sprawling in the dust. But he could barely stand himself and had to lean against the postern gate to steady himself.

What could he do anyway? Thom was Edith's husband: she was his to do with as he pleased. Rafi's fingers curled at his sides. He couldn't bear the thought of it. She had called Le Cran's marriage a love match. This was none such. The two walked apart, with Thom leaning towards her every so often to push her forward. She would stumble, then move away from him again.

Sir. She had put him so far away. For his sake, he didn't care, but for her – what would Thom do to her if he'd known they'd been laughing together only a few minutes before?

Jesu, a few minutes, was that all it had taken to turn light to dark? He thought of the bed they'd planted, the rows of sage and tansy, parsley and his beloved marjoram. To begin with they'd been neat, ordered, precise, like the dots he used to mark on vellum before scribing words in a straight line, with ink such as the apothecary had been making in his alembic. And then gradually the neatness had disintegrated, loosening as their words had softened.

When the tansy flowers blossomed, he wondered how well they would work if he crushed the yellow petals and mixed them with oil. But he would have to wait until late summer before they emerged into the sun, and he had hoped he would have gone home by then.

Home. He looked around, at the abbey and the mill pond, across the stream and back towards the cathedral. Where was home now? Not above a tavern in Winchester, but if not there, then where did he belong?

'What the hell do you think you're doing?'

Roger was leaning against the wall between the abbey and Colebrook Street. A ring of keys was looped through his belt. Rafi had been so bound up in his own misery he'd paid no heed to anything else. Roger could have been watching him for some time. At the sight of him, Rafi felt a simmering of rage.

'Going about my business,' he replied, curtly.

'Lurking behind walls and spying on young women.'

'Indeed I am not. And I could ask you the same question.'

Roger pushed away from the wall and stepped forward. The lines etched into the side of his mouth lessened as he smiled.

'Since you ask, I am collecting rent. Here, and over yonder.' Roger nodded towards Tanner Street. 'Your little friend lives in one of our cottages.'

The simmering became a boiling cauldron. 'Do not let me stop you.'

Roger unhooked the keys, slowly and deliberately. 'We are considerate, but that is not true of all landlords. If they do not pay, the bailiff will enter. It is a sorry sight.'

'I do not doubt that you enjoy the spectacle.' Rafi clenched his fists.

Roger sprang forward, lithe as a snake, giving Rafi no chance to dodge. His hand closed around the younger man's throat, pressing against the windpipe.

'Leave young Agnes be. And keep away from the abbey. I've told you before . . .'

Rafi pushed him away. 'So you followed me, did you?'

'I go where I will, as I told you I would.'

'I have not even spoken to the girl.' Rafi coughed and tried to swallow.

Roger grinned. 'You'll need a little physick for that cough, but be careful where you find it. I saw you wave; I saw you watching her. So I say again, keep away from here.'

'Is this what you do all day, sniff at my heels like a mutt?'

'Among other things. And if I see you here again I won't wait quietly this time.'

'You cannot tell me what to do.'

'For now. But I will, soon enough.'

'Do not count on it.'

'We'll see.' Roger looked up at the sky, briefly. 'Any day now, I reckon.'

They stared at each other, neither giving way. And then Roger stood aside, bowing in mockery.

Rafi could not stop himself. 'You cannot drive me away from the abbey. Your master does not own the church here. And nor does he own Agnes.'

To Rafi's surprise, Roger paled. Then he gathered himself and jabbed Rafi in the chest. 'Keep away from her, I'm warning you.' His eyes narrowed. 'How many women do you need, eh? I thought you were chasing Edith's skirts, but it seems one is not enough. And she a married woman. But it is Agnes you're spying on now.'

Roger smirked, his grey eyes cold. 'I know your game. Pick on the young and vulnerable, or even worse, put horns on a husband without caring how it places his wife in harm's way. Well, Thom can deal with Edith. But you do Agnes any harm and, I swear, I will kill you, you hear me?'

Rafi did not answer. He could see from the look on Roger's face that he meant it.

'A married woman, and the adopted daughter of an abbess. Shame on you. Word gets around quickly, you know. We'll see if anyone is prepared to help you after this. I would never have believed it of you, but your lechery will become public knowledge now.'

Roger stormed off as Rafi fell back against the wall, stomach roiling like a butter churn. How could he fight this? Not a single door had opened and now Roger would ensure the rest were even more tightly bolted against him.

And Edith. Ah, Edith.

What had been so vibrant had fallen still and flat. She was afraid of Thom; that much was clear. And Rafi had been dismissed, reduced to anonymity. He understood why, and while he had no wish to be a stranger, he had no wish to place her in harm's way. An afternoon such as this would not be repeated; it could not be.

But there was nothing in the world he would rather do than speak with her again.

Chapter 12

Rafi had no enthusiasm for further searching that day. After Roger had left him coughing and spluttering against the wall, he'd wandered back along the high street, tripping over shop signs and earning a mouthful of expletives for his troubles.

He had thought to pass through the Durngate and look for moss, so that he could make paint, and throw his heart onto parchment. But it wouldn't have taken his mind off his distress. It would have made things worse. How could he forget what had happened if he went to the very place Edith herself frequented to gather her curatives? What if she had been there? What if Thom followed her?

He didn't truly understand why he felt hollow or why it took so much effort to lift one foot in front of the other. He supposed he was what Adam would call 'lovesick', something he'd never expected to experience. It was just his luck he felt all of the symptoms but with no hope of remedy. He would have to pray that the fever broke soon.

He spent the evening drinking far more than he'd ever drunk and sleeping badly because of it. When he woke, his tongue was glued to the top of his mouth and his head thumped as if a wild boar was stampeding on his brains. He was mildly ashamed he'd succumbed to self-pity and could barely make eye contact with Serlo as he left the Chequers.

In such low spirits, he made his way to the guildhall. He was not going to risk the abbey, not today at least. He needed more time to recover himself. Even thinking about the events of yesterday made him tremble.

The guildhall was a two-storey building, with a whitewashed plaster exterior criss-crossed with dark timber. There were two fine horses tethered to a post outside but the ground in front of the door was churned up and the lack of proper drain covers meant that here, as almost everywhere on the high street, admission to the building would result in stinking, damp breeches. The door was closed, but Rafi tried the heavy metal ring anyway, clinging on to it as he slithered across the threshold. Closed, but not locked. Good. This was one building he would enter before Roger barred his way. He hoped it would make the steward chew on a nettle with rage when he found out.

The ground floor was strewn with sweet rushes and expensive furniture, polished tables and seats. Rafi could hear voices above, muffled and low, but the ground floor was empty save for the guild clerk seated behind a desk near the stairs.

Rafi's shoes, breeches, shirt and tunic were scrutinised by the clerk who made no attempt to hide his curiosity. Rafi was shabby below the knees but so was everyone in Winchester. Whatever criteria had been set was satisfied. The clerk finished his assessment and smiled amenably, asking Rafi his business.

'I wish to find some information about a seal. If I could show it to you and ask if you have seen such a thing before?'

'Well . . . I could look, I suppose.' The clerk ran his tongue over his front teeth. 'But then that would distract me from my duties and my time will have been wasted.'

'I can pay you for your time.'

'Well, in that case . . .' The clerk removed his hands from the papers in front of him and pushed his chair back. 'Let me take a look.'

Rafi leaned forward to make it easier to get the locket over his head. The stampeding behind his eyes intensified and he stumbled forward, steadying himself against the clerk's desk.

'Mind you don't smudge those papers!' snapped the clerk.

Jesu, he would do more than smudge them! Rafi swallowed down the bile, hoping he did not vomit all over the records the clerk had been making.

Records. The names of the men currently on the upper floor.

Rafi blinked. His headache was making his eyes play tricks, surely.

There were three names written vertically on the parchment, and three wax seals horizontal. Th. De Hoyville; Peter Fayre; Hugh Le Cran.

Le Cran was upstairs? Well, that would make sense. He had been mayor and was now still an influential citizen. Mayor of the staple, as Edith had informed him only yesterday.

Edith. Rafi swayed again. The clerk glared at him.

'Apologies.' This was no good. He would be thrown out if he didn't watch himself.

'What are you staring at?'

'Sorry, those marks . . .' Wax seals. They were no bigger than the size of a ring, which was no doubt what had made them. A ring worn on the finger with a seal matrix embedded. It was a common enough accessory, and could vary quite drastically in size. It was the one in the middle that transfixed him. He leaned forward to get a better look.

'That is none of your business.' The clerk moved the paper out of the way and placed it in a drawer.'

Which name was it? The one in the middle – Peter Fayre. But were the marks on the top of the page in the same order as the names down the side?

'Are they . . .'

The clerk stood up. 'Who are you?' He narrowed his eyes. 'Is your name Dubois, by any chance?'

'Why . . . How did you . . .?' Roger. He'd got here first after all.

'I'm afraid you'll have to leave. Now.'

'No . . . I . . .'

Rafi and the clerk looked upward. There were soft steps on the floor above them, steps that began to descend the stairs. Dark boots, a fine three-quarter-length tunic, a velvet cap on dark hair. Young. Younger than Rafi had been expecting. He knew who it was. Edith had said the man was handsome and Rafi was still as annoyed by that as he had been yesterday.

Hugh Le Cran, standing on the stairs and yes, he was handsome, there was no getting away from it. If Rafi painted him it would be as an archangel; forbidding, masterful. But dishonest as the day was long. He'd stick a forked tail on him and make his face fat. He wouldn't be handsome if Rafi had anything to do with it.

Le Cran frowned. Rafi realised he'd been grinding his teeth. He had never expected to feel jealous of another man's looks and he wasn't enjoying the experience at all.

'Do you have a good reason for disturbing guild business, Dubois? I assume that's who you are, yes?' said Le Cran. 'I very much hope you do, otherwise I shall be most unimpressed.'

'I have been asked not to let him in.' The clerk bowed. 'Your steward—'

Le Cran held up his hand. The clerk clamped his mouth shut.

'Well.' Le Cran looked down on Rafi from his vantage point. 'That is the matter closed, then. If those are my steward's instructions then I commend him. Please leave.'

Rafi stepped forward. 'You have no right to—'

'Right now, if you would be so kind.'

Rafi had every intention of leaving. Nothing else could be achieved here. But he stayed a moment longer, irritated that Le Cran's face bore not a single sign of the dishonesty that dwelt

130

within him, but unable to look away until the clerk elbowed him in the ribs and as good as kicked him through the door.

If his head did not hurt so much, and if his heart had been less heavy, Rafi might have skipped through the pig swill and dirt of the high street instead of looking downward to keep the sun from his sore eyes. Roger would hear about the exchange that had just taken place and think he'd won a fine victory. Rafi had been banished from the guildhall, which was what Roger had wanted. But the truth was, Rafi had found something on that piece of paper that would make his task here much easier, so there was some satisfaction in a small victory of his own over his tormentor.

Three names, one of which he could dismiss. He already knew that Le Cran held a vintner's seal: Roger bore such a badge on his tunic. So that left Peter Fayre and Thomas De Hoyville.

Rafi had not scrutinised all three seals closely; there had not been the opportunity. He needed to see the one in the middle again. He needed to be sure of what he had seen.

A bird. Holding a stone aloft in its claw. Unlike the seal he carried, the bird was solitary, and that was what prevented Rafi from shouting to all the saints that he'd found his man. It wasn't quite his seal. Almost, but not quite.

But it was close enough for him to want to seek out Peter Fayre and Thomas De Hoyville.

Maybe the soul of the dead soldier would soon be at peace.

And you, Maman. I will know the name of the man who took you and Christophe. I am close.

He is within my reach.

Chapter 13

Rafi sat at a trestle table in the Chequers, digging his feet into the uneven ground as hard as he could to stop his stool from toppling over. He was covered in pastry crumbs, which he idly brushed away while savaging the remains of the potpie in front of him. He hadn't realised how ravenously hungry he was until he'd come back to the inn. He had hoped to find some respite in his room to gather his thoughts. He was yet to reach the foot of the stairs that led up to the gallery overlooking the firepit in the centre of the inn, where lodgings were kept for paying guests. The smell of potpies and griddle cakes had been too much.

Serlo had laughed at the sight of him.

'Pale and sickly, young Rafi. Your first cloudy head I reckon. I knew you were no Fleming before you even told me. They know how to hold their ale. You, my lad, can barely hold a cup of piss.'

'I can hold a pie, though.'

'Ho! That you can.'

The headache and the dry mouth he could live with. Were it not for the dent in his heart, this would have been the best day Rafi had had for a long while. A good plate of food before him and a step closer to finding the seal owner. More than a step, surely? He was cutting through the forest at last. He smiled. This pie was good; this day was . . . almost good. He was close; he knew he was.

He asked Serlo about the two men, Hoyville and Fayre.

Serlo wiped his sleeve over his face. He'd spent most of the morning turning a pig over the firepit and looked as well basted as the dead animal.

'Hoyville is up from Romsey. Sheep is where his purse is pointed. Fayre, he's Winchester all right. Young son, Mark. Rivals of your friend Le Cran.'

'He's not my friend.' Rafi's teeth began to grind again.

Serlo's sweaty eyebrows shot up. 'Ohh! What has burst since this morn, when you slunk out of here like a man with a snipe caught in his craw?'

'A snipe in his . . . what?'

Rafi would never understand the vagaries of the local tongue, no matter how clever he was with languages. English in England was nothing like the English he'd learned in Ghent, but he supposed merchants trying to curry favour with Van Loo would speak more formally than an innkeeper as skilful at hospitality as Serlo. Master merchant, master mason, gongfermour or alewife, he dealt with them all day every day, and his success was measured in the popularity of his inn. It was unrivalled in Winchester, and with good reason.

'Oh, never you mind, young Rafi. Just give me the telling.'

Rafi smiled. 'I met Le Cran this morning. Our encounter was not entirely friendly.'

'Friendly is not a word I would put with him. But give him his due, he's a clever one. He built that family up from disaster, and he caught Joan too.' Serlo patted his heart. 'That did give me pause. A lovelier woman you'd be hard pressed to find. If she took him on, he must have something to recommend him other than his purse, for she was rich enough in her own right not to care for that. Must be more under his coat than coin, eh?'

Rafi scowled. Le Cran must have blinded her to his faults with his fine calves and velvet cap.

'Are you well there? You are chewing leather.'

'He seemed very . . . very fair.'

Damn him to the pit of hell.

Serlo grinned. 'He is. But Joan is also very fair. And she has a good head on even shoulders. Her first husband was very old and infirm and she was as loyal and true to him as any woman could be. If she has a warmer bed now, I'm not likely to begrudge her.'

Rafi's cheeks burned. He should not let his jealousy cloud his judgement. It was not Hugh's fault that Edith had called him handsome. 'Well, Fayre, then. I think he may know about my seal.'

'That is fine progress!' Serlo clapped Rafi on the back so hard he nearly pushed him headfirst through the table.

'I hope so. I would like to meet with this Peter Fayre.'

Serlo's face fell. 'That might not be possible for a few weeks at least. He and the boy Mark are abroad in London, and he is a widower so there is no wife to speak of. He will have sent his steward to do his business. I'm sorry, lad.'

Rafi's mood was not as light as it had been a moment ago. A few weeks? He had no desire to stay here for that long, not with Roger biting his ankles and a soldier chasing him for information he didn't have. But, perhaps he could talk to Fayre's steward.

'Look now, have you tried the castle? Fayre may use one of the clerks there. If you can use your wits they might let you in.'

Rafi shook his head. 'Not yet, but I did intend to.'

Serlo dashed over to the firepit where one side of the spit pig had begun to char. 'Well, finish that pie and get your fine boots up there. No good buying fancy footwear if you're not going to use it, is there?' Serlo coughed. 'I think this animal is on its way to the eternal pyre. Lucifer could not do as much damage as I have done, prattling with you all day. Begone, Rafi, before demons descend on my kitchen.'

Taking Serlo's advice, Rafi headed for the entrance to the castle, which was through an arch just inside the Westgate. He predicted that Roger would make an appearance, for surely the steward would not be able to stop himself from gloating. He had been fully aware that the man was following him; he hadn't even been bothered to hide it. Sure enough, there he was, an ever-present menace, leaning against the castle walls, examining his fingernails.

'Good day, Master Dubois. Walking off your embarrassment, I see.'

'If you like. 'Tis a nice day for it.'

Roger scowled. 'I did warn you. But you can always change your mind. The offer is still open.'

'Thank you, but no.'

'Hmph. Well, if you have a mind to enter the castle you may struggle to get past the clerk,' Roger said, nodding towards the entrance.

Damn. Well, there had still been something of use at the guildhall for all that Roger had tried to stop him getting in, so maybe his luck would hold. Rafi could see a clerk in the doorway, beside an open window. Perhaps the clerk would be called away at some point. It would help if Roger wasn't hanging around like a dose of the pox.

'I was actually going for a walk,' lied Rafi.

'A walk? Do you take me for a fool?' Roger pushed himself away from the wall and smiled. 'I've secured the castle so please, be my guest. I have better things to do than watch you make a fool of yourself.' Roger gestured towards the entrance. 'Off you go, then.'

Roger was so secure in his victory he left Rafi standing by the castle entrance and strode down the high street as if walking on clouds.

The clerk had been watching the entire exchange, and smiled expectantly as Rafi approached.

'You can't come in.'

Rafi groaned. 'Where is the . . .'

'You can't come in.'

This was pointless. What was he to do now? He would have to wait, discreetly. If that's what it took, then so be it. But not here, not where the clerk could see him. Behind the entrance, where he had come in. The clerk would surely lose interest soon enough.

The bells rang the quarter-hour. Then another quarter. By the sixth clamour Rafi was on the point of giving up but then noticed that the clerk was no longer at his post. Nor was he in the courtyard. Rafi edged through the arch. Other than a few officials hurrying between buildings, robes flapping behind them, there was no one here to pay him any heed.

He stepped lightly across the open space, trying to look as if he belonged. He was nearly at the great hall now. If the clerk was lurking just inside, his journey would end here, but while there was a chance, Rafi was going to take it.

He swallowed. There was someone there, an elderly man, his arms filled with books that he was sliding onto a shelf. But no sign of the clerk. Not yet anyway. Rafi clenched his fists and strode forward, praying that Roger had not warned more than just the solitary clerk who had been guarding the entrance.

One of the books slipped from the shelf and clattered to the tiled floor.

Rafi dashed forward. 'Here. Let me help . . . oh!'

Rafi held the book carefully, running his fingers over the embossed title. It was the *Summa Theologica*, a work he knew very well. 'You have Aquinas!'

'What is that you say?' The older man shuffled forward.

'I spent much time with that book. I scribed many parts of it. The *quinque viae* . . .'

'I see.' The old man stepped forward into the light and inspected Rafi. 'Once a novice, eh?'

'Yes. Well, not quite but . . .'

'You were here earlier with Writel, were you not? I saw you from the window. You are new here, I think?'

There was a corridor just behind the old man. At any moment the clerk might return. Dare he lie? Could he do such a thing? The hairs on the back of his neck began to prickle. He could not do this; it was wrong. But now the old man was staring at him intently.

'I . . .'

A door, a door opening, the hiss of a bolt being drawn into place. It might be the clerk. Rafi was unable to see. The corridor was dark. But there were footsteps now.

'Yes. New. I was sent by Master Writel to . . . to look at some records of . . . trade with a Master De Hoyville . . .' The footsteps paused. There was a muttering of expletives and then the footsteps faded again.

'Why didn't you say so? Come this way. What is your name? I am Thurstin.'

How could he do this? Thurstin was so amenable. Rafi's hands trembled slightly as he followed him into the office. The window he had seen from the courtyard was still open. The room was filled with books and scrolls; two desks were placed by the window, the light slanting onto the scratched surfaces. Thurstin removed his hat, beneath which he wore a white coif, the laces tied loosely under his chin. A sprinkling of grey hair stuck out beneath the edges.

'Well then, young man, what can I do for you?'

Rafi took a deep breath. There was a pain in his chest. Guilt. It must be guilt.

'Oh dear. Here, sit down. Are you sickening for something?' Thurstin passed Rafi a mug of weak ale. 'Drink this. Take your time.'

This was making things worse. Thurstin was kind, so kind. And, there was something about him that reminded Rafi of Brother Johannes. But he had to know. That clerk might come back. Roger might come back.

'I am well, thank you. I . . . I am sorry.' Yes, he was sorry. Sorry that he was having to lie to this kind scrivener.

'Well, let us see.' Thurstin edged towards a pile of boxes under the window. 'Hoyville. Yes. I had heard your master is entering into a business association with Master Hoyville, a plot of land I believe. I expect you have come to see the deeds of ownership?'

His master. Hugh Le Cran. Rafi ran his palm over his forehead. 'Yes. And . . . and Master Fayre too.'

'Ah! Peter Fayre. I have known him for many years, and your master too, of course.'

Thurstin removed the uppermost boxes in the pile and put them to one side, then grasped the next two, shuffling them across the desk towards Rafi. 'Here we are. I expect Master Le Cran will be collecting the rents from this plot from now on, if he is buying?'

Rafi could do nothing more than nod. He had spoken too many lies already.

'Proof of ownership will be in there, and the details of the residents. It is De Hoyville's land, but it adjoins that of Fayre. I should have known Le Cran would have sent someone – I was informed of the particulars only today and of course filed the papers immediately. Your master likes everything to be in order.'

This must have been what they were doing at the guildhall, finalising the sale of land. Well, they would have signed and sealed the agreement. Rafi had only to look at the signatures for Hoyville and Fayre – and their seals – and he could be out of here before his guilt got the better of him.

He did not know what made him ask, what put the thought into his head at that moment. A restless spirit, reaching out to him from long ago, guiding his path? Or intuition. Or plain luck.

'I was asked to see Le C . . . my master's papers too, to make sure nothing was missed.'

Thurstin hesitated. Rafi shifted in his seat. Had he given himself away, somehow? But then the scrivener went back to the pile of boxes and Rafi let his breath escape.

'It is unlike your master to miss anything. I am surprised he would need to check again.'

'I am keen to . . . to make a good impression.' Where were these lies coming from? Rafi was appalled by his own behaviour.

The box was placed beneath the two already on the desk. Thurstin peered closely at him, but said no more.

'I will leave you to check. I am sure you will find nothing amiss.'

Thurstin took his seat at the other desk. There was a row of dip pens lined up on a small table to Thurstin's right, and a small paring knife. Rafi knew the tools well. A pen would break a dozen times a day, so a good clerk or novice always had a knife to hand, to sharpen a new quill and correct his mistakes. Thurstin picked up a quill and began scratching at a piece of parchment.

Three boxes. He opened the first one. It took but a few seconds to conclude that the bird seal did not belong to Peter Fayre.

Rafi opened the second box. De Hoyville. As Serlo had said, his business seemed to be mainly in wool, with a little property in Winchester. The land he intended to sell to Le Cran was near the drapery and included several shops and a number of private dwellings. The rental from these alone would make a man very comfortable indeed. The agreement was signed and sealed with . . . three hares. This couldn't be right. Rafi checked again but no matter how he tried to make the hares look like birds, they steadfastly refused to grow wings.

The third box. It sat across the table from him. Le Cran. He didn't want to have anything to do with it. Any number of deceptions might be found inside. He visualised the face of the man who had looked down his nose at him in the guildhall. Le Cran hadn't *looked* like a dissembler, but if he were a good one he would surely be able to hide it. Rafi recalled the velvet cap and the dark hair. Brown eyes, which hadn't seemed cruel. In fact, they'd held him steady. Rafi blinked the image away. He could do without having that man's face in his head. Handsome bastard.

He pulled the box towards him.

'All in order?'

Rafi nodded. 'Yes. The other two signatories have made their mark.'

'You will find nothing amiss with your master's agreement.' Thurstin went back to his scratching.

Rafi rubbed his hands on his breeches and then opened the box.

It held a large amount of correspondence relating to property sales. Everywhere, the vintner's seal, exactly the same design as the one on Roger's badge. Perhaps he should look in Fayre's box again. Perhaps he had missed something. He cast a quick glance at Thurstin. The scrivener was completely focused on his writing.

Rafi frowned. He must have made a mistake. Maybe he wanted to see his bird so much he'd imagined it. But he had been so certain. A single bird, and . . . what was this? Where had he seen this before?

Three feathers.

That was the mark on the badge the soldier had worn, the one who had attacked him in Hammond's Passage. What was it doing in here? Hadn't Roger asked him to find out who the soldier was working for? If the soldier bore this mark, and this mark was mixed in among Le Cran's other documents, then Roger would have a pretty good idea who he was. This made no sense.

Rafi quickly pulled the document out from the bottom of the box. It was a request from the Earl of Arundel to the merchant H. Le Cran for payment of £200 sent five years ago.

Owed unto me by yr. brother, Wm.

The earl's mark, and then the three feathers beside William's name.

William? That was the elder Le Cran brother, the one Van Loo had once mentioned. He had almost lost the family fortune, Rafi remembered now. But if the feather badge belonged to William Le Cran, then it was he who must have sent a soldier to Winchester to find incriminating information about Hugh. A family feud? Dear God, he had been caught up in a feud between these two devil brothers and lost a tooth into the bargain. Well, this was not his business and he had no desire to get involved. There was no bird seal in here. The promising information from this morning had taken him nowhere. He closed the box, disappointed.

'All done?'

Rafi nodded. 'All in order.'

'I would have expected no less.'

'I . . .' Rafi wished he hadn't lied to Thurstin. It sat ill with him. And it had all been for nothing, which made the crime even worse. Unless . . .

'What is it, young man?'

'I was expecting to see a different seal.'

Thurstin knitted his brows together. 'Oh?'

'Was there another signatory?'

'Another signatory?'

Rafi swallowed. 'Yes. I saw the seals at the guildhall while Le . . . my master was in attendance. I don't see it here.'

'The guildhall?' Thurstin put his quill down and clasped his hands together on the desk. 'Can you describe the seal to me?'

'I can draw it.'

Thurstin wordlessly pushed a piece of paper across the desk, his eyes not leaving Rafi's face. The paper was used for wiping excess ink from the quill. There were dark streaks and blotches on the surface, but enough space to draw.

Rafi took the quill that Thurstin gave him and with guilty hands drew the solitary bird with the stone.

Thurstin held the paper up to the light and scrutinised it. 'You have a good eye.' He smoothed the paper out on the desk. 'But you don't work for Master Le Cran, do you?'

'I . . .'

'I did think it a little odd, you asking to check his papers. But I thought that as you were new, or so you said, you didn't realise how thorough he is. He would have checked and double-checked, and then checked again. I let it go, because you might have been overly eager to please.'

Rafi's head dropped. He couldn't look Thurstin in the eye. But how had he given himself away? What was it about the drawing?

'This mark is part of a tapestry. It's a rather magnificent piece, which of course it would be. It hangs in the hallway of a house in Minster Street. You can't miss it. I expect you can guess which house I'm referring to?'

Rafi groaned.

'You would have seen it if you worked there, of course. The matching seal is used rarely; the usual Le Cran seal is a barrel and grapes. But he does use this on occasion, mainly when the matter concerns transactions outside his regular business – land, property and such like. So I expect he did use it today at the guildhall to say he was in attendance. But it's never used on formal deeds, and you'd know that if he'd asked you to check his papers, because he'd have told you.'

Rafi raised his head, ashamed. 'I did see it in the guildhall.'

'I have no doubt you did, but that's what gave you away. Master Le Cran always attends alone, and on the rare occasions he is accompanied, it would be with his steward only. 'Tis a shame. I would have liked to talk to you about the *Summa*, and you're clearly a bright young man. I wish you'd been honest with me. I would have happily told you what that mark was. It has been displayed in the hall for as long as I've known the family, thirteen or fourteen years. This deception was unnecessary.'

'One bird?'

Thurstin shook his head. 'What is this now? I'm going to have to ask you to leave.'

'But . . . please. Is it just one bird, or were there others?'

Thurstin sighed. 'Master Le Cran carries one bird, yes. 'Tis the only one remaining.'

'I'm sorry.' Rafi could hear himself mumbling. 'I'm truly sorry.'

'Yes, I do believe you are.'

Rafi stumbled into the courtyard. It was quiet now. He would have to walk across the yard feeling the scrivener's disapproving eyes on his back. It was no more than he deserved.

The Westgate would close soon, once the curfew bell tolled. Rafi was back on the high street again, the castle wall behind him. He pressed his back against it, feeling the cool stone through his tunic. His skin was warm; his lies had made him sweat. What would he do now that the trail he had been following had run out?

There were the bells on the quarter hour again. One more remaining before the gates closed for the evening.

One remaining.

Wait. If he had been less intent on running wildly out of the scrivener's room maybe he'd have thought harder on what was being said.

Le Cran had one bird, but it was *the only one remaining*. That is what Thurstin had said. What did that mean? Were there others, and where were they now? How many? Was this something to do with Le Cran after all?

Rafi rubbed his brow. Le Cran's bird must be part of a flock.

A flock. Family? But William's seal was of three feathers.

Rafi could not bear the prospect of having to approach Hugh Le Cran. But if he wanted answers, then it seemed he might have to. And he had something to bargain with. He knew who was trying to incriminate Le Cran, and now, he was prepared to tell him who that was.

But Rafi would demand information in return.

If one bird remained, where were the others? Who were the others?

He would offer William Le Cran's name, in exchange for the path to open once more.

Chapter 14

Rafi needed to think. Painting or drawing was his usual method for calming and ordering his thoughts, but he still had so little material. At least he knew where to find moss though; through the Durngate, up on the marsh.

What had she said?

Between supper and curfew.

She may be there now, gathering her stores in the place she'd spoken of, Danemarch Mead, just outside the city. He would have been there with her, maybe, had Thom not dashed his hopes and desires so cruelly yesterday.

Edith. He so longed to speak with her and lay out this mystery. Just telling her would have shone a light where he saw none. It would have sparkled. He saw her now; hair poking out from her headdress, catching between her lips and making her brush it away with the back of her hand. He saw her push the dibber into the soil and gently drop sprigs of mint and thyme into the spaces before stroking the earth over them. He would crumble to earth forever just to have her stroke him with the same tenderness. It felt like an age ago. He wished it were now.

He had a little moss and some buttercups in his room, which he was soaking in oil. Green and yellow. But not enough. He could not go to the marshes when she was there; it would be wrong. But he would go soon, during the day, when she would not be troubled by him. Willow bark, water violet and kingcups. They would make good colours. Perhaps he could make her a sign, for her stall. But then . . . he shook his head. It would give Thom too many suspicions and she would suffer because of it.

Damn this, what was he to do? He could not forget her, but he would have to. He had come here for one purpose, and whatever he might have found, that day in the garden, he would have to put away.

Rafi headed for the steps to his room. He had no desire to drink Edith out of his thoughts as had happened the other day. The Chequers was busy again – many apprentices made their way here after the shutters were drawn down on shopfronts, after carts were put away and horses fed and watered. Some finer citizens came here, too. There was ale, but also some higher quality wines, mead and melomel. Serlo catered to everyone. Seats and tables were arranged carefully; there were doors leading into private eating areas for those who could afford them. For himself, Rafi tended to remain in the big room with the firepit. It could become unbearably hot in the evening, and the smoke from the tallow candles and spitting fat made his eyes sting, but the voices and chatter were comforting.

There was one voice here he recognised, and which called to him just as he put his foot on the stair.

Adam.

'Here! Over here!'

Well, it seemed Adam was in better spirits than he had been the last time they'd met. Even so, Rafi was hesitant. What Edith had told him in the garden that day, about how he had abandoned Ailith, without so much as a goodbye, had disappointed Rafi greatly.

Adam was seated near the firepit. The heat was intense. Rafi removed his tunic.

'I hear you had a little trouble at the meat market? I didn't have you down as the brawling kind.'

Rafi smiled despite himself. 'I lost a tooth but gained a reputation.'

'Aye! And you tumbled Mistress Alice to boot!'

'I did no such thing!' It was as well the heat was so intense to explain his blushes, which he was sure could be seen from as far away as Salisbury.

'I jest, you big fool. I bet she tried, though.' Adam laughed. 'How are you, man, how goes this search of yours?'

Where to begin? 'I think Le Cran might know something but I can't be sure.'

'Le Cran?' Adam shook his head and patted the badge he wore. 'This is his mark. We all wear it.'

'He has another. Not quite the same as the one I hold, but close enough to make me curious.'

Adam lifted his mug. There was a pewter jug on the table between them. Rafi narrowed his eyes – surely Adam was not going to drink all of this?

'Don't look like that. Serlo said you went rolling up the stairs this week, so you are in no position to condemn me.'

'I did not realise the ale was so strong.'

Adam's face fell. 'Aye.'

Rafi could have kicked himself. Serlo had told him that Ailith provided some of their ale. He should have thought before he spoke.

'Sorry, I . . .'

''Tis not your fault. This is one of hers. I would know it anywhere and it is damned fine ale.'

'I would have thought that you were not allowed out.' Rafi tried to change the subject. 'Did you not warn me that Le Cran was much stricter than Van Loo?'

'He would be if he were here. He has business in Southampton and will be there until the morrow. May as well take advantage.' Adam refilled his mug. 'So, tell me. How did you come to learn of this second seal?'

Rafi bit his lip. 'I asked Thurstin, one of the clerks at the castle.'

Adam put his mug down and grinned. 'You're hiding something. Did you climb in through the window in the middle of the night? That would be funny.'

'Well, not quite.'

Adam clapped his hands together. 'Why, Rafi, what have you done?'

What he had done was wrong. Perhaps Adam's condemnation was to be his punishment. He deserved it, and more.

'I pretended to work for Le Cran. It was the only way I could go through the papers I needed to see.'

'You lied?'

Rafi scratched the back of his neck and gazed intently at the firepit until the smoke defeated him. 'There was no other way.'

'You lied. I thought you didn't know how to lie?'

'I have always known how to lie. I have simply chosen to avoid doing so where possible.'

'This is more than just a plain lie. You pretended to be someone else entirely and as good as stole information! And you looked scornfully at me because I didn't tell you about the woolsacks. You can put your saintly garb away for evermore. You no longer have the fitting of it.'

As if he didn't already know that. He rested his elbows on the table and put his head in his hands. 'Do not remind me.'

'I did say, didn't I? That one day you would step off your path if necessity asked it of you.'

Rafi well remembered – that day they had arrived in Winchester. Adam had asked how far would he go to find out who owned that seal. He knew now that he would lie, and even prolong that lie. How quickly he had changed.

'I take no pride in it.'

'Aye, well. I do. You're learning fast. Will you talk to Le Cran, then?'

'I will. He wants to know about the man who attacked me. I think his brother has something to do with it.'

Adam looked up sharply. 'His brother? But he is banished to Salisbury.'

'Banished?' This must be to do with the loss of the family fortune. 'What did he do? I hear he nearly ruined his father.'

Adam overfilled his mug. 'There was more than just that. He came back from the wars without his brother . . .'

'Le Cran was in France?'

'Hugh? No, no. Remember, I told you there was another brother, Richard, the middle son. After Richard died in France, William ate through the family coffers. Their father was ill by then. It was said his heart was broken when Richard died, and Hugh was too young to do anything about it. Richard was the one who had kept William under control, but with him gone . . .'

Rafi waited while Adam gulped his drink down. He hoped his friend would be sated, but it seemed not. Another mug was overfilled. He would need to prompt Adam to finish this tale before he became insensible. If he were to approach Le Cran, the more he knew the better.

'So . . .' Adam was slurring now. He leaned across the table. Ale mingled with smoke and made Rafi's eyes tingle. 'One of the sisters from the abbey went missing. Found next day in a terrible state. It was William. That's when he was disinherited and banished, and Hugh took over the business. He was very young at the time. Hugh paid the abbess a large sum of money and had the nun placed in the abbey at Wherwell.'

Rafi grunted. 'I expect he wanted to keep her out of the way.'

Adam shook his head. 'No. She didn't want to stay in Winchester after what had happened. Master Hugh gave an endowment to the abbess at Wherwell to take care of her and keep her safe. They would have taken the sister anyway but . . .' Adam shrugged. 'Master Hugh is no saint, but he is not all bad.'

Rafi rubbed his eyes. 'I see.'

'And you' – Adam prodded him in the shoulder – 'are no devil, but you are not all good.'

No. No, he was not.

'He is a . . . a good master. Is it so bad, what he does? That tax would only go on the king's wars. Is it not better spent on fine cloth and fine ladies? None have died in the making of a bliaut, Rafi. And he treats us fairly. Not like our fat friend in Ghent.' Adam was struggling to keep his head upright.

'Come. Let me walk you back to the . . .'

There were two men, their outlines shimmering through the heat haze. One of them raised his cup and nodded. The smoke hurt Rafi's eyes but he recognised the figure only too well.

Adam followed his gaze.

'Oh! It's Stefan!'

Rafi raised his eyebrows. 'You know him?'

'He bought two fine cloaks from the drapery this morning.'

'Adam, be careful.'

Adam slammed his cup on the table. 'Can I not have friends of my own, eh?'

'Of course. But he . . .'

'Let it go. Fine cloaks they were. The finest . . . finest cloaks.'

It was impossible to see Stefan's expression through the smoky veil. The firepit was between them, the ribbon of heat distorted the man on the other side. He raised his cup to Rafi again.

'Finesht . . .' Adam pushed his cup aside. 'To hell with this . . . betrayal. This is hers. It tastes of her. Whore.'

'Come on, Adam. Let me walk you back to Minster Street.' Rafi needed to get Adam away from the keen eyes of Stefan, away from the smirks and disapproval. When Roger found out about this, as he would, Adam would rue the day he had been born. Best get him out of here before he made things worse.

'I don't need your help.'

Rafi offered it anyway. Adam slumped against him, almost knocking him off his feet. It was like supporting an ox, although Rafi suspected an ox would have more grace and mobility than the stumbling, slurring man whose bulk now leaned into him.

He got Adam almost as far as the alleyway that led through to the marketplace. It would be a short walk from there to Minster Street and Adam's bed, assuming Roger didn't catch him and send him to sleep in the stables.

'Aha!' Adam pushed Rafi aside. They had reached the Helle.

'No, Adam. Let us get you home.'

'You are not . . . my . . . mother.' Adam shouldered the door open. Lights flickered at the bottom of the stairs; the narrow steps would be a challenge to the soberest of men. If Adam descended into the depths, he would not return this side of morning. Not without help.

But this was as far as Rafi was prepared to go. 'No, Adam. You have drunk too much already.'

'Do not . . . tell me . . . what to do. Go talk to . . . Edith in her garden . . .' Adam pushed Rafi, then pushed him again. Then a third time. Each push jolted Rafi's shoulder, jerked his head back, reminded him of the pain in his jaw, which had not yet fully receded.

'What did you say?' Rafi tasted blood. The jarring had reopened the barely healed hole in his gum.

'I saw you on Colebrook Street. I was . . . delivering a . . . passing by . . . how you have . .' Adam leaned in through the door of the Helle, catching himself on the lintel, precariously balancing at the mouth of iniquity. 'How you have changed. Well, tumble her, if you may . . . She is . . . she is . .' Adam lost his footing, sliding backwards first, so that he fell on his backside three or four stairs down. He lay, horizontally, blocking the entrance. 'Come, come down. Come down with me.'

Rafi shook his head but Adam did not see. He shuffled

downward, descending into the bowels of the tavern. He would have forgotten what he said in the morning, had probably already forgotten, but Rafi would not.

To hell with Adam and his foolishness and his coarse tongue. How dare he speak of Edith like that? Let him take the consequences of his drunkenness. Rafi would not be there to guide him home this time, as he had so often in Ghent.

But . . . if Adam had seen them, then who else? Gossip, chatter – would it wind its way to Thom, burrow into the space they called home? And what then . . . what then?

Rafi's boots thudded through the passageway, taking him out into the deserted marketplace. It was darkening already; the evening mantel grew heavy. The cathedral was quiet, for it was well past compline now. A few hours earlier, this would have been alive with traders, commerce, noise. Edith's stall, it would be just a short distance from where he now stood. And where he now walked.

He was in the space she occupied by day. He closed his eyes. Nothing. A light breeze, the tang of late spring, but nothing more. But then, as he breathed, the faint warmth of spice.

Cinnamon. Her cinnamon.

Rafi opened his eyes. The nightwatchman was approaching from the direction of Minster Street, taking in the cathedral precincts as he did his rounds. Rafi kneeled and stroked the earth where her feet trod each day, as she had stroked the earth in the garden. He let his hand rest there, pressing hard into the ground, not heeding the tears that fell onto his fingers.

Curse Adam. Curse Stefan. And curse Thom.

The nightwatchman was nearly upon him. Rafi sighed. He would be admonished if he stayed here, wandering outside the cathedral after curfew. And it was as well he returned to his room. He would approach Le Cran tomorrow, so he had best plan what to say. And his jaw ached again. Serlo had left the valerian from a few days before. It would ease him to a dreamless sleep.

The high street was empty now, although the Chequers was lively enough. The table opposite the firepit was unoccupied. Stefan and his friend had gone.

Chapter 15

Rafi hesitated outside the house on Minster Street, craning his neck as his eyes travelled from bottom to top.

In the herb garden, just opposite the stable, everything was still, save for the bees that darted among the lavender heads. So much peace in this place: he could close his eyes and be back in the cloister at St Michael's, five years gone in an instant. And that scent: lavender for pillow herbs and perfume. He was standing beside his mother now in their little cottage garden, cutting the purple heads for drying, their hands covered in powder. He was here for her, as much as he was here for the soldier.

A dark door, heavy oak, metal hinges wide and strong. It opened before he had a chance to knock.

'Less than a week.'

There was little point in a retort. 'I wish to see Master Le Cran.'

Roger pulled the door open fully. 'This way.'

Rafi was led into the hall. Sweet herbs were strewn on polished tiles, a long table taking up the centre of the room. The windows at the far end of the hall had alcoves, with padded seats to sit and enjoy the view of the large garden at the back of the house.

There were stairs to his left, leading up to a gallery. The kitchens and scullery led off to the side, and there was also another door, of heavy oak behind which, he assumed, Le Cran lay in wait.

And there, hanging on a wall just behind the table, the tapestry that Thurstin had told him about. It was in the shape of a pennant and displayed just the one bird. The stone was, as ever, held aloft in the claw. Perhaps he had been mistaken; the bird was not as plump as the one on his seal, less like a duck or goose, more like a heron. But this was the closest he had been to something similar. It was possible that his seal had been made by someone less skilled than whoever had fashioned the tapestry. That, or he was clutching at straws.

This was nothing like Van Loo's house. Not only was it tidy, not only were the furnishings correctly chosen and carefully placed, but it smelled fresh. It did not have the all-pervading stink of the river they had grown used to in Ghent. Everything here was pristine. He rubbed the back of his neck and tried not to make eye contact with Roger.

Roger glided across the hall as if he were made of liquid. His feet barely made a sound. He rapped on the oak door and stepped back.

'Enter.'

Roger turned the metal ring handle and gestured to Rafi to step inside.

This was like walking into a wasps' nest. Roger hovered behind him, likely to sting at any moment, and before him was Master Le Cran. At least the man was seated this time. It was marginally better than having him stare down his nose, although it was still not worth rejoicing about.

Le Cran wore his velvet cap, resting lightly on raven-black hair flecked grey at the temples. Rafi was as annoyed by Le Cran's looks as he had been in the guildhall. He glared.

'What on earth are you doing?'

Rafi had to say something, if only to prevent himself looking like a madman. 'I believe you wished to speak with me.'

Le Cran nodded. 'Yes. You may have some information. If you can tell me anything at all about the man who attacked you, then please do so.'

'I may. But you might also have some information for me.'

'Well, who shall give way first?' Le Cran started toying with some jettons that were piled up in neat rows on his desk next to a silver scale and balance.

Rafi would rather Le Cran went first. He didn't trust him to reciprocate. If the information about the feather badge was of no use to him, there would be no incentive to answer Rafi's questions.

'You are very quiet.' Le Cran removed his cap, brushing it and laying it neatly on the table. Apart from the small flecks of grey that had been evident at his temples, the rest of Le Cran's hair was as dark as his fringe. Without the cap, he looked even younger than Rafi had first assumed. Not much more than thirty.

'Perhaps our original conclusion was correct. Writel managed to convince me that you were probably not a spy. Probably. Your silence is very troubling though. *Si vous êtes venu ici pour m'espionner, je vous conseillerais fortement de réfléchir à nouveau.*'

'You speak . . .'

Le Cran rolled his eyes. 'Of course I do.'

Rafi breathed deeply. Le Cran was intimidating but if he really thought Rafi were a spy he would have had him arrested by now. 'Well, I am not here for any nefarious purpose, I can assure you.'

'No, I do not think you are,' said Le Cran, observing him keenly. 'So, tell me, what do you wish to know?'

'Your tapestry—'

'What in God's name are you babbling about?' Roger growled.

Le Cran held up his hand. 'Go on.'

'Is there one with more birds on it?'

The silence was heavier than an anchor. It sank, further and further, pulling Rafi down with it. What had he said? Le Cran's expression had not changed, but Roger looked as if he had been winded by a blow to the guts.

'No.' It had taken Le Cran too long to answer. Much too long.

Rafi's locket was with him. He could take it out and show it to Le Cran. He had shown Serlo and Adam; he would have shown Thurstin under different circumstances. His palms were sweating. There was something amiss here, something his instinct forced him to listen to.

He is lying.

If he showed Le Cran the seal, Le Cran would lie.

'Then . . . I must have been mistaken.'

'Mistaken? About what?'

What could he say? Roger already knew he was looking for the man who killed his mother so if he strayed too far from the truth he would be caught out.

'My mother . . . she was killed by someone wearing a badge with a horse and two chickens.'

The anchor was raised.

'Can you not tell a chicken from a crane?' Le Cran wrinkled his nose. 'And a horse, there is no horse on the tapestry outside.'

'It might have been a wolf.' Lying was coming naturally to him now.

Le Cran shook his head. 'You cannot even tell a horse from a wolf? I was led to believe you were clever.'

Roger laughed. Rafi scowled at him.

'Well, we have answered your question. Now. Tell us what you know about the man who attacked you. Why did he wish to know of me?'

'I do not know. But I can tell you that he was wearing a badge with three feathers on it.'

The anchor dropped again. Rapidly. The silence in the room was so deep Rafi's breathing began to slow. Again, Le Cran's expression did not change, but there was a momentary pinching at the corners of his mouth.

'Three?'

'Yes. Your brother's mark, I believe?'

'And how do you know this? Oh yes, your snooping did not go unnoticed. You could have got Thurstin into a lot of trouble. Were it not for the fact that he has served this family well for so many years, I could have had him dismissed for showing you documents that should have been confidential.'

'I am not proud of myself. But he . . .' Rafi glared at Roger. 'He was being as helpful as . . . as an empty quiver of arrows.'

Le Cran held up his hand again, cutting off whatever barb Roger had been about to throw.

'It is indeed my brother's mark.' The merchant took a pile of jettons to pieces and then rebuilt it, neatly, seemingly oblivious to the discomfiture his prolonged silence was causing.

'We have not got off to a good start, you and I. You have shown a certain ingenuity. And you kept your mouth shut when it would have been easier not to.' Le Cran shot a brief glance at Roger. 'I need people like you. Not to mention the fact that you speak, what – English, French, Flemish, and have reading and writing?'

'And a little Castilian and Italian. And Latin, of course.'

Again, that swift look towards Roger. 'You would be safer working for me.'

Safer?

'I would prefer not to. I have no desire to stay long in Winchester.'

'For a short while then, but not as an apprentice. I need a courier. Someone who can listen and understand what he hears. Someone who can read and understand what is on the page. You would be wise to accept.'

'I have already said I am not a spy, and nor do I wish to become one.'

Le Cran leaned forward. 'You would find it a lot easier to uncover your horse-wolf and chickens without my steward standing in your way. You know he is relentless.'

'I am well aware of his talents, but no. Thank you.'

'You are making a mistake, but so be it.' Le Cran nodded his dismissal. 'You may go now. If you change your mind, and I strongly advise it, then speak to my steward. He will find you.'

Roger pushed Rafi into the hall and shut the door quietly. 'Idiot boy.'

Rafi was confronted once more by the pennant. Apart from the build of the bird, the similarities were striking. The posture, the angle of the claw, the stone. But, damn it, there was only one bird.

'Why would you think that a chicken?' growled Roger. 'It is nothing like. It is a crane, a play on the family name. All the brothers had one. Is it not obvious?'

Roger stood in front of the tapestry, deliberately blocking it. He was frowning more ferociously than usual. 'Why are you being so pig-brained? He can protect you.'

'I do not need protection, and besides, you have already shown me how useless your protection is.' Rafi squeezed past Roger to get another look at the pennant.

Roger took a step back and blocked him again. 'I will keep doing this, and if you try to climb over me I shall tear the whole thing down and strangle you with it.'

'No doubt your relentless talents make you capable of such things.'

'Your tongue is so sharp you could pare a stake with it.' Roger folded his arms. 'Accept his offer. Were you to work for him, I would have more concern for your welfare if you were attacked again.'

Rafi shook his head. 'No. You want me to lure this man to you. I am bait, that is all. Why does William not send him to attack you?'

'He already knows he would get nothing out of me.'

'Not all your secrets are so well kept.'

Roger narrowed his eyes. 'What do you mean?'

'Just . . .' Rafi wished he had kept his mouth shut. Roger was standing very still, his body held tight, something vicious about to strike.

'I heard about what happened at the abbey.'

The steward stepped forward, grasping Rafi by the shoulders, his fingers digging in hard, pressing against the collarbone. 'What did you hear?'

'The . . . the nun who was attacked, and sent away . . . let go!'

Roger loosened immediately, like a rope pulling free from a chain. He removed his hands, much to Rafi's relief. 'It is no secret. But unlike you, people do not gossip about it anymore.'

What nest had he just poked? If everyone knew about William Le Cran's banishment, if it was so far in the past, then there was no need for such a reaction. Such anger, to be so quickly replaced with . . . relief.

Relief, that was it. Relief that the secret Rafi had alluded to was in fact no secret at all. An old wound, perhaps, but not a fatal one.

Which must mean that there was something else, something that connected Roger to the abbey and which he was determined to keep hidden. Perhaps Edith's suspicion was correct and Agnes was indeed Roger's child. But where would Roger get the money to pay for her endowment?

Rafi was still trying to think of plausible explanations as he walked towards the Durngate, hoping that a little time away from the city would clear his head. But it did not seem to be working.

He had given Le Cran all the information he had, yet the merchant was still keen to press him into service. It was true that Rafi could be used to bring Stefan into the open again, but since they already knew who Stefan was working for, they could take it up with William themselves when all was said and done. They had no real need of him.

Rafi had no interest in a fraternal feud. All he cared about was the seal, and a possible connection with the bird on the pennant. It was the reaction to his questions that had piqued his interest, not Le Cran's disagreements with his objectionable brother.

'All the brothers had one.'

If only Roger had not changed the subject. If only Rafi had not been so intent on getting closer to the tapestry, he would have paid more heed to what the steward had said. All the brothers had one. Rafi did not know how many birds there would be on his seal were it ever to be reunited with the other half. But he knew there was more than one.

What if there were three, on a family seal? One for William, one for Richard, one for Hugh?

Rafi sighed. Perhaps he was looking for things that were not there. The birds on his seal lacked the graceful, flowing lines of the crane on the tapestry. Ducks. Adam had said they looked like ducks. And there was no tree on the pennant, not even a leaf.

No, he was trying too hard. His mind was making a picture that his eye did not truly see.

He was at the Durngate now. Between curfew and supper, she had said. She would not be here. It was too early. But she would walk this way in the evening. Perhaps along this very path. He trudged around stagnant pools on Knights Meadow. Willow bark, kingcups and water violet. He picked some of the petals and tore off some of the bark, securing them in his purse, and then sat where the grass was less boggy, away from the marshy outlands along the Itchen. The city was below him, the cathedral and abbey standing at the east end, near the silver ribbon of the river.

The abbey. What was the lie, what was it that unsettled Roger so greatly?

He could not get the thought out of his mind, that Roger knew something important. A simple question – were there other birds – had thrown the steward off balance.

Rafi did not need to open his locket to look at the matrix. He could have drawn it with his eyes closed, and did so now, in his mind. The symmetry, the position of the complete bird and the placing of what was left of the second one . . .

If he extended the round, three would fit perfectly.

William. Richard. Hugh.

William, the disgraced elder son; Hugh, the saviour of the

family business; and Richard. What little Rafi knew was that Richard had died in France, and his manservant, Roger, had . . .

Oh Jesu. Not just anywhere in France . . . not just anywhere. What had Roger said, when they had first met? He was a bowman, and he was at Crécy – is that where his master had died, in a forest?

Rafi held his hands out in front of him. They were shaking. If he stood up he would fall down. He breathed deeply; no cinnamon this time, but there was a clump of moss in the grass near where he sat. It made him think of Edith again. Moss, for her little poultices, for the green of her eyes. The thought agitated him, but in a different way to thoughts of Roger. Preferable, of course, and his hands soon shook less.

Rafi summoned his memories, ones he preferred to keep at bay. That terrible night in the forest, losing his mother, losing Christophe. The scenes had haunted him ever since. He could not see Roger in any of them. Too slight, too rangy of build. But he was hiding something, something beyond what Le Cran was hiding. And neither of them were going to tell him anything unless he found it out for himself.

Perhaps he should take Le Cran's offer. If he worked in the household he could rummage around more fruitfully than not. But he did not think he could stomach it. For the first time in his life he could go where he pleased, with no one to tell him what to do. Once Le Cran had him, his time would no longer be his own.

Whatever Le Cran said, whatever assurances he offered, Rafi knew what he wanted. Someone who could listen and understand? Someone who was more than a courier, who was little more than a spy? How much would he have to dissemble? Could he pretend to be that which he was not: a cloth-eared boy, unable to understand the language of others, yet all the while translating quietly, listening around corners and against keyholes to the tales he would bring back to his master? Yet had he not already proved that he could lie – to Thurstin, and to Le Cran himself.

Roger held the key; Rafi was sure of it. Perhaps he should do a little hunting of his own. About time Roger knew how it felt. And he would hold on to freedom for a little longer even though it seemed that one way or another his fate was tied up with Master Le Cran, at least for now. At least until he learned more.

Whichever path he chose, the way ahead was full of shadows and lies.

Chapter 16

After leaving the marshes and meandering along the squelchy bank of the Itchen, Rafi let his options turn over and over in his mind and came to the conclusion that he did not like any of them. If the clue to the seal was hidden in the house in Minster Street, his time would be best served devising a plan to uncover it. There were two options: either break into the house or agree to work for Le Cran. He was confident that he would fail spectacularly in the former, and the latter held no appeal. As for Stefan, there was little he could do about that, though if he kept himself in the open and stayed inside the inn at night, then it would reduce Stefan's opportunity for mischief. Rafi ran his tongue around his mouth. The flesh around his missing tooth was still spongy. He did not plan on losing another if he could help it.

It was a beautiful day, warm for spring. Sitting in the spot where Edith was wont to spend time had cheered him despite the futility of the situation. He had a number of new ingredients to add to his collection of paint materials, and fewer paths to consider. It could turn out that he was completely wrong, that the bird on his seal really was a duck, that the three Le Cran brothers had their own individual representations of it and that no family seal existed with all three birds together. But there was no harm pursuing his theory, and if it annoyed Roger to see him hanging around where he shouldn't, then all the better.

With this gratifying thought keeping him amused, Rafi chose to skirt around the outside of the city and stretch his legs instead of re-entering at the Durngate. Keeping to the opposite side of the Itchen, he walked back through the orchards and cottages that lay just beyond the marshes, heading for the Eastgate.

And there, striding out of the abbey and away from the city, was his nemesis, Roger.

Time to go a-hunting.

Rafi assumed Roger was now about his normal duties, perhaps collecting rent. From what Rafi had learned, Le Cran owned multiple cottages and houses all over the city, and probably without. Including, Rafi now remembered, Edith's house.

Rafi stamped his feet as he walked. Yes. Roger had insinuated that he could set the bailiffs on her if he wished. Well, damn him to hell. It would give Rafi great pleasure to cause Roger as much discomfort as possible.

Roger passed through the Eastgate looking neither left nor right. From what Rafi could see of his face from here, he was angrier than usual.

Good. Let him boil with rage. With luck it would kill him.

The hill beyond the gate was steep and wove in a broad sweep over and above the city. There were more houses here, orchards and gardens, so Rafi had plenty of opportunity to huddle behind walls and gates without the risk of being seen. At a bend in the road, Rafi lost sight of Roger so hurried on, the White Boar Inn up ahead nestling on the corner. The path split: either follow the hill as it wove its way upward, or go back and snake left along the drover path, which was the one Rafi chose.

The hill was gentler here. The church of St John rose before him, built into the slope, sitting high above the city. Rafi feared that he had lost his quarry, but the church called to him and he could not resist. Winchester lay below him, the spires he had seen from the west road striking up into the heavens, the Itchen twisting down from the marshes at Winnall, past the abbey and flowing out to St Cross.

He heard the footsteps behind him too late. Before he had a chance to turn he had been picked up by his shirt, legs and arms dangling like a kitten held by the scruff of its neck.

'Nice view. You should take a closer look.'

Rafi was flung headfirst towards a hawthorn that stood on the slope next to the church. His hands came out instinctively, the flesh quickly punctured and torn by the spikes. He turned his head to one side to avoid losing an eye but the shoulder of his shirt was ripped, one of the thorns getting stuck in his upper arm. The sharp stinging in his palms made him cry out.

'Jesu!'

Stefan stood over him. 'It seems you don't work for Le Cran after all. You should have told me.'

'I . . . did.' Rafi wriggled away from the hawthorn as best he could, wiping the rivulets of blood from his hands onto his breeches.

'Perhaps you could ask one of your friends to get me the information instead. The stupid one – what's his name? Adam Bixham. If you can't persuade him, I might be able to. I did try, but he got too drunk too quickly. I might have to try a different method.'

Rafi fell back against the hawthorn, scratching his hands again.

'They say,' said Stefan, 'that the crown of thorns was made out of hawthorn.' He brushed one of the leaves gently with his thumb. 'A few sprigs of this might look nice on him, don't you think?'

'Leave him alone.' Rafi was lifted again, held a hair's breadth from the cruel barbs, close enough to feel their teeth pressing against his shirt.

'Tell me what to do one more time and you'll be impaled on knives, not thorns.' Stefan swung Rafi around and threw him onto the grass next to the church door. 'Tell your superstitious friend to give us what we ask for, or we'll send him to hell to meet his devils.'

A final kick to Rafi's shin for good measure, and Stefan headed down the hill, back into the city.

Rafi pulled the splinter from his arm as best he could with trembling fingers. It bled a little, but he got all of it out. His hands hurt more – dozens of punctures, some quite deep, blood already drying on the skin. There would be holy water in the church. It would clean and maybe even purify his wounds. He held his hands up. They were shaking.

He entered St John's by the north door, getting the iron ring twisted as he tried to shut the latch properly, his hands stinging too much to hold the metal for more than a second. In the end he left the latch jammed across the wooden frame.

Once inside, Rafi dipped his wounded hands into the shallow holy water bowl. The blood swirled into the water, turning it a pale pink. He apologised to St John as the stinging began to subside and he let out a long sigh. He shook his hands to dry them, breathing deeply. As he was about to sit on one of the benches, the latch began to rattle and the ring slowly twisted. The sound echoed through the empty church.

Please God, no!

Rafi had seen Stefan walk away but who was to say he would not come back? He would not dare raise his hand in a church, surely, though Rafi had no wish to find out.

He would have to hide, and quickly. The ring was stuck but whoever was trying to get in was determined to do so and began shoving against the door. Where to hide? There, by the Lady altar in the south-east corner of the church. There was a parclose screen that separated it from the nave. He slid quickly behind it. The top half was intricately carved with geometric patterns, open and transparent, but the lower half was thankfully solid. There was an empty stone coffin in the corner, slightly raised on a low wooden trestle. He dived underneath, lying flat along the floor. There was barely any room to wriggle and the bottom of the coffin bore down on him, almost touching his nose. When he breathed in, his chest nearly brushed the stone above, but there was nowhere else to hide. Unless someone deliberately chose to look under here, he should remain undetected.

The door finally swung open, clattering back on its hinges.

'Have we lost him?'

Rafi had never been so relieved to hear Roger's voice.

Footsteps along the aisle of the church, the sound coarse on the stone floor. It became clear there were two people.

Rafi's mouth dried. Stefan. Was Roger in league with his master's enemies?

'So, nothing new. Nothing in the past week?' Roger's voice was sharp.

'No.' A man's voice. Accented. Rafi closed his eyes. It was not Stefan. This man was French.

'I knew this would happen.' Roger sounded agitated.

'What of the girl, the pretty one?'

'We have moved her out of the house.'

The stranger sighed. 'Good. And Mistress Joan?'

'A problem. We cannot so easily dispose of her.'

Rafi drew in his breath. Joan was Hugh's wife. Dispose of her? Was Roger trying to kill her?

'And the master . . .'

'Knows there is a problem.' Roger sighed. 'But does not yet know the extent of it.'

'Ah!'

'And now she is with child. I fear this will make things worse.'

The stranger spoke again. 'William set his two hunting dogs loose nearly a month back. They are still running with their noses to the ground, or at least they were when I left this morning.'

'It seems they are here. Van Loo's apprentice confirmed it.' Roger groaned. 'Damnation. I've not been able to track them down since one of them attacked him.'

'That is because they don't want you to. Assassins know how to hide their faces. If they want you to see them, then you will.'

Rafi hardly dared breathe. He could not afford to be discovered. He did not understand the significance of what he had heard, but he knew it spelled danger for Joan Le Cran.

'Well,' said the stranger. 'Perhaps this is for the best. It is a boil that has long needed lancing. Once the child arrives I fear what might happen.'

'No!' Roger's voice echoed sharply around the church. 'I will deal with it.'

'They are watching already.'

'Aye. But watching isn't the same as doing.'

'For now. He wants money again – you know that.'

Roger muttered. It sounded like a curse, a curse in a holy place. Rafi winced. 'He always wants money, Jehan.'

'Let him rot. I would.'

'And then what? He would become desperate. It is better this way. The master will pay William's debts and all will be well again.'

'For a short while only. Threats are one thing, but now they have attacked someone because they thought he worked for you. Will they stop with one? I don't think so and neither do you. Le Cran has a right to be prepared. You and I are the only people who know how far William will go. You must tell Le Cran everything. A wild beast cannot be tamed, Writel, and I am . . .'

Jehan paused. Rafi clenched his fists. He had tried to stifle a cough, and in doing so he had moved, ever so slightly, but the stone floor was littered with dust and tiny particles of gravel. The sound of them dislodging had seemed like a thunderclap.

'What is it?'

'I thought I heard something.'

There was silence for a moment, Rafi's heart beating so loudly he could hear nothing else but the thump of it in his ears. He tried not to move. He could not run now; he had to stay tight.

'Ah, damned bird, look?' Roger sounded relieved.

Jehan mumbled something that Rafi could not hear; his heart was still battering his chest.

'Here.' There was a clink of coins. 'Your purse . . .'

'I will do what I can,' said Jehan.

'Farewell.' It was Roger, the direction of his voice had moved. He was leaving.

The door opened. Rafi remained where he was, silent and still. His heart was slowly coming under control. He would wait another few moments; he could hear nothing, but he could not be sure whether Jehan had followed Roger or if he was still in the church.

'J'entends une souris. Ou peut-être c'était un rat.'

Rafi shivered. If Jehan was trying to flush him out, then he would have to come and get him. He heard nothing more. Jehan was not moving, either towards him nor out of the church.

There was a bird; Roger was right. Rafi could hear it cawing.

'Ah! Shoo! Shoo!' An indignant squawk followed. Then footsteps. Then a warning.

'Fais attention, petite souris.'

And the door was closed. Rafi could hear the metal ring being twisted, and Jehan cursing it. The curses were coming from outside now, the door rattling and finally closing. Then, the sound of footsteps walking away.

Rafi lay on the floor of the chapel, shaking and sweating. He was going to be sick. He wriggled out from under the tomb, shirt stuck to his back. He waited for his breath to grow calm, for his heart to return to a steady rhythm. The nausea began to pass now that he was no longer enclosed and he lay on his back for a moment. If Jehan was outside lurking to see if there really was a rat in the building, he would make him wait.

Rafi hobbled towards the aisle and sat on a bench just inside the north door. He couldn't leave anyway as his legs were like water. The ring on the door was tilted slightly; the priest needed to fix it. But it was what lay above and to the side that had his mouth hanging open with wonder.

The paintings on the side of the north door were extraordinary and ran the full length of the wall. A bishop, hand raised in blessing, yellow braid and patterning on his robes and sleeves. And St Anthony, St Peter and St John. The workmanship was beautiful. He leaned back, his palms flat against the bench. There was something rough carved there, under his hands, something cut into the wood. He rubbed his fingers across the jagged marks. VV. The sign against witches and devils, right here, in a church.

Whoever had marked it had not done a very good job because there was a devil above the north door. Squeezed against the ceiling, looking down between the saints on either side of him, the devil lurked above the head of every worshipper who came through this entrance, waiting to catch an impure soul. Vivid red, with wicked eyes and a lascivious grin, the carving in the wood offered no protection. The demon was already inside.

And outside there were two more, turning their malice away from him and towards Adam. He would have to speak to Adam as soon as he could, warn him that his new friends were not friends at all and meant him harm.

But there was a third one too. A man who pretended to be loyal to his master but who spoke of his mistress as a problem, one who needed to be 'disposed of'. What was this boil that needed to be lanced? It was something Le Cran did not know about and which Roger wished to conceal. As he wished to conceal something from Rafi also.

Rafi stared into the eyes of the beast above the door. Roger Writel, the black heart behind a façade of loyalty.

The worst devil of them all.

Chapter 17

Rafi knew as soon as he entered the room that something was wrong. The rushes had been disturbed and whoever had moved them hadn't bothered to put the wooden boards back in place. Rafi kept a small amount of money in his purse, and the rest he had hidden here in the gap, which he kept covered by a loose board and which was now exposed – and empty. Whoever had taken his money was already long gone.

He squeezed his fingers inside the gap, still hoping that he had forgotten to put the board back this morning. The money would be there; it had to be. There were a few coins left, ones that had rolled into the furthest corners of the hole. His fingers scrabbled to find as many of them as he could, but it was a pitiful amount.

No. No, no, no! This could not happen! He had paid Serlo until the end of this week but then what was he to do? He could barely pay for his supper with the small amount of money he had left. How was he going to survive?

All of Mevrouw Schellekens' pretty florins gone. His freedom: gone.

Gone for good. He rested his head on the floor and howled.

Roger. It had to be Roger. The litany of crimes was so long now. Roger had caused his book to be burned, had not lifted a finger to help when Stefan was smashing his teeth to pieces, accused him of stalking Agnes, threatened to call the bailiff on Edith. And now Roger had dealt the final blow. He had stolen the last of the money.

Bastard. By all the saints, he would make him pay for this.

But however long he stared at the gap, Rafi was not going to make the money reappear. He had to do something; he had to prove Roger's guilt. There would have been enough time for Roger to have walked back, broken into the room and stolen the florins. Rafi had had to walk slowly back from the church, way behind Roger. His leg still hurt where Stefan had kicked him.

'You don't look too happy, young man.' Serlo's round face peered up from the depths of the cellar at the sound of Rafi's footsteps.

'I have been robbed.'

'What?' Serlo put down his brush and clambered up, banging his head on the low lintel and swearing.

'Has Roger Writel been here?'

Serlo shook his head. 'No. And he wouldn't do such a thing. I mayn't like him, but he wouldn't do that.'

'I am not so sure.'

Serlo looked at him sternly. 'No, I don't believe he would. And you should put that thought from your mind.'

'Then who has?'

'The door is locked, young Rafi. We have had the cart with casks of ale, some herbs delivered. That is all.' He rubbed his head. 'Oh.'

'Yes?'

'We had the rushes cleaned and swept, as you asked. But they were delivered by our regular supplier. No strangers have been in.'

'Who supplies your rushes?'

'Why, Mistress Edith, of course.'

Edith? Had she been in his room? Rafi was too embarrassed

to ask for fear his cheeks would burn and give Serlo more cause for gossip. And not for one moment did he believe she would do such a thing anyway. He closed his eyes and sighed.

'Come on, sit. I'll bring you some bread and cheese and a little slice of pig.'

Rafi opened his mouth to speak.

Serlo held up his hand. 'No, I will not charge. You've brought me good company and I'm sorry this has happened here. It's partly my responsibility. Go. Sit.'

Rafi was touched by Serlo's kindness, but he could not eat, and later, sleep eluded him. His thoughts tumbled one after the other, none staying long enough for him to bring clarity. As soon as he tried, the next one pushed its way through. In the end, he got up and sat on his bed, his head in his hands.

He counted the remaining coins again. It wasn't enough to last him more than a few days.

He threw himself back down on the mattress. He had thought he was making progress this morning, that his fate was bound to that of Le Cran somehow. Now his jaw and hands were still sore from being picked up like a doll and thrown at a tree, but that was the least of his problems. All his money. The clink in his purse signified but a few pennies remaining.

There was only one place where he could go now, but he would no longer be his own master. He punched his pillow angrily. He had had time and a little freedom but now he'd lost them, along with his fortune.

How long had Roger said it would take? A week. And a week it had been, give or take. Roger had been remarkably prescient. Uncannily prescient.

'He will make sure things are wretched for me now,' Rafi whispered miserably to himself as he waited for dawn to come. But then came the realisation that he could make things wretched for Roger too. He would uncover what Roger was about, what devious plan he had for Joan. Rafi could afford a little humility in the meantime if it helped him uncover Roger's guilt.

And so it was, when next morning Rafi, head bowed, walked slowly up the path to Hugh's door. Roger had it opened before Rafi had even raised his hand to knock.

'Tragic. No, really. Quite, quite tragic. Has it really been a week? I should be a fortune teller.'

You will not rile me. I shall play you as you have played me.

Rafi forced a slight nod as Roger stood aside and, after a brief hesitation, he entered.

A dark-haired woman sat by a recessed window in the hall. Her face was framed by a veil of white linen shot through with silver stitching and attached to a velvet barbette. She smiled at him, revealing a slight cleft in her upper lip, which he thought suited her. This must be Joan Le Cran.

Rafi waited. Joan looked at Roger and raised her eyebrows, but Roger remained where he was.

This time, Rafi was not led towards Le Cran's room. This time, the heavy oak door was opened from inside, the space filled by the tall, lean figure of the man himself, his shirt clean and crisp under a sage-coloured tunic. Le Cran leaned against the door frame and folded his arms.

Rafi stood straight, with his hands behind his back. Like a lamb to the slaughter.

'We meet again, Raphael Dubois. We meet again.'

Chapter 18

Everything was new and clean. The boots, so much better than the shoes he had bought. Soft woollen hose, a doublet with an undyed linen shirt beneath. They put his own new clothes to shame. And a velvet cap. Velvet! He kept touching it, so rich and fine. He wore it at a jaunty angle; he could not help himself.

The hostile reception Rafi had expected from Le Cran never materialised. Le Cran had got what he wanted. Rafi knew it, Le Cran knew it and the merchant chose to let the victory hang silently between them. The courier's uniform had already been made. Le Cran had produced it wordlessly from a chest in his room. It had been a perfect fit.

Fancy clothes or no, Rafi was not going to forgive Roger. With his money stolen, Rafi's fate was sealed. He was absolutely certain that Roger had engineered everything. Rafi would watch him as keenly as a falcon from now on.

As well as clothes, Le Cran had presented Rafi with a silver misericord dagger, polished and lethal.

'Tuck it inside your boot.'

Joan had tried to stay her husband's hand. 'Is he to be a

diplomat or a killer?'

'More of one than the other, I hope. But still.' Le Cran laid the dagger across Rafi's palm. 'One can never take too many precautions.'

'Well, my welcome shall not include weaponry.' Joan glanced at her husband. 'May I borrow our new courier?'

Le Cran smiled. Rafi had never seen him smile properly before and was both mesmerised and annoyed by it.

'Come, Master Dubois. I believe you are something of an artist?'

'Oh . . . no.'

'Nonsense! Roger saw something you made for John Marsh. He said it was . . .' Joan scrunched up her eyes. 'What is the word?'

'Monstrous?' suggested Le Cran.

Oh no! The rats, hanging from the firepit. The woman stabbing Marsh in the guts. Rafi's face was so hot Serlo would have been able to cook a griddle cake on each cheek.

'Do not listen to him!' Joan turned to her husband, who responded with a gentle shake of the head. 'But I have something smaller in mind. I believe you used to illustrate books?'

'Well yes, I . . .'

'Excellent!'

'No limited range of colours for this task, you hear me, Dubois?' warned Le Cran. 'Come, we shall show you the matter at hand.' He waved his wife through the door then gestured for Rafi to follow behind them.

'You have been mixing vegetables and flowers, I hear,' said Joan, guiding them through a door built into some panelling in the hallway. 'We can do better than that, I am sure.'

Le Cran had wasted no time gathering information. Adam knew about Rafi's time in the monastery, and Serlo had seen him collecting materials for paint. He remembered what Thurstin had said – Le Cran would check, and check again.

Rafi followed Joan and Master Le Cran up a narrow, twisted staircase, hidden in the walls of the house, to the room at the very top. He now stood in the turret, which he had seen from the marketplace when he had first arrived.

'See, here . . .' Joan opened a chest, full of powdered pigments neatly held in small wooden boxes and jars, pens, brushes, all new and untouched.

Rafi stared at this box of wonders, his fingers twitching. It was all he could do to stop himself snatching up this glittering treasure trove and hugging it like it was a precious child.

Clothes, tailored and ready for him, and now this. He shook his head. He had thought everything was within his control, but he had been wrong. Le Cran had hooked him days ago and had merely waited until it was time to net him. Peering into the box, Rafi felt his heart leap with excitement. He couldn't help himself. If he was caught, then he was caught firm.

Joan was watching him, waiting for his reaction. Her gentle smile told him that his pleasure was written all too clearly on his face.

Hugh Le Cran moved forward. 'You should be at ease now, my lady.' He placed a tender hand on the swell of her belly. 'Here, sit.'

Rafi felt out of place, embarrassed by the gentle exchange between the two. This was not the master as he was downstairs in the office, or in the guildhall, chiding him.

'Thank you.' Joan sat on the cushioned seat next to the window. Her tapestry hoops and materials were on a chest by the wall, her bodkins and her small scissors. And she could look out over the garden, cathedral and the whole of the eastern end of the city.

Joan picked up a hoop, her needle jabbing back and forth, her movements precise. 'Master Dubois, tell me of your time in the monastery. Did you enjoy working on your books? For I have a very particular task in mind for you.'

Rafi hesitated.

'Speak,' urged Le Cran. 'Tell your mistress what she asks of you.'

Rafi told her, haltingly, of his time at St Michael's, paring pens, scratching the parchment pricker across the vellum to make neat, straight lines for writing. She continued with her sewing, scrutinising the fabric, but it was clear that she was listening intently. She had fastened her tumble of dark hair under her veil with a quatrefoil pin of amber. And the indentation on her lip. It was only slight, the mark of the hare.

'Here, now.' Joan pointed at a bookshelf when he had finished. Aquinas, a missal, and a slightly battered book of hours that Le Cran picked off the shelf and handed to her.

'This belonged to my mother, and her mother before her.'

Joan sat with it in the window seat, her deep blue gown falling in rich folds and pooling on the floor, her bodice criss-crossed with silver thread. Underneath, a shift of finest batiste. She looked like one of the women Rafi was sure he would encounter in the book she held.

'So, this letter here,' she pointed. 'And here . . .' She turned the pages carefully. 'They have faded so much. Can you bring them back to life for me?'

Rafi hesitated again.

''Tis a simple question, Dubois,' said Le Cran. 'Look at the book, man.'

Rafi touched the cracked leaf around the lettering; there was enough colour left to see what was required. No lapis, fortunately, although Le Cran could probably have afforded the expense. Not even ultramarine. Brown, ochre, deep greens, carmine. He nodded. 'Yes. I think I can.'

'Oh, splendid.' Joan put the book on her lap and clasped her hands. 'But this must stay here. You can work on it when I am not here, but it cannot leave the room. But please, we shall reward you with a trip to the parchmenter and here, I shall give you this brush, to use as you will.'

Her dress rustled as she walked to the box of treasures. She held the brush with a flourish. 'Take this, and any of the other brushes you like. Far better than a dagger.' She smiled.

'Thank you!'

He scrutinised the pig bristles, so neatly held together, each one perfectly cut. Even though his palms still hurt a little from the hawthorn, he was glad to be holding a brush again. He gazed again at the array of materials made available to him. Any illustrator would be blessed to have such things.

But for a brief moment, he thought of the bedraggled piece of moss he had picked from Danemarch Mead. It made him feel heartsore and lonely. He and Edith could not be friends, and it hurt him. He would have swapped these jars and powders for one of her simples in a heartbeat. But he would not compromise her, or himself, and would keep away from the Durngate in the evening.

'Well,' said Joan, standing beside her husband. 'You have given me an artist. All I need now is to have my maid back again.'

Le Cran raised his hands. 'Soon, I promise.'

Joan glanced at him reproachfully. 'I will hold you to that. I miss her.'

Le Cran bowed his head, then took her hand and pressed it to her lips. 'I have duties to attend to, madam.' He looked at Rafi, who made to leave with him.

'He can start now, can he not?' said Joan. 'Send Beth up to me. She can sit with me while he works.'

'As you wish.'

So Joan's maid, Ailith, had been sent away. Roger had said as much in the church. But not forever, it seemed. Had she done something wrong? Why had Jehan asked about her?

Rafi took the opportunity to gaze out the window, trying to work out what Ailith had to do with the conversation in the church. The view was what the turret had been built for. The cathedral was so clear, and there was the abbey, sitting in the shadows; in the distance the orchards he had walked through yesterday.

And something else.

Two men, standing on the high street. One with a bag over his shoulder, the other with his hood pulled up. Rafi froze, his hand

179

tight on the shaft of the brush. Stefan and his friend.

What devilry were they about this time? They were very close to the drapery; anyone walking from there to Minster Street would see them in an instant. They were hiding in plain sight.

And then, a third man joined them. Rafi pushed at his fringe and leaned even further out of the window.

It was Thom.

What the hell was going on? Thom? He surely wasn't involved in this – he was a drunken lout, a bully, a . . .

'Are you well?'

Rafi dropped his brush. 'Yes, I . . .'

'It is a wonderful view, is it not?'

'It is, yes.' It had been, until he'd seen Stefan and his friend, and until Thom had sullied it even further. There had to be a reason for him to be speaking so amiably to Stefan and his companion. If he could have hit Thom by throwing his misericord dagger from here, then he was not sure he'd be able to stop himself.

Joan tilted her head. 'I cannot hear anyone coming up, so it seems that my husband has not been able to find Beth. Well, perhaps you had best get settled into the workshop first, and then return later.'

'Oh, of course, Mistress.'

He took his leave of her, finding his way, fretting over what he had just witnessed.

The workshop was so far removed from Van Loo's room in Ghent it was like another world entirely. The lodgings for the apprentices were as good as the ones Van Loo shared with his wife and family. Tidier and cleaner, two sweeping brushes, a pail for water, mattresses held on shelves on the wall so that the dust from daily toil didn't cling to them.

Roger was inside and scowled at him as he entered.

'Adam! Cedric! Find somewhere to put this creature and be quick about it. If he's not at work by the time I get back, I'll dock you both a day's pay and kick your arses for good measure. Get to it.'

Adam made a crude gesture at the door Roger slammed behind himself.

'Just like before, eh?' Adam said.

It was very like before, even down to the items held on the large table in the centre of the room, which he had seen before in another life. The colours were beautiful, golden and red and luscious. He saw the weaving of Mathys and the stitching of Vincent in every cut of fibre.

'Well, look at you. Very fancy!' Adam grinned. 'But for the love of Saint Ann take that ridiculous cap off.'

Rafi patted the velvet and pretended to consider. 'No.'

'You are becoming vain. And it makes you look like a juggler.'

'And what sort of juggler wears a velvet cap like this?'

'A bad one.'

'This is indeed fancy.' The young apprentice, Cedric, walked around Rafi, appraising all angles. 'And what is this? A new badge?' He patted Rafi's doublet. 'Well.' He sucked the breath between his teeth. 'This is new livery. Well stitched.'

'How about you finish with that yellow dress that is *still* sitting there doing nothing of any merit?'

Adam pointed over Cedric's shoulder at the fabric on the table.

Cedric tutted. 'It belongs to the mistress and I do not know how to do it justice. I need to think carefully. It is quality.'

'You could get twenty hats out of that. Good ones.'

'Don't be so foolish.' Cedric snorted.

'It is wonderful.' Rafi stroked it.

'It is indeed fine!' Cedric batted Rafi's hand away. 'So kindly leave it alone. It is as well I unpicked the pearls from the neck before that brute over there spent them in the Hellhole.'

Rafi and Adam exchanged glances while Cedric went back to the door Roger had slammed shut. It opened onto the shopfront where Cedric could keep an eye on passing custom. 'Don't let him make you do all his work,' he said, taking the dress with him into the shop.

Adam nodded at Rafi. 'He is easy to tease but in fairness, he is a genius with a bodkin.'

Adam checked that the door was closed behind Cedric, then the latch on the door to the yard outside. He pulled at the window shutters, fixing and unfixing the clasp several times. When he had finally satisfied himself that the room was secure he pushed Rafi into the corner, as far away from any entrances as possible.

They were surrounded by boxes and crates, ells of broadcloth, chalon blankets folded and stacked on top of each other. Adam paced to and fro, biting on his lip so hard that he drew blood. What had happened since Cedric had left the room? This sour mood was very sudden.

'What is it?' Rafi asked.

'You have always been a good friend to me, from that first day I arrived in Ghent and spoke not a word of Flemish. I depended on you then.'

Was this something to do with Ailith? Had Adam had a fight with his brother and knocked him senseless?

Adam picked up a tray of bodkins and threads and put it back down again. 'The other night, after we spoke, I . . .'

The last time Rafi had seen Adam, they had not parted on good terms. He would prefer not to remember the words Adam had spoken outside the Helle, nor the pushing and jostling he had endured.

'What has happened, Adam?'

Adam began to whisper. 'I was pursued by ghosts, monks near the graveyard. They cursed me!'

'Cursed—'

'Cursed. They said Beelzebub would find me and . . . they would come for me again and drag me to hell.' He glanced towards the door to the shop. 'Cedric was awake. He heard me knock on the door. If he had been a moment later . . .'

Your superstitious friend.

So. Stefan had already got to him.

182

'Adam, I know who it was that chased you that night and they were not ghosts. They were men. It was Stefan, and his friend.'

Adam shook his head. 'No, no. Stefan and Fulke wouldn't do that. Why would they?'

'For the same reason as this.' Rafi rubbed his cheek, which was still bruised. 'I told you in the Chequers, but you were . . . a little forgetful.'

'Stefan did that?' Adam knitted his brows together. 'No, I don't believe that. Are you jealous, that I have new friends? You've spent little time with me since you returned, perhaps it's you who has new friends.'

'What? No!'

Adam bit his lip again. 'I was at the postern, near Shite Lane. I saw you, following Edith into one of the abbey gardens. Made friends with her very quickly, didn't you?'

So that was it. Now Adam was sober the truth was clear. He was jealous. He wanted Rafi's friendship to himself.

'She needed some help; that is all.'

'Help? Is that what you call it?'

Rafi got to his feet. 'I am not going to listen to this any longer.'

Adam tugged at Rafi's sleeve. 'No! Don't go. I'm sorry. I've been . . .'

Adam was pale. There were dark rings under his eyes. This was not the result of drinking too much; he always shook the effects off very quickly the following day. There was something more to this.

'Very well.'

Adam smiled weakly. 'I've been all at sea since I found out about my brother and . . . her.'

'Have you not made your peace yet?'

Adam shook his head. 'No, and nor will I. I'll not forgive them, not ever. But I'm sorry for what I said. And . . . tread carefully. Edith has a husband and he's not very—'

'I know.' Rafi pulled at the threads on the tray. 'I've encountered

Thom, and wish I hadn't. Which is why you must not spread rumours.'

'I would never! I would not wish to hurt Edith. I was angry with you. I'm sorry.'

Rafi pushed the tray to one side. He did not want to talk about Edith. 'So, these ghosts?'

Adam nodded. 'I walked along the side of the graveyard after I left the Helle and back to the workhouse. The gate was locked. I had to climb up and one of them . . . bit me.'

'He *bit* you?'

'Be quiet, for the love of God!' Cedric rapped his knuckles smartly on other side of the door.

Rafi and Adam fell silent until they heard Cedric's footsteps move away. Adam slowly rolled up the leg of his breeches. An angry, circular mark was visible on the back of his calf. Rafi peered at it. In the low light it was difficult to see, but he could definitely make out the faint trace of teeth marks.

'I pulled my leg as hard as I could, but he had his hands around my ankle. He would not let go. He said he was going to cut my foot off and feed it to the pigs.'

'How did you . . .'

Adam shuddered. 'He reached for his knife. For a moment he had only one hand on me so I pulled away as hard as I could. And then I jumped off the gate and ran, back to the workshop.'

'Jesu! You are sure they followed you from the graveyard?'

Adam nodded.

'They are ingenious ghosts, are they not.'

Adam sat back and narrowed his eyes. 'You think this is fine sport, do you?'

'No, no I do not. I think you have been ill-used by men masquerading as spirits, men who are trying to disrupt and cause confusion in this house.'

It was obvious. Stefan and Fulke had followed them after they'd left the Chequers. They had waited for Rafi to walk into the cathedral grounds, then entered the Helle to find Adam. They had learned his weaknesses and played on them. Adam would have passed by the side of the graveyard to get home. It would have been dark, Adam had been drunk, and it would have been easy for them.

The statues on the cathedral that Adam had spoken of, the fear of dying unshriven – Adam was scared. Scared of demons and death and darkness. When coupled with his weakness for drink, Adam was at his most vulnerable, and it was there they had wounded him.

Adam shook his head. 'Why would they do that? Why would they wait in the graveyard for me? How did they even know I'd be there?'

'They followed you after you left the Helle.'

Rafi flinched at Adam's look of disdain. 'This is mad conspiracy. I believed you to be clever but you're not. I see what you're trying to do, trying to soothe me by spinning a tale, but it won't work. If you think I can believe this, then you take me for a fool. They were demons. Don't try to call me a liar.'

'One of them bit you, Adam. Bit you and threatened to cut your foot off. Are those the actions of a demon?'

Adam folded his arms. 'I see you doubt me.'

Of course, Adam did not know the full story about William Le Cran and the men he had sent to Winchester to scatter discord in his brother's house. That was a tale Rafi would have to tell and make Adam see sense. But now Adam's mind was set, and he would be a hard man to convince without losing face in the process.

'I believe you were followed by Stefan and Fulke, not by ghosts or demons. But finish your tale. Mayhap you'll change my mind.'

'How very gracious of you.' Adam paused. 'Very well. After Cedric returned to bed, I kept my candle burning. They would have known I was awake. I heard it, a crackle of paper and the sound of something sliding under the door. I knew it was them.

They were outside, outside the door only inches from where I lay.'

Adam pulled a folded note from his cuff. 'Here. This is what was pushed under the door.' Adam smoothed the paper on the table in front of them. He slid it across the polished wood towards Rafi.

Rafi nodded. 'Let us see, then.'

Adam's face had taken on a sickly tinge. The very sight of the note had unmanned him. Fear. Fear of ghosts in a graveyard who were no ghosts at all. The dead did not write messages and push them under doors. Rafi would need to tread gently if he were to unravel the knot they had placed in Adam's mind.

To Le Cran and his mistress
A gift shall be delivered
Tu a . . . m Nuntius

'What does it mean?' hissed Adam.

Rafi was thinking. 'I am not sure. Part of it is missing. You are the message, maybe? Nuntius.'

'That doesn't make sense.'

'Nuntius . . . nuntius. Information. Message. Let me think . . . courier.'

They fell silent.

'Courier? That's you.' Adam spoke first.

Rafi shook his head. 'If you received this the night you were chased, it cannot be me. I was no courier then, nor like to be.'

'Until your money was stolen.'

'Well, if they stole it . . .' Rafi rubbed his forehead. 'If they stole it then they cannot be ghosts, can they? Ghosts do not rip up floorboards and steal purses. And besides, there was no guarantee I would stay here after my money was gone. I could just as easily have gone back to Flanders.'

He left out the fact that he did not believe that it was Stefan and Fulke who had robbed him. He was quite sure that it was a sour-faced steward who was the guilty party. 'Thus, they would have to predict my course of action. How would they know I would come here, or that Le Cran would take me or that, even if

186

he did, he would ask me to be his courier. That has all happened today. How could they have named me "Nuntius" before this date? It cannot be me.'

'They are demons!' Adam stood up so fast his chair crashed backwards. He righted it and sat again, but he could not stay still. He looked around and then dropped his voice. 'They can see into men's minds.'

'Does Stefan look like a demon?'

'You're doing it again. I know what chased me.'

'Adam, I tell you they are not spectres, they are corporeal.'

Adam was clenching and unclenching his fists.

'Can I take this to Le Cran?' Rafi began to fold the note.

'Take it. I don't want it near me.'

'There is a tale here, Adam, but it is a long one. I shall tell you everything tonight, I promise. And then mayhap we can start to undo the web.' He paused. Perhaps if he appealed to Adam's vanity he would have better luck than trying to appeal to his reason.

'I will need you, Adam. I cannot fix this on my own, but once I have it laid out before you perhaps you can help me make sense of it.'

Rafi tucked the note into the leather bag around his waist. He patted Adam's shoulder, noticing that his friend had begun to look more like his old self.

'I would rather fight soldiers than demons, if you really think that's the truth?'

'I do, and when you have heard it all, you will sleep well again. But now it's urgent that I take this to Le Cran.'

Adam nodded. 'I'll make myself busy in the meantime.'

Rafi smiled. 'Perhaps you could make those yellow hats while I see what Le Cran has to say?'

'It would keep me indoors at least, and I'd enjoy the spectacle of Cedric's face when he saw them.'

'All will be well, Adam. And now, I had better do the job Le Cran is paying me for.'

Adam grinned. 'Begone then. With your foolish finery.'

'Adam! Fetch Mistress Litton's gown. The siskin and damask. She is here to collect it. Hurry!' Cedric battered on the door.

'Ah, Mistress Litton. I will give her a private audience if she wishes to try her gown on in here.'

'Go! Before Cedric gets a battering ram.'

Rafi stepped outside. His first mission as a messenger and it was not one that would bring any pleasure to his master. This was a dangerous escalation in Stefan and Fulke's activities if they had moved their target from the apprentices to Joan. And how did Thom fit into their plans? For they would be using him for some scheme, Rafi would bet on it. They would find his weakness, too, as they had found Adam's. It surely wasn't Edith; Thom had shown no affection for her.

The sun was warm, and the lavender had burst like joyful purple clouds along the path, but Rafi was too lost in thought to notice as he made his way out of the yard and into Minster Street. He didn't see the barrel rolling towards him until it hit him hard in the shins.

'Ow! What the . . .' He stopped dead. Edith had just walked through the Minstergate from the direction of the market. She almost smiled. Almost, but then her eyes darted towards her husband, standing against the wall.

'Oh, sorry. Did that hit you? What a shame. My apologies.' Thom spat the words.

Rafi pushed the barrel to one side, where it rolled along the road before resting gently against the side of Le Cran's yard. He stared at it. He stared at it so he wouldn't have to look at her.

'Quiet, aren't you?' said Thom. 'I suppose you're too good to talk to the likes of us, what with your frills and dancing outfit.'

Rafi's head jerked up. Thom moved very deliberately towards Edith. His thin, mousy hair was pushed back from his face. He might have been pleasant to look at once, but now his skin was mottled from too much ale, and one of his front teeth was missing. Rafi recognised him for what he was. A weak man, a bully. And now he was hiding behind his powerful friends and had a swagger in his step. It would go ill with him. They would use him for whatever malicious plan they had in mind, then discard him. He would not play the coxcomb so quickly then.

Rafi removed his cap, twisting it between his hands, feeling the soft velvet. His new leather boots were warm and sturdy, the wool of his hose brushed and well fitted. Hers was a ragged dress, a patched wimple. He swallowed his anger. It would do her no favours if he gave vent to it.

'Those must have cost a fair few florins, or did Le Cran buy them for you? Has he provided a jewelled collar as well, so he can keep you on a lead?'

Rafi's hands stilled.

A *fair few florins*.

He knew he should not look at her; he knew it would give him away. But he felt her presence too keenly, too close to his heart for wisdom to prevail.

She was hunched into herself, keeping her head down. Her eyes were on the ground, and she did not attempt to raise them.

'What are you gawping at?' Thom spat the words.

Rafi willed her to look up.

'Her, I expect. Well.' Thom tilted his head towards her. 'If you haven't already, you can have her for an hour, or two.' He held his hand under Rafi's nose. 'A shilling, I reckon – she must be worth that at least.'

Edith's cry of distress cut Rafi to the quick. He had never hit anyone in his life, had never sought trouble – he was too slight to be a challenge for those who thrived on it. He made poor sport – but in his mind he plunged his new dagger into Thom's chest. A split-second vision, that was all. He felt it in the set of his jaw as it clenched, in the pain as his nails dug into his wounded palms.

He felt it, and Thom saw it.

'Whoa there, calm down. See, wife, you're not even worth a

shilling.'

Edith finally caught his eye over Thom's shoulder. She shook her head, the movement so quick Rafi almost missed it, but he understood. It was as he feared. If he angered Thom, she would bear the brunt. Her hair, as ever, was poking out of her wimple, but she left it as it was, her usual gesture of irritation with it, a gesture that made him smile, nowhere to be seen. She let it hang there, her hands clasped together below her waist.

'Edith, run along.'

Edith began shuffling down Minster Street towards the high street. She did not look where she was going, just watched her feet.

Thom pushed Rafi against the wall. 'You will not do a thing. You can't. And even if you wanted to, she's my wife and there is nothing you can do about it.' He straightened. 'I have friends and you will have to answer to them if you cuckold me – unless you pay for the pleasure, of course. Now let me pass. I have a delivery to make to your kitchens. Whatever Nell makes with this, I hope it bloody chokes you.'

He spat at Rafi's feet and pushed the barrel down to the gate. Nell, the cook, would admit him to the kitchen. Rafi couldn't bear to think of that man anywhere near the house or workshop.

Rafi's anger had fled with Edith. Now he wanted nothing more than to find her. He had intended to make his way to the wool staple where Le Cran would be found, but while Thom was otherwise occupied, Rafi had a window of opportunity. He would be fast, before Thom saw them. She had been humiliated in front of him; he needed to speak to her. He had promised himself not to approach her, knowing that his resolve would be sorely tested, his good intentions stretched like goatskin on a parchmenter's frame. Until it snapped.

There was no sign of her towards the Nunnaminster. Nor was she west, on the road that would take her towards the staple where he was headed. She must be already lost in the maze of streets near the God Begot House and down past the Chequers, or perhaps she had gone back to the market. But no . . . there. There she was, walking quickly and with purpose, down the alleyway near the Tabard. He brushed people aside as he sought to close the distance. He ignored Mal's cry of greeting. His foot caught on a breadbasket that had been discarded in a cartwheel channel on the high street. On he went, down the alleyway, narrow and busy, past the stockfishmonger stall, holding his nose.

She was heading along Parchment Street. He could catch her if he put his mind to it. He jogged along the side of the streams where the dyers washed their newly coloured fabrics, the surplus colours threading through the water. On he followed. At the end of Parchment Street, as she was about to cross the squelchy pathway that led further towards the north wall, she stopped, her back to him. Without knowing why, he stopped too.

There was nothing between them now but a muddied street, jumbled with people ducking between horses and sheep. Two long strides and he'd be with her. She was not moving; he would catch her. But he chose not to. He was close enough to see the movement of her shoulders as she breathed, the tiny tremble of her hand as it brushed against her skirt. And still, he waited.

She turned then. Her face pale and her eyes bright with tears, and again the shake of the head. She didn't want to be followed. He moved his lips:

Come with me.

Come with him where? Back to Minster Street? Away from Winchester altogether? Another city, another country?

She shook her head again and carried on, not looking back.

He would not follow if she didn't wish him to, but he silently beseeched her to turn round one more time. She was at a cottage now. Ailith was sitting outside. There was a pole sticking out of the ground with a sling attached in which baby Judith was suspended, the breeze gently rocking her back and forth as she slept. Edith stroked the baby's cheek. Ailith was speaking, then twisted in her seat and when she saw Rafi, she waved him away.

191

The gesture was not unkindly done but the message was clear. He was not needed. He had made a mistake in following her. He was sick to his stomach. He was ashamed and frightened for her.

What if Thom had not tarried with Nell and instead followed him? What if Stefan had seen them? He would use her against him; she would become a pawn.

Jesu, what had he just done?

He had to forget her. He had to. But if he was to do that successfully, he had to want to forget her.

It was an impossibility. But it was a necessity.

He had a job to do, one that could lead him to the answers he sought. He had to focus on that, focus on getting away from here. For her sake.

Rafi turned west and made his way to the staple. He saw her face over and over, her humiliation, her shame. He had to put it out of his mind. This would not help matters.

Le Cran was waiting for him, drumming his fingers on a large desk while two merchants squabbled over the weight of a woolsack. He looked almost relieved to see Rafi and beckoned to him.

'These people are exceptionally tiresome. It is a matter of an ounce, and they will be here all day arguing over it.' Le Cran watched the two merchants closely, the side of his mouth twitching every time one of them spoke.

To Rafi, the sacks looked much of a muchness. The staple clerk was loading each one onto the tron, the city scales that were used for measuring woolsacks and other goods so that duties could be levied on them. It took up most of the centre of the room.

'It is below the limit!' complained one of the merchants.

Le Cran looked towards the ceiling and muttered.

''Tis above,' insisted the clerk.

'Sweet Jesu!' Le Cran rolled his eyes. 'Remove a handful of the fleece, then. A wisp, a fingerful, a morsel, however much you like. But for the love of St Clement, quit your squabbling.'

'But this is my clip. I am not going to remove a single strand!'

'Then pay the tax on it and be done. The presager is waiting.'

A bored-looking man in a grey cloak stood by the tron with a barrow.

The merchant paced back and forth and then kicked the woolsack with such force it slid across the room. Le Cran raised an eyebrow.

'Very good. You have cleaned the floor.'

'You could let this pass.' The merchant glared at him. 'The tron may measure false!'

'It is accurate!' the clerk protested.

'Make your choice and leave. And that goes for you too.' Le Cran waved his hand dismissively at the second merchant.

'Hurry up, will you, I haven't got all day.' The presager was growing impatient.

'They hurt my ears,' said Le Cran, gesturing towards the large window that offered a view of the castle. 'Come this way. They are quite insufferable.'

The arguing began again. The clerk removed the woolsacks and dragged them towards the door, pursued by the fractious merchants. The presager started to load his goods hastily onto the tron while he had a chance.

'So. You are here because you have something for me?'

Rafi nodded.

'Diligent already. Well, let me have it, then.'

'I . . . this was pushed under the door some days ago . . . it mentions the mistress.'

'And no one thought to bring it to me until today?' Le Cran snatched the note from Rafi's hands. He stood by the open window and read it, his face stony. The light from the afternoon sun poured into the room as Le Cran held the paper up to read. Rafi frowned and edged closer to his master. There was a mark at the bottom that he had missed earlier when Adam had shown it to him. Here, the light had found a secret, a trace of something.

Le Cran turned on him. 'What is this?' His mouth was drawn

in a tight line. 'Some sort of message? A message in the form of a human? Is that right?'

'I think so, Master. I believe that is what it might mean.'

Le Cran nodded. 'Please prepare to leave for Salisbury on the morrow.'

'Salisbury? But why?'

'Do not question me.' Le Cran silenced him with a look. 'Roger will explain. Be packed and ready by dawn.'

Rafi nodded, bewildered. 'May I . . .'

'What is it?'

'The paper, may I read the message once more?'

'I doubt it will have altered since the last time you saw it, but if you must.' Le Cran thrust it at him.

Rafi held the note up to the light. Yes, it was as he thought. There was an imprint there as if something had been resting on the corner of the paper. Something circular. He pressed the note against his face as he held it this way and that, trying to find the best angle. And then he saw it.

The paper fell through his fingers, fluttering to his feet and landing on his new boots.

'Pick it up, man, for goodness' sake!'

Rafi stood dumbly, looking at the paper. His body had been hollowed out, and he was made of air.

'What is the matter with you? Get out of here, go on. Make haste and sort out your affairs. Go!'

Rafi did not know how he put one foot in front of the other; his body seemed to move of its own accord. By the time he became aware of his surroundings he was at the other end of the city, at the Nunnaminster, outside the gate as the bell rang for nones.

The nuns were walking in a line into the abbey. Domneva was at the back, with Agnes. The nun's piercing stare was far from friendly. Agnes waved. He waved back without thinking. Domneva glared at him. He stopped waving.

They filed into the grey building, the towers thrusting skyward, the pond glinting as the sun bounced off the surface. It was a picture of bounty and serenity, the very opposite of how he felt.

The paper Le Cran had held up to the light. A circular outline. A tree. A tree and part of a bird. The images he knew as intimately as the lines on his palm, but always incomplete.

Until now.

Now he saw the whole tree, the trunk spreading upwards to bountiful leaves and strong branches and not one, but three birds.

He touched his chest. The locket nestled against his skin and he could feel it with his fingers through the fabric. And inside the locket, the jagged remains of the seal matrix given to him so many years ago.

He had found it. Surely there could be no other seal so closely matched to his? Three birds. Three brothers. William, Hugh, Richard. And the tree that held them, that must be . . .

Bring it to my father.

The soldier's dying words. Richard's dying words, for who else could it be?

But he needed the name around the outside of the seal. The lettering hadn't been clear enough on the paper, and that was what Rafi needed to uncover, the final piece in the mystery. He had tried once and had been lied to. Before he took his questions back to Le Cran, he needed more proof. If he had the name, then the lies would fall on stony ground.

Other than Le Cran and Roger, who would know who owned the seal, and who would know truly where Richard had fallen? There was one such. One who had worked for the family for many years. One that Rafi had lied to.

Thurstin.

It could not wait until Rafi got back from Salisbury. He would approach Thurstin now. At worst, the scrivener would tell him to leave. He had to try.

He was a step from the truth. Such a short step, so close to finding who killed Richard.

And Maman. And Christophe.

He should rejoice that the journey was almost over.

Instead, he felt as if a stone had been tied around his neck.

Chapter 19

Thurstin was still in the castle even though it was long past nones. The clerk who had previously guarded the door like an enraged wasp now stood aside to let Rafi pass.

'Aren't you going to have me thrown out?'

The clerk shrugged. 'Writel says you work for him now. You can go where you like.'

If only he'd been allowed such liberty a few short days ago, how differently things might have turned out. The lies he had told to Thurstin wouldn't have been necessary. As it was, he stood in front of the scrivener, hardly able to meet his eye.

'Which boxes will you rummage through this time, hmmm?'

Rafi shuffled his feet. 'Master Thurstin, I apologise for misleading you.'

Thurstin sat at his customary desk beneath the window. The daylight would shine directly on to the worksurface, but now, as it grew late, candles would be required for reading. Candles which, if tallow, would fill so small a room with smoke and smart the eyes. Thurstin looked at the parchment in front of him, but he wasn't reading. The sparse, white stubble on his chin stuck up like wheat stalks after harvest.

'You wear Master Le Cran's livery.'

'Yes. I really do work for him now.'

Thurstin nodded. 'So Writel told me. And I take it you're not just here to apologise?'

'No.' It felt churlish to admit it, but Rafi did not want to insult Thurstin by being anything less than completely honest. 'I have a seal I want you to look at. Half of it anyway. I'd be grateful for any information you could give me.'

Thurstin nodded towards the desk Rafi had sat at before. 'Very well. Let me see.'

Thurstin carefully examined the half disc that Rafi gave him. He pushed it back across the desk and shook his head. 'This is not familiar to me.'

'But . . .'

'You think I should recognise it?'

'I . . . the bird on there. And the bird on Master Le Cran's tapestry—'

'Are not remotely the same. Your seal shows a squat bird, like a duck. It is certainly not a crane. And there is no tree on your master's seal.'

Always a duck. He would eat the wretched bird as soon as look at it again.

'But today I saw a mark on a paper that looks like mine. Le Cran has it and . . .'

Thurstin smiled kindly. 'Perhaps it did look like yours, but I am telling you the truth. I have never seen anything like this in your master's possession, nor on any of the correspondence I have dealt with since I have been his clerk. A vintner's mark, or one crane – that is all. What you saw today must belong to someone else.'

Rafi put the seal back in the locket. Tears of frustration stung his eyes.

'Where did you get it?' asked Thurstin.

'A soldier gave it to me. He died very shortly afterwards. He begged me to find his father and explain what had happened. The soldier who died, he . . . tried to save my mother. But she died, too.' Rafi blinked the tears away as best he could. 'This is the only clue I have.'

'Where was this?' Thurstin's voice was soft.

'Crécy. I was very young at the time. We were hiding in a forest.'

'And you thought it might belong to Master Le Cran? But he was here when the battle took place.'

Rafi shook his head. His fingers curled around the locket, the only link he had with his past, with his family. 'I thought it belonged to his father. The tree, you see, the tree with many branches, or sons in this case.'

'But . . .' Thurstin was staring at Rafi intently. 'If Hugh was here, and his father was here, how would this seal end up in a forest?'

'His brother. Richard. If all the brothers have a crane, and the cranes belong to the tree, and Richard was at Crécy, then . . .'

Thurstin shook his head. 'I think you have let your imagination run away with you. Richard did die at Crécy; that much is true. But not in a forest. He fell in battle. Writel was witness to it. He can tell you if you dare ask him.'

Rafi let his forehead sink to the desk. 'But . . . it has to be Richard.'

'Are you not just seeing what you want to see? You have convinced yourself that this is the Le Cran seal because a few pieces fit. But the pieces, such as they are, don't fit in the right place. Richard was very unlucky; English losses were light that day. But Writel accounted for him. He died on the field of battle. Writel would have collected Richard's possessions and brought them back home. I'm sorry.'

Rafi lifted his head. Thurstin sat very still, watching him. There was no sophistry here, no evasion. Thurstin was telling the truth.

'So, I must start again.' Rafi put the locket back around his neck. It felt heavier. For the first time in his life, he resented having to wear it.

'Why did you choose to leave the religious life?'

Rafi was not expecting the question. 'I . . . I was only there by accident. And I'm not really the religious type.'

Thurstin smiled. 'Not the lying type either, although you gave it a valiant attempt.'

Rafi squirmed in his seat.

'Your search will be easier now. That badge you wear, that will open doors. Le Cran will treat you well if you serve him well. With your talents, you will thrive with him.'

'Talents? If they filled a dish it would be paltry fare.'

Thurstin began to close the shutters on the window. 'Writel thinks very highly of you.'

'Roger? I . . .' Rafi began to wonder if Thurstin wasn't a master liar after all.

The shutters were secured. Thurstin now turned to tidying the papers on his desk, scattering sand across the ink to make sure everything was dry. 'He says you are brave, although he also says you would do well to sharpen your tongue less often.'

Brave? Well. He had always been braver than Christophe, for all his cousin was two years older. It was why he'd handed Christophe the scapular that night. The talisman that did not work.

He thought again of Thurstin's words as he returned to the workshop. Was he really seeing only what he wanted to see? Perhaps. But even if the seal did not belong to Le Cran, the shadow of it had appeared on that note. That note came from William Le Cran. Thurstin was not William's clerk, so if William had a different seal to his brother, Thurstin might not know about it. And if not William, then perhaps it belonged to whoever had pushed the note under Adam's door.

Stefan.

Rafi shook his head. That would be too much of a coincidence. Unless . . .

Roger had said that Stefan looked like a soldier. Maybe he had been with William at Crécy, and they had retained their association. That could mean that the man in the forest wasn't Richard, but one of Stefan's relatives instead, carrying their family seal, which now appeared on a note Stefan may, or may not, have written. But how in the name of all that was holy was he to investigate Stefan's background without earning a fist to the mouth and a broken head?

Rafi was growling with frustration by the time he arrived back at the workshop. But his annoyance was as nothing compared to Cedric's.

'Stop playing games, Adam. Put it back.'

The apprentices' living quarters were in disarray; cots pulled from the wall, books and ledgers piled onto the tables while Cedric searched the shelves.

Rafi waited by the doorway, looking questioningly at Adam, who shrugged.

'Someone has stolen the mistress's dress. We've searched the shop and it's nowhere to be found so why we are searching here I do not know. Our friend here thinks it was me. Our friend needs to think again.'

Rafi set his things down carefully on his mattress. He had been to the parchmenter on the way back from the staple. As Joan had promised, some paper had been put to one side for him, along with a few extra surprises – pens, goose feathers, a paring knife, ink, more brushes. He had carried his bundle of treasures home in his leather bag. It had been the one bright spot in an otherwise bewildering and unhappy day.

And now another theft. Two in as many days. First his money and now the dress. He let the cogs in his brain spin, staring into space while a picture began to form.

'Cedric?'

'Mmm?' Cedric continued to scrabble behind the shelves.

'There was a delivery to the kitchen today.'

'There is always a delivery.'

'Specifically, from the spicer.'

'Edith?'

The sound of her name pulled at his heart. 'No.'

'It is only ever her.'

Adam nudged Rafi with an elbow. 'What's on your mind?'

'I saw her husband this morning, on his way to the kitchen.'

Cedric stopped what he was doing. 'Now I come to think of it, Rafi is right. It was that ghoul of a husband today.' He scratched his head. 'I thought it was a bit odd at the time. He . . .' Cedric's eyes opened wide.

'What is it?' Rafi was alert.

'He delivered the rushes.'

Rushes for the floor. Strewn over broken boards. The picture was becoming clearer. Rafi waited for Cedric to finish.

'Edith brings them to Nell. It is Nell who comes in and leaves the barrow.'

Cedric pointed to the corner. A wooden barrow sat with an empty sack hanging over the side.

'We lay them out. Well, I do.' Cedric glared at Adam. 'That one there is either too drunk or too lazy to bother.'

'But today?' Rafi could already guess.

'Today the ghoul delivered and offered to do the scattering. Adam was in the shop, you were at the staple, and I was busy . . .'

'So you left him to it?'

'I was always here!' protested Cedric.

'As if that makes a difference,' muttered Adam.

Cedric sat heavily at the table and slapped his hand against his forehead. 'Oh no . . . I . . . I brought the dress in here last night. I didn't want to leave it in the shop unattended.' He groaned.

So Thom was delivering the rushes in Edith's place. It would be easy to check with Serlo if it had been Thom, not Edith, who had entered Rafi's room at the Chequers. And if it had, then this put a new complexion on things. Perhaps the list of crimes Roger had committed might not be as long as Rafi had given him credit for.

'I think we need to make a delivery of our own then,' said Adam, punching his fist into his palm.

Rafi held up his hand. 'No, not yet. There is more at play here. Let me think. And we have no proof.'

'Who needs proof?'

'No, Adam. Rash actions have consequences. Think first.' It was what he was doing, after all. Caution had stopped him showing his seal to Le Cran. He needed to stay at the heart of this household if he were to uncover the truth for himself, and he needed Adam to adopt the same tactic. If Stefan was using Thom as a thief, then it would be best to let them think their activities remained undiscovered. Charging headlong into a fight would give too much away.

'That bastard deserves a kicking anyway. And as for you . . .' Adam pointed at Cedric. 'You dull-witted collop. What were you thinking—'

'I could not have put it better myself.'

The three of them fell silent. Rafi quickly slipped his papers under the brown tapet that covered his bed as Roger slid into the room. They should have been more careful. Writel occupied the space that separated the apprentices' rooms from the main body of the master's house. To get to Le Cran, you had to either walk outside and around to the front or cross the steward's threshold and risk rousing the human mastiff. A mangy, ill-tempered one. With sharp ears.

'Just reminding you, Dubois.' Roger's eyes darted briefly to the mattress. 'You had better be ready by dawn tomorrow. And if you are not in the yard, I shall drag you there myself.'

'Is that all?'

Roger turned to Adam. 'Would you like to find your wages short this week? I thought not. Then keep your tongue from rattling in that empty head of yours.'

'Idiot!' hissed Adam after Roger had left. 'What if he'd heard?

203

The master will separate our bowels from our arses and throw them in the Itchen if he finds out.'

'Well, he didn't,' shot back Cedric. 'Let us retrieve the item ourselves or at least prove that the ghoul has it.'

'And how do you propose to do that, you boil-brained lump?'

'We know where he lives. I'm sure we could break in . . .'

'Break in? And frighten his wife and her children to death? You're more of a dungpipe than I thought.'

'Well, what's your clever idea then?'

Rafi sat, blocking out the voices, trying to think. Thom was working with William Le Cran's men, and now he could guess why. They were using him as a thief. He had access to the spaces they could not get to as easily.

If it was Thom who had delivered the rushes to the Chequers, then it was Thom who had stolen his purse. *A fair few florins*, he'd said only this morning. And Rafi would bet those fair few florins that Thom had taken it not because he had been ordered to by William's men, but because he was emboldened. They could not have chosen a better dupe. He would carry out their bidding and cause trouble of his own while he was about it.

The dress, however, was another matter. What could they possibly want with Joan's old dress, especially since the pearls around the neck had been removed?

Adam and Cedric were still arguing, quietly, in case Roger heard them. Rafi sat back on his bed. There was nothing he could do about Thom now anyway. Tomorrow he was set for Salisbury and still had no idea why.

If it had something to do with the writer of that note, there would almost certainly be a risk of danger. Rafi had already lost a tooth and Adam had bite marks on his leg. What if he were injured this time, or worse?

But whoever had written that note had rested a seal on the paper, which had left an imprint; a seal that was so close to the one Rafi carried that he was convinced it would give him the answers he sought. Who had written it? William Le Cran, or perhaps Stefan or Fulke, soldiers who may have been at Crécy and who now worked for William.

He still felt, deep down, that the answer lay with Le Cran. He was still convinced it was Richard who had died in the forest that day.

He did not believe that Thurstin had lied. But Roger might have lied about the manner of Richard's death, and there would be no reason for Thurstin to doubt him.

What if I see only what I want to see?

The note was taking him to Salisbury for good or ill. He would have to pray that he found the evidence he so longed for.

Chapter 20

Le Cran had told him to put his affairs in order. What affairs did he have? He had no family, and his only friends were here in this room. He belonged nowhere and to no one.

He had been alone for more than fifteen years.

He had left a door ajar in his heart but held out little hope that it would ever fully open. He had promised Adam that he would talk to him and explain everything he knew about William Le Cran, but something else lay more heavily on his mind.

Against his better judgement, Rafi chose to walk along the path that led across the Waldytch, into the mead, where the silence curled around the reeds and marsh lilies.

He had eaten with the others. Dark rye bread, cheese, the last of his daily share of ale – he'd given half of his to Adam who would no longer leave the workshop once the shutters closed and who hadn't seen the inside of an inn since he'd been attacked. Adam had swooped upon Rafi's offering with delight. He and Cedric then engaged themselves in a game of hangman's gully, the wooden dice clattering on the tabletop as they threw. Rafi had retired to his corner with his brush and parchment. He painted in the shallow light from the candle for a while, pausing now and then as Adam teased and Cedric bit like a fish wriggling on a hook. If he closed his eyes, he could be back in Ghent, watching Adam bait Mathys, using his poor Flemish as an excuse for pretending he didn't understand the rules, and winning every time.

But Rafi was here, in Winchester, and the world was different now. His troubles weighed on his heart. But at least there was some brightness in the generosity of his mistress, Joan, and he transferred that brightness to the page before him.

He sat back and appraised his work. The May Queen. The moss he had collected had been used for the dark leaves plaited and intertwined with tansy and buttercups around her head, hair falling across her eyes, her feet bare as she stood in a golden meadow.

She would never see this, but he painted anyway. He let his hand hover over her face for a moment, then blew out the candle.

He pushed the painting in the space under the bed. Adam and Cedric barely looked up as he let himself out.

There were still a few hours of light left as he headed down Parchment Street. He reached the north-east side of the city and passed through the Durngate then along the outer perimeter and across the ditch. She would not be here. Not after what had happened.

The still, green water was alive with pond skaters. The reeds, thick and reaching up to Rafi's waist, rustled as a light breeze took them. There were foxes in the meadowland too; he could smell the musty scent, catching in his throat. The days were growing longer. The cottages near the abbey at Hyde were just about visible from here, and beyond that were the green striped fields above the hamlet of Headbourne Worthy.

He skirted around Knights Meadow and over to Dutton Bridge where he stopped to look back over the path he'd just walked. The city was full of spires, dozens and dozens of them. Crows dived and gathered together on rooftops, dark dots over the cathedral and abbey. He could see St Lawrence's church, and St Peter de Macellis where the curfew bell rang out. The spires he'd seen as he and Adam arrived from Southampton. It already felt like a lifetime ago.

The light was softening now, turning silver-grey. There was a mist rising from the marsh, ghostly and white. He wasn't scared. Unlike Adam, he had no fear of the supernatural. So he knew that the figure approaching from the south-east, where the light was poorer, was not a ghost.

She held a basket in one hand, a small knife in the other. She kept her head low, watching the ground for plants and useful things, things that might be missed if she didn't step carefully. She squatted near a small pool, cutting and then raising her bounty, inspecting it. She placed it in the basket and then, glancing behind her quickly, she untied her wimple and bunched it up in her apron, letting her hair run as wild as it liked without her having to fret and curse as it worked its way free.

She was the woman in the picture. He could almost see the wreath of flowers he'd made for her, resting on the hair that he had imagined so perfectly.

A deep sadness filled him. She had not wanted him to follow her, and he had truly believed she meant it, especially now. Yet he had come here because he couldn't stay away, because even if she had not chosen this evening to walk in the same place as he, being here would have brought him closer to her. The realisation of what he had done made the breath stop in his throat. He had been foolish; rash and foolish. Thom's suspicions must have been roused today and he could have followed her. He had put her at risk because of his own selfish desires, which had blinded him to her position.

He would have to slip away before she saw him.

But he was already too late.

She touched her hair self-consciously at the sight of him, glancing down at the crumpled headdress, considering it. She shrugged. She stood where she was, keeping the distance between them. They held each other's gaze for a few moments and then she beckoned to him, drawing him to a part of the northern fields.

'I thought I would find some new plants here.' She bent towards a clump of grass, holding her knife firmly.

She cut, the knife moving back and forth quickly and precisely.

'I am sorry,' Rafi said quietly.

She paused.

'I did not think to find you here, otherwise I would not have come.'

'You did not? But I came here because I always do, and you knew of this . . .' She went back to her work. 'But it is I who should apologise. You were insulted and mocked.'

'It was not at your hand.'

She stood. 'Kingcups.' The waxy golden flower nestled in her palm. 'Look. Something is growing near that tree.'

There was a thick oak tree, standing by the edge of the meadow. The knife came out again, slicing gently. She held up a delicate plant with pretty yellow leaves. 'Adder's tongue, see?'

The plant lay on her open palm.

'I am leaving tomorrow.'

She put the flower in her basket. 'Oh. Well. You will have a better journey this time, I hope. Will Adam be going too?'

'No. I am not bound for Ghent. I am to be sent to Salisbury, but I have not been told the reason for it.'

She smiled. 'That is not too far. I thought you were to leave us forever.'

Maybe that is how it will be.

'I hope not. But . . .' He took a deep breath and removed the chain from around his neck. 'I think I will find the rest of this, or at least a clue.'

She tilted her head. 'A clue?' She peered at the locket in his hand.

'My mother was killed many years ago, when I was a boy. The

man who tried to save her left me this.' He opened the locket. There it was, a half circle of soft metal with his bird and his tree and his memories. 'This was his mark. I saw that mark this morning on a letter. The imprint anyway. And I gave the letter to Le Cran.'

Edith gasped. 'Killed . . . I'm so sorry.'

Her eyes filled with tears. He wished he could brush them away, comfort her, hold her. Instead, he had to wait for her to compose herself.

'And now he sends you to Salisbury.'

Rafi nodded. 'The two are linked.'

'You think Le Cran has something to do with it?'

Rafi shook his head. 'I don't know. All I know is that it is not my master's mark.'

'If he's part of this, you must tread carefully.' She closed his fingers around the locket, holding her hand over his for a moment.

He looked away. 'I . . . almost want him to be innocent. Joan is very kind to me. And there is something about him.'

'Yes, there is.' She shivered.

He took his cloak and put it around her.

'Oh, how warm this is.' She smiled. 'You don't want to get it dirty. My clothes are none too clean.'

'I care not.'

He tied the fastening at her neck, looking at her hair as it brushed against the woollen fabric. He longed to hold her, but did not dare. It was enough that she was here, that he was here.

'What's your name?' Her breath was against his chest. 'Your real name.'

'Raphael. We gave each other small names in Ghent.'

Matt, Vin, Will, Jac – he could still see their faces and hear their laughter. And Raphael had become Rafi.

'I prefer Raphael. Like the guardian angel.'

'It's what my mother always called me.'

Angele Dei.

Marianne. The mother lost to him for so long. He didn't know

210

how he had survived without her, and yet he had. He didn't know how he could survive without Edith, and yet he must.

'There are two soldiers. I think they were the same men who delivered the letter with the mark on it. I think they will be waiting in Salisbury, and I fear . . .'

She gasped and looked up at him, her eyes wide. 'No!' She was trembling. 'Not again.' It was almost a whisper.

There was a patch of grass under the tree. He gestured to it with his hand and she stood with him beneath the wide branches, their backs against the trunk, leaning towards each other but never touching. Never touching.

'Again?'

She closed her eyes. 'My husband, Will. He too worked for Le Cran. Three years ago, just before Leof was born, he . . . We had very little. He would take any job, especially with another mouth to feed.' She paused. 'He was loading Le Cran's ship in Southampton when he fell. He . . .'

Rafi could see the silvery track from her eyes as the tears fell.

'The *Lady Cecily*?'

She nodded.

'Now I know why you don't like the name or any like it.' The plant she had ripped up so viciously in the abbey garden that day. Sweet cicely.

'It is silly, *n'est-ce pas*?'

It took him a moment for the words to sink in. He stared at her. 'Where did you learn to speak French?'

She looked at him, confused. 'I didn't.'

'You just did.'

She raised her eyebrows. 'Oh! I think I've heard someone say it at the abbey. Is it really French?'

He nodded. 'I can teach you some more.'

'When you get back from Salisbury?'

He nodded.

'Speaking of the abbey, that day we spent . . . the plants were dug up. The whole patch trampled. We don't know who did it. I'm sorry.'

Roger! He had threatened Rafi that day, behaved in a way that went over and beyond his usual peevishness. Something about the abbey always seemed to aggravate him and Rafi had never been able to work out why.

'I will never forget that afternoon. I felt . . .' How could he tell her what he felt? Curse Thom, curse Roger. None of this would matter if Edith was free. He could tell her then; he'd never stop telling her.

'I remember when you first arrived.' She smiled. 'You were bumping into everyone. Now, you have a fine cloak and a badge. And you are different.'

'The city has changed me. You have—'

'I like it here,' Edith interrupted. 'I often go to the water meadows, but I like this view of the city best. It is good to get away from the stink of Tanner Street.' She clenched her fists in her lap. 'And it is good to get away from Thom.'

He waited.

'I should have told you, but . . .' She looked up. 'I didn't see why it would matter. And when I realised it did, it was too late. Something about that day in the garden, something changed.'

He closed his eyes. He could not imagine what it must be like for her. His own father had died not long before he had lost his mother, but still he remembered happiness, joy, love. It broke his heart that he would freely give all of those gifts to Edith but he could not.

'I married Thom because . . . I didn't think I would find someone to look after us and I couldn't manage on my own. He was kind, at first. He pretended to be. Once we were wed . . . I would have been better off alone as he is worse than . . .'

He took her hand.

'What solace is there for a woman like me?' Her voice was anguished. 'With Adam gone, what choice did Ailith have? What will Agnes do if she decides to leave the abbey? What could I do? Even Joan was not free to choose. A rich woman and she still had to pay for the king's permission to marry whomsoever she chose. It is not right.'

'And what is a woman like you?'

'A widow, poor, plain, with three young children to feed.'

'You are not plain.'

'I cannot even keep my hair tidy.'

He touched it without thinking. Burnished copper. 'It is better than the gold or silver on any manuscript I have ever seen; beautiful in itself, and even more beautiful on you.'

She started to cry and he pulled her head onto his shoulder, holding her close.

They sat in silence for a little while longer, waiting for the curfew bell, looking out over Danemarch Mead and along the silver line of the river that led across the marshes and into the smoke-coiled city below.

Chapter 21

Edith knocked gently on the door of Hilda's cottage. Her sister opened it almost immediately, her finger resting on her lips as she ushered Edith inside.

The three children were asleep on one mattress on the floor, Simon next to the wall, his dark hair tousled and swept back from his face; Tilly in the middle, thumb in her mouth, her head snuggled against Simon's shoulder; and at the end, little Leof, both his arms thrown over his head, his lips parted gently.

'They've been asleep for over an hour,' whispered Hilda. 'Perhaps it is best if we leave them here. I am on my own this evening; it is no trouble.'

Edith reached for her sister's hand. 'Thank you.'

'You can stay too, Edith.'

Edith shook her head. 'You know he will not allow that. If he batters on the door, the children will waken and it will be distressing for all of us.'

Hilda took Edith's other hand. 'I wish you—'

'Don't. Because it does no good wishing for what we cannot have.'

A dozen or so spindle whorls were lined up in order of size on the table near the tiny window. Edith smiled. 'Tilly?'

'She's been counting again. She's such a clever girl.'

Darling Tilly. Much good it would do her.

Edith leaned over the children, kissed each one on the cheek and then hugged Hilda. 'It is best if I go before . . .' She felt her sister's arms tighten around her.

The cottage was quiet when she entered. Dark and cold. There was movement behind the sacking curtain that separated the storeroom from the kitchen and sleeping area. It had once been a bedroom when Will was alive, and the children had slept in the kitchen where it was warmer. Edith and her husband had kept each other warm well enough. Now, it was full of barrels and crates and sacks, produce she had not bought nor wanted. Wasteful, expensive items that she could not sell. He'd squandered what had been left of the money she and Will had saved.

He heard her close the door and appeared from behind the curtain. 'You have crawled back to me, then.'

She didn't answer.

'I know you were with him. I saw the sad milksop on his way up there earlier. Waiting for you, was he?'

She reached for a bag of powder douce, left lying carelessly on a chair near the hearth. She'd made at least ten before she going out but couldn't remember where she'd put the rest of them. The storeroom, probably. She would gather them and take them to the stall tomorrow.

'Do not ignore me.'

She turned. The cord was already in his hand.

She held up the pouch. 'I need to make some more of these. They sell well.'

He grabbed her arm and squeezed it until she cried out. 'We don't need them anymore. I threw the other ones on the fire. I must have overlooked this one.' He pulled it out of her hands and threw it onto the embers. The smell of wild garlic and cinnamon

215

smoked through the tiny room. What should have been put in a pot had been wasted and burned for nothing.

'They sell better than anything else.'

'As I said. We don't need them anymore. We don't need the stall. I don't need you or your pathetic powders and potions.'

She swallowed.

'I knew he wouldn't stay away for long. I saw how he looked at you at the abbey. And today – he'd have you for nothing, the fool.' He wrapped the cord around her waist and pulled her into the storeroom; he pulled so hard that she fell forward against the doorway and hit her cheek.

She put her hand up to her face. No bleeding, but there would be a bruise. She could make a comfrey and yarrow poultice, which would stop the swelling if she applied it quickly enough. She counted the leaves in her head, the quantity of boiling water required, the time she would need to keep the cloth pressed against her skin.

'I have no use for you now. I have no use for this.' Thom swept his arm around the barrels in the storeroom.

Edith was barely listening to him. Yarrow and comfrey. A linen cloth. Hot water left to cool. Apply it gently over the place where it hurt.

She saw the pot in her mind's eye, where she would boil the water and the leaves. It was an earthenware pot, left on the cold embers above the cinder tray. Heavy, used for pottage and watery soup, beans, turnips. If she took it now and smashed it down on his head, who would be any the wiser? Drunk, and he fell over, she would tell the coroner. But now she saw herself pick up the pot, saw herself bashing it against his skull, crushing bone into brain, not once, but over and over and over, because she knew that once she started, she would not be able to stop. For herself, for all her children, but especially for Tilly.

'I asked you for his purse and you failed me. Well, no matter. I've done better for myself than you ever managed. I can get a pretty dress and ribbons for Tilly, for when she's older. I don't need the stall anymore. I work for a different master now. You . . .' He looked her up and down with a sneer. 'You are nothing more than my servant and as such, you will sleep in here from now on. I will sleep in the kitchen where it is warm. With the children. In time, they'll treat you like a servant too.' He grinned. 'And if you speak to him again, he'll suffer for it.'

In her head, she made a potion. Henbane, masked with honey mead and the heat of ground pepper. Sweet and hot. A trace, that was all she needed. She would send Tilly away first. Ailith had said her mother needed help, and Tilly could count already. Domneva would not notice if she took a little poppy seed. Maybe that was better, poppy seed in his ale, enough to send him to sleep forever.

He had pushed her onto the floor and kneeled beside her, holding her wrists. She curled herself tight inside, into a hard ball, hard as rock.

'You disobeyed me, Edith. You went to him anyway. That was your last chance.'

He stood over her now. She stared towards the barrels, and beyond to where something glistened, close to the wattle wall. She looked away immediately; she did not want him to know.

'You'll sleep here now on the floor, like a dog in a kennel.'

She nearly laughed. It was less of a punishment than he thought. She would be free of his stinking body close to her at night.

Her eye and cheek were beginning to swell, but she could see him well enough. He'd been drinking; she could smell it. How easy, she thought, how easy.

'Remember, wife, I have friends. They don't use words. Do I make myself clear?'

He left her, pulling the sacking curtain across the doorway. She heard him lie down on the mattress. He would be asleep in minutes.

She waited. There was the faintest flicker of light from the tallow candle in the kitchen. It would burn down soon. She needed it before it guttered out. Finally, he snored, and she eased herself up as quietly as she could. The candle was on the wall just inside the kitchen. Taking care not to burn the curtain, she returned with it to the storeroom. She balanced it carefully on a barrel. There wasn't much light left in it.

She would have to move one of the barrels. Quietly, quietly as she could. She pushed at the ground with her toe, trying to dislodge the glistening thing. She nearly gasped and had to cover her mouth with her hands.

A tiny cut of expensive yellow cloth, and a single seed pearl hanging from a frayed thread. It looked as if it had been hacked and sliced in no sensible manner. There was an open purse pushed further under the barrel. She knew immediately whose it was.

'Bastard.' She took the empty purse and stroked the soft leather, holding it against her bruised cheek as if it could soothe, but the memory of his touch was not enough to heal. She didn't know whether to take it or not. Would Thom come back for it? She couldn't risk it. He could sell it even if it didn't bring more than a shilling at most. She tucked it back under the barrel.

But the pearl. What was she to do with the pearl? This must have been dropped by accident. It was so small and easy to miss. She ripped it from the cloth. There was no way Thom would have left this here had he known. He would have sold it. It was worth far more than just a shilling.

She rolled the pearl around in her palm as the candle began to gutter and die. She took the thread from the fabric and put it in her shoe with the pearl. She would use the thread to sew the pearl into her dress and keep it safe. And then, she would run. She would take her children first to Ailith's mother in Hyde; they could shelter there for a day or two at least. She would sell the pearl, and then they would leave. Go to Southampton, or even London. They could melt into a big city, and Thom would never find them. He would not even look.

She lay back on the musty earth. The candle had died now.

Being on her own, even on a hard, earth floor, was a relief. Her eyes closed, but she didn't sleep. Her mind went back three years, to just before Leof was born.

The boat that Will had been loading with wine and woolsacks. It would have been bound for Ghent, sailing along the Scheldt to dock at a warehouse on the Leie. A Flemish merchant's apprentices would have unloaded what her husband had placed in the hold on that awful day. Perhaps Rafi had been there, ready to tally the goods and mark off the amount in the ledger, not knowing that he was counting, perhaps, the last sack that her husband had held before he'd slipped and fallen.

Her tears fell silently. One love stolen from her, and one she could never have. But in denying herself that love, she would keep him safe.

Chapter 22

Rafi was ready well before dawn. It was no hardship to rise ahead of the sun as he'd done for many years at St Michael's. Roger need not have worried.

Ned brought the palfrey out. It was pearl grey with soft brown eyes. Roger's mount was dark like cinnamon. Ned waited, sleeves rolled up, shirt open, oblivious to the morning chill. He smiled at Rafi. They hadn't spoken since Rafi saw him through the gate with Ailith on his very first day here, but there had never been any sense of animosity. Rafi smiled back. When he returned from Salisbury, he would try and help mend the breach that had opened between the two brothers. He knew what it was like to lose a family and he wouldn't wish it on his friend.

The palfrey was equipped with a shiny leather saddle with a bag attached. A purse hanger with an amber pendant tied to the harness, polished until it shone. She was a gentle-looking horse, but her ears were forward, and her movements were keen.

There were two other men, wide charcoal-coloured cloaks spread out behind them. They were mounted on sturdy rounceys and ambled out of the stable yard without a word, nodding to Rafi as they passed. The cloaks rippled on the rumps of their mounts as they turned into the white-misted street, heading west. They were both armed.

Rafi patted the bag at his side – a parcel of oatcakes from Nell and one other item, which Roger had insisted on. The misericord dagger.

'I expect you will chop your own fingers off with it, but no matter. Take it.'

Roger handed Rafi the reins to the palfrey, mounted his horse and waited.

'Are you going to tell me . . .' Rafi started.

'Just a little snooping around; that is all. Time enough for talk. Get your backside in the saddle and keep quiet until Salisbury. I mean it,' Roger warned.

'Why the armed—'

'Ever heard of thieves? Of course we have an armed escort, you dolt.'

Rafi wriggled on the saddle until he got as comfortable as he could. Roger was clenching his jaw and Rafi could see the outline of his bones and teeth.

Roger nudged with his heel, the horse nodded and shook his head and then followed the path the two rounceys had taken, with Rafi bringing up the rear.

They left by the Westgate, heading first towards Andover before turning in the direction of Stockbridge, passing the gallows where Roger slowed very deliberately.

The wooden platform was scuffed and poorly maintained, and the trapdoor looked barely able to support the poor victim destined to fall through its maw. All was mercifully quiet this morning, but even so, Rafi shivered as he urged his horse forward. He was glad of his cloak, the one that had been wrapped around Edith the evening before. It was a great comfort to him.

It would have been a poor attempt by Roger to unnerve him on any other day, but on an empty road at dawn, heading out on a path that may contain thieves as Roger had warned, it was enough to make him feel uneasy. He appreciated the effort Roger had put into the endeavour but didn't much feel like commending him for it.

As they reached Sparsholt, the green leaves of the crabwood flickered with the light of the climbing sun. They were at Stockbridge a little over three hours after leaving Minster Street. Roger dismounted wordlessly by a clump of trees, turned his back on Rafi, relieved himself, then ate one of the oatcakes Nell had given him. He offered Rafi a drink of his ale without looking at him, then got back in the saddle. They hadn't spoken since leaving the stable yard.

They picked up the Salisbury road, now making a slight southerly turn until they could see the distant line of the Avon, with the spire of the cathedral shimmering on the horizon. Graceful where Winchester's cathedral was squat, Salisbury pointed up into the heavens, tapering like a thread pulled into the clouds.

There were sheep on the common pastures. 'Fine wool,' observed Roger, his first words since they had left Winchester behind them and likely to be his last as he showed no inclination to add any further comment. The green shaded strips of farms along the route fascinated Rafi. How would he paint that? How many different shades of green, and brown, and earth? It gave him something to take his mind off Roger's surly presence and his own unease.

As the sun rose higher, Rafi reluctantly removed his cloak and attached the neat roll to the bag that hung from behind his saddle. He liked having it close because Edith had worn it, but he would pass out if he didn't strip to his shirt. The sun was blistering.

Roger turned them south once more, and they crossed the river at a ford, reaching a small hamlet in the afternoon.

'Odstock. This way.'

Rafi followed Roger towards a small alehouse, sitting on the outskirts of the hamlet. The Lamb was well kept and clean, but otherwise empty.

'Writel,' the rosy-faced innkeeper greeted him as they entered.

'Sit,' hissed Roger, pushing Rafi towards a low bench in the corner.

'How goes it?' Roger leaned towards the innkeeper but the room was so small Rafi could hear everything anyway. There was no point in Roger keeping his voice down.

The innkeeper looked over Roger's shoulder towards Rafi.

'Don't mind him.'

The taverner raised his eyebrows. 'Slight fellow.'

'In brain as well as stature,' growled Roger.

Rafi hid a smile.

'Things are lively, let us put it like that.'

Roger nodded, his face grim. 'And the earl?'

'In attendance.'

'Hmm. That could work either for us or against us.' Roger inclined his head towards Rafi. 'You may come in useful after all, then. Or not, as the case may be.'

'I appreciate the clarity,' said Rafi.

The innkeeper smirked. 'Slight, but spirited.'

Roger shook his head. 'Idiotic, if the previous few days are anything to go by, but never mind. Have you anything better than ale?'

'Always, Writel. Le Cran keeps a good cellar.'

The innkeeper disappeared into the undercroft, returning with a glass bottle.

'Enough for one each.'

Roger took the bottle and two wooden goblets, sliding into the seat beside Rafi.

'This is a very quiet alehouse indeed,' Rafi said as Roger poured the mellow liquid into his cup.

Roger took a sip, swilling the wine around his mouth and holding it for a few seconds. He topped up his cup and then pushed the rest of the bottle towards Rafi.

'Are you going to tell me—'

'Drink. You won't die of it.'

Rafi did as he was told. The wine was smooth and rich, unexpectedly fine in an alehouse in the middle of nowhere.

'The Lamb doesn't serve much ale,' Roger confirmed.

'So I see.'

'Its primary purpose is to keep an eye on the manor we're about to visit.'

Rafi was happy to stay here all day. He'd never tasted wine as fine as this.

'It is Lepe. It is Spanish, and it is costly, so try not to develop a taste for it.'

Roger finished his drink. Rafi pointed to the bottle. 'No, you have it. There is enough for two.'

Rafi bade the final cupful a fond farewell, eyeing Roger as he did so. Like Rafi, the steward was down to his shirt, sweat dripping from his forehead, the linen cloth sticking to his back and chest. There was a scar poking above the neckline, an old one as far as Rafi could tell, almost smooth against Roger's pale skin. He was all muscle, not an ounce of fat on him. It wasn't obvious when he was fully clad but once that bulk was stripped away, Roger was lithe and athletic. Rafi was somewhat taken by surprise.

Roger scowled. 'What are you looking at?'

'Nothing of note.'

'Are you not going to ask who owns the manor?'

Rafi shrugged. 'You told me not to ask questions.'

Roger ran his hand along his jaw. His face was rough; the action sounded like a brush sweeping across a tiled church floor.

'It belongs to William Le Cran.'

Rafi let the information sink in, gripping the table as the room began to swim. It could have been the wine, strong on an empty stomach that was already knotted.

The weight of the locket felt heavy against Rafi's chest. William Le Cran. William Le Cran, the master's older brother. The man who had sent Stefan and Fulke. He might not have been the one

224

who had broken Rafi's teeth and or scared Adam half to death, but it was William who had sent the men who had.

Roger was staring at him. 'Too strong for your taste, I see.'

It isn't the wine.

'We are here to pay William's debt to the Earl of Arundel. We shouldn't have to, of course; he has an allowance which should more than cover his household expenses. But . . . let us say he has expensive tastes.'

'I see.'

'And alas,' Roger continued, 'even though our master is providing him with funds, he finds it amusing to play silly games with us. Unfortunately, I cannot anticipate what those games are because he chooses to conduct his business in a language I don't fully understand. He also, rather predictably, won't reveal what he's up to anyway, not when I'm around. A servant, though, a servant will go unnoticed.'

Rafi moistened his lips. He looked longingly at the empty bottle.

Roger sighed. 'I don't need another drunk apprentice on my hands. I have enough trouble with Adam already.' He twisted the stopper back in the wine bottle. 'So, this is where you come in. We could have conducted this business some time ago had you not been so stubborn.'

Two goblets of Lepe and Rafi marched right through the door Roger had just opened.

'That did not justify what you did to me.' Rafi banged his hand on the table so hard the bottle shook. 'I could have lived with Marsh throwing me into the street, but I lost something precious and . . .'

Roger held up his hands. 'That was unfortunate, I grant you. I didn't mean for that to happen.'

Rafi couldn't stop. 'And the little patch of garden. Such a small thing, but such spite. Did you not even care? Sister Domneva, Edith, they were trying to do something good for the people who lived there, but you destroyed it.'

Rafi had gone over Roger's crimes many times in the silence of his room and the rage had been building.

Roger stared at him, perplexed. 'I have no idea what you are talking about. I have not touched your wretched garden or your stupid weeds. And I didn't steal your money either – don't think I don't know why you eventually came crawling to Minster Street. Perhaps the person who took your purse rampaged over your precious pots and plants as well. Did you think of that?'

Rafi had thought of that and had already conceded that Thom had most likely stolen his purse. But he'd convinced himself that Roger was responsible for everything else, and it was hard to change such a firmly held conviction.

'Apart from which' – Roger had raised his voice, growing as angry as Rafi – 'I told you over and over again to leave the abbey alone, and that warning still stands. It is a command now, from your master's steward. You should have done as you were told.'

There was silence. Roger stared straight ahead, and Rafi fixed his eyes on his shoes.

Rafi didn't regret saying what he'd just said; it had festered for too long. And oddly enough he believed Roger. But he didn't think Thom had anything to do with the garden. It would have taken more effort than a sly and lazy man like Thom was capable of. And where was the profit in it?

'Dubois?'

Rafi's head jerked up. Roger's mouth was set in a tight line, his grey eyes cold.

'We have work to do. Let us go about it and be done.'

'What would you have of me?'

Roger patted his breeches. 'There are two hundred pounds in here.'

Owed unto me by yr. brother, Wm.

The note in the box he'd seen in Thurstin's office. But that was from five years ago. How many loans had there been? William must be bleeding his brother dry.

'This is what William owes the Earl of Arundel and what he cannot afford to pay.'

'But why has the earl lent him so much money?'

Roger slumped back in his seat. 'They have some bond, forged in France many years ago. I don't know the whole story and I don't care, but when William asks for a loan, Arundel gives him one.'

'Why not let him pay his own debts?'

Roger growled. 'His profligacy makes him incapable of doing so. Our master bears the burden.'

'Then let the earl chase him for payment.'

'And drag the Le Cran name into the mud? And earn us the reputation of acting in bad faith? No.' Roger shook his head. 'No. We would all be tarnished.'

'But . . .' Hugh Le Cran was well educated and fluent in French himself, or whatever language it was that William thought to obscure his dealings with. It would only take him a few hours to get here, as they had. 'Why does our master not come here and speak with his brother himself?'

Roger glared. 'Because William's temper is unpredictable, and violent,' he said. 'He is not of sound mind. He is a very dangerous man, and you are a very foolish boy.'

'So foolish,' retorted Rafi, 'that I am the only one capable of doing the master's bidding in this matter.'

Roger nodded. 'Aye, and I'm not convinced you're capable, but here we are. Your master and his brother are not on good terms, and you've already meddled enough to know why.'

The nun. The nun who had been moved to the abbey at Wherwell.

'I wouldn't put it past William to murder Hugh where he stood; hence, the two must be kept apart. So let me tell you what you are to do. And for the love of Saint Swithun, pay attention.'

As Rafi had expected, he was to snoop around the manor. Listening at doors. Standing quietly in the shadows – a servant, no more, no less. Easily ignored and invisible.

Rafi remembered how distasteful he'd once found the suggestion that he had to dissemble for a living. No longer. He'd do it. He would follow Roger into the lair and once in, he'd search in hidden places, hunting for the seal that had made that mark on the paper. He'd spy for the devil if he had to.

The path leading to the manor was a dark one. It cut through woodland on the edge of Cranbourne Chase, leading them into an isolated spot away from Odstock and two miles from Salisbury itself. On the fringes of the city, it was a domain of its own. The building was bigger than Le Cran's Winchester townhouse, stone-built and strong, a thick wall around the perimeter. It was like a fortress. To keep visitors out, or to keep William Le Cran pinned inside?

The bond with Arundel had been forged on a battlefield in France, Roger had said. What was it? Had Arundel killed Richard? Had William somehow found out? Why else would Arundel loan money to such a wastrel – blackmail?

But it was a loan, not a gift. And Hugh had to pay each time. If William were blackmailing Arundel, there'd be no obligation to pay the money back.

Rafi's fingers curled around the reins, the gentle thump of the horse's hooves vibrating through his body.

Think. Think. That night in the forest. A forest just like the one they were in now. The dread, rumbling through the leaves towards them. And two men. An English mercenary and an English soldier.

But what if it hadn't been a mercenary? It was night, and Rafi had been under leaves and branches; how easy it would be for a child to make a mistake. And now he remembered, they'd seemed to know each other – the soldier had moved in for an embrace.

They must know each other. They must be friends.

How could he have forgotten? Friends. He'd thought they were friends. He'd never once imagined . . .

Brothers.

A bond forged on a battlefield. There'd been so many battles; William could have been at any of them. It could have been Poitiers, or Calais or Auberoche. It didn't have to be Crécy; it didn't have to be fifteen years ago, it didn't have to be that forest clearing.

It did not have to be William Le Cran.

But if it was, Rafi would know.

Chapter 23

The rounceys were tethered on the edge of the woods, close together in a patch of trees. The riders watched them pass in silence, nodding to Roger. Their thick woollen cloaks were folded on the ground to keep them warm should the night prove chilly, their bags rolled into pillows. Their weapons were by their sides, within an inch of them.

'They're not just protecting us from thieves, are they?' asked Rafi uneasily.

'No harm in caution if we need to make a quick exit.'

They passed through the gate and dismounted before the door. Nobody came to take their horses. Roger waited for a few moments before striding away, leaving Rafi on his own.

He didn't have long to wait; Roger returned briskly with a pale-faced boy of about fourteen.

'I will check on the stabling anon, so make sure you look after them properly.'

The boy scowled at Roger, but as he took the reins of both horses, his face softened. He led the two mounts away very gently and calmly.

'He knows what he's doing, but he's lazy.' Roger raised his hand and knocked sharply on the door.

There came the sound of ferocious barking as the wooden bar was raised behind the double door. What manner of place was this? More a fortified building than a home. But if its occupants were familiar with life on a battlefield, then perhaps it suited them to have it this way. It was late afternoon now but they could surely expect a bite to eat and a bed for the night. How long they were intended to stay, Rafi couldn't say. Roger had not enlightened him.

The entrance hall was large and dark with an enormous table taking up the centre of the room. The windows were small, and the shutters closed tight, so the gloom was by design. You could lose all sense of time here. There was no natural light from without, and rushlights were flickering as if it was already dark outside.

The barking had come from a pair of talbots standing upright beside the fire, one grey, one black as pitch. The grey had an open maw, teeth visible. He didn't look friendly but did not move from his spot. Well trained, at least.

As Rafi's eyes adjusted to the dim interior, there was a movement from the head of the table.

'Writel. Finally.' The voice was a whisper, but it carried well enough in the high vaulted room, echoing across the hallway.

Roger walked forward. Rafi remained where he was. The steward was rigid; he moved as if someone were pushing him. His fists were clenched behind his back. Rafi didn't think it was fear. It was anger.

'You may as well give the money to Arundel directly. He will be down anon. We have a seat made ready for you but we were not expecting you to bring a lapdog.'

Rafi kept his eyes down and his head low. The voice was still a whisper. Had the man lost the power of speech, or was he deliberately making himself hard to hear?

Roger still hadn't spoken, but now he turned and gestured with his head towards the corner of the room where a narrow wooden bench was set. Rafi seated himself obediently and waited. It was darker here than in the rest of the hall. This was where the servants would eat.

Rafi tried to focus on the figure at the top table, but the shadows hid his features. In form, he was bulky – either corpulent or muscular, it was impossible to tell which. Rafi needed to see his face, but couldn't make it out. He shrank back against the wall, melding into the fabric of the building then took the hood from the satchel at his side and put it on, pulling it over his head and shoulders.

It wasn't long before two servants appeared with dishes, which they placed at one end of the table, near where William Le Cran had positioned himself. Only three for supper then. Roger, Le Cran and the man who emerged onto the gallery over the hall, stood for a moment observing the table below, and then made his way down the stairs.

This had to be the earl, a stout man in his fifties with grey hair and a jowly face. He wore a purple tunic, the royal colour few were allowed. A belt, trimmed with a gold buckle, held a long dagger close to his side. He did not look happy.

Roger stood as the earl took his seat.

'Good evening, Writel.'

'My lord.' Roger bowed and then sat.

'Eat,' whispered William, gesturing at the food impatiently.

The three men ate in silence. Two servants came and sat with Rafi, offering him a trencher full of soup, which he took gratefully. Neither of them engaged him in conversation and once the meal was done they cleared what was left of the trenchers, returned with wine, which they placed at the top table, and vanished into the kitchen. Rafi was left in the shadows alone. The earl hadn't once looked in his direction and William seemed to have forgotten he was there.

'So, you have what I am owed?' The earl's voice was gruff.

Roger gave him the purse.

'Very good.'

'If you will pardon me, my lord,' said Roger, pushing his chair back.

'No, no, have some wine.' The whisper managed to be sinister.

'If he says he wants to leave, then let him. You may go, Writel.'

'Thank you, my lord.'

Roger walked down the hall, not looking to either side of him. As he passed Rafi's bench, he put his finger to his lips.

William's wheedling voice followed him, but he wasn't speaking English. He would not want Roger to eavesdrop, which Roger would surely make it his business to do. It was time for Rafi to listen, and remember.

'He deliberately humiliates me. I should not have to run to him for money.'

'Indeed.' Arundel sounded weary. 'But nor should you keep running to me.'

'He profits from my inheritance. And now he has a child on the way to keep me from what is mine. It is unjust.'

Arundel sighed. 'Your conduct is what kept you from what was yours. Your behaviour was unbecoming. You attacked a nun, William. A nun.'

'It was not as he said, it was not at all what he said. My brother lied to get rid of me. Did he not persuade our father to pay for the woman to be moved to the abbey at Wherwell? Is that not an admission of guilt?' The whisper grew hoarser.

Arundel put his goblet down heavily. 'Or the act of someone trying to repair the damage to his family's reputation. It is no wonder your father disowned you.'

'He lied about me to my father. That is why I was undone. My brother stabbed me in the back.' He was slurring his words.

The earl grunted. 'Perhaps, or perhaps it would be best if you were more prudent with your money. Prudent enough not to need mine.'

William shifted in his chair and leaned forward.

'Listen to me.' Arundel held up his hand and reverted to English. 'I am grateful for what you did for me on the way to Calais. Had you not pulled me out of the river, I would have drowned. You will always have my gratitude, but this has gone on too long. Look at this place. It is cold, few servants, the rooms are barely furnished. But you pay for bodyguards with my money. Mercenaries. Don't think I don't know it. This is an easy life for them and I have no doubt they get bored, and bored mercenaries are dangerous. And this . . .' Arundel picked up the pitcher of wine. 'Expensive, plentiful. If you kept your affairs in order, I would mind less. But this?'

William sniffed. 'I have told you, I will come into my own very soon.'

'Then you no longer need me. Live on your allowance until you are the wealthy man you say you will be.'

'But . . .' William started forward. Rafi held his breath. A few inches more and William's face would catch the light from the candles. But no. He threw himself back in his chair. 'I need to keep Fulke and Stefan for another four months, and my allowance is not enough.'

Arundel stood up abruptly, the legs of his chair scraping across the stone flags. 'I am sorry. I cannot help you any longer. I bid you goodnight now. My room is cold; it is uncomfortable; the fire is unlit. I shall use this to bring me what little warmth I can find.'

The earl took the pitcher and went up the stairs.

William clapped his hands. Rafi shrank back as far as he could, making himself as small as possible, pulling his hands into the sleeves of his tunic in case the whiteness of his flesh stood out against the dark wall.

The man who answered William's summons was Fulke.

'Fulke. Fulke.' The whisper didn't carry far, but it roused the dogs who scampered to their feet from their place in front of the empty fire.

Fulke sat indolently in the chair the earl had vacated.

234

'What have you discovered for me?' asked William.

'There are two others. They are hiding somewhere but we will soon flush them out.'

'Good.' William clapped his hands again. One of the servants appeared with a replacement pitcher.

'They have been brought in to protect the lady wife,' said Fulke, putting his feet on the table.

'Kill them. It will take my dear brother a while to find a couple more. Let him run around like a chicken in a coop while he fusses over her safety.'

'And then?'

'And then we take the apprentices, one by one. And then we take Writel . . .'

'Writel? You aim high.'

'I will aim higher still once he has gone.'

'The woman?'

'And the brat will die with her. Two for the price of one.' William's laugh turned into a pitiful wheeze. 'But we need to act quickly.'

'Our payment . . .'

'Is assured.'

'He will pay?' Fulke nodded to the room above the hall to which Arundel had retired.

'Does it matter?' William's voice faltered. 'Once I have my inheritance you will be handsomely rewarded. Arundel can damn himself to hell for all I care.'

Fulke reached for one of the silver dishes on the table. He tipped the contents onto the floor. 'I will take this,' he said, 'as a down payment. Just in case you do not make good what you owe us.'

'You doubt me?'

Fulke didn't answer but moved towards the pantry calling for wine, slapping the silver dish on the side of his thigh.

Rafi was left on his own with William who continued to drink, full goblets downed at speed. His head grew heavy, and he slumped forward. Reaching for the flagon he tipped one of the mazers over and started swearing. His cup rolled along the table, rasping against the wood.

'God damn!'

William reached for a pewter candlestick the better to search for his cup. He found it, filled it, drank the contents in one go and then fell forward in a stupor. Within minutes, he was snoring.

The noise was strange to Rafi's ears and made him wince. It was more of a wheeze than a snore, a harsh gasp for breath.

William had moved the candlestick to hunt for his cup, and now the light flickered in the holder beside him. Rafi could finally see him, the close-cut dark hair, eyes closed tight, mouth open. There was a strange mark on his neck, a poorly healed wound, jagged and darker than the surrounding skin. His chin was turned in a way that obscured the full extent of the injury. But his face was illuminated.

He looked nothing like Hugh, and Rafi couldn't remember the dead soldier's face well enough to say if there was any resemblance there either.

One face Rafi did remember though. The one belonging to the man who'd taken three lives without mercy fifteen years ago.

It was the face of William Le Cran.

Chapter 24

Rafi stood over William's prone figure. Even though his eyes were blurred by tears, he was absolutely certain. The man was older and heavier, but it was him without a doubt. Rafi backed away. He had no desire to look upon William any longer. He had seen enough.

He had expected to feel anger or hatred, but there was just sorrow and a numbness in his chest. He had found his man, but what was he to do? Kill him as he slept? He had his misericord dagger with him, but the dogs would be upon him before the deed was done. He would be struck down by Fulke and possibly provide the excuse needed to kill Roger while they were about it. No. Caution was required, even now as he stood within striking distance of the man who had torn his life apart.

And he had a promise to fulfil. Richard Le Cran deserved justice, assuming the dead soldier really was Richard. Any revenge would have to come later.

The name on the seal, he needed the name on the seal. If he could conclusively tie it to the Le Cran family then how could they deny it? The seal must be here. It had to be.

He just needed that last clue.

'Who is there?'

Rafi jumped. The half-eaten trencher he'd been holding fell to the floor with a damp thud.

'*Allez*! Pick it up or the dog will have it!'

William stirred but didn't wake. Rafi followed the voice into the kitchen. He found it hard to turn his back on William, but he had to present an orderly face. He had to listen and discover and not let his emotions cloud his judgement.

The kitchen was a little more welcoming than the hall, but only just. It was untidy, raw meat left out of the cold store and going grey around the edges, food waste piled in a corner, glasses sticky with wine and ale. But also a large pot, bubbling gently, smelling of goodness.

'Well now. The little mouse has appeared. Or is it a rat?' The man's accent held the cadence of the grey Atlantic, the wild and rocky coast of Brittany. Rafi had heard it before as he had cowered in the Lady Chapel of St John's.

'A mouse, I fear.'

The man smiled. 'I am Jehan. But you know that.'

'Yes. I am Raphael.'

Jehan nodded. 'And I know that. I saw your boot was sticking out from under the coffin after Roger left. You should learn to hide better. Come. Let me find you something.'

Jehan poked at a few pots, frowning. 'Not much left, but there is some soup.' He poured a steaming mugful from the pot into a wooden bowl. The smell of it made Rafi hungry all over again. 'Some bread too, better than what you've just picked off the floor.'

'Thank you.'

'So.' Jehan sat opposite him, hands pressed flat on the table. 'You seem fascinated by the monster out there.' He jerked his head towards the hall.

Rafi didn't answer. He packed the bread into his mouth, watching Jehan cautiously. The man was slender, with salt and pepper hair, dark eyes. He had moved around the kitchen easily,

238

appearing supple, but on closer inspection, he was older than Rafi had initially thought.

Jehan folded his arms and scrutinised Rafi as thoroughly as Rafi had scrutinised him. 'He's asleep, but his thugs are about.'

Rafi dipped his bread slowly into the soup, biding his time. He drew a breath. 'Thugs? Both of them?'

'Yes.'

Stefan.

Jehan leaned forward and dropped his voice. 'I have another master, Raphael. You have heard me speak with Writel. You need not fear me.'

'I did not like what I heard.'

Jehan shrugged. 'A half story is not the same as a full story.'

Rafi raised the bread to his mouth, some of the warm, brown liquid dropping onto his arm and staining his sleeve. He looked beyond Jehan, to a shadow growing in size as it approached the pantry. His sigh of relief, when it came, was louder than he expected it to be.

'So?' Roger remained where he was, outlined against the doorway. Strings of garlic, bags of barley and herbs lined up against the walls behind him. William Le Cran stocked a good kitchen. Or rather, Hugh stocked a good kitchen for him.

Rafi kept his voice as low as he could. 'He is going to kill you.'

Roger sucked in his cheeks and then nodded. 'And?'

'I will not see it, alas. They will come for the apprentices first.'

'Not funny, Dubois.'

'I did not mean it as a joke. And once you are gone—'

Roger held up his hand. 'Do you know why? Why he has chosen now?'

'The Earl of Arundel is not going to give him any more money. His brother has a lot of it and he wants it.'

'He has always wanted it.'

'That may be true,' said Rafi. 'But now the mistress is with child it puts him at one remove from what he sees as rightfully his. Come September, the heir will no longer be William, and he desires to stop that happening.'

Roger sighed. 'And he thinks he could take over the business? That would never have worked. No one will deal with William. No one. And besides, our master would simply employ new clerks and apprentices if William kills all the existing ones.'

'I am touched that we mean so much to you.' Rafi thought about the fist that had slammed into his face, and the fear in Adam's eyes when he recalled being attacked in the graveyard. 'But if all the clerks and apprentices are dead who would want to take their place? I would not want to work for someone if it meant I'd be eviscerated within the week.'

'Why the sudden change of . . . ah!' Roger flopped onto a chair and rubbed his chin. 'I see now. With the earl no longer sending him purses of coin, he can't pay his lackeys.'

'He needs to kill his way to the coffers as fast as he can. And I would not want Stefan or Fulke coming after me for wages I can no longer pay. I'd be on the receiving end of a lot worse than a punch or a prickly tree.'

Roger frowned. 'A prickly . . . a what?'

'Never mind. I've just remembered something. They know about the others who came with us.'

Roger paled. 'Jesu.'

Jehan waved his hands. 'They will do nothing. They only pick on the weak. Your men will see them off.'

'You'd better hope so.'

'This one here.' Jehan pointed at Rafi. 'He seems peculiarly interested in the bastard out there.'

Rafi picked at his bread.

'Are you sure you can trust him?'

Roger's grey eyes met Rafi's. For a few moments there was silence as the two men stared at each other.

'Yes.' Roger nodded. 'I trust him.'

Trust? Roger trusted him? But could that trust be returned?

It would have to be. Rafi's life might depend on it.

Roger got straight to the point. 'What were they talking about earlier?'

Rafi shrugged. 'Hugh Le Cran is a coward who has lied to take his inheritance. William will get even one day. It was a litany of self-pity.'

'That does not surprise me. But what we need now is proof. He plans to kill us all? Until Master Le Cran has that proof in his hands, he will be reluctant to move against his own flesh and blood.' Roger shook his head. 'In spite of everything.'

So that was it, was it? He was supposed to search the house looking for evidence that might not even exist. But then, he intended to search the house in any case, looking for a seal, which also might not exist.

'You don't need me to do this,' said Rafi. 'Surely Jehan can . . .'

'Jehan can do many things but he can't be caught rummaging through correspondence.'

'But I can? Expendable, I suppose.'

'No, not expendable. Invisible. He will call for me, not you. Your absence will not be noted, but mine will, as will Jehan's. And we need him to keep his position here.'

'Very well. Tomorrow—'

'We don't have tomorrow. We leave in the morning. He is in his cups. His room will be empty. The dogs will stay with him down here.'

'In that case, where should I . . .'

Roger suddenly ducked behind the door.

'Well, well. The lapdog is chatting to a fellow traitor.'

It was Fulke.

'*Ne dis rien,*' said Jehan. *Don't say anything.*

Fulke kicked at Jehan's chair. 'I should have killed more of your countrymen when I had a chance. I should hang you, you and your friend here.'

He swept his hand across the table, knocking Rafi's bowl of

soup onto the floor. He leaned over and pushed his face into Rafi's.
'Perhaps I will. Perhaps I will string you up like a trussed chicken
and leave you to swing. Do not think Writel would save you.'

Rafi watched the pool of rich soup congealing on the rushes.

'Where is he? Where is the interfering arselicker?'

'Find him yourself,' said Rafi.

Fulke grabbed at the collar of Rafi's shirt and lifted him off his
chair like a rag doll. 'One step out of line and you are a dead man.'
He let go, Rafi falling heavily back into his seat, his throat dry.

Fulke shook his head, then turned and left.

'This,' observed Jehan after the footsteps had died away, 'is
what your master's money is paying for.'

Rafi coughed and adjusted his clothing. 'Who are they?'

'Soldiers with nothing better to do. Bored soldiers are dangerous
soldiers. They are hired hands; that is all. They have no loyalty
but take the coin and cause mischief on his behalf.'

'They are not old family friends of William's?'

'I doubt it.'

So, unlikely to be linked to that forest clearing. This put them
another step away from being the seal owners. Not that Rafi had
ever truly believed it to be related to either of them in the first
place.

Rafi drank the ale Jehan offered him, grateful. His throat was
hurting.

'There is a reason the earl is wealthy. He doesn't borrow what
he can't pay back. Unlike our friend out there.'

Jehan continued to speak in his native tongue. It was doubtful
that Roger, still hiding in the buttery, would understand much
of what they were saying.

'Your friend, Roger. Hates that bastard as much as anyone,'
said Jehan.

'I guessed as much.'

'I have been here a long time, Master Raphael. Roger has been
with the family since he was a boy. He was the personal servant of

Richard Le Cran, and now Hugh. He has never forgiven William for returning from France when Richard did not. The resentment has never gone away. He feels it still. You can see it every time he is here. The better brother died.'

'He would kill him?'

'Undoubtedly. Only his loyalty to Hugh stops him.'

'So would I,' whispered Rafi.

Jehan raised his eyebrows. 'I knew there was something. What has he done to you? Are you another one whose sister or wife or sweetheart has fallen foul of that devil out there?'

'I . . .'

'It is why he has no voice. Survived battles and a siege, ended up being stabbed through the throat when he got home. It was bound to happen one day. Maybe the next time, the job will be finished properly. There are husbands, brothers, fathers out there who would happily try if they had the chance.'

'And sons,' said Rafi.

'Ah.' Jehan poured himself a cup of ale. 'I am sorry.'

'He killed her.'

Jehan nodded. 'He has always done as he pleases. They say he rescued the earl from a river during a heavy storm. I have no idea how true that is. He would not do anything unless there were some gain in it, and he has fed off the gratitude of the earl ever since. It wouldn't surprise me if he'd pushed Arundel in, if only to give himself a chance to play the rescuing hero.' Jehan sipped slowly. 'What was her name?'

Rafi closed his eyes. William's face, cruel and hard, the moonlight shining through the trees as he pulled Rafi's mother away forever.

'Marianne. Her name was Marianne.'

When Rafi opened his eyes, Roger was in the doorway.

'I am going to my quarters,' he said gruffly. 'There is a room set aside for me on the first floor, on the corner above the yard. William's room is on the upper floor. There is a staircase directly above here.' Roger pointed at the ceiling. 'It will take you up to his chamber, which will be empty, as you can probably guess.'

The sound of wheezing was still audible.

'Go round by the door at the back,' said Jehan. 'Through the buttery. There is a staircase outside, which takes you up to an entrance the first floor. I have left it open. You are less likely to meet any undesirables.'

Roger nodded. 'Rafi, there is a cot in my room for you when you have . . . finished with your enquiries.' He turned to go, then paused. 'Be careful. He is not worth your life.'

Rafi stepped into the yard. The moon was full although half hidden behind a cloud. There was enough light to see the stairway Jehan had told him would be there. Rafi shivered, the skin on the back of his neck prickling, beads of sweat forming on his brow. He wiped them away with the sleeve of his shirt. He would do this, no matter how foolhardy and dangerous it might be. He'd come too far to walk away now.

His hands were damp on the railings, but he got himself up the stairs and back inside through the door Jehan had left unlocked. He was grateful now that William paid so little regard to homely comforts. The lack of light was welcome. No candles, rushlights or cressets lined the hallway, just a blanket of darkness that wrapped itself around him as he edged forward. He was stealthy, light on his feet, and his steps were silent. He would make a better thief than Roger or Jehan, although it wasn't a role he'd play willingly. He reached the end of the corridor, directly above the kitchen where Roger had said the door to the room at the top of the house could be found. Rafi couldn't see. He ran his hands along the wall. No door. No gaps. There were footsteps though. Descending.

Rafi pressed himself flat against the wall and edged away from the direction of the noise. His hand felt something, solid and wooden. A table, with a covering. There was a bowl made out of something like pewter just in front of the table. It wobbled slightly, the noise like thunder in the silent corridor. Rafi ducked underneath the table, hoping the cloth and the darkness would keep him obscured.

A door opened just where he'd been standing. The hallway was lit dimly now from the light in the room above.

Stefan.

Stefan stopped by the table where, to Rafi's horror, he moved the bowl. Rafi winced. Stefan must have heard him just now.

The bowl moved again, a scraping noise as if it were being pushed across the corridor. Then the sound of clothes being adjusted – a belt being loosened. Rafi prepared to take flight, doubting he would get far even if he did. But if Stefan were readying his sword, there was no other choice.

There was splashing, a gentle trickling against pewter as Stefan relieved himself into the bowl with a sigh. Rafi held his breath.

Jesu, this was taking forever. How much had Stefan had to drink?

At last Stefan took the stairway back down to the buttery and Rafi gasped loudly, his breath bursting out of him. A few seconds later and they'd have come face to face. At least he knew William was still downstairs. He didn't know, however, if Stefan would come back.

The light from the doorway now marked his path. A narrow stairway taking him into William's lair. There could be something up there that gave away William's plans, proved his bad faith and finally forced Hugh to act. But there was only one way up and one way down. If Stefan came back, Rafi would be trapped.

It was worth it though. Worth it if it finished William off once and for all. Rafi pushed against the door and went up.

Candles held on metal spikes lit the room, scorch marks staining the walls. Tallow had fallen in globules on the floor. It didn't look as if the room had been cleaned for some time; it was untidy as well as dirty, like the rest of the house – from the rushes to the furniture to the cups and plates and hangings. The only servants Rafi had seen, bringing food from the kitchen, had melted away before the meal was finished. There were no women.

The smell of heated animal fat was unpleasant, but at least Rafi could see. There was little care here, but the furniture was very fine. A scarlet coverlet shot through with gold thread that hung half on, half off a plump feather mattress, sheets of fine Rennes linen, a walnut chest and shelves. The shelf was stacked with letters, some sealed, some open, some yet unsent. If there was anything here of use, he would find it.

Rafi's fingers flicked through the letters and scrolls, his eyes skimming the contents – household accounts, bills unpaid, complaints from a merchant in Salisbury for damage to his property, and then . . .

A letter from Arundel dated March, rejecting a plea for money. More beseeching, cajoling words in response, begging for a loan until Michaelmas. *When my fortune will be at hand.*

'Your brother's fortune,' whispered Rafi, noting that the letter had never been sent. Arundel had made his intentions clear.

Rafi took the letter addressed to Arundel, and stuffed it inside his tunic. There was a note, in the same hand as the one sent to Adam. *I trust your lady wife enjoyed her gift.*

There was one last tattered piece of paper, beside the others, weighted down with a sticky goblet of sour wine. A list. All the members of Hugh's household, their names and their occupations.

Adam, apprentice. Raphael?

Of course, they'd not known Rafi had been employed by Le Cran when the list was made.

Cedric, apprentice. John, carter. Ned, stable hand, Ailith, maid.

At least twenty names, all the way up to Roger, Joan and Hugh. Some names were underlined.

There was an instruction at the top.

Mark their graves.

Adam, Ned, Raphael, Roger, Joan and Hugh.

Two apprentices and a stable hand – enough to sow fear in

the household and send the rest running. Roger – chief of Hugh's servants. Without him the fear would be less easy to contain. And Joan and Hugh. The entire Le Cran business would fall if Hugh was removed, and his heir with him.

This was what Rafi needed. This was William's intent, in his own hand. They had him now.

Rafi checked the shelves again in case he had missed anything that would help in his own search for answers. Down at the bottom was an applewood box, not big enough for correspondence. The lid had a raised section in the centre, inlaid with a diamond of oakwood and carved with flowers and acorns. It rested in Rafi's palm, small and light. Inside was a silver signet ring, face down in velvet padding. Gently, Rafi pulled it from its soft bed. The disc looked large enough to cover the lower half of the finger. He turned the band so that he could see the face of the ring.

ulligiS.

The word hit him in the guts.

'Steady,' he whispered. *Sigillu* was a common marking. It merely meant seal, that was all. He closed his eyes. There might be disappointment, or discovery. He didn't know which one he feared most.

Maman.

He needed her strength. But it was his own strength that had driven him here, his own courage and his love for her and Christophe. He would do this for both of them.

Rafi knew the curve and line of every mark, the position of the leaves, how the feet of the bird pointed forward. He would use his hands, not his eyes.

Gently, his fingers moved over the ring. He paused, catching his breath as he felt a tree. And then, at last, he felt the rest of the tree. And now the second bird, not just the rump, but the whole creature, same as the first one. And underneath those two, a third, all three identical, all with bumps under their feet. Not bumps. They were stones. He'd seen this motif before, on the pennant in

Minster Street. Stones held aloft in the claw of the bird spoke of watchfulness. Rafi almost didn't dare follow the words around the edge. He reached the letter 'S', where his thumb had always stopped, forever imagining the form the next letters would take. He had them now, in his hand. He did not have to guess anymore. He finally opened his eyes.

enarC sinoguH ulligiS
Sigillu Hugonis Crane
Seal of Hugh Crane.

The ring fell from his hand and clattered onto the floor where it rolled under the bed.

Thurstin. Thurstin had lied to him. But . . . Thurstin was Le Cran's clerk. Perhaps he'd lied out of loyalty.

Hugh Crane. The dying man had asked for the half to be returned to his father. Master Le Cran must be named after him. But it did not matter, this was all the proof he needed. The seal belonged to the family, the family the soldier had told him to find. It had to be him. No other pieces would fit so well.

It was Richard.

And William had killed him.

Rafi sank onto the rumpled bed and tried to stop shaking. Fifteen years, and he had ended up here. His mother, Christophe – murdered by a disgraced and banished son, a drunk. A man who had killed his own brother and would not hesitate to murder the last remaining one.

If only . . . if only he had not let go of Christophe's hand. If only he . . .

He could have been mistaken, but he thought he heard something. Slowly, he rose to his feet, alert now. There it was again. The whispered breathing and a foot on the stairs. He waited. There was a long pause but then it came again. Someone was climbing upwards. The footsteps were hesitant, but they kept coming.

William.

There was nowhere to hide. There was nowhere to go. No

hangings, no closet.

Rafi opened the shutters and stepped onto a small ledge. The night air came like a cold slap. It made him tremble, so much that he feared he might fall. The stables were so far below, built around a stone courtyard. If he fell, he would be killed. His stomach turned, but there was no other alternative. The footsteps had nearly reached the top of the stairs.

He pressed himself against the cold stone of the building thanking God for the moonlight. He'd left his cloak in the kitchen and longed for it now. Someone came to the window. He heard the high-pitched whistling noise. William.

'Who opened these bastard shutters?'

The whispering voice was so close. The voice of his mother's murderer.

The shutters were closed, rattling as William tried to hook the clasp securely for the night. Rafi was stuck now. He could neither go back inside nor stay here all night. He shuffled along the ledge, which worked its way around the whole of the top floor of the house. He bit his bottom lip and kept going, slowly sliding one foot along the ledge, his hands stretched out, feeling along the stone wall. He was no longer over the stable; he was near the rooms on the first floor, close to the corner of the building. There was a platform below, sticking out in front of one of the windows. Fifteen feet, he reckoned. Maybe a little more. Still far, but not as bad as the sheer drop outside William's room.

He didn't think he could do it. He was sure Adam would be exhilarated by the thought of adventure, as he was that night on the boat, sliding down the rope into the murky darkness. But had the captain not picked him up and forced him over the side, Rafi would never have left the *Lady Cecily* on his own.

There was no captain now.

If he died . . . if he fell, Rafi at least knew who had killed his mother. What he'd come here to find, he had found. What else was there?

And then, despite the cold and the fear, he knew. There *was* something. Someone.

Edith. Even if they couldn't be together, he could protect her from a distance, keep her safe if he could.

Angele Dei.

That night in the forest to here. Edith had his heart now. Always. He had to make it to the platform. He couldn't bear it if he never saw her face again.

'Well,' said Rafi to the air. 'This angel had better have good wings.'

If he could hang on to the side of the ledge, the fall would be shorter still. He edged along further, his legs hollow. He was above the platform now. He had just about enough room to turn so that his face was to the wall, then he slowly slid down until he was kneeling on the ledge. He would have to grip the base of it with his hands and pray that his arms could take his weight. The shelf was wide enough, but he couldn't dangle here for long.

He had no idea who was below, but he hoped it was Roger. He could still fall and break his neck or the platform might lead to one of the soldiers' rooms. But he couldn't go back. He would have to pray to every saint in heaven that it was Roger who found him.

He leaned forward, resting his weight on his elbows, and let his legs go over. The muscles in his upper arms began to feel the strain as he held his position for a few seconds, feet in mid-air.

Then he let go.

He bent his legs as he landed, but went over on his left arm, grazing his palm. The jolt sent a wave of pain through him, up his wrist and along his forearm. He could move it, but only just. His wrist felt the agony.

The platform was broader and more stable than the ledge. It would be possible to curl up in the corner for a few hours and wait until morning, trying to bite the pain down.

There were shutters on the wall here too. Roger had said his room was on the corner, but what if it was a different corner?

There were two on either side of the yard. He had no idea which one this was; he was disorientated. He could risk knocking, but if this wasn't Roger's room he might find himself in even worse trouble. He wriggled on his stomach towards the window and tried to peer in through the crack, but there was only a dim flickering inside, not enough to see. Apart from a shadow, which loomed up suddenly, blocking out what light there was. The shadow was moving towards him. Rafi rolled back against the wall. If the shutters opened outward, they might shield him.

They did open outwards, but they did not shield him. For the second time that day he was grateful for the sight of Roger.

'What the hell are you doing here?'

Roger reached for Rafi's arm to drag him inside and Rafi nearly fainted with the pain.

'Come, quickly. You look pale as a ghost.'

Another cold room, with unclean rushes. But a blanket, which Roger draped over him, and a cup of mead. Roger waited while Rafi sipped it, feeling the honey warmth slide down his throat and into his belly, calming him. He pulled the blanket tighter.

'I did . . . find something,' he said at last. He bit down on the rim of the cup. Even a blanket and some mead could not stop the sudden shaking that overcame him.

Roger took the rushlight from the wall and held it over Rafi's arm. 'In good time. Can you move it?'

'A little. It is my wrist.'

'But your arm, can you move your arm?'

Rafi twisted his arm gingerly, left and right.

'Let me see. Try not to cry out.'

Roger lifted Rafi's fingers, one by one. 'Not broken.' He put his hand lightly around Rafi's wrist and gently rotated. Rafi winced.

'Twisted.' Roger took the tapet from the end of the bed, ripping it in half. 'Hold still.' He bound Rafi's wrist. 'It will hurt in the morning.'

'More, you mean.'

251

Roger put the rushlight back and stood up. 'What on earth were you thinking?'

'I was in William's room when he decided to sober up and go to bed.'

'Jesu!'

'Indeed.'

'So you threw yourself out the window. I see.'

'I would have preferred to use the stairs but I fancied a change.'

Roger raised an eyebrow, then quickly moved towards the door, pressing his ear against the dark wood. He put his fingers to his lips.

Rafi couldn't hear anything but waited, nursing his wrist, which was throbbing violently.

'Our friend Fulke doing a final prowl before retiring. I expect the other one is on guard duty tonight.' Roger glanced down at Rafi's hand. 'You were lucky.'

'So much good fortune I barely know what to do with it.'

'Foolish boy.' Roger tilted his head towards the door again. 'Gone. Speak quietly and tell me.' He sat close.

'It is much worse than we thought. He ran out of money in March, for that is when he started writing begging letters to the earl for more. He won't last until September if he can't pay those two.'

'The letters were not kindly received?'

'No.' Rafi gestured to his tunic. 'I have them here.'

Roger nodded. 'Which is why he has grown more audacious.'

'But . . .' Rafi gritted his teeth as he accidentally hit his arm against the side of the cot. 'I said it was worse than we thought – it is worse than we could ever have imagined. There is a list. The names of everyone in Hugh's household with a mark by some of them, including the mistress.'

'Did you get it?'

'Yes.'

Roger smacked his fist into his palm. 'Then we have him. Now our master will act. Here, I will carry the documents. I have two good arms. You only have one. Besides, they wouldn't dare molest me. You, on the other hand . . .'

Rafi waited while Roger put the documents into a pouch hidden under his tunic then shook his head. 'But what more did he need? The last note I delivered mentioned the mistress, surely . . .?'

'Loyalty.' Roger pressed his ear against the door. 'He knows what William is like but from a distance he can ignore it. He would hesitate to move against his brother out of respect for his father's memory. But this is a clear threat, a direct threat to the lives of his wife and child. He will not hesitate now. You have done good work.'

'But surely William would hang for murder? The crimes could not go unnoticed.'

Roger didn't agree. 'Money can buy you a lot of justice and William would think he could use it to buy his way out of trouble. There are many who are envious of our master's wealth and would happily make a bargain with William. And slice up his land and property for themselves. William would be no match for them. He would risk it anyway. He is not the most . . . rational of men.'

Rafi had seen what happened when William was crossed.

Roger poured Rafi another cup of mead. 'Here, drink this down. It may help you sleep through the discomfort.'

Rafi drank, but slowly this time. Roger was watching him. 'I could not understand all you said to Jehan, but I guessed some of it. I am truly sorry.'

Rafi hid his face behind his cup. It would be difficult for Roger to see his expression clearly in the poor light, but his emotions were raw after all that had happened and some of it would be obvious.

Roger didn't pursue the matter. 'You should sleep, or try to. You did well, Dubois.' He rolled himself up in his cloak and lay inside the door. The loyal mastiff.

Rafi touched the locket around his neck as he always did before he went to sleep. The mystery was all but solved now, but the habit would be with him for the rest of his days.

He could hear Roger breathing, unevenly. Still awake. His expression of regret had been genuine, and Rafi was touched by it.

'What did he do to you?' Rafi wondered if he should have thought twice before asking, but there had been something in Roger's face when he had appeared from the buttery.

'It doesn't matter. It was in the past. Get some sleep, Dubois, and stop asking questions. No more talking.'

Edith had said, in the garden that day, that Roger treated Agnes like his own daughter. Maybe that was it. Roger's wife or sweetheart had fallen victim to William, like the many Jehan had hinted at. William's daughter, a by-blow, with Roger protecting her until she came of age. It would explain why Roger hated William so much. Where was Roger's wife now? Had she been killed, or died in childbirth? Only Roger knew the truth and Rafi doubted he would tell him.

No wonder Roger prowled around the abbey. The steward was protecting not only Agnes but also Hugh's reputation. Hugh couldn't possibly know. If Agnes was William's daughter, then she was Hugh's niece. Would Hugh leave her in an abbey? Or maybe he did know – perhaps Hugh was Agnes's mysterious benefactor. She was well looked after, well protected. It all suddenly made sense.

Rafi settled back. The mead had made him feel more relaxed and less rigid, but his arm was very sore. Roger had bound the wrist expertly, and it was held firm and secure, but the pain had gone right through him. He had to think; he had to decide what to do once he got back to Winchester.

It would seem that his quest was over. He had found a copy of his seal; he knew whose name was on it. But to be certain, he would ask Roger tomorrow, to make sure he had the name right. And if he was right, and that seal belonged to Hugh's father, then that would confirm Richard's identity.

How, how was Rafi ever going to explain this to his master? Roger had told Thurstin that Richard died in battle. It was what he would surely have told Hugh?

There was some solace in mourning a heroic death. But this? Slain by his brother in cold blood. It would shatter the memory into a thousand pieces.

But for Rafi, Richard had died trying to save a woman he did not know for one simple reason. He was an honourable man. There should be solace in that.

Sigillu Hugonis Crane.

Roger was wrong. It did matter. It would always matter. The past would never lie still.

Chapter 25

There was no sign of William when they rose at dawn the following morning, nor of Fulke or Stefan.

'You won't see William this side of noon,' said Jehan, ladling some barley porridge into their bowls. It was plain but warming and would keep them going until they reached Winchester.

'Aye,' grunted Roger, finishing his food and pushing the bowl away. 'Might as well make our way to the stable. The horses will not be brought round.'

'Godspeed, Writel.'

'We'll need it.'

They travelled back the same way they had come but Rafi struggled to keep up this time. He could ride, but not well, and his arm was injured. Roger must have realised because he slowed, and waited for him. He was his usual taciturn self again, grey clothes to match his demeanour. But Rafi had begun to reassess him. Yes, Roger had caused him pain and trouble, but he had also looked after him last night. It was Roger who had bound his arm, given him the blanket and gone without.

And then there was Agnes. If she was not Roger's daughter,

then she belonged to someone precious to him. Rafi had so many questions and each answer would, he hoped, shed new light on what he'd discovered in Salisbury.

'What happened at Crécy?' He addressed Roger's back so didn't see the man's expression. The growl told him enough.

'Did William fight too?'

Roger slowed to a gentle walk. 'Yes. But I was not his servant.'

'You were the servant of Richard Le Cran?'

'Oh, how you apprentices love to gossip.' They rode on a little further. 'Yes.'

'He died in battle?'

Roger tilted his face to the sky. 'Yes.'

'What happened?'

Roger wheeled the palfrey around sharply, his face grim. He rode back towards Rafi. Rafi felt a flicker of alarm. He'd gone too far. But then Roger let the rein drop into his lap and shook his head, then his shoulders sagged. 'Of course, you will be curious. You would have been what – five or six?'

Rafi waited.

'There is not much to tell. We were in the Prince of Wales's division, with Arundel. We were separated. Richard was a man at arms; I was a simple archer. We were in the vanguard so bore the brunt of the French charge. We held them off, and lost very few men, but still . . . we lost some. I saw him, on foot by then. William still had a horse. It was raining; there was mud, Richard slipped. I . . . did not see him again. That is all.'

Rafi rode on in silence, drawing level with Roger who kept adjusting his pace. It was cooler today, and Rafi was grateful that the sweltering heat of yesterday had passed. The spire was behind them. Rafi looked around a few times, but he was glad to turn his back on Salisbury.

'Wrist holding up?'

Rafi nodded. It wasn't holding up, it was sore, but there was nothing he could do about it.

Rafi opened his mouth, and Roger held up his hand. 'Your questions are becoming tiresome, Dubois.'

'I have but one more.'

'I said enough.'

'The answer need only be one word.'

'God's teeth, but you are vexatious! Say your piece, then, and be silent after.'

'What was the master's father called? What was his name?'

Roger glared at him. 'Is that it?'

Rafi nodded.

'Hugh. Now quit your babbling.'

Hugonis.

There was the proof. He had it now.

They reached Stockbridge, gently guiding the horses uphill. Rafi was sweating now. The effort of riding jogged his wrist no matter how well Roger had bound it. He held it limply in front of him, resting it on the palfrey's soft neck.

To his relief, Roger stopped them under some shade and pulled out a costrel filled with ale.

Rafi drank enough to wet his dry mouth, then handed the costrel back to Roger.

'I went to the kitchen.' He had gone with Cedric and Adam, to ask Nell about the rushes. 'Nell said that Mistress Joan would make the master merry again.'

Roger drank the remains of the ale and wiped his mouth. 'Aye. I believe she will.'

'I heard you in the church.'

'Did you now.'

'What you said about Mistress Joan, about her being a problem . . ?'

Roger rolled his eyes. 'You dolt. A problem in that she was in danger, and 'tis the danger that is the problem, not the mistress. Let that teach you to flap your ears where you should not!'

'Oh.' Rafi blushed.

Roger had said they wouldn't stop, but that was before it became apparent that Rafi was struggling to keep up. They were both silent. Rafi rested against the tree and tried to work his way through the web he was now caught in while Roger stood looking back at Salisbury, his arms folded. He too was deep in thought.

'I don't know where you are from,' said Roger finally, pulling the horses towards them and holding out the reins to Rafi. 'But there were many camp followers and women in farms and villages. I understood enough of what you said to Jehan. He killed her, you said. I got that much. From your age at the time, I would guess your mother.'

Roger was mounted now, holding Rafi's palfrey for him as he struggled into the saddle. 'I was never William's man but I will not allow any more harm to come to you. The family has wronged you – I have wronged you – but please, keep this from the master. He has found happiness again. Your mother . . . I will try to make amends. I know our master would want to, but he has borne enough of William's sins. It is the least I can do.'

They didn't speak again until they reached the same hill that Rafi and Adam had descended not much more than a week ago. Winchester lay before him once more. It looked very different now.

Rafi had one more question. 'William had a signet ring with what looked like a seal matrix on it. It was in a box . . .'

Roger turned. 'Did he now?'

'Three birds against a tree and shield. Are they . . .?'

Roger smiled. 'Yes, you asked about this before. Three cranes. Three brothers. The ring belonged to the master's father. We have not seen it since he died, a year or so after William came back from France. I expect William took it from his finger. It would not surprise me.'

'Why did you lie to me?'

Roger shook his head. 'The three birds were sundered when Richard fell. His father couldn't bear to look at it. Our master was broken-hearted. He placed the ring on his father's finger when he died, to bury with him. Your questions . . . you were opening a wound, Rafi. A wound that hasn't healed.'

The birds. Longer-limbed and more elegant than the birds on his own matrix. He must have been carrying an older, cruder copy all these years. The true matrix had been on the hand of the dead father. Three birds with one claw holding a stone aloft. Rafi understood the meaning. If the watchful crane fell asleep, his stone would drop and he would wake up. Always on guard, ever vigilant.

'Did you not wonder why I asked?'

'I saw that you were taken by the tapestry. I knew you were looking for clues to your mother's death. A bird is not such a rare symbol.'

'Why were you so insistent that I worked for you? That day . . . you clearly both thought I was a fool.'

'We thought you naïve, dangerously so. But no fool. Your master genuinely does appreciate your learning. And we wanted you to work for us because . . . we both suspected that William's men would come for you again, and it would be easier for us to protect you if you were within our household. As I have said – your master takes on his brother's sins and tries to right them.'

'Fine show of protecting me, letting me take a beating.'

Roger scratched his ear. 'Aye. I maybe could have stopped that. But to be honest, you'd been so irritating I thought you deserved it.'

'What in God's name!'

'But mainly, I wanted to keep an eye on you. You were trampling all over the place like a wild ox and leaving a mess everywhere you went.'

Roger flicked his reins, letting the horse guide them down the gentle hill that led to the Westgate. 'Well, at least we know now. The master gave up looking for that ring years ago. He never used it again after Richard died anyway. Was it in a small box, perchance, with acorns and leaves?'

'Yes. The very same.'

Perhaps Thurstin hadn't lied, then, if he'd become Le Cran's legal clerk just after Richard died. The seal would no longer have been in use.

Roger looked at him sternly. 'That box too belonged to his father. Well, William can keep it. Let it stay in Salisbury. It no longer matters.'

Chapter 26

But it did matter, more than anything. What was he to do? Where did his loyalty lie? With his master, whose wounds would be reopened if the circumstances of Richard's death were to come to light? Would it not be better to let the past die, to let it go?

But what of his loyalty to Richard, the man he'd prayed with and held on to as the life ebbed away? The man he'd made a promise to, the man who had tried to save his mother.

He would have to choose one or the other, between the living and the dead; either spare his master, or lay the wound raw.

And what of his heart? What of Edith? If the way was clear he would walk – no, run; he would run to her. Yet what could he say – that he would protect her, from a distance? That was no protection at all.

He loved her. She had been there with him that night on the ledge, his source of courage. He could offer her an escape, with her children. They could go anywhere. He had thought to go to Castile or Milan – well, why not with Edith? It was wrong; he knew it was wrong. He, of all people, understood the sanctity of rites spoken in the sight of God. She had a husband.

You cannot sunder a man from his wife.

Yet, at the thought of it, his blood pounded and he was filled with such hope, and a desire that shook him. It was as wrong to leave her in such a dire situation as it was to take her from it.

He would ask her.

Come away with me, Edith.

Roger had gone to Le Cran immediately after returning from Salisbury. Alone. The following day he dropped a bag of coins in Rafi's hand in the yard without saying a word. As Adam had always said, you could grow rich working for Le Cran if you were loyal and worked hard.

By noon, Rafi still hadn't decided what to do but his anger began to burn – anger at the injustice that allowed William to lie and cheat and hurt, and anger at himself for twisting and turning on whether he should stop it. Roger had spoken of family loyalty. William had shown none. If the list of names still wasn't enough to push Hugh to move against his brother, then the truth of Richard's death would surely be the final nail in William's coffin.

Le Cran would be at the guildhall today, but he would return for supper. Tonight, then. He would talk to Le Cran tonight and tell him everything.

Rafi sat in Joan's turret, finishing off the flaked lettering in her book, waiting for the hours to pass until he summoned the courage to face his master.

'Oh my. How dark the sky has become all of a sudden.' Joan put her embroidery down, frowning as she looked anxiously at the clouds.

'I will close the shutters, Mistress,' said the maid, Beth.

Rafi shook himself. He hadn't even noticed the light changing, he had been so absorbed in his thoughts. He quickly moved his desk back from the window and removed the book so as not to risk getting it wet.

'I can do it,' said Rafi.

The rain was blowing into the room now, the wind had picked

up. Rafi felt the spray on his face as he leaned out to pull the shutters tight. He revelled in the coolness of the breeze. It had been muggy all day, so that even moving from one side of the room to the other caused sweat to break out. He allowed a few more drops of rain fall onto his forehead, letting his gaze sweep down the length of the high street.

There she was, two children by her side and one in her arms, rushing along by the postern gate towards Colebrook. This was his chance – he had to tell her what was in his mind before he lost sight of her once more. He tied the shutters as fast as he could, his fingers clumsy, so clumsy.

'Rafi, are you—'

'Sorry, Mistress, I have to . . .' He shook his head dumbly at her, reached for his cloak and then fled, down the spiral stairs. She called after him, not angrily, but he didn't answer. He just ran as fast as he could, through the house, out along the lavender path.

He slid as he stepped into the street. In this rain his cloak would not keep the wet out for long and he rolled it under his arm. Through the Minstergate he ran, into the cathedral grounds and straight through the market. Everyone was running for shelter, the rain was heavy now, drenching the canopies that protected the stalls, the water pouring from them in a torrent.

He was at the postern gate. She had paused between the narrow houses that ran along the side of the Nunnaminster. She was gathering the children, ready to make a dash for Tanner Street, pressed hard against the wall to where the muddied path was still a little dry.

'Wait!'

She turned, her face wet. Leof was huddled against her chest, Simon and Tilly holding on to her skirt. Their clothes were so thin, his heart ached for them.

'No, don't come near.' She looked around, wide-eyed.

'Edith, I need to speak to you.'

She shook her head, her arms tightening around Leof.

'Edith. Let me at least give you this.' He held out the cloak.
'Keep away.'

'You will be drenched. Please.'

Her face tightened. 'I stole your money. I stole it. It was me.'

Rafi felt her words like a thorn in his heart. 'I do not believe you.'

'Believe me. Why else would I speak with you all those times, or . . . or walk in the marshland? You surely did not think I desired your company? I—'

'I don't know, Edith. But you did not do it so you could take the opportunity to rob me.'

'You were so easy to steal from.'

He nodded. 'Aye. That I was.'

She looked up. The first rumble of thunder had come. Leof started to cry.

'You can tell me to go away; you can tell me this is what you wish. You do not need to lie to make it so.'

She bowed her head. She was sobbing quietly.

'Edith, listen. Come with me, I can . . .' The clap of thunder was louder now, drowning out his words.

She shook her head. 'It is impossible. I cannot stay. We cannot stay.' Leof was still crying. 'You, and . . .' She glanced down at Tilly. 'There is danger unless I take the four of us away from here. Today. Tonight.'

'Then let me take you. If there is danger, then we can leave it behind.'

'I cannot do that to you. I do not have the right. I am not free.' She muffled a sob in Leof's hair.

'Edith, I . . .'

She took a step back. 'If it were possible then, for your own sake, I beg you.'

The rain was still coming and the wind had risen, stirring the clouds into an angry storm. The lightning flickered, the sour yellow light illuminating her suddenly. She was soaked through.

Rafi handed the cloak to Simon. The boy hesitated for a

moment and then took it, draping it around his mother's shoulders. Leof huddled under the soft brown folds.

'See, already you make better use of it than I. It is perfect for you, *n'est-ce pas?*'

Her eyes were wet. Rain mixed with tears. She tried to smile, her wimple flattened onto her head by the downpour, her hair, loose and untidy as ever, darkened by it. He would remember her like this always.

'I . . .' Her words were lost to him as the wind took them.

He closed the gap between them then. 'I would never leave your side, I would—'

She spoke softly. 'If I were free, then I would never leave yours.'

Rafi felt her hand rest lightly on his cheek for a moment. He covered it with his own, turned his lips to her palm.

'You are a good man, Raphael. Find someone to love. And be happy.'

She chivvied the children away, clinging onto Leof, the other two running ahead. The street was awash with mud; the brook had burst through the wooden drainage slats and ran like a flood out towards the Eastgate. The four of them crossed gingerly, skirts and feet darkened by the deluge. Simon turned once and waved shyly, but Edith kept moving ahead with Leof and Tilly. He knew in his heart that she meant what she had said. She was lost to him.

'I have already found someone to love,' he called as the rain and wind battered him.

But she could not hear him.

Chapter 27

The rain eased gradually, but the sky remained dark. One by one the apprentices came back to Minster Street from the shops and stalls where they had taken shelter. But not Adam. Supper came and went, but Rafi could not eat. Every time he closed his eyes he saw her, that last weak smile, her tears. He couldn't bear the thought of losing her. Surely she wouldn't leave on such a treacherous night. If she were on her own then maybe, but not with the children.

The curfew bell rang out. Still Adam had not returned. Rafi began to get worried, as did Cedric, who had seen Adam last.

'He went out on the master's business,' Cedric informed Rafi.

'Do you know where? Perhaps he has come to some harm. I could go and look for him if I knew where to start.'

Cedric shrugged. 'I don't know. The ghoul didn't say.'

Rafi narrowed his eyes. 'Thom? Why would the master ask him to pass instructions to Adam?'

'It did seem odd.' Cedric paled. 'But he was very convincing. And . . .'

'And?'

'I think Adam saw an opportunity to kick his arse for stealing Mistress Joan's dress.'

Rafi groaned. 'Assuming he *did* steal it! Oh Cedric, this is very bad. If they have got into a fight . . .'

Or if someone else has used Thom as bait.

Rafi ran to the kitchens. He looked in the buttery, in the pantry, in the cellar, where he found Nell. She'd seen Roger, yes. He was outside with Ned helping them secure the stabling for the horses, which had been blown across the yard by the wind.

Rafi thanked her and ran outside. He had no wish to alarm Ned, but he had to tell Roger what was going on.

'What is it?' Roger was instantly alert.

Rafi nodded towards Ned and shook his head, but Ned saw him.

'Well?' Ned let go of his barrow.

'Did you, or the master, ask Thom to deliver a message to Adam today?' asked Rafi.

'Thom?' Roger was scornful. 'I would sooner deliver a sack of shit to my own mother as a gift.'

Rafi's heart sank. 'Then Adam has been sent on a false errand and has not yet returned.'

'Then he will be in the nearest tavern,' said Ned.

Rafi and Roger looked at each other. Adam had been avoiding inns since he'd been attacked. Ned had not spoken to his brother for so long he was unaware of his changed habits.

'There may be no need for concern.' Roger spoke calmly now. 'It is only Thom making mischief. Probably wanted to lift Adam's purse and now they've fought.'

Rafi took a deep breath. 'I saw Thom from the mistress's room. Before we went to Salisbury.' He glanced briefly at Ned before addressing Roger again. 'He was talking to Stefan.'

'Jesu.' Roger blinked. 'Get back to the workshop. I will tell the master.'

Rafi stood firm. 'Let me help.'

'No.'

'But—'

'No!' Roger's face darkened. 'They are here. If they bring danger then you are in the path of it.'

'As are you.'

'Apprentices first. You said so yourself.' Roger was not going to back down.

'You ain't stopping me, though.' Ned kicked the barrow to one side and pulled a sleeveless jerkin over his shirt. 'I see from your faces that something's amiss. He's my brother. I'll go find him.'

Roger hesitated. 'Very well. Wait here.'

'Who is Stefan?' Ned took a pitchfork from behind the hay in the nearest stable. Like Adam he was built like a bear, but unlike his brother he had not grown soft. Ned worked outdoors, lifting and carrying. The sight of him with a pitchfork would frighten most sane people.

'A hired thug. He is here to make trouble for the master by—'

'By what?'

Rafi could not meet Ned's eye.

Roger came around from the side of the house, accompanied by the two men who had travelled ahead the day they had left for Salisbury. 'Hal and Gilbert. Hal, you and I will search together, we will go towards the Eastgate, and then south to Kingsgate. Ned, Gilbert – take the stretch to Westgate and then along the Northgate and down to the Durngate.'

Ned and Gilbert left immediately, Gilbert with a concealed blade, Ned with his fork.

'Go, Rafi,' said Roger. 'Go back to the workshop.'

'What is to stop me coming back out again after you have left?'

'That would be very selfish of you as we would then need to search for two of you.' Roger scowled. 'Do as I say. Think of the mistress – we'll need people here as well as searching for Adam.'

'Hal can do that. Look at him. If Fulke or Stefan come here, which of us do you think would put up a better fight of it?'

Roger's shoulders sagged. 'Damn you, Dubois. Very well. Come, but so help me if you don't stay close I'll have you hung up over the Westgate by your breeches. Hurry up.'

It didn't take long to find Adam. It was almost as if he were meant to be found. As Rafi and Roger reached the postern gate leading to the abbey, they saw the open door of the chantry chapel, flapping back and forth in the wind. Roger pulled at his belt.

'Damn!'

There was a figure standing by the chapel, a silent sentinel. Domneva.

Her dark eyes narrowed at the sight of Rafi and she took a step back.

'Sorry, Sister,' said Roger. 'My keys have gone. The keys to this damn . . . sorry . . . to this chapel.'

Domneva pointed at the open door, still staring at Rafi, then gestured downward.

'The charnel?' Roger frowned.

Sweet Jesu, surely not? Had they put Adam in the charnel house, with the bones of the dead?

VV.

It was engraved on the windowsill by Adam's bed. The ward against evil. How cruel, to hide him here.

Rafi pushed Roger aside and took the stairs, two at a time. It was such a small space, Adam was easy to spot. He'd been placed in the far corner, on his back. They'd arranged him so he was facing a wall of skulls, dozens of them piled high on shelves reaching up to the ceiling. He would have been terrified.

'Adam!' Rafi was on his knees by Adam's side. 'Adam!' He pressed his ear to Adam's chest.

'Is he . . .?'

The slightest breath, barely worth the name, but . . . 'Just. We need to get him back to the workshop.'

'Take his legs. I'll take the top half of him.' Roger had already lifted Adam's shoulders from the floor, dragging him towards the stairs.

Domneva had gone by the time Rafi and Roger got Adam out of the charnel house and onto the rain-soaked grass outside. It was an effort to pick him up between them once more. Their hands and clothes were so wet, and not just with rain. Roger's sleeves were marked red where he'd held Adam's shoulders. The wind had risen once more, sprinkles of rain landing gently on Rafi's hands and face. By the time they'd reached Minster Street, the sprinkles had turned to heavy drops. Adam's hair was a matted mess of blood, the rain smearing his face like crimson wash. Rafi's fingers kept slipping on Adam's breeches, one leg freeing itself from his grasp as they nearly fell over the threshold.

Ned had returned already, his shirt discarded over a chair, a pool of water forming beneath. He crossed himself as Adam was brought inside.

'Onto the bed, quickly,' Roger ordered, as he and Rafi laid Adam gently on the mattress.

Ned stayed close, his hands over his brother's.

'Raise the hue and cry!' ordered Roger. 'Gilbert, Hal – quickly! And find Mistress Edith.' Roger glanced across at Rafi. 'He needs help. The apothecary is too ill to call.'

The silent guards melted away into the night. They would head towards the Eastgate and call out the alderman. There would be a search party now. Whoever did this would be hunted.

They wouldn't be found. They'd be long gone by now. And Edith would not come. Why did Roger not call for a surgeon, if the apothecary was indisposed?

The light flickered from the torch attached to the holder in the wall, casting faint shadows over Adam's pale and sickly face and the top of his shirt. Rafi leaned forward. What was this? Something yellow. Yes, it was yellow, bright yellow cloth.

Rafi moved closer, kneeling beside Ned and pushing Adam's shirt open at the neck just a little bit. He pulled on the cloth, which gave itself up easily.

'Cedric?'

Cedric shuffled forward and peered at the thing in Rafi's hand. He gasped. 'That is part of the mistress's dress!'

'You two will have some explaining to do later,' growled Roger.

The snippet of dress had been cut crudely and sewn onto a piece of stuffed linen resembling the form of a woman. A plain doll like one would give to a child, extravagantly dressed with expensive fabric. The doll had a swollen belly, the intention clear. Joan's dress on a mannikin of her pregnant body. There was a note tucked into the bodice, but the rain had washed the words away, and the paper was a sodden mess. But they didn't need a note to tell them that this was a message in itself.

I trust your lady wife enjoyed her gift.

It was Adam. The gift of the doll was to be delivered on Adam's corpse. Adam was the messenger.

Nuntius.

'Where was he?' asked Ned.

'Under the chantry chapel.'

'Under? You mean . . .'

Rafi nodded. 'In the charnel house.'

'How did they get the key – it's always locked, is it not?' Cedric was clutching the doll, almost in tears.

'Mine went missing this morning,' said Roger. 'The abbey chaplain has one, as does the abbess, and I have the third. Or I did.'

This morning. When Thom had been here to pass on the master's non-existent instructions. He had taken the key, then entered the abbey grounds. It would have been quieter than usual because of the rain, and the darkness of the clouds all day would have given him some cover. He'd either unlocked the chapel himself, or left the key somewhere it could be easily found by his new friends – Stefan and Fulke.

'He has gone too far this time,' muttered Roger.

How much did they pay him? Rafi wondered. Or had Stefan

used his fists as persuasion?

Adam opened his eyes. He couldn't move his head, but he could see his brother. 'It hurts.'

Ned leaned over him. 'I am here now!'

'Ned . . . I am so sorry.'

Ned held his brother's hand fast.

'I didn't love her enough. But you, you always did. I deserve this.'

'Nay, you do not.' Ned stroked his brother's bloody forehead. 'Is no matter. We both love you, and Judith will . . .' Ned bowed his head, tears falling onto Adam's bruised neck and shoulder.

Rafi didn't turn when the door opened. She had come. If she'd planned to leave tonight the rain must have stopped her; perhaps she had left the children with her sister for one last night. He was keenly aware of her standing behind him. He tried to focus on Adam and Ned, but he saw only her. The hem of her dress brushed the floor beside him as gently as her hand had brushed his cheek only a few hours ago.

He gave up his place to her at Adam's side. It was painful, being in such a confined space, not able to speak to her. She smelled of rain and faint traces of warm spice. Like home, long ago, a tiny kitchen full of nourishment and safety and love. He'd never longed for anything so much.

She sat by Adam, and her face tightened as she opened his shirt and ripped at his sleeve. The stab wound was deep, slicing from left shoulder to just above the left breast. They had meant to kill him. Edith took a deep breath then removed the sacking from the bag that protected her medicines.

She asked for linen cloths, wine and warm water, and once Cedric had brought them to her the room hushed as she worked. Edith cleaned the wound carefully with wine while yarrow soaked in the water. When she was satisfied that the wound was clean, she took the yarrow from the bowl and pressed it into the place where the knife had entered the flesh. The linen cloth she used as binding. She washed Adam's face and dampened his hair, the blood staining the pillow beneath him.

Ned kneeled on the floor, his hand still holding that of his brother.

'Can you lift his head?'

Gently, Ned put his arm around Adam, trying not to disturb the bandage that Edith had wrapped around his arm and neck. She had a small bottle with a lip. She encouraged Adam to drink, but it was difficult. Even with Ned taking his weight, holding his head up was painful for him.

The dark liquid went down, though. She nodded when it had all gone.

'Valerian,' she said. 'It will help you sleep.'

She got up. Roger pulled her to one side. 'Will he live?'

'How long was he untended?'

Roger raised his hands. 'A few hours . . . I cannot be sure.'

Edith looked back at Adam, her face grave. 'He is young and strong, but if there is corruption . . . The wound is deep at the shoulder. If it suppurates, the yarrow will draw it out, but it must be applied every day. Warm it in water as I have done, and press it into the flesh. You had better pray that you found him in time.' She put her arm through her basket. 'I must go.'

'Wait.' Roger stepped forward. 'Hal will escort you home.'

She tilted her head. 'I . . . am not going home.'

'Your children?' Roger frowned.

'Are in the infirmary.'

Rafi saw her half turn towards him but then change her mind.

'They are well?' He shouldn't ask.

She turned now, her green eyes on his. 'They are well.'

Roger gestured to Hal. 'Do not let her go alone.'

She shook her head. 'I will come to no harm. It's just a short walk.' But Hal followed her and wouldn't let her go by herself.

'Go as well,' said Roger immediately the door had closed. 'Speak to her as you must, stay in sight of Hal and do not return here alone. Stay together.'

'Why are you—'

'Take an opportunity when it is offered, Dubois, and do not question why.'

But the opportunity didn't materialise.

'Rafi, Rafi.' It was Adam, his voice weak.

Rafi's hand was on the metal ring of the door. He began to turn it.

'I am . . . I need you to say the words. Remember, you promised me if I was dying, you would say the words.'

Rafi pressed his forehead against the heavy oak door. He had to leave now if he was to catch her.

'I beg you . . .' The voice was fading.

Rafi dropped the handle.

He was not a priest and had never become a monk, but he had seen the rite performed before and he did what he could. There was a cross above the fireplace, and some oil in one of the cressets. It seemed to comfort Adam who fell into a deep sleep once Rafi had finished.

Ned was given two straw mattresses, which were laid on top of each other beside Adam's bed. He settled himself there and would not be moved, even when offered a more comfortable cot on a frame on the other side of the room.

Rafi sat on his bed, knees drawn up under his chin, back against the wall. It was too late. He had missed her. If Adam had not called, what would he have done? Her children well, but in the infirmary, at this time of the evening? Had Thom hurt one of them? The questions came fast, and he could answer none of them, and he had lost his chance to ask.

Hal and Gilbert had gone back to the main house to await further instructions from their master, and there were other servants and a new hound, which lay on a soft rug outside the Le Cran bedroom. Joan was well guarded. And Rafi had learned that Ailith and the baby were with her.

Roger, Cedric and Rafi didn't speak or even look at each other. They had retreated to their own corners of the workshop, deep in thought. Roger did not go back to his private room but stayed with the apprentices. He had taken the doll and thrown it in the fire, watching it burn.

Adam's breathing steadied as he slept, but Rafi grew more and more angry in his corner. How much more pain was William going to inflict? One brother dead and another besieged in his own home, his wife in danger. Marianne, Christophe and now Adam.

Rafi retrieved his painting from beneath the bed, the colours dim in the poor light. Edith was lost to him. His mother was lost to him. Maybe Adam would die. There was nothing left to lose now. So be it.

He put the painting in some sacking, noting that Roger had dropped off beside the fire, his head drooping. Cedric was curled on his cot with his face towards the wall, sniffing every so often. Ned was awake but fully focused on his brother.

They didn't see him leave. The yard was empty and the rain was nothing more than a hard drizzle. He walked along Minster Street and out onto the high street, turning right towards the Eastgate. He could see the outline of the abbey, hear the rush of the Itchen as it ran past the city wall. The stone towers loomed up into the moonlit sky, deep blue-grey. There was little light from inside, but although the moon was beginning to wane, it was still bright, a poacher's moon, or it would be when the rain clouds finally scudded away. It was enough to guide him around the side of Colebrook Street.

He climbed onto the abbey wall, around the back of a house, shinning onto the tiled roof, praying he wouldn't dislodge one and alert someone inside. From there, he jumped down inside the wall that skirted the Nunnaminster.

He should not be here. This was a violation, and he trembled at the thought of what he was doing.

The storm had wreaked havoc. The ground was slippery. Great

drops of rain still shook from the leaves as he passed. He pressed his painting close to his chest.

He knocked on the infirmary door. A scurry of movement inside, and then a small peephole opened. It was Domneva. She blinked in disbelief and then her dark eyes grew wide. She must be horrified. But he couldn't leave without a word.

'I must speak to Edith.'

Domneva shook her head.

'I know she is in there.' He didn't care how desperate he sounded.

'Please, you must go.' Edith was just inside the door now, her voice stricken.

'I know, and I am going. But I have to leave you something. I will place it against the door.'

'Where . . . Where are you going?'

Why would she ask if she didn't care? He stared at the door, willing it to open.

'To do what I should have done in Salisbury. I found him, Edith, and I walked away. I've spent too many years playing safe, and because of me, Adam is . . .'

It was his fault. It was all his fault. He should have told Le Cran earlier; he should have gone to him as soon as they got back from Salisbury instead of prevaricating like he always did. They could have secured the drapery sooner, made sure all the apprentices were indoors, warned them. But he had not and now he had to make amends.

'I am going to finish this, Edith.'

He heard her sob. She was close to the door. Only a piece of wood separated them.

'Don't worry, my dearest Edith. I run very fast and they'll never catch me.' He heard her sob even more and pressed his lips to the cold wood.

'You told me to find somebody to love. Well, that is at least one thing I have managed to do.'

277

He pushed the painting against the door. 'Sister Domneva, please look after her.'

The nun did not answer and he did not expect her to. His behaviour had been unforgivable.

He knew where he could slip through the Westgate; Raymond the saddler had told him, and not only that, had told him where the stable was. Rafi slithered out, a slim, dark shape sliding down a bank and scrabbling up the other side, wincing whenever he jogged his injured arm. Raymond's grey mare was tethered in a dilapidated barn, near an even more dilapidated hut. Shushing the animal as best he could, he led her gently away from the city, towards the Stockbridge road.

There were trees to give him cover almost immediately, but he didn't go in too deep. Even with moonlight, the leaves closed in and he could not see his way, and the ground was wet and treacherous. He would keep near the edge of the path, ready to turn into the woods if he had to.

He would follow the road west to Salisbury.

Chapter 28

Edith pressed her palm against the door long after Rafi had gone. Leof and Tilly were sleeping in two of the beds usually reserved for Domneva's patients. Simon was awake, watching his mother guardedly. When she finally sat by his bed and dried her tears, he pressed his hand silently into hers.

Domneva had seemed frozen while Rafi had been outside but now turned her attention back to the former cellaress Sister Eleanor, who lay in a bed at the farthest end of the infirmary. Because of the gravity of Eleanor's condition, Domneva had not remained in the abbey after compline and thus, when Edith had battered on the door, she had been there to let her in.

Edith had been so grateful to see Domneva's face. She had not wanted to run to the abbey first, but had come here to the infirmary where she felt safer. The door was locked with a key and an iron bar, and the exit at the other end, where Eleanor lay, led directly into the abbey. It, too, was locked. The keys hung on a belt at Domneva's waist.

Domneva had taken one look at Edith before admitting her, ushering the children in and shushing them so as not to wake the patient. She had put her hand against Edith's bruised cheek.

'What are you going to do?'

'Ailith's mother. She will take us for a few days. If the storm had not broken we would be there now, but the river has burst its banks; we can't get across the marshes. We can't walk through the high street in case . . . in case Thom sees us.' Edith gestured towards the two younger children. 'It was all planned, everything. We had somewhere to go, somewhere ready, and then the storm and . . . he came back just as we were about to leave.' She began to sob and gulp. All that planning, anticipation and dread, all had come to naught because the storm had defeated her.

Domneva put her arm around Edith and gently guided her to one of the beds. Taking a blanket, she wrapped it around Edith's shoulders and began to rub some warmth into her shivering body.

'He burned everything, Sister, and then he left again. He thinks we are still in the cottage. He will come looking . . .' Edith shivered.

'He will not find you.'

'He didn't destroy everything. Rafi gave us . . .' She closed her eyes and saw his face. The same dark hair, the same earnest eyes she'd seen when he had first walked past the stall. Then, he had been like Adam's pet, walking through the market as if he owed everyone an apology. She put her hand to her cheek, the hand he had kissed a few hours earlier. Now, he was as earnest as before, as kind, but she had seen his love. He had asked her to come away with him – how he'd changed, that he would dare to ask. His love was as fierce as hers. She had seen it in him.

'The cloak?' asked Domneva.

Edith nodded. She'd hidden it in a store barrel and Thom had not found it.

She rummaged under her skirts, ripping open a secret pocket sewn into her kirtle. 'And this.' She held her palm out to Domneva who raised her eyebrows.

A pearl.

They had been staring at the pearl, the key to Edith's freedom, when Rafi had knocked on the door. And now he'd gone.

She'd lost him.

A blast of fresh air lifted the hangings on the window shutters as Domneva pulled the door open. The sacking fell onto the floor, the top of the painting revealing itself at the neck of the parcel. Domneva took it out, carefully, a small square of parchment hammered onto a thin piece of timber.

Edith watched in silence as the nun's eyes ran over the drawing in her hands. The only sound came from Eleanor, her breathing laboured. Tilly and Leof still slept peacefully in their beds. She was used to silence from Domneva, nevertheless she was taken aback by the intensity of the nun's eyes. Glancing at the worktop, Edith saw the pot of valerian she'd borrowed for Adam still open on a dish, and a clay pot filled with crushed henbane. She pushed it to the furthest reaches of the table. It would not do if Tilly or Leof put their curious fingers in it.

Domneva turned the painting round, thrusting it into Edith's hands.

'Oh!' Edith gasped. It was a picture of her. How could this be? She looked happy and calm and somehow bright. If this was how he saw her . . .

'I'm not like this.' The tears blurred her eyes.

'You are,' said Domneva. 'You do not see it. But he does.'

'I am not.'

Domneva sighed. 'It is there. This is what you are.' She paused. 'Do you love the boy?'

Edith nodded miserably. 'Truly, I do.' Simon held her hand tighter.

The painting. She could barely hold it. How had she gone from that woman, to where she was now? She turned her head so that Simon would not see her cry again and the painting slipped from her hand.

Domneva reached forward to grab it as it fell face down towards the floor. She frowned, staring at the back of the painting, at the plain wood. She held it in front of her face as if looking hard into a mirror.

'What is it?' Edith started forward. The nun looked as if she'd seen a ghost.

'RD.' Domneva held it towards Edith. There were the initials, signed with a flourish.

'Yes. That is his name.'

'RD.' Domneva repeated, and then took a three-legged stool from under the worktop, sat heavily on it and placed the drawing on the table. Face down. She held her palm over the letters.

'Are you well, Sister?'

Domneva closed her eyes. 'What is RD?'

Edith was confused now. 'His name.'

'His full name.'

Edith was beginning to grow concerned for Domneva who had turned a deathly shade of white. The black-clad nun now had both her palms on the board. She sat like a statue at the table, the place where she held command, mixing, pounding, teaching, healing. She'd been rendered powerless by the sight of those two letters.

'It is Rafi . . .' Edith corrected herself. 'No, sorry. Raphael. Raphael Dubois.'

Edith was taken aback by what happened next. At first, Domneva simply clasped her hands in her lap and said nothing. And then the hands came up to her veil, which she unclasped and removed very gently, leaving nothing but a white linen cap, which fastened under her chin. This, too she removed.

She looked so young to Edith. The veil and the uniform of a nun aged her, and even though it had always been obvious from her skin and the brightness of her eyes that she was younger than she seemed, Edith had always viewed her as someone like Nell – much older, motherly. A taciturn woman in a dark, shuttered building who spoke little and had a capacity for healing greater than any surgeon. And she was so beautiful.

Beautiful and familiar.

Edith felt a chill. Something was happening; the night had burst open and was falling in on them both.

Or was it the knocking on the door, as someone pounded the timber with his fists.

Domneva roused herself and went to the peephole. 'Stop. There are sick people here.'

Edith could hear Roger's voice. Frantic. 'Where is he? Where is that fool of a boy?'

'Not here.'

Edith was unprepared for Domneva opening the door and allowing Roger to enter. A man, in the infirmary this late, with a guard. The abbess would be horrified when she found out, as she surely would. Roger had keys, of course he had keys. He looked after the chantry and collected rents from some of the houses that backed onto the abbey. But even so, it was after compline; the doors were closed. He should not be here.

Roger stared at Domneva, at her bare head and short cropped brown hair. He opened his mouth, but no words came.

'You have to find him. You have to find him and bring him back here,' said Domneva.

He jolted back to the present. 'I would if I knew where he was.'

'He's gone back to Salisbury,' said Edith.

Roger groaned. 'On foot?'

Edith nodded.

'He won't get far then.'

'No, he won't,' said Domneva. 'Send him,' she nodded at Gilbert.

Gilbert was at the door immediately, his hand on the latch. As Roger turned to follow, Domneva stood in front of him, blocking his passage. 'No.'

Gilbert waited. Roger nodded at him over Domneva's head. 'Find him. By all that is holy, find him.'

The breeze swept in as Gilbert closed the door behind him. Roger drew the bolt across, his expression grave.

'The truth now, Roger.'

Edith sat on her hands. It was so. The sky really was going to fall in on them all.

'Sister, I don't think . . .' Roger glanced at Edith.

'What did he look like, the boy in the clearing?'

Edith took a sharp breath.

'I . . ?'

'No, you can tell me. The truth. Do not hold back.'

'I can't . . .' Roger clung to the worktop.

He is falling, thought Edith. He is falling. We all are.

'You can and you will. Everything.' Domneva was relentless.

'Domneva . . .'

'Was he fair, dark?'

Roger dropped his head. 'It was hard to tell.'

'His injuries were so bad?'

Roger's knuckles were white. 'Yes. I'm sorry. I didn't want to look . . . and it was dark.'

'Then you can tell me if he was big, or small. Plump, like a goose, or slender like an ermine?'

'A goose, I suppose. More goose than ermine. You never asked me.' Roger looked as if he were about to weep. 'Why are you asking me now?'

'I never asked you because you gave me this.' Domneva drew a piece of cloth from underneath her dress, a small square held with brown cord.

It was a scapular.

'My son wore this and never took it off. He said he was too scared to take it off in case something bad happened to him.'

'I'm sorry,' said Roger.

'But he was always so much braver than he believed himself to be. Always. Otherwise, he would have kept it with him that night. But he must have given it up, given it to someone less brave.'

Roger looked up, realisation dawning.

Domneva smiled and placed her hand on his. 'What is my name, Roger?'

'You never told me. You didn't speak for months. And then we came here and you were Domneva.' Roger sat heavily on the stool at the end of the worktable.

Domneva nodded towards Edith. 'I think she knows.'

Roger's face was anguished. Edith knew why. He had unwittingly let Domneva live a lie for fifteen years and had only just found out what he had done.

Edith shook her head. 'You say it, Domneva. It is your name. You say it.'

Domneva took both of Roger's hands in hers and looked into his face as she stood over him. He was weeping where she was composed. *She is stronger than all of us,* thought Edith.

'My name is Marianne. Marianne Dubois.'

Chapter 29

It was not Gilbert; Gilbert had left when he had been bidden. So who was it, who was outside now? Roger roused himself and went to the peephole. Edith heard him cursing, regaining his sense of himself as he remembered he still had work to do before the night was over.

'One moment.' Roger stepped outside, holding the door slightly open behind him.

'Your husband is wandering around near the chantry. He appears to be in his cups. Oh, he's changed his mind. He is away to the Abbess Bridge. Perhaps he thinks he can swim over the river. Good luck to him. With good fortune on our side, he'll drown. The waters are high and fast after the storm.'

He turned then. 'I am sorry, Edith, I should not have said that.'

Edith looked at the children and shrugged. Even Simon was fast asleep now, his head lolling on her shoulder.

'Does he know you are here?'

'Who would tell him? The only people who know were in the workshop when you brought Adam in.'

'Good. Keep the door locked then, and let's hope he falls into a ditch.'

Roger tightened his belt. There was a small dagger tucked close to his hip.

As he opened the door, he looked over at Domneva. 'I will find Rafi. I am responsible for this.'

Domneva shook her head. 'You are not.'

'You thought he was dead because of me.'

'You saved us, Roger. If I had thought my son lived that night, I would have fought. I'd have fought to get back to him. Would William not have killed me for it?'

Roger looked down at his feet. He nodded. 'He does not like to be defied.'

She reached for his hand. 'Then do not blame yourself. But bring him back to me. He cannot have gone far. Does Gilbert have a mount?'

'Yes. But I do not. So I had better hurry and get one.' He raised her fingers to his lips and kissed them. She drew back. He bowed. 'Madam, Edith. I will bring him home.'

Domneva sprang into action as soon as Roger had gone. 'Edith, you can look after Sister Eleanor for me?'

'Yes, of course. But where are you going?'

'I need to see Mother Molins. She will want to know of Sister Eleanor's condition and will also have questions of me. I do not think your husband's presence will have gone unnoticed, nor that of Roger. I will only be gone a short while.'

'Please be careful.'

Domneva tried to smile. 'It is only a short distance, n'est-ce pas?'

Edith stared at her.

Domneva replaced the cap and veil, fastening them quickly under her chin, the white cap hidden under the folds of black, her face as good as hidden too. Leaning down she took a small bottle from a rack under the dispensary table. Ale, thought Edith, mead?

'I shall bring this to Mother Molins.' Domneva glanced over at Sister Eleanor. 'How do you think she is? Go see.'

Edith laid Simon gently on the cot and then moved towards the nun, whose wrinkled face was like wax against the pillow. Eleanor's breathing had calmed and she looked restful. She would last the night, but maybe not for much longer than that.

'Lock the door after me.'

Domneva clutched the bottle to her chest, the veil fully secured now. She was a nun again; the striking woman had been replaced by an anonymous matron.

'Edith, tell me once more. Do you love him?'

'Yes.'

Domneva paused. 'The plants.'

Edith tilted her head, confused.

'It was me. I watched that day, when you were in the garden. I saw what was happening. I feared for you. So I dug them up, to keep him away.'

Edith had nothing to say. Nothing could shock her anymore.

'We will plant them again, and they will grow.'

After Domneva had left, Edith pulled the coverlet over Eleanor and went back to sit with her children. She had placed Simon beside Tilly and she had snuggled against him in her sleep. Edith stroked his cheek. Her children. And Will's. How proud he would have been of them, never complaining, kind to each other and obedient, except perhaps Leof who got away with more mischief than the other two.

How had Domneva not recognised her own son? Though if she believed him to be dead, she would not be looking for him. Edith remembered now that he'd never come into the infirmary and Domneva had never strayed into the garden when he was there. Perhaps he'd reminded her of something lost, but that was all.

There was no sound from outside now; even the dripping from the leaves had ceased. It might be lively on the high street, in the taverns and inns, even after the curfew bell, but in there, in the sanctuary of the Nunnaminster, all was calm. Edith looked around absently. The dispensary worktable was clear, the dish and cup she had pushed away earlier were nowhere to be seen. And Domneva had not left through the door to the abbey, which would be the quickest route to Mother Molins.

She had gone outside.

Edith's stomach began to churn and bubble; her mind whirred. The sky had further to fall this night.

She lay on the cot beside Leof, calm now. She could see the painting from here, propped up against the stool. The cloak Rafi had given her, which had been drenched earlier, was hanging on a peg near where Domneva kept her gardening gauntlets and cutters, dripping gently onto a piece of sacking on the floor. She glanced once more at the dispensary table to make sure, then she closed her eyes, still awake, keeping vigil for Eleanor. And for Rafi.

The pot of henbane had gone.

Chapter 30

Thom was relieving himself in the pond when Domneva found him. He sullied everything he touched, even the water the nuns used for washing clothes and making ale. She was disgusted by him. She would be glad to be rid of him.

He was so drunk he didn't see her approach. She could have pushed him into the pond easily enough, but she wanted to be absolutely sure. He heard her as soon as she pulled the stopper out of the bottle, a noise he recognised only too well.

'What're you doing here, you foul witch?'

She edged closer towards the pond.

It was deep enough and big enough for ducks to nest there, ducks that Leof had played with only a few days ago. Leof and Agnes. And in the garden that day, just over the wall, Edith and Raphael. Her son, only she hadn't known it then. She had felt something though, when she looked at him. At the time she'd thought it was fear; the two of them had edged closer and closer as the afternoon had worn on. They had been reckless. Edith and Raphael, heads bent, hands hard at work. Hearts working harder. She'd seen it.

When he'd stared at her from a distance, she'd felt another kind of fear. She'd thought she was going mad.

She was at the very edge of the pond now. The water lapped at her hem. No one would notice anything amiss when she returned to the abbey; the ground was already so wet.

As murders went, it was easy. She didn't need to say a word. He saw the bottle in her hand and took it for ale. The henbane acted almost immediately, it was so potent.

The convulsions lasted only a few minutes and then he was gone.

The ground was wet and slippery and it was easy to push him so that his face rested in the water.

She removed the poison bottle and reattached it to her belt, then took a second one, which she opened, spilling half the contents and leaving it lying on its side near Thom's clawed hand. Weak ale and valerian. What a shame that she'd lost it on her way to Mother Molins's room. If only she hadn't gone into the grounds to get some fresh air instead of going through the passage at the back of the infirmary. A terrible mistake, but the ground was treacherous and she must have dropped the remedy when she slipped.

A tragic accident. They'd pray for his soul in the abbey.

She had her own prayer, here and now.

'One less bastard to hurt a woman again.'

She hoped her words followed him to hell.

Chapter 31

Rafi emerged from dense, damp woodland. Across the open stretch of farmland before him rose the faint outline of a cathedral spire lit ghost-grey by the moon. Salisbury. The sky was so clear he could hardly believe the storm that had battered Winchester only a short time ago. He hadn't stopped once since he'd slithered through the city wall and stolen Raymond's horse. The hours had passed without him noticing.

He was grateful to reach more enclosed space as he rode down to Odstock. The approach to Le Cran's manor was hemmed in by trees and dark places, like a forest from his past.

The sodden earth silenced his footsteps as he dismounted and led Raymond's horse as close to the entrance as he dared. Goat willow, wych elm, hawthorn; they smelled fresh and alive. He slipped as he went, stumbling in the mud and tripping over the gnarled roots of oaks that pushed through the earth like thick snakes slithering one over the other. It would not do to fall. He would need to tread more carefully.

He pulled his hood forward to cover as much of his face as he could. He would be a shadow in shadow, under the leaves as he had been all those years ago. The misericord was tucked into his boot, hard against the cloth of his leggings. He thanked Le Cran now for forcing him to take it. A paintbrush was a fine thing, but it was useless here where none could help him if he were waylaid.

As the breeze rifled through the trees Rafi heard a sound. An animal? A fox, or maybe a screech owl. He waited for a few moments but all remained quiet. He walked more slowly, finally reaching the very edge of the wall that opened into the manor courtyard. Moonlight was gradually being replaced by grainy pre-dawn light. He had to get inside fast before the household awoke. He tethered Raymond's horse to a chain loop hammered into the outer wall. Good. He hadn't wanted to bring the beast inside. He leaned his head against the animal's neck, not that such a gesture could make up for the indignity of being dragged out of a warm shelter and forced to canter cross country on what was probably a fool's errand.

Then the noise came again. It was human. A muffled voice, then a thud, then silence.

Rafi pressed his back against the wall. What the hell had made that noise? It was silent again, eerily silent. Perhaps it had been the stable hand, tripping over something. Or maybe Jehan, emptying slops from the kitchen. It was unlikely this early, especially in a household that seemed to rise late. But not impossible. He waited, listened. All was still. Another step and he'd be in the open. He would need to make a decision soon; he couldn't stand here forever. He'd have to either make a dash to the kitchen where he hoped to find Jehan, or go home.

He closed his eyes and prayed for courage as Raymond's horse lifted her head. The movement raised the metal ring, which fell back against the stone wall. Rafi held his breath; still no sound came from the courtyard. If anyone had been there, they must have gone.

Rafi didn't even have time to gasp as a leather-clad hand pulled at his arm while another clamped tightly over his mouth and nose;

no time to struggle as Fulke's arms encircled him from behind.

'Well, well. We meet again.'

Rafi couldn't reach for his dagger. He could barely breathe. If his mouth and nostrils were covered for much longer . . .

The sky began to spin as he looked up, swirling into a blurred circle of brightness. He needed to breathe.

Fulke lifted his hand from Rafi's mouth and instead jerked both his arms back. Rafi feared they'd be torn from their sockets. His lungs screamed as he gulped for air. Fulke pushed him. His knee smashed onto a sharp rock and he cried out.

'I didn't expect to get two chickens in a row,' said Fulke. 'We were going to pluck you one by one, space you out a bit so you panicked in the coop, but no matter.'

Fulke tugged Rafi's hair, forcing his head up. 'You're not going to run away, are you? You'd miss all the fun. The stage is already set, after all. We weren't expecting an audience, but here you are.'

There was nowhere else Rafi could look. Fulke had twisted his head towards the corner of the stable yard. There was a man lying on his side, hands tied behind his back, his words silenced by a horse's bit that had been rammed into his mouth.

William Le Cran.

Sweet Jesu!

'Leave him to me.'

There was a hand on the neck of Rafi's surcoat, pulling it tight, pulling him to his feet. Rafi was again struggling for breath. He couldn't put his weight on his leg; his knee was shattered. He screamed and was thrown to the ground. His eyes travelled up to the heavens, into the face of his tormentor.

Stefan. He walked in a circle around Rafi and then squatted in front of him, just like he had in that alley in Winchester.

Stefan leaned in. 'You should have gone back to Ghent.'

Rafi didn't need to ask why. He had seen his own name on the list.

'Why are you here?' Stefan narrowed his eyes.

294

'I . . .'

Stefan pressed a fist into Rafi's knee. The pain was greater than anything he had felt before. Death itself could not feel worse than this.

'I don't really want to know. But it saves us a trip.' Stefan sighed and shook his head. 'The thing is, we've not been paid. Big brother William said he would reward us, but he hasn't.'

Stefan walked over to William's prostrate body. He kicked him in the stomach and William groaned. 'Thinking about it, I don't believe he ever will. All that trouble we went to with the fair-haired lout yesterday and what thanks did we get?' The boot went into William's face this time. 'So, we're going to have to ask his little brother to make good the debt. I don't think he will either, well, not without persuasion. Fulke?'

'What about this one?' Fulke had emerged from behind Rafi.

Stefan shrugged. 'He's not likely to run anywhere.'

Fulke lifted William so the man was on his knees. There was blood pouring from his head, and from his mouth where Stefan had kicked him, the steel of the bit cutting through his lips.

'Let's hear him beg.'

Fulke untied the leather straps that held the gag in William's mouth. William coughed, spat a mouthful of blood and tried to speak.

Stefan cupped his hand behind his ear. 'What's that? I can't hear you.'

William started to sob. Rafi cringed at the sound. He remembered William's voice near his ear, the night he'd been hiding on the ledge outside William's room. The stink of his breath and the stench of him.

'Shall we kill him, Raphael Dubois? I have the strangest of feelings that you came here to kill him yourself. A lot of people would be grateful to you. Writel, and little brother too, I suspect. What say you? You don't look like much of a killer but you could play the judge well enough.'

Rafi lay on his side in the dirt. He was in too much pain to care anymore. William was going to die regardless. Rafi had come here to do it after all, and had expected to be cut down in the process. That someone else was going to do the killing made no odds. Rafi knew his end would follow soon enough. If justice was to be served did it matter if it was by his hand, or Stefan's?

'Raph . . . Raphael. M . . . mercy.'

There was fear in William's voice. Fear in his tear-streaked and bloodied face. Rafi felt no pity for him.

'You showed no mercy to my mother, nor my cousin. You showed none to your own brother. You will get nothing from me.'

'Who are you? P . . . please! Raphael . . .'

'You have no right to say my name!'

Rafi heard his mother scream. He saw Christophe, lying on the forest floor. He saw his own hand, holding on to a dying man.

Adam said I would lie and cheat to find the man who took my mother.

But would he kill?

Why would he have come here if he hadn't thought himself capable of doing so?

'Well? Will you plead for him?'

Once more, Rafi thought of his mother. One last time he heard her before he answered Stefan. 'No.'

William began to struggle, blood spraying from his ruined mouth.

'Quite the ruthless one, aren't you?'

Rafi shook his head. 'You're going to do it anyway.'

'Yes. I do believe I am.'

William had no time to struggle further. His head was pulled back and the knife drawn across his neck before he would have even seen the blade. Face down in a pool of blood, he'd died more quickly than his brother. Less painfully. But there would be no *Angele Dei* this time.

My turn now.

'What shall we do with you, foolish boy?' Stefan wiped his knife across his thigh.

Foolish boy? How many times had Roger called him that?

'I think we should make an example of you, as we did with the fair-haired lout. Deliver your carcass in a sack to the kitchens. That'll make the maids scream very prettily.' Stefan grinned. 'With luck it'll be all it takes to get little brother to pay our wages and then we can be off. Not much luck for you, of course.'

'He will hunt you down – you know that?'

'He'll have to find us first, and we'll be long gone.'

Rafi nodded towards the knife in Stefan's hand. 'Just be done with it, then.'

Stefan frowned. 'Oh no. If I'm to transport you back to Winchester in a sack I don't want blood everywhere. It would ruin the surprise.'

Rafi's head sank into the ground. He longed for this to be over. If he could run he would have tried, but his leg was as good as useless. The pain from his knee throbbed through his body with the beating of his heart.

'Fulke. Hang him. It's clean.'

Rafi started to pray. He knew the words. He had said them this afternoon over Adam's bed, and now he was saying them for himself.

'Prayers won't help you, boy,' said Fulke, lifting Rafi off the ground with one hand and dragging him towards the stables. A beam ran from one end of the building to the other. Fulke dumped Rafi on a bale of hay, oblivious to Rafi's screams as his knee twisted beneath him.

Bridles, leather straps, saddles. Rope. Fulke slung a length over the bar, catching one end of it to form a noose. The other end trailed on the ground. Someone would pull it, with Rafi on the other end of it.

It was Stefan who secured the noose under Rafi's jawbone as Fulke held him tight.

Rafi began to tremble, so hard that Fulke had to hold him tighter. Rafi could feel the man's muscles, strong enough to hold him like this for hours and barely feel a twinge in those arms. And his face, Rafi could see it more clearly now in the grey light. Square, clean-shaven, short cropped hair. Those eyes, so dark, no feeling at all.

Stefan moved back and took the other end of the rope.

Fulke held him a little longer. Rafi couldn't bear to look at him. He thought of Edith, her green eyes, so full of expression, so bright. Everything about her was bright; she was lit from within. He had tried to capture that, but the essence of it was elusive. It would only ever have been a poor copy. He would never see her again. She would probably be gone by the time he was found. She would never even know he was dead.

And his mother, he tried to remember her, that last look as she had faded into the trees, her hands slipping from his.

His feet were lifted off the ground. Stefan had pulled the rope taut as Fulke let go. Rafi spun, slowly, his throat burning, the blood rushing in his ears. Nearly a full turn, the breath almost extinguished. There was noise, but it could have been his heart and lungs exploding and forcing the last of the life out of him. He spun back to his starting point. Was this delirium? He was getting lower, just a fraction, but he could feel the ground against his toes.

The beam had begun to bend with his weight. The wood splintered and the rope slipped through the broken strut, taking Rafi with it. Rafi's scream tore at his ruined throat as he fell onto his shattered knee. Fulke turned, cursing.

'I'll send you to hell the easy way.' The knife was out, a glittering point against the ghost of dawn.

Rafi couldn't move; his leg was useless. The stable roof would surely fall in. They would be crushed to death, both of them.

Rafi lay with one end of the rope in his hands, the other around his neck. He was dizzy and still struggling to breathe. Nothing he did would make a difference – he was going to die here. Why make a useless attempt to hold off the inevitable? That was how he'd lived his life, always doing the right thing, always walking away, thinking too much and acting too little. Because of him, Adam had nearly died, he'd let Van Loo bully him for five years, he'd waited too long get on a boat to England. If he'd come here earlier, he'd have met Edith before . . . before Thom . . .

His right arm came up and he whipped at Fulke's leg with the rope as hard as he could.

He wasn't afraid anymore. He wasn't the boy in the forest, or the young man on the quayside, barely able to hold a crate knife. He had no time left on this earth; hesitation was a weakness he could no longer afford.

'Whoreson!' Fulke recoiled, then raised the knife again.

The blow never landed.

Fulke's hand opened and the knife fell, skittering across the straw-covered floor. Fulke slumped forward, the arrow still quivering between his shoulder blades.

The bowman stood only a few feet away, calmly holding his weapon, a second arrow already nocked and ready to fly.

The archer from Crécy. Roger Writel.

Rafi rolled onto his back. The stable roof was beginning to buckle. A hand dragged him away, out of harm, onto the ground outside the stable just as the entire roof crashed onto the spot where he'd lain, covering Fulke in a cloud of dust and broken wood.

He hadn't realised that he was crying. Roger stood over him now, or at least he thought it was Roger. The silhouette had a disapproving stance to it, if such a thing were possible, so it was a reasonable enough assumption.

'Managed to . . . rescue me this time . . . Wri . . .'

Roger's hand passed over his brow. It was so cool. He'd not known he was so feverish.

'You foolish boy. I said I'd protect you.'

'I don't . . . need a guardian . . . I'm Rapha . . .' Who was he?

Where was he? Roger was fading; the sky was fading. Dawn seemed so bright; everything was bright.

Roger was talking again 'Gilbert! Gilbert! Let the other one go. We need to get Rafi out of here. He's in a bad way. Quickly!'

The voice was receding. Had it even been Roger's voice? His throat, it was closing again, he couldn't breathe. He couldn't . . .

'Rafi, sweet Jesu, don't go.'

Was Roger the last memory he would have? But then he saw Edith again, those green eyes, the unruly auburn hair plastered to her face as the rain poured, drifting away with her as he closed his eyes and sank into darkness.

Chapter 32

The road was dusty, hot. The boy was thirsty. There were black-berries on the bushes along the way, clusters of ripe and unripe fruit, encircled by thorns that scratched him. He chose the darkest ones he could find, otherwise the fruit was too sharp and bitter. When the deep purple pearls burst on his tongue, they gave him some relief from thirst, but not for long. His tongue felt thick in his mouth, pushing against his teeth and against the back of his neck, making him gag. He needed something to drink.

There was a bird ahead of him, shimmering in the heat haze. A big bird. A giant crow, or raven maybe. It was getting bigger, black, hazy in the light. It was coming towards him. He looked around; perhaps he could hide in the bushes.

He scrabbled at the unforgiving leaves, the thorns flaying his soft skin, leaving criss-crossed scratches that filled up with shallow rivers of blood. He brushed them away and kept scrabbling. The bird was still getting bigger; it would find him and carry him away.

So thirsty. He stopped for a moment and took another handful of dark berries, cramming them into his mouth, tasting the blood as it came off his hand. He burrowed as far in as he could, paying no heed to the branches lashing against his cheeks.

His throat hurt so much; it was so dry. His mother would have given him a warm drink, honey, something soothing, something to ease the pain. All he had were berries.

He lay still and closed his eyes. If he did not move, the bird would go away. He had done this before when a robin or sparrow hopped about in his mother's garden. If he was completely still, they did not see him and pecked at the ground close to his face while he watched the sheen of their wings and the ripple of their feathers. Even the plain birds were beautiful, deep brown and mottled, blue black or deepest black of night. This bird would be the same.

The light behind his eyes got darker as if a cloud had passed across the sun, but he kept them closed. He hardly dared breathe, but the darkness did not go away, and now something was pulling at him. Hands. They were hands, not wings.

A tall, thin man stood over him. He was wearing a long, dark cloak, dusty from the road, and a dark hood placed loosely on his head. As the man leaned forward, the hood fell down, revealing the tonsured skull.

'Come. I will not hurt you.'

The monk smiled. His face was wrinkled and kind. His eyes were a watery blue, washed out, almost grey.

'I am Brother Johannes.' The monk took a pair of gloves from his scrip and tried to clear space away from the thorns, working calmly, smiling, the sweat gathering on his upper lip and forehead.

'Now then, see. No more scratches. I can reach you.'

Johannes extended his hands, and the boy felt himself being lifted, up, up into the light. His mouth was so dry, his eyes hurt, his head throbbed. He gulped a mouthful of nothing and his throat constricted.

Gently, Johannes laid him on the ground and kneeled beside him, holding his head while he dripped some weak ale onto the parched lips.

The boy rested his head against the rough sleeve of the monk. He closed his eyes, feeling himself being lifted once more into Johannes' arms as the monk carried him away and into a new life.

Chapter 33

Rafi heard a whisper. 'Johannes.' It had come from him, the merest wisp of sound.

He opened his eyes. Someone was sitting beside him in a room he didn't recognise. He coughed. His jaw ached. He tried to open his mouth, but it felt alien to him. His lips were swollen; his teeth and gums throbbed. His eyes. He had to close them again. Trying to move them so he could look around the room made them hurt, they were so dry.

He was awake but helpless. Even turning his head on the pillow was an effort.

'Raphael?'

He didn't recognise her voice. Her dress shuffled as she moved, there was a clink of a pot or a cup from somewhere in the room, and then she was near him and he could feel her breath on his cheek.

'I will move your head forward very slowly. I am putting another pillow underneath you. I will be as gentle as I can.'

He wanted to scream, but knew even if he tried, no sound would have come. It was all over very quickly, thank the good

Lord. He was propped up a little now. Her arm came around his shoulders.

'Try this, my dear Raphael.'

He tried. The juice, when it came, was warm and sweet. It filled his mouth with softness and felt wonderful.

'Good, good.' She squeezed a cloth and wiped his eyes. She was an angel, whoever she was.

He blinked the excess moisture away. He could see her now. The girl from the abbey. Agnes. She looked different. Her hair was no longer hidden away; it lay dark and sleek on the crown of her head, tumbling down her back untied. Her dress was more elegant than the clothes she had worn the day he had seen her by the abbey pond playing with Leof. She had a pale yellow surcoat over a blue gown, held at the waist with a velvet belt embroidered with silver thread. She looked like one of the princesses in Joan's book. She had stroked his hand and called him dear. What was happening?

He tried to say her name, but she put her finger on his lips, shushing him. 'Do not speak too much. Save that for later.' She looked around as the door opened and she smiled. 'A visitor already.'

Hugh Le Cran stood by the bed, his face stern as usual, his eyes fixed on the patient. Rafi shrank into the mattress in the hope that he might disappear forever.

Le Cran rolled his eyes. Rafi envied him the ability to do so. 'You can't hide from me so I'm none too sure why you would bother. How are you?'

'Don't ask him questions.' Agnes frowned at him. 'I have forbidden him to speak.'

'Just as well I suppose. His inane babble has always been rather tiresome.'

Agnes tutted and busied herself with a pipkin, which she was warming in a bowl of hot water by the bed.

'Well, you look a bit better, which is not saying much. This is what happens when you get yourself strung up in a foolish attempt to murder my brother. Let that be a lesson to you, should you try such japes again.'

Jesu.

'Oh, no need to worry, I'm not cross. I never liked him anyway.' Le Cran almost smiled. 'There are quite a few people who will be delighted to know you are awake. Extraordinary, considering how much trouble you've put them all to. I shall spread the good news. Agnes, do you need an extra pair of hands?'

'We have everything planned, thank you. I, Ailith, Nell, Mistress Joan and . . .'

'All these women fussing over you, Dubois. You will be the envy of Winchester.'

Le Cran patted Agnes on the shoulder before he left. Such a familiar gesture. Familial. So, he had been right all along. Agnes was William's illegitimate child, and now it seemed the truth was out in the open. Roger must have told his master after all.

Agnes and Nell tended to him for a few more days, the girl barely leaving his side. He asked her why she was here and not at the abbey, but all she would say was that she'd turned fourteen and had chosen to leave. She fussed over him, would not let anyone else give him medicine. His leg was bound, but not as painful as he'd feared it might be. If he was careful and used the stick Agnes gave him, he was able to take a few turns around the upper floors and look over the gallery into the hall. The tapestry was hung where it had always been, guarding the wall opposite Le Cran's office.

Nell brought food up from the kitchen: meat broths, coddled eggs, bread soaked in warm milk and glasses of Lepe because 'Roger says you like it'.

From Agnes, care; from Nell, food. From Roger, bits and pieces of news to fill in what had happened after Rafi had lost consciousness.

Fulke was dead, which was no surprise, and Stefan had vanished. The search party had not been able to find him. Three days they'd hunted him in the area around Salisbury, and in the city itself but none had seen him, nor had he been seen in Winchester. The manor had been ransacked and anything of value taken – silver plate, linen, what weaponry William had possessed. Probably not worth as much as Stefan might have hoped to extract from Hugh, but not an insignificant amount. But the fear remained that he might return, and two more men had joined Gilbert and Hal as guards.

Adam lived, and would recover.

Of Edith, he had learned very little despite his questions. When he asked Agnes, she was evasive, as was Roger. Finally, this morning, Agnes said that Master Le Cran wanted to talk to him, and would tell him everything. They had merely wanted to wait a few days until Rafi had recovered, until the valerian he'd been given to help him sleep had fully worn off.

Rafi needed to talk to Le Cran too. The truth about Agnes may well be out in the open, but there was still more, the truth he'd been about to reveal before Adam had gone missing.

He wanted to rid himself of the burden. He needed to be free of it.

It was time.

Chapter 34

Agnes was waiting for him at the top of the stairs like an anxious parent.

'Do not worry, Agnes. I must walk further than the gallery. My legs will forget what they are supposed to do, and my knee is much better.'

Agnes responded by throwing her arms around him. As if this was not surprise enough, she reached into her apron. 'We had to take this,' she said, 'but I kept it safe.'

Rafi stared down at the item in her hand. A silver locket. His silver locket. He'd not even noticed that it had been missing.

'It had cut into your neck,' she explained.

He remembered now. Fulke had dragged him into the stable by the scruff of the neck. It had caused Rafi's shirt and the chain of his locket to ride up and begin to choke him.

He looped it over his head, marvelling that he had not noticed its absence. As he reached the bottom of the stairs, he took in his surroundings, familiar now. The wide hall, still clean and swept and beautiful, the window seat where Mistress Joan had been sitting on the day he'd returned after his money had been stolen.

Beyond, he could see a corner of the garden, fully alive now, not dormant as it had been when he had arrived in Winchester. The lavender was green and fresh with fluffy purple heads, roses of damask and white petals bloomed against the wall. And the herb garden was a bright patchwork of all the shades of green he could ever imagine. Mint, sage, rosemary. He smiled. His mother would have spent all summer in a garden like that one.

He pushed open the door to Le Cran's office. There were more people waiting for him than he'd expected. Hugh, of course, and Roger, but also Mistress Joan and . . . the abbey nurse, Domneva.

Domneva stared at him. She stared and stared. He'd never seen her face clearly before – he still could not, it was almost entirely concealed by her wimple. But he could see her eyes.

He was lost. His head swam. He swayed, and Roger caught him. 'Perhaps it is too soon . . .'

Rafi shook his head. 'No. I am here now.'

He sat. She watched his every move.

'I've learned something I did not know before.' Le Cran came straight to the point. 'Something I perhaps would have preferred not to hear, but I can't unhear it now and can only try to fix what has been broken.'

Le Cran removed his cap, not a hair out of place underneath. For thirteen years he had controlled his father's fortune and kept his elder brother at bay. It was no wonder he found it difficult to trust. But he had Joan now. She sat quietly beside him, her padded chair pushed back from the table to allow for the swell of her belly. One hand she held lightly over her stomach, the other was on her husband's desk, close to him, should he need it.

'For many years my steward has withheld something from me which, had he seen fit to explain fully, might have spared a lot of pain.'

Roger shifted uncomfortably. 'Master, I—'

Le Cran held up his hand. 'I know. You did it for my father's sake. The truth would have sent him to his grave earlier than

Richard's death eventually did. I understand.' He sighed. 'But you could have told me, once he'd gone.'

'Too much time had passed. You believed your brother had died honourably and that seemed to help you grieve and . . .'

'And you tried to deal with it yourself and spare me. Your intentions were good but you were mistaken. Well, it is done now.' Le Cran shook his head. 'How do we tell you the truth, Raphael Dubois? For I am at a loss.'

Rafi cleared his throat. 'I already know. I was there. Your brother . . .' He stopped. Roger, Le Cran and Joan had all turned to Domneva.

'You do not know,' whispered Roger.

Rafi swallowed.

'Here.' Joan took a cup and gestured to Roger to press it into Rafi's hands. 'You are not yet healed. Rest your voice if you need to, and drink this.'

Rafi took it. His hand shook so much the wine sloshed out of the pewter cup and onto his tunic. He stared at it, the damp spot darkening. He put the cup on the floor because he could not trust himself to hold it. He felt a warm hand take his, a hand he knew. He watched the patch, seeping into the tabby cloth. He should try and get it out before it dried.

The hand squeezed his. He squeezed it back. Her eyes had not left him all this time.

'*Mon petit.*'

His nose tingled. He wiped it with his sleeve. And then drops fell from his eyes and splashed onto the patch, making it even bigger. Tears and more tears, and he couldn't stop them.

'Maman?'

Wordlessly, she unfastened her wimple, leaving nothing but a plain cap with lacings under the chin. This, too, she removed. He knew for sure it was her even before she put her arms around him. And then he breathed her in, days past suddenly rushing to meet him. Her hair smelled of summer. They couldn't stay like this forever. He could not cry any more as his throat ached from it, and she could not hold him and bend in such an awkward position. He stood, and took her hands and pulled her upright. He would never let her fade away again.

Roger took the cup from the floor and gave it back to Rafi. 'Drink now. You know you should never waste Lepe.'

Rafi smiled weakly. 'It is costly.'

Roger patted Rafi's shoulder and then walked to the window.

'Speak, then,' ordered Le Cran.

Roger bowed his head.

'It will be well, Roger.' Marianne spoke softly, as softly as Rafi remembered.

Roger took a deep breath. 'Richard did not slip and fall as I told you.' He looked apologetically at Rafi. 'He spent the evening after the battle trying to control his brother. William was beyond control. There was a madness on him which I'd seen before. He could not be stopped.'

Le Cran poured himself a cup of wine. There was a slight tremor as he held it to his lips.

'I couldn't find Richard, but I found William,' Roger continued. 'He was . . . I tried to stop him.'

'He struck you. I thought you would not get up,' said Marianne.

'I nearly didn't. When I came to, he was . . .' Roger looked at Marianne. He shook his head. 'I . . .'

'It doesn't matter. It is done now.'

Nobody moved while Roger tried to compose himself. 'He was going to take her with him. I asked where Richard was and he said he'd left him behind. I had to think quickly. I needed to find Richard and I wanted to get Marianne to safety. I knew he had finished with her . . . for now. I had time. I thought . . . I thought if I had Richard with me then between the two of us we could subdue him. And so I ran back to the clearing as fast as I could. And he was there. He was already dead. And the boy . . .'

Rafi spoke slowly. 'So it was you. I saw you take my scapular from Christophe.'

'There was nobody there.' Roger frowned. 'I would have seen you.'

'I am invisible, remember. Maman told me to hide. She knew—'

Roger shook his head. 'It cannot be.'

Rafi pulled the chain slowly from around his neck and placed it on the table in front of Le Cran. He would never wear it again. Richard's message had finally been delivered.

'The other half of the seal matrix is in there,' Rafi told Roger. 'You looked for it when you searched Richard's body, but he had already given it to me.'

Le Cran stood, his cup nearly tipping over. 'You spoke to him? He was alive?'

Rafi retook his mother's hand. 'I am sorry, Maman. You told me to stay hidden.' He turned back to Le Cran. 'He didn't want to be alone.'

Le Cran put his hands over his face. 'What did he say?'

'He told me to find his father and give him that.' Rafi nodded towards the locket.

'So that was the reason you came here.' Le Cran took the locket and rubbed his thumb along the clasp.

'Yes. That is why I got on board the *Lady Cecily*.'

'I'm glad I did not throw you in jail after all.' Le Cran still had not opened the clasp.

'I prayed with him.' Rafi needed his master to know. 'He was not alone.'

Le Cran refilled his cup and drank until it was empty. The tremor was stronger. 'What prayer did you give him?'

'He asked my name. He said, as people often do, that it was one of the guardian angels.' Edith had said it too, the night they'd hunted for flowers on Knights Meadow. His heart felt heavy. 'So, that is the prayer I gave him, the one I knew best then, and the one I still say every night. I stretched out my hand to his and said the *Angele Dei* until . . . until the end.'

Le Cran finally reached for Joan. 'Then I thank you for it.'

But Rafi had not finished. 'You screamed.' He turned to his mother. 'I heard you scream. And then there was silence and I thought you were dead.'

'I screamed because he gave me this.' Domneva pulled the scapular from around her neck. 'I thought you were dead. I didn't know you had given it to Christophe.'

'I wanted her to have something,' Roger began to explain. 'William was already leading her away and she was struggling because she wanted to get back to you. I had no choice but to follow as a servant of the Le Cran house, but I knew that if she kept trying to run back into the clearing that he'd kill her. I thought the dead boy was her son, and I thought if she had something of his . . . I don't know. I pushed it into her hand when William wasn't looking. I was confused. My master was dead.'

Roger's face was a mask of anguish. Rafi did not know whether to be angry or to pity him. Roger, the man who had persecuted him and then saved his life.

'But . . . then . . .' Rafi frowned. 'Where is the other half of the matrix, the half you took from Richard's body?'

Roger sighed. 'William took it from me. He took it and . . . threw it into a river.'

Le Cran buried his face in his hands again and his shoulders shook. Joan leaned in towards him and rested her head gently against his neck.

''Tis a pity,' said Rafi quietly. 'I carried it for so long. I would have liked to have seen the rest of it. The bird had less grace than the one on the ring I found in William's room; for a long time I thought it was a duck. Almost as if an infant had fashioned it.'

Le Cran uncovered his face and put the locket carefully back on the table. 'Not quite an infant,' he said. 'But I was no more than eight or nine, and my hand was never as skilful as yours, Raphael Dubois.'

Rafi remembered Adam's words in Ghent, the day before everything had changed.

It looks like a child's hand made it.

Le Cran finally opened the locket. He smiled. 'I drew it. It was a game, to mimic the seal my father had. Richard filled in the words and the tree, to make the thing look more real, and to indulge me. He was ever attentive to me.' He stroked the matrix gently. 'My father cast it for our amusement. When he left for France, Richard took it with him as a memento. It is no surprise that William destroyed what little there was of it.' He stared at the broken remains on the table, all that was left of the token he'd made with his beloved brother.

Rafi's master. The last of the three birds, the one who had held the stone aloft for the longest. Ever vigilant.

'Finish it, Roger.' Le Cran smiled as Joan gently stroked his cheek.

'Domneva?' Roger looked to her.

'Yes. Yes, Roger. Tell him.'

Rafi felt his mother grip his fingers once more. He pushed his chair closer to her and took both her hands in his, waiting. He could not bear the thought of being parted from her ever again.

'We moved on to Calais, to the siege,' Roger continued. 'We were there over winter. William hated it. In spring he walked away. He just . . . left. I had to follow. Your mother had nowhere to go, so I looked after her, brought her on board ship.'

'All of his pay, everything,' said Domneva. 'Tell them. Everything you had. They did not want me on board.'

'He'd lost interest in her by then. I took her to the Green Dragon in Southampton.' Roger nodded at Le Cran. 'Your father's inn.'

Rafi knew it. It was the one he and Adam had stayed in after the *Lady Cecily* had dropped them overboard.

'I told them to look after her. They knew who I was; they took it as an order from Le Cran and didn't question it. She had to stay somewhere safe for a while. She had lost everything because of William. I couldn't leave her.' Roger looked at Le Cran. 'Your father gave me a handsome purse, for services to his son.'

Domneva pressed Rafi's hands. 'Roger gave it all to the abbey. To take me . . . and . . . my child.'

Rafi knew immediately. His heart leaped in his chest. There was no surprise or confusion; there was simply joy. The girl who had hugged him and called him dear. He knew.

'My daughter,' said Domneva. 'To be adopted by the abbess, and for me to live in quiet and solitude.'

Agnes.

The realisation that he had a sister broke like a wave against him and began to wash some of his pain away. Agnes. If he had to choose a sister . . . sweet, magnificent Agnes. His eyes were damp again.

'I thought maybe William had done something to you,' he told Roger. 'To your wife or someone you loved, and she had died and you took care of Agnes and . . .'

'There was no wife.' Roger stared at Domneva.

But there was someone you loved.

'There is more.' Joan spoke at last. 'It concerns you alone and what you do with the information is in your hands. Roger, please?'

'The night we found you,' began Roger. 'We called first at the infirmary. After you had left, Thom came looking for Edith.'

Rafi's heart sank. What had Thom done to her? Dear God, please let him not have killed her.

'He was very drunk, which was not in itself unusual. It seems he managed to get hold of a bottle of the abbess's sleeping draught.'

Domneva's voice was cold. 'Mother Molins does not sleep well. It is very unfortunate.'

Roger paused. 'Sister Domneva would normally go through the abbey, but unfortunately she could not find the key. She had no choice but to go through the grounds. Of course, the rain had made everything treacherous. She slipped and the bottle rolled away.'

'I went back to get another one, and by the time I made my way across to the abbey again, there he was.' Domneva shrugged.

'The bottle was beside him on the grass, empty. He had already drowned by the time she found him.'

Roger and Domneva looked at each other.

Le Cran sniffed. 'The coroner was very clear. An accident, nothing more.'

William, and now Thom. They had hurt the people he loved and they were gone. And Edith was free. But . . . he had not seen her since that night. Agnes, Nell, even Roger, but never Edith. She must have gone before Thom was found, and no one had been able to find her. She had not been by his side.

'She is waiting for you to get better.' Joan was smiling at him. She was still here? Please God let this be true!

'She . . . she didn't leave?'

'Heavens, no!' Roger said.

'But, where has she been?'

'Delivering medicine to the door for you. Rafi, have the last of your brains finally fallen out of your cloth ears? She's newly widowed. How d'you think it would have looked, you foolish boy!'

Roger's look of exasperation was the best thing Rafi had seen all day.

His mother put her hand on his forehead. 'You look pale. Not feverish but . . . you are tired. You must go up to your sister, and you let her take care of you. You are still weak.'

'*Oui*, Maman.' He wanted nothing more than to sink back into his bed. He could rest easy now. Edith was here; she'd waited for him.

'And you, Maman?'

'The abbey. It is where I belong. I have peace, and my children are safe and close to me.' She smiled. 'It is enough.'

Chapter 35

Rafi grinned as Agnes ran towards him, down past the market to Colebrook where he waited for her. She was carrying her basket, her long hair tied back but not covered, wearing a pretty gown of damask silk. His intended mission to find Edith had been put back for a few more days. After the revelations in Le Cran's office, Rafi had been overcome with exhaustion, as if the lifting of the burden he'd carried for so long had weakened him.

But now he felt strong again and had moved back into the workshop with Cedric and a recuperating Adam. It was like being back in Ghent, sharing a room with his friend. But this time, there was no chain around his neck, tying him to the past.

Rafi didn't miss the locket. It had been replaced with so much more. A mother, a sister, and a woman he could now love freely.

'So, what next, sister?' He loved saying the word. *Sister.*

'Well, we have a shop to stock, so let us not waste any more time.'

The old apothecary had died only a few days ago and Joan, realising that her niece had far too much talent to go to waste, had persuaded Le Cran to purchase the shop and give it to Rafi and Agnes. One to provide medicine, one to provide paint and ink. They would look after each other. It was perfect.

'Where to then, sister?'

'Well, I need some moss. It makes a wonderful poultice, with yarrow for bruises. How about the water meadows, south of here.' She pointed down past the cathedral. The water meadows stretched out just a short way behind it, all the way to St Catherine's Hill. He had not walked that way before, but he was sure it would be full of as many good things as he had found elsewhere. But not today.

'You are teasing.'

She looked up at him, her brown eyes wide. 'Surely you cannot think so little of me?' She laughed. 'Very well, let's find it near Hyde. I wonder what else we will discover there?'

That which I long for most.

'Come.' She placed her hand gently on his sleeve. 'Lean on me if your leg gets too sore. I'm stronger than I look.'

Rafi began to tremble. As they reached the Durngate, he trembled even more.

The last time he'd been here was the evening before he left for Salisbury. Today, the marshes and meadows were less foreboding with the sun shining on the grass and the reeds and the water, and he could see Hyde Abbey more clearly. He had wanted to visit, and had never found the time. Well, no more. He could put that right now. He could put everything right.

Three children were playing just by the Dutton Bridge. A boy, and a girl with frizzy auburn hair holding the youngest of the children by the hand.

'Why, it's Tilly and Simon!' cried Agnes. 'And Leof. Leof!'

Leof waved and came running towards her.

Their mother was with them, standing at a short distance. Like Agnes, she held a basket. The breeze blew her apron and her dress, the water from the river already darkening the bottom of it. Her hair poked untidily out of her wimple. She raised her hand as if to wave, then lowered it again when she saw Rafi. And then a gust of wind took her headdress, whipping it away from her, her hair tumbling and tangled as she turned around and about to find it, with Simon and Tilly dancing after, all three of them laughing as it fell into the stream. It bobbed for a bit and then sank. She shrugged and put her hands on her hips, looking over towards Leof who was safely holding on to Agnes's hand. And then she turned to Rafi.

Rafi waved shyly at her across the meadow, his heart in his mouth.

She waved back and smiled.

It was a smile that reached her eyes.

Historical Notes

Most of the characters in this novel are fictitious but some did live in the city at the time.

Hugh Le Cran was Mayor of Winchester several times from the 1360s onwards. He was also the Sheriff and Mayor of the Staple. He was married to Joan, the widow of John Cuppyng. Hugh and Joan had a son, John. After Joan's death, Le Cran married again. He did own many properties in the city including, at one point, the Tabard (and the Chequers). He also did owe the Earl of Arundel £200. The reason I've given for the loan is pure speculation.

Le Cran died in 1401.

The suggestion that the drainage system was badly maintained was my doing – there were rules and fines and while the rules were often broken, as per dye frequently being tipped into the brooks by the local dyers, there was yet some sense of civic responsibility. I was hoping that Le Cran would fix it all in his usual and efficient manner when he became mayor but the situation never arose. Perhaps it will come in another book; who can say.

The seal in this novel is based on the real one he held, and can be found in the Winchester Records Office.

Roger Writel was one of Le Cran's servants so I turned him into his steward.

Serlo was a butcher who lived in Winchester in the previous century. I chose him as the landlord of the Chequers because I liked his name. I'm only sorry that I'll never try one of his pies.

The Helle was a cellar next door to St Lawrence's church. It is close to where the Buttercross is today.

Thurstin was a real Winchester clerk.

Mother Margaret Molins was the Abbess of St Mary's Abbey from 1349 to 1364. The abbey was dissolved by Henry VIII and little remains, although there are some foundations near the car park in Colebrook Street (and yes, there was an area near Colebrook known as Shite Lane). The charnel chapel was probably on the site of where the Abbey Gardens public toilets are today.

In 1370 a nun was abducted from the abbey. I moved that event back a few years and made William Le Cran responsible.

The devil's face can still be seen leering from above the north door in St John's church which is, to my mind, one of the love-liest buildings in Winchester. You can get some great views of the city if you walk up nearby St Giles Hill. Much of the original painting in the church has been damaged but the devilish face is still there, along with the two saints he mocks. It is there that I learned of the 'VV' mark against witchcraft from a local historical research team who were carrying out a medieval graffiti study on the day I was there.

The yarrow recipe, which Edith uses to soothe Adam's wound, is taken from Hildegard von Bingen's *Physica*.

Acknowledgements

Jericho writers – the staff, the online courses, the support, the forum – all of it was invaluable.

People from the internet who live in my phone – Kevin and Sigourney who beta read, and Rich who answered a torrent of queries about medieval weaponry.

Dr Cindy Wood, University of Winchester. She agreed to meet me for tea and cake in the cathedral refectory and enlightened me on abbey life for women in the middle ages. If I've messed any of it up, it's on my head, not hers.

The researcher from the Hampshire Medieval Graffiti survey who just so happened to be in St John's church the day I visited. I realised the church was having an open day (there was tea, so obviously I went) but had no idea he'd be there too. Talk about serendipity. He showed me some of the graffiti around the bell-tower, with some explanations as to what it might mean. It was such a privilege.

Dr Sally L, who knows how to get a woman back on her feet.

Debs and Jim from the Poetry Pharmacy.

To Kate Mills at HarperCollins for saying yes and being so

supportive.

Finally, the boys. They'll never read the book but they're incredibly enthusiastic about it all and frankly, what more could I ask for?

Dear Reader,

We hope you enjoyed reading this book. If you did, we'd be so appreciative if you left a review. It really helps us and the author to bring more books like this to you.

Here at HQ Digital we are dedicated to publishing fiction that will keep you turning the pages into the early hours. Don't want to miss a thing? To find out more about our books, promotions, discover exclusive content and enter competitions you can keep in touch in the following ways:

JOIN OUR COMMUNITY:

Sign up to our new email newsletter: http://smarturl.it/SignUpHQ

Read our new blog www.hqstories.co.uk

🐦 https://twitter.com/HQStories

f www.facebook.com/HQStories

BUDDING WRITER?

We're also looking for authors to join the HQ Digital family!
Find out more here:

https://www.hqstories.co.uk/want-to-write-for-us/

Thanks for reading, from the HQ Digital team